WAGON TRACKS

ACROSS KANSAS

George Edward Moon

Order this book online at www.trafford.com
or email orders@trafford.com

Most Trafford titles are also available at major online book retailers.

Printed in the United States of America.

ISBN: 978-1-4907-5242-6 (sc)
ISBN: 978-1-4907-5244-0 (hc)
ISBN: 978-1-4907-5243-3 (e)

Library of Congress Control Number: 2014922130

Trafford rev. 01/07/2015

Trafford
PUBLISHING® www.trafford.com

North America & international
toll-free: 1 888 232 4444 (USA & Canada)
fax: 812 355 4082

ACKNOWLEDGEMENTS

Much of the information regarding the American Plains Indians was taken from the excellent internet site Wikipedia, the free encyclopedia.

Other sources were: *"Our Hearts Fell to the Ground"* edited by Colin G. Calloway; *"The Plains Indians"* by Paul H. Carlson; *"The Contested Plains"* by Elliot West; *"Plains Indian History and Culture"* by John C. Ewers; *"Native North America"* by Larry J. Zimmerman and Brian Leigh Molyneaux; *"The Long Death; The Last Days of the Plains Indians"* by Ralph K. Andrist; *"Nez Perce Country"* by Alvin M. Josephy Jr.; *"Method and Theory in American Archaeology"* by Gordon R. Willey and Philip Phillips; *"What Do We Know About The Plains Indians?"* by Dr. Colin Taylor; *"Daily Life in a Plains Indian Village 1868"* by Michael Bad Hand Terry; *"The Native Americans an Illustrated History"* by David Hurst Thomas, Jay Miller, Richard White, Peter Nabokov, and Philip J. Deloria and Illustrated by Alvin M. Josephy Jr.; *"The American Indian"* by Colin F. Taylor; *"The Last Conquistador, Juan de Oñate and the Settling of the Far Southwest"* by Marc Simmons; *"The Cheyenne Indians, Their History and*

Lifeways" by George Bird Grinnell; *"Living Through The Plains Indian Wars, 1864-1890"* by Andrew Langley.

All of which provided the content for me to set the stage for Wagon Tracks, a story in which the Plains Indians play an important part.

PREFACE

Wagon Tracks is a continuation of the Tennessee Mountain Man saga. Abel Strawn, one of Jack Leffingwell's sharpshooters, has an opportunity to acquire land in the western Kansas Territory. President Andrew Johnson gave amnesty to all southern soldiers before leaving office. As a result, former Confederates now qualify for the Homestead Act's land giveaway. On the surface, it seems like a good opportunity for him and his wife, Amanda. At the moment, they live with the senior Strawns in the Methodist Minister's parsonage, provided by the church. Abel functions as assistant minister serving the youth in the congregation. Settling in Kansas would give them land and a log home of their own.

After hearing Abel's story, Jack did not discourage his friend from accepting the offer presented to him. If the account was factual, it was surely an opportunity. After four years, spent together in the war, Jack Leffingwell knew the ability of his friend.

His principal concern was those people resenting a settler on the land in which they historically claim as their own. While the Civil War was being fought, the tawny inhabitants were less vengeful. The idea of whites killing whites was pleasing. It's true, that some fought on the side of the North and others the

South, however, most remained on the sidelines and cheered the onslaught.

Now that hostilities between the states have ended, a persistent queue of wagons can be seen daily, as more settlers encroach upon the land of the red man's forefathers. For centuries, these noble savages of the plains have battled each other when a foreign tribe impinged their hunting grounds or sacred territory. Today, dauntless white men, led by the belching black smoke of the iron horse, trespass and take a firm hold of land belonging to those who settled first.

INTRODUCTION

W ho are these people who live as nomads, while others of
their kind have evolved to a more agricultural way of life
and move less often? From where did these migratory hunters
originate? To answer such questions we must look back to the
end of the last Ice Age, about 20,000 years ago. During the
last glacial period most of the earth's northern hemisphere was
covered with a frozen water sheet. In Canada, the covering was
almost two miles thick blocking any possible movement by
humanity through the interior. The formation of such enormous
amounts of ice caused the Bering and Chukchi Seas to drop some
400 feet, exposing the land beneath the Bering Strait. Scientists
refer to this terrain as Beringia, an ancient subcontinent uniting
the eastern and western hemispheres. This bridge of land was
a treeless, grassy tundra over 1000 miles wide and served as a
route of human migration to the Americas. Once the North
American glaciers began to melt, they no longer blocked the way
southward. Occurring about 15,000 years ago, several groups of
big-game hunters from Siberia followed their prey, along ice-free
corridors drifting southward to the Rockies, taking advantage
of more moderate weather along the mountain base. Eventually,
their route funneled them into the Northern Great Plains. By
now, with the ice sheets melting, the Bering Land Bridge is once

again submerged beneath the Bering Strait and no longer serves as a walkway into America.

Due to the nature of nomadic culture, archeologists have found little evidence of these early Americans. The first important discovery site was found in 1932, near Clovis, New Mexico. Toolkits were discovered exhibiting fluted stone projectile points ranging in length from 1½ to 5 inches. Exactly how these points were attached is unknown. Most likely, they were tied to a wooden or bone foreshaft that worked loose from the spear shaft once the projectile head was buried in its prey. Since no earlier evidence has been found, it appears that this culture, called Clovis, just magically appeared; nonetheless, logic tells us Clovis technology had to evolve from previous experience. Perhaps it took place back in Asia or, at least, while on route to America. Up until now it remains an unsolved mystery.

Lasting until about 11,000 years ago, the Clovis culture gave way to several more localized regional cultures. One of which is called the Folsom Complex. Primarily, it is a continuation of the Clovis people but identifiable by their particular unique projectile tips and hunting methods. The improved points had thinner blades and much reduced in size when compared with those from the Clovis culture. It's been suggested such weapons were designed to facilitate hafting to a spear prong. It's also likely the Folsom points were in response to a new weapon—the atlatl. This hunting accessory increased the length and leverage of the hunter's arm, causing the spear to be thrown farther and with increased velocity. The manner or technique by which these huntsmen of the plains stalked their prey may have been discovered when an excavation in Colorado unearthed a 10,000-year-old bison kill site. Remains of about 300 animals were found in a gully. Apparently, the bison were driven into the ravine where they would be more easily dispatched. Possibly at a time when the gulch was filled with snow, hindering their movement. In order to conduct this type hunt, careful planning and coordination was needed to bring groups together for a common advantage. Once the kill was harvested, Folsom hunters would return to their various bands and tribes. Considering they sought seasonal game, gatherings would have widely separated after the resources were depleted. Limited evidence makes it difficult to draw sharp boundaries; however, archeologists believe the Folsom culture lasted 1,000 years, and then blended into a number of various Paleo-Indian traditions.

It also was the period when many of the *megafauna* or large animals abruptly disappeared. Mastodons, mammoths, giant ground sloth, and horses, became extinct as did the carnivores that preyed upon them—short face bear, Alaskan lions, saber-tooth cats, and dire wolves. The exact reason for their demise eludes a solid scientific conclusion.

We do know that while the descendents from Siberia frequently changed their residence, the climate also underwent a rapid alteration. The warming period was abruptly interrupted by a return to glacial conditions bringing both cold temperatures and drought—referred to as the Big Freeze or Younger Dryas stadial. After which, the climate entered another warming trend having a dramatic effect on vegetation and grazing animals. Average temperatures climbed by 45° Fahrenheit over a 50-year duration. The grasslands moved northward, replacing the habitat of the mammoth with one more suitable to bison herds. The species, at the time, *Bison Antiquus*, was much larger than the modern bison. Standing 7½ feet tall, 15 feet in length, and weighing 3,500 pounds, they roamed the grasslands in great numbers. Nevertheless, the changing habitat did not serve them as well as their smaller cousins and they, too, succumbed to the pending fate of the larger beasts.

While the extinction of the large *megafauna* is considered sudden in scientific terms, it took place over a 1,000-year period of time. Grazing animals could not thrive on the tall dry grass, brought about during extended periods of parchedness. Accordingly, their numbers progressively got smaller at a time when nomadic hunters grew more efficient in their skills.

The carnivores suffered for lack of prey, especially the saber-toothed cats. With their enormous, bladelike upper canine teeth, extending more than 7 inches below the lower jaw, they were perfectly designed to bring down mammoths. These heavily muscled cats needed to open their jaws extremely wide in order to allow the canines to be used. In other words, a huge target was required. Once the large *megafauna* disappeared, saber-toothed cats began to starve. Ironically, due to the same enormous canines, they may not have been able to even bite smaller game.

Since the beginning of time, the fundamental character of the world is one of constant change. It is a shifting system of transitory events shading over into one another. In order for the life forms to survive, they must adapt to the ecological transformation. Humans are a good example. When *megafauna* were no longer prevalent, some primitive groups continued to concentrate toward the open plains and bison hunting, while others adapted to hunting and foraging in the Rocky Mountain foothills. Different life styles were emerging. More permanent groups began to form. Bands of 25 to 100 people were maintained. These groups were composed of several nuclear families more complex than the assemblages of earlier times. People began making different kinds of tools. Implements for grinding seed and nuts, woven baskets, and nets for fishing were now being devised. This interval dating from about 8,000 to 4,000 years ago is commonly called the *Archaic Period*[1]. The more populated bands were likely to have someone acting as headperson who led discussions and served as mediator in disputes. Such persons had no coercive power, therefore, relied on charisma and respect accorded to the position.

Exchange of raw materials and finished artifacts occurred years before, but, mostly irregular and between random individuals. It's not until the *Archaic Period* that substantial economic exchange took place. In fact, as populations moved into more ecological niches and societies, trade began

---

[1] One of the stages given by Gordon R. Willey and Philip Phillips in their book, Method and Theory in American Archaeology. The other stages are: Lithic, Archaic, Formative, Classic, and Post Classic.

to flourish. Accordingly, with increases in population, trade became an important factor in the transformation of *Archaic* cultures into different, more sophisticated forms. At this time, historians witnessed the blooming and profusion of many different lifeways and a spreading out across the North American Continent, filling in virtually every environmental zone. In some areas, people simply intensified already existing survival practices. Those in the plains, for example, continued to hunt the buffalo, while moving their homes as the seasons changed. In other areas, where large game was lacking, people were forced to seek smaller quarry and supplement with a wide range of plant food. In some regions, fish and shellfish became staple food.

From about 3,000 to 1,500 years ago we entered into a Neo-Indian period defined by Gordon Willey and Philip Phillips as the *Formative Stage*. The *Formative* cultures development level featured achievement in such areas as pottery, weaving, and food production. At this time, agriculture came into focus as part of a well established settlement life. Certain cultures evolved into permanent towns and villages. These settlements grew larger and began to be surrounded by smaller satellite communities. Dwellings appear more permanent or at least semi-permanent. The populace exhibited a social class hierarchy, which included elites, nobles, commoners, poor, and wandering nomads.

Bison *antiquus* was a massive animal that failed to survive the *Pleistocene* period. It was 25% larger than modern bison reaching 7.5 feet tall, 15 feet long, and weighed 3,800 pounds. It gave rise to Bison *bison*, the American buffalo of today.

Political and religious foundations were represented by the presence of pyramidal mound-based temples. Those early Americans, who migrated eastward into the woodlands, represented the most significant mound-based discoveries. Because of the mounds, archeologists learned a great deal about the controlled civilization and how it lived.

Cultural development took place as several small gathering-and-hunting tribes came together in the river valleys. Over time, the regular social interaction and economic exchange created a degree of genial ranking and increased ceremonialism, especially when it came to burial and considering the afterlife.

With the arrival of additional bands, the subsistence patterns became more complex. For example, even though they hunted turkey, seasonal waterfowl, and deer, a greater reliance on agriculture took place. People relied heavily on seasonal crops, growing maize, squashes, and beans. The new subsistence pattern transformed the culture. Settlements became more complex. Formal arrangements of house groupings were located around open plazas in order to accommodate an increasing populace. The inhabitants became known as mound builders.

One of the most significant discoveries of mound-based culture took place near the confluence of the Mississippi, Missouri, and Illinois Rivers. Although the inhabitants left no written records, other items such as symbols on pottery, shell, copper, wood, and stone gave archeologists a pattern to describe a planned community with a sophisticated society, featuring elaborate burial mounds. This ancient city is called Cahokia[2] and covers about 6 square miles. Within its confines are about 120 man-made earthen mounds, each differing in size and function. Considering how it all came about is nearly unfathomable. Over a period of decades, thousands of workers had to move over 50 million cubic feet of earth, carried in woven baskets.

---

[2] The city's original name is unknown. It acquired the name Cahokia later, after a clan of Illiniwek people living in the area during the 17th century.

The most outstanding structure and central focus of the city is a massive platform mound named *Monks Mound—(named after a community of Trappist monks that resided in the area once Euroamericans arrived)*. Standing 10 stories tall, it is the largest man-made earthen mound in the United States. Over the course of several centuries, and at least 10 construction episodes, the mound grew in elevation. Archeological unearthing on the top of *Monks Mound* revealed evidence of a large structure measuring about 105 feet long and 48 feet wide. A building this size could have been 50 feet tall and would be seen throughout the city. Obviously, it was an edifice of prominence and possibly either a temple or home of a principal leader. Adjacent to the mound was a large plaza where sporting events or public rituals may have taken place. In addition to this plaza, three other very large parks surrounded *Monks Mound,* placed in the cardinal directions to the east, west, and south. All part of the sophisticated engineering displayed throughout the excavation.

The discovery at a site west of *Monks Mound* was both unusual and thought provoking. It contained postholes that appeared to form a timber circle. The placement of posts marked solstices and equinoxes similar to England's famous circles at Stonehenge and Woodhenge. Scientific analysis supports the hypothesis that the location of these posts was by design. Interest in the sun's seasonal movements was conceivably for agricultural purposes; however, determining planting time may not have been their only concern.

Cahokia was the most important center for the early *Formative* Indian cultures that migrated across what are now the Midwest, Eastern, and Southeastern United States. It maintained trade links with communities as far away as the Great Lakes to the north and the Gulf Coast to the south. Such commodities as copper, Mill Creek chert[3], and whelk shells readily changed hands. Mill Creek chert, a rock resembling flint, consisted essentially of translucent and various colored quartz. It was

---

[3] Mill Creek chert was used extensively for the production of utilitarian tools such as hoes and spades.

used in the production of hoes, a high demand tool for farmers around Cahokia and other communities. By controlling the manufacturing and distribution of such hand tools, Cahokia established an important economic activity that allowed the city to thrive.

Before the year 1050 only about 1,000 people claimed Cahokia as their home; however, shortly thereafter it is estimated that the population quickly grew to around 40,000 inhabitants. At that point, Cahokia was facing the problems of adequate food supply and, just as important, maintaining waste disposal and appropriate sanitation. Scientists have pointed at this, as well as other environmental factors, causing the great city's decline after the year 1300 AD. It was abandoned more than a century before Europeans arrived in North America.

Evolving out of the *Formative* culture is what's referred to as the *Classic Stage*. From about 1500 to 1200 years ago, it marks the beginning of urban life in the native Americas. South American cities became the nuclei of political and religious governments. Construction of the temples and public buildings are now larger and more elaborate. There is a much higher order of craftsmanship. Archeologists note improvement in ceramics, weaving, stone work, and carving. Craft specialization has become more apparent as excavations have unearthed different burial goods, varying art styles, and improved architecture.

According to Willey and Phillips, following the *Classic* culture, the *Postclassic Stage* occurred from 1200 years ago to modern times. Migrations continued, causing population shifts. Societies became more secular as they faced times of unrest and war. The *Postclassic* civilizations are generally dated in the last six hundred years or so preceding the presence of armored horsemen, who arrived by boat and claimed the land underfoot for Spain— circa 1500 AD.

While native Indians, across the Americas, advanced their culture into agriculture, urban life, and political prominence, those living on the Great Plains continued a lifestyle unchanged greatly by the passing of time. They lived in an area that ranged from the Mississippi River to the Rocky Mountains and from Canada to Mexico. The Plains Indians are divided into two overlapping groups, each dealing with the undertaking of agriculture. Most bands were part time farmers living in villages along the rivers where the soil was both fertile and easy to work. On the open plains the land was impossible to farm. Stone tools couldn't penetrate the entangled layer in the grasslands. Roots of the matted grasses grew 10 feet deep and had a tenacious grip on the soil. These inconstant farming tribes raised corn, beans, and squash while gathering wild plants and continuing their hunting practices for game. Their larger game consisted of deer, elk and bison; however, being on foot and following the seasonal pattern of the buffalo was difficult. Early Americans would disguise themselves by wearing animal hides and quietly stalking the humpback beasts. Most likely a corral was previously constructed and part of the herd stampeded into it. Another technique was to select a favorable cliff and chase the beasts over the edge. In both cases, it became easier to incapacitate the animals for eventual slaughter.

Several different clans would join in the hunt. In cases where the hunt was joined by other tribes, speaking different languages, they communicated by using sign language. Semi-nomadic Plains Indians used their dogs as pack animals, thus limiting the amount being carried and distance covered. The load was dragged on a travois, consisting of two trailing poles, harnessed to the dog, with a platform at the opposite end. Due to the limitations of canine draft animals, their burden naturally became lighter. Materials for living on the hunt allowed for only a small temporary shelter. Accordingly, once the game was harvested, people quickly returned to their villages.

A second group of original plainsmen were primarily hunters. While their women sought wild plants, such as Indian turnip, the men primarily pursued the buffalo. Similar to the part-time farming tribes, bison became the chief source of food and all the items made from their hide and bone.

Typical among these nomadic hunters were the Sioux and Blackfoot Indians who ranged across large areas of the northern Great Plains. The region was semi-arid and covered by short grasses, ideal grazing for the American bison. While men were hunters, women took on different roles. Besides gathering wild foods, they cooked, made clothing, and were responsible for erecting tepees—a frequent activity considering the tepees required dismantling each time the tribe moved.

Basically, the plains culture continued unchanged until the first white man came on the scene. In 1492, Christopher Columbus, a Genoese sailing under a Spanish flag, stumbled on the Bahamas while seeking a shorter route to the East Indies. His discovery resulted in three more voyages. On his second expedition he sailed with 17 ships, 1200 men, and supplies to establish permanent colonies in the New World. Among the passengers were priests, farmers, soldiers, and a few horses— ten mares and fifteen stallions. Along with exploration, the Spanish goal now included establishing continuous settlements and missions dedicated to converting the natives to Christianity. While Columbus may have been the first to reintroduce horses in America, it will take a few years before there is enough to be significant. However, King Ferdinand ordered that future expeditions carried all horses possible to stock the islands with Spain's best breeding animals.

The Spaniards were the most successful of all the explorers who came to the New World. These searchers and conquistadors probed from the Caribbean to South America on foot and horseback. Many of the conquistadors were mounted on their own horses— animals of excellent quality and breeding. Others acquired them from the islands.

Men with such names as Hernán Cortés, Francisco Pizarro, Hernando De Soto, Vasco Núñez de Balboa and Juan Ponce de Leon foraged their way northward establishing settlements and rule under various Flags of Spain; each bringing a quantity of horses for the purpose of farming and reproduction. In 1500, Captain Diego De Velázquez was appointed governor of Cuba and took eighty horses from his ranches of Espanola with him. Later, he brought more chargers and established the Bayamo Ranch from where conquistadors, sailing to North and South America, supplied their mounts. By the time King Ferdinand placed an embargo on exporting horses in the year 1520, the islands furnished nearly all equines thereafter, which went to the New World.

While each had a hand in it, probably the Spanish adventurer most responsible for the reintroduction of the horse to the American Plains was Hernán Cortés de Monroy y Pizzaro. Born to a lesser nobility, Cortés chose to pursue a livelihood in the New World. Accurate descriptions of Cortés, as to his personality and motivations, are sketchy. We know that he went first to Hispaniola then Cuba where he received an *encomienda*[4]. Once news arrived of a bonanza of silver and gold, found along the southeast coast of Mexico, the governor of Cuba, Diego Velázquez appointed Cortés to lead an expedition into the mainland. Within a month, Cortés was able to gather 6 ships and 300 men.

At the last moment, due to a personal enmity between the governor and Cortés, the expedition charter was revoked. Cortés ignored the orders and went ahead in an act of open mutiny.

At the point of departure in 1519 his expedition had grown to about 11 ships, 500 men, 20 horses, and a small number of cannons. He landed first at Tabasco and defeated the natives in battle. It was there, Cortés learned of Montezuma, emperor of the vast Aztec empire, possessor of immense riches, and living in a city called Tenochtitlan (Mexico City). After lingering a short time at Tabasco, Cortés sailed up the coast to take command of Veracruz, a crescent-shaped strip of land between the Sierra Madre Mountains to the west and the Gulf of Mexico to the east.

---

[4] A system to regulate Native American labor. It was designed to protect natives from other warring tribes, instruct them in the Spanish language, and teach the Catholic faith. Many natives were forced to do hard labor under the punishment of death.

He now dismissed the influence of the Cuban governor and placed himself directly under the authority of King Charles. Determined to deal with any disaffection and ideas of retreat, he scuttled his ships, effectively stranding the expedition in Mexico and committing his entire forces to survive by conquest. While in Veracruz, he met some subordinates of the Aztecs and tried to arrange a meeting with Montezuma. Failing to organize a meeting, Cortés set out for the Mexican interior. By now, he had learned there was political unrest and bitter resentment by many of the subjugated natives, who were forced to pay tribute to the Aztecs and Montezuma. While its inhabitants defended each territory along the route, their efforts were futile against the armored conquistadors mounted on horseback. Many of the conquered natives became his followers and when Cortés entered the capital city, over 6,000 had joined the Spaniards.

Awed by men wearing protective armor and riding strange animals equally covered with metal carapace, Montezuma believed Cortés to be a god and patron of the Aztec priesthood. Accordingly, the emperor greeted him with friendship and great respect. Cortés, on the other hand, was intoxicated by previous events and assumed the attitude of a conqueror rather than a guest. That demeanor irritated some of the Aztecs and they assaulted the Spaniards. Cortés quickly seized Montezuma, placed him in irons, and delivered him to the headquarters of his troops. Threatened with instant death, Montezuma was forced to acknowledge himself and his subjects, vassals of King Charles V, and to relinquish a large amount of gold. A short time later, seventeen of those who made the attack were rounded up and burned to death in front of the palace, a serious act of retribution and harsh warning against repeating similar aggression.

Now, Cortés was master of Tenochtitlan, however, Spanish politics and rancor was to plague him throughout his meteoric career. Back in Cuba, Governor Diego Velázquez was relentless in his efforts to discredit his antagonist. He pursued his attacks in Spain through Bishop Juan Rodriguez de Fonseca and the

Council of the Indies. Cortés countered by sending lengthy dispatches directly to King Charles.

While still savoring his triumph over Montezuma, Cortés learned from the coast that a much larger party of Spaniards had arrived. Governor Velázquez had sent Pánfilo de Narváez, commanding 900 men, 80 horses, and a dozen cannon, to arrest Cortés and bring him back to Cuba to stand trial for insubordination, mutiny, and treason. Cortés found himself in a quandary with few options. If arrested and convicted, he would most surely be executed, considering his hostile relationship with Diego Velázquez.

Historians, in their attempt to better understand the character of Cortés, are most likely unanimous when it came to bravery. If there is an outstanding fault, it must be his heedless disregard for caution. In the face of pending expulsion, the rash conquistador assembled 140 Spanish soldiers and placed them under the command of Pedro Alvarado. They, and a number of loyal natives, were given the task of holding the city while Cortés set out to face Narvaez.

Rushing to the Mexican coast, he was able to gather a few additional reinforcements; even so, it probably brought together only 250 men by the time he reached his adversary. Facing overwhelming numbers, Cortés used his smaller force in a surprise night attack. Catching his opponent off guard, he was able to capture Narváez and take him prisoner. With their leader restrained, Cortés told the defeated soldiers about the riches of Tenochtitlan and promised them a share. They agreed to join him and prepared for a quick return to the city of gold.

Near the time of departure, messengers arrived with news of a disaster in Tenochtitlan. A terrible massacre had taken place in which 600 Mexican nobles had been slain. The capital was ablaze with fires of an insurrection. Pedro Alvarado, in charge while Cortés was absent, had granted permission for the natives to celebrate the feast of their war-god in the courtyard of the palace where the Spaniards were quartered. While the defenseless nobles were dancing in celebration, Alvarado's soldiers attacked them.

Whatever the excuses were given for Alvarado's actions, the slain aristocrat's bodies were stripped, reaping a rich harvest of jewels. After the dead nobles were thrust without the walls, the infuriated populace stormed the confines in retaliation. Montezuma, himself, was unable to quell their attack of vengeance. This was the state of affairs when Cortés arrived at the causeway leading to the capital. The Aztecs were aware of his coming and allowed the troops to enter unimpeded. Cortés marched quickly to the central square and found the gates of the palace closed. Alvarado appeared, and after learning that Cortés was still in command, ordered the gates open for his countrymen to enter. This is exactly what the Aztecs had planned; get the hated invaders together and destroy them. The city contained about 300,000 people of which 60,000 were warriors willing to sacrifice their lives in order to annihilate the Spaniards. Cortés' forces were less than 1,800 armed soldiers and some 8,000 native allies—chiefly Tlaxcalan warriors. The Spaniards, facing overwhelming numbers and a perpetual onslaught, now must contend with a siege. The Aztecs cut off all supply of food and water making starvation a strong possibility. Once the Aztecs were convinced all the Spaniards were within the palace walls, they resumed their relentless attack. Wave after wave of human undulation besieged the palace periphery, only to be temporarily stayed by Spanish cannon and musketry. There was no need for the soldiers to take aim. By reloading and firing aimlessly, they would hit one of the swarming hordes.

Thousands surrounded the palace and took positions atop higher structures so that a continuous rain of missiles fell upon those within the confines. On the third day, after failing several military counter moves, Cortés knew that capture or surrender meant immediate death by sacrifice on the temple altar. As a last ditch effort, he organized a group, made up of his bravest cavaliers, to storm the great temple and control its priests. The exalted temple commanded the entire area around the palace and served as the center of attack on the enemy below. With nearly 600 Mexicans standing on the summit platform, hurling large stones and delivering every sort of missile, it now became the focus of the Spanish leader.

Three hundred soldiers were assigned the task, while 3,000 Tlaxcalan battled the gathering crowds of Aztecs. The conquistadors passed around the terraced slopes five times before they finally gained the elevated platform. Aztec warriors rallied around their imperiled priests and nobles, while nearly 5,000 rushed into the surrounding enclosure and up the steps of the pyramid. Now, from the highest pinnacle, Cortés held a strategic advantage. With their impenetrable steel armor, the courageous conquistadors were able to withstand the onslaught of those shrieking in defiance.

The battle raged for hours before Cortés succeeded in setting fire to the temples of the gods. More than 500 Aztecs were slain, while fifty Spaniards lost their life and nearly all were exhibiting bloody wounds. Thinking the destruction of the temples would prove to the Aztecs that their gods were impotent proved wrong. It only increased their rage, as they stubbornly disputed the passage back to the palace. Once behind the protective walls of the palace, Cortés called for a meeting with the few remaining nobles. The indomitable Aztecs would not hear of peace; they wanted war until the bitter end.

Facing overwhelming numbers and disastrous defeat, he summoned Montezuma and asked him to beg his countrymen to end their attacks, after which the Spaniards would withdraw from the city. When Montezuma went before the nobles and made the plea, they refused and let loose a shower of arrows and stones; one of which struck their former chief and, later, proved fatal. That proved to be the *causa finalis*. The situation was no longer tenable and to remain meant certain death. Reluctantly, Cortés must accept a disparaging defeat and retreat from the battle.

The shortest route to the mainland was the causeway leading to Tacuba—a section northwest of Tenochtitlan. The Aztecs had previously destroyed all the bridges across the canals, in order to hinder any attempt at escape. To accommodate this, Cortés ordered a pontoon be constructed and placed fifty handpicked soldiers in charge. Unfortunately, there are three canals to cross and only one floating platform. Cortés had divided his small army into three units; the first of which contained the artillery, prisoners, the king's portion from Montezuma's treasure, and most of the baggage. Cortés led the second group; giving him the advantage to observe both front and back.

Just before midnight the palace gates were thrown open and into the darkened outer grounds emerged the remainder of a once proud legion. They progressed as quietly as possible under the gloomy drizzle of rain, encouraged by the puzzling silence of their enemy. Everything changed once they reached the first canal and began positioning the pontoon bridge. Aztec sentinels signaled the alarm, followed by the blowing of horns, and sounding the great drum above the war-god's altar. Immediately, the heavens exploded with a cloudburst of missiles falling on the heads of the huddled brigade. Many of whom had discarded their armor in order to ford the waterway. The lone pontoon was firmly wedged and impossible to move. Despire the fact, the vanguard dashed forward only to be halted by the second canal.

Amid the brutal barrage of burning coals, arrows, and darts, Cortés managed to inch his army forward; primarily by crawling over the slain men and horses. On every side, the triumphant Aztecs were hewing at the defenseless soldiers with their obsidian broadswords and javelins. Rows of canoes, filled with warriors, dragged as many prisoners as they could reach, back to the sacrificial stone, to have their hearts torn from their bodies. It was short of a miracle that a single soldier escaped; nevertheless, nearly two thirds of the cavaliers managed to get through. Over 500 were slain, along with 4,000 loyal Tlaxcalan natives. All the artillery and ammunition was lost. Even the muskets were thrown away during the frantic withdrawal. Now, the long journey to Tlaxcala lay ahead.

The Aztecs decided not to follow them; probably because they satisfied their blood lust and now concentrated on sacrificing prisoners. Cortés' destination lay nearly 100 miles away. Halting only long enough to sleep and dress their wounds, the valiant conquistadors embarked on a march that will take a full week. It was a week in which they were assailed by threatening shouts from hostile savages every step of the way. Finally, after passing through a mountain gap, they faced an immense horde, numbering over 100,000 warriors, gathered in full battle attire.

For the longest moment, the two armies faced each other in silence. Waving plumes and weapons, gleaming in the sun, extended as far as the eye could see. Then, the familiar sound of battle cries began to swell. The Spaniards were convinced their end had come. Cortés had no cannon, few muskets, and little ammunition. Combat was mainly hand to hand. Outnumbered one hundred to one, the outcome was never in doubt; but, Cortés managed to see the principal leader and knowing the reverence with which the Aztecs regarded their cacique, formed a wedge of horsemen and pierced the crowd until he reached their chief. By pinning him to the ground and waving the royal banner, the angry Aztecs gave up the contest and fled the field. It was a great victory, but with so few survivors, they did not dare to follow it up and resumed the march to Tlaxcala.

All homes were opened to the Spaniards when they arrived at Tlaxcala. The friendly natives provided nurses and surgeons to help bring the battle worn army back to health. Soon, Cortés was strong enough to begin scheming to recapture the Aztec capital. It will take time for his convalescing troops to regain their fighting condition; meanwhile, Cortés sent for reinforcements from the coast. Vessels frequently arrived with men and supplies in order to continue the colonization along the coast. They possessed large quantities of war material, and their crews were easily convinced to join the popular conquistador.

Over the next five months, he gradually gathered a larger army than the one which originally invaded Tenochtitlan. He devised a new battle plan to begin his conquest. Forays were sent out to capture the territories surrounding Tlaxcala. The native tribes fought hard against the invaders but their primitive weapons were inferior to Spanish cannon and musketry. These somewhat minor victories fit into his overall plan to siege and capture his main objective—Tenochtitlan. By securing the area outside the Tlaxcalan territory, potential allies for the Aztecs will be removed. While cutting off all tributary cities and towns from Tenochtitlan, Cortés and his gallant soldiers fought many perilous battles. In defense of their homeland, tribal inhabitants sallied against them by the thousands; nevertheless, Cortés remained dauntless and steadfast in his quest. His widening circle of triumph now included Texcoco and the great lake by the same name, on which the capital rests.

While the conquistadors were on the march and fighting, other workmen were constantly employed. Auxiliaries had cut timbers from the Tlaxcalan forests in order to construct brigantines, which will serve to permit an attack by water. And, from Villa Rica, on the coast, iron-works and rigging was brought to Texcoco. All these components had been hand carried by native burden-bearers. Ships were put together with deliberate speed and launched at the end of April. The siege of Tenochtitlan had begun.

Cortés now commanded a much greater force than he had previously, when his undertaking ended with the stigma of failure and retreat. The embarrassment haunted his dreams for months afterward and reinforced his vengeance during the waking hours. His refitted army was composed of nearly 900 soldiers. And, when on the march, it displayed a cavalry of 90 armored men and horses, 100 musketeers and cross-bowmen, followed by 700 infantry, armed with lance and sword. Making the force even more auspicious, they were being accompanied by 70,000 Tlaxcalan allies.

For weeks Aztec sentries had observed the activity across the lake—the massing of men building boats and reported to Guatemotzin[5], their new emperor. Only 23 years old, he was well

---

[5]   The son-in-law of Montezuma named Guatano or Guatemotzin and trained by war chiefs.

beyond his actual age in leadership ability. While Cortés planned the attack, he devised a strategy for defensive ambush.

Some habits, however, are difficult to break; for, as soon as Cortés' brigantines moved in the water, the Aztecs let loose their war-canoes. An immense fleet of shrieking warriors hastened forward, cutting the surface with powerful strokes of their paddles. The resonance of their battle cry was all too familiar to Cortés, as he liberated the brigantines to meet them. Each square-rigged watercraft was armed with cannon in the bow and made up with a crew of twenty-five men. Aztec war-canoes were no match for the heavier Spanish vessels. The brigantines plowed forward, overturning and crushing all in their path. Cannon fire splintered the remainder until only flotsam littered the choppy lake surface. Young Guatemotzin suffered his first military defeat; albeit, a naval contest. His genius was best demonstrated wherever the conquistadors attacked, as they found themselves surrounded by hordes of Aztecs repelling their advance. Cortés counteracted by apportioning his army into three units and attacking the smaller towns and outposts encircling the capital city. The inhabitants were no match for the Spaniards, advancing by both land and water. With the perimeter subdued and controlled, Cortés could now stage a siege. He set up his command camp closest to Tenochtitlan and cut off the supply of food and water. Over the next few days, the enemy within the besieged boundaries grew quieter; a sure sign the blockade was working. This tactic didn't fit well with soldiers who relished direct combat; and, after a few weeks, they clamored for an advance in force. Against better judgment, Cortés finally conceded.

Supported by thousands of Tlaxcalan war-canoes and a reunified army force, the Spaniards proceeded along the causeways. Guatemotzin, unknown to the aggressors, had prepared for any straightforward assault. And, as the Spaniards and their hosts advanced, the Aztecs feigned a retreat and drew their enemies into the great plaza. Now, Cortés found himself wedged in by the undisciplined Tlaxcalans who were crowding forward. Suddenly, the emperor's great horn was sounded and Aztec warriors burst from their places of hiding with incredible wrath. At first, escape was prevented by the masses of allies lodged between them and the safety of their command camp. Besiegers were slaughtered by the hundreds; and, amid the booming drumbeat, blaring horns, and deafening shrieks of the howling savages, the clangor was so loud no orders could be heard. Nearly 100 soldiers were dragged away to the war-god's temple for sacrifice.

Cortés had remained with the rear-guard; however, hurried forward when he heard the tumult of retreat. After reaching his retracting troops, he found himself caught in the press and plight. Quatemotzin's warriors pulled Cortés from his horse and dragged him toward their waiting canoes. Were it not for Spanish soldiers recognizing the struggle, Cortés would have been another sacrifice on that terrible altar. His men managed to defeat the abductors and affect his release.

Narrowly escaping the unthinkable, Cortés withdrew his shattered army back to the protective walls of Xoloc, his command headquarters; all the while being pursued by the Aztecs to the very gates.

Respect for young emperor Guatemotzin has grown considerably. While the booming resonance of the great drum sounded off in the distance, the Spanish army reorganized and rallied to revive Cortés' original scheme. The captains apparently had lost their enthusiasm for another frontal attack and became more willing to follow their leader's plan. Now, the general advance concentrated on destroying all the buildings in front of them and filling the causeway hollows with their debris. Hordes of Tlaxcalan allies eagerly joined in the destruction of the city. Progress became easier as the effects of the siege took hold. Tenochtitlan was entirely blockaded and the inhabitant's supplies of food and water completely cut off. Famine and pestilence killed by the thousands.

Cortés finally regained the central plaza and sent messengers to Guatemotzin asking for his surrender. He rejected them all with scorn, as he and his nobles retreated farther into the corner of the city unoccupied by the Spaniards. It was a minor irritation for Cortés, who now controlled Lake Texcoco with his brigantines. Any warrior canoes in their path moved away quickly with no resistance. One such canoe drew the attention of the brigantine's captain. It seemed to contain persons of notability, and as the Spanish archers took aim with their bows, a shout was heard from the canoe stating that the emperor was among them. The capture of Guatemotzin signaled the siege was over and Tenochtitlan belonged to Cortés. His victory marked the fall of the Aztec empire.

After a battle, lasting seventy-five days, Cortés had become the de facto civil and military ruler of a huge territory called New Spain or Mexico. The full account of his victory had to wait nearly a year as he concentrated on rebuilding the city he once claimed to be the most beautiful in the world. In a letter sent to King Charles V, he described the events in brutal detail.

News of conquests and forwarded treasures to the King made the valiant hero very popular in Spain; despite the continuous attack by the territorial executive of Cuba. Cortés was officially named governor and captain general of New Spain in 1523.

Restless desire for exploration moved him to undertake an expedition to Honduras from 1524 to 1526 with marginal results.

Two years later, due to the political maneuvering of his enemy in Cuba—Diego Velázquez, Cortés was ordered to relinquish the leadership of Mexico and return to Spain. After appealing to the King, he was made marquis of the Valley of Oaxaca in southern Mexico and reappointed captain general; although, not restored to civil governorship. While involved in other explorations, he was never able to reclaim the prestige he once possessed. The champion explorer eventually retired to a small estate near Seville, in the south of Spain.

I had previously stated that the Spanish adventurer most responsible for the reintroduction of the horse into the American Plains was Hernán Cortés. While he and his men mainly brought their own horses, some did break loose and run wild. In itself, it was not enough to be significant. The fact that Cortés conquered Mexico set the stage for future mainland colonies. And those intrepid adventurers who followed, i.e., Francisco Vásques de Coronado, Hernando De Soto, Don Juan de Oñate y Salazar, and others, paved the way for colonial population and expanding greater numbers of horse herds in northern Mexico and North America.

The first contributor of consequence may have been Francisco Vásquez de Coronado who brought 558 horses with him on his 1539-1542 expeditions. At the time, Indians of these regions probably perceived of horses, but had never actually seen one. Only two of Coronado's horses were mares; unlikely making him the source of any Great Plains horse culture.

In 1592, Don Juan de Oñate brought 7,000 head of livestock with him when he came north to establish a colony in New Mexico. He undertook a large expedition to the Great Plains in 1601 with 350 horses and mules. Among the horses were many mares. Oñate's excursion was plagued with harmful setbacks from the beginning. Actually, the Basque Conquistador's expedition was at a costly standstill for many months.

Don Juan de Onate...In 1598, Onate led an expedition of 500 settlers on a northward march into the upper Rio Grand Valley of New Mexico. He established the first European settlement west of the Mississippi. His entourage consisted of seven-thousand head of livestock...beef cattle, spare oxen, horses, pack mules, donkeys, sheep and goats. While previous explorers brought mainly stallions, Onate delivered mares which led to the population of wild herds.

His political enemies denied approval to move forward; and, after nearly a year, prospective colonists became discouraged and fled back south—an act of mutiny in the eyes of the Spanish authority. Be that as it may, during the extended delays, many horses broke free and joined wild herds.

* * *

Horses revolutionized the Plains Indian's way of life. It made an emphatic change in their culture by allowing their owners to hunt, trade, and wage war more effectively. In search of bison herds, they were able to travel faster over longer distances. The Plains Indians could now overtake the stampeding humpbacks and make the kill while on their ponies. It did require shortening their bows to three feet to accommodate being on horseback.

Horses permitted bigger tepees. Additional possessions could be conveyed, not to mention transporting their old and sick, which otherwise would have been abandoned. No longer relying on dogs to carry belongings, horse owners can now maintain larger supplies of food.

Horses soon became the foundation of status systems by changing formerly equal societies into class ranking based on horse ownership. A wealthy family might own as many as thirty horses, but only one or two would be good enough to be ridden into battle. And, while horse ownership had elevated social status, nearly all groups of Native people integrated use of the equine into their culture. Many became very capable horse-breeding tribes led by Comanches, Lakotas, Cheyenne, and Nez Perce. The later, in particular, became master horse-breeders and are credited for developing one of the first distinctive American breeds— the Appaloosa.

Other tribes were not that interested in conducting their own selective breeding. On the other hand, they sought out desirable horses through acquisition and quickly weeded out those with undesirable traits.

By the 1800s the region in the southwest supported nearly two million wild horses; however, as the frontier moved northward through the Plains, the numbers were greatly reduced. Harsh northern winters have a negative effect on reproduction and, heavy snowfall over the grassland made feeding difficult, resulting in severe winter losses. Finally, large horse herds affected the southern region's delicate ecological balance as they competed with native species for water and grass. Not only did horses exact a toll on the environment, it required considerable labor to take care of the herd. Rich men took several wives and captives to manage their new found livestock.

The overexploited river valleys pushed bison herds farther north into the Plains; perhaps, signaling an early reason for the future decline of the massive buffalo herds.

CHAPTER ONE

T he year is 1868. The South's economy was in ruins. Massive war costs took a grave toll on its financial framework. With the Civil War primarily fought in the South, many of the major cities were either destroyed or severely damaged. Their courthouses had burned to the ground along with documents for the various legal relationships in the communities. And, beyond the obvious physical destruction, losses in human capital, such as knowledge, useful social attributes, and desire, had reduced the ability to perform the required labor to produce economic value. Furthermore, slaves were now free under Federal mandate; however, white planters lacked necessary capital to pay the freedmen workers to bring in the crops.

Farms were in disrepair. The prewar stock of horses, mules, and cattle was much depleted. In fact, 40 percent of the South's livestock had been killed.

After Abraham Lincoln was assassinated, Vice President Andrew Johnson became president. The new president shared Lincoln's belief concerning reintroduction of the Confederacy back into the Union. Because of his lenient approach in handling the rebels, Johnson became an opponent of the radicals in Congress. The Republicans won the critical mid-term election of 1866 and overcame Andrew Johnson's vetoes.

In 1867, with a two-thirds majority in both houses, Congress removed the civilian governments in the South and put into effect the Radical Republican's Reconstruction plan under the supervision of the U.S. Army. In part, it allowed for an immoderate coalition of freed slaves, scalawags (local whites), and carpetbaggers (recent arrivals) to take control of the Southern States' governments. Many were unqualified for positions of authority and ill prepared for the important task ahead.

Now, with full control of both houses of Congress, the Radical Republicans impeached President Johnson and almost removed him from office in 1868, were it not for a single vote.

Considering the prevailing political climate, there was no way Andrew Johnson would run for reelection. His parting gesture was to give a presidential pardon to the Confederate soldiers. While this act infuriated the Republicans, it was a time for celebration in the south. Up 'til now, Confederate veterans were prevented from receiving many rights of citizenship. Thanks to the "Tennessee Tailor" the majority of their rights are returned.

* * *

In spite of the ravages of the Reconstruction, Jack Leffingwell has managed to improve the farm to the point of profitability. He and Melvin Kaufman overcame odious restrictions; and, with the hard work of both families, not only produced adequate crops but increased the animal herds as well.

In Tennessee, the month of October still clings tenaciously to the passing of summer. The autumnal deception is betrayed by the brilliant colors of the dying tree leaves. This most pleasant visual phenomenon is due to the presence of accessory leaf pigments that normally assist the plants during photosynthesis by capturing specific wavelengths of sunlight. These pigments become visible when the leaf dies in the fall, giving an array of beautiful red, orange, and yellow coloration.

With the harvest completed, the children, as well as Abigail and Hope, sense a mounting excitement in anticipation of fall visitors. Within the week, Horace and Grace Waterman will arrive by train from Richmond, Virginia, along with Hope's 12-year-old sister, Susan, and plan to stay for three weeks. Their visits occur at least twice each year. The Watermans look forward to spending time with their daughter and perhaps more so with their two-year-old granddaughter, Rebecca. Susan loves her sister but is also looking forward to being with her sidekick Sarah Jane. The young girls are the same age and share the inquisitive nature of preteens.

Jack and Melvin anticipate seeing their Civil War companion, Abel Strawn and his wife Amanda. The Strawns also have a two-year-old daughter whom they christened, Abigail and call Abby. The twenty-mile trip will be covered in a chaise carriage borrowed from one of the Methodist Church parishioners. Of late, Abel has been troubled with an irksome dilemma and needs to discuss it with Jack before making any decision. Jack Leffingwell has the innate ability to see beneath the surface of most problems and Abel won't take on a venture of this magnitude without first seeking Jack's counsel.

By now, Grace Waterman has become more used to her daughter's house. The unadorned cabin came as a shocking surprise upon her first visit. After witnessing how much her daughter loved it and the manner in which Horace made himself at home, she accepted the rustic dwelling but could never get accustomed to not having better oil lamps. Her Richmond fixtures were more elaborate than the common lamps found on the farm. The fumes from Hope's lighting devices made her eyes burn. Grace failed to realize that it would be more than seventy years before such instruments were no longer being used. While fuel, wicks, and mantles will improve, many rural areas will not have electric power until after the Second World War.

Horace Waterman, on the other hand, took delight with the farm, especially in the misty autumn mornings. He loved to take his coffee on the front porch and listen to Hope's roosters, announcing the sunrise by dueling each other in a reveille contest. There appeared to be more poultry than when he and

Grace last stayed. Strolling over to the henhouse, he observed newly hatched chicks in close formation round their mother. In addition, several bantams were pecking the ground for bits of overlooked grain. They were joined by a few guinea fowl with the same idea. Finally, Horace took another sip from his coffee mug and smiled to himself when a large turkey made his appearance in the fenced in coop. Clipped wing feathers told him the bird's destiny awaited a certain Thursday in November.

Hope's chicken venture had turned into a dependable source of revenue. It provided enough hard cash to allow for purchasing the occasional notion item plus, putting a little away for the proverbial rainy day. After being chased by one of the roosters, she became an old hand at sexing newborn chicks.

Returning to his favorite chair on the porch, Horace was joined by his son-in-law, Melvin Kaufman. The two men sat in silence for a minute or so when Horace said, "Your poultry livestock has increased appreciably from when we were here last."

"Hope gets all the credit for that," Melvin replied proudly. "She has taken to the rural life like a duck takes to water. Did you notice we put chicken wire on top the fence?"

"As a matter of fact, I did," Horace confessed. "It seemed odd until I saw the turkey."

"That turkey isn't the main reason. We have all kinds of owls around the farm and, with Hope raising chickens for eggs and such, the hatchlings presented an easy meal for the hooters."

"I never gave the owls any thought. With so much natural timber around the farm, baby chicks would be a habitual source of prey for them," Horace agreed, while swirling the remainder of lukewarm coffee before taking his final swig.

"Can I get you a hot refill?" asked Melvin.

"No thanks son, I can smell bacon frying. So it won't be long before we eat breakfast," Horace answered frankly as he stood facing the kitchen screen door. At that moment the image of Hope was viewed behind the meshwork and she asserted, "Breakfast is on the Table."

* * *

A short distance away a similar scene was taking place. The young girls assisted Abigail in preparing the morning repast. Sarah Jane and her buddy, Susan Waterman, were relishing one of the few times they could act grownup. Keeping an eye on the little boys was another but not nearly as fulfilling as making breakfast. Susan worked the biscuit cutter, Sarah Jane turned the bacon, and Abigail tended the eggs just to be safe. Jack liked his easy over.

"Where's daddy?" inquired Sarah Jane.

"He's out doing the morning chores," replied her mother.

"Is he going to gather the eggs?"

"Most likely, your father has the boys with him. You girls talked half the night and didn't get up very early," Abigail reminded. The expression on the youngsters' faces indicated their disappointment and also determination against these circumstances being repeated.

"Jack Junior and Jozef aren't very good when it comes to gathering eggs. They are afraid to look under the hens if they don't leave the nest right away," Sarah Jane said calmly.

"Why is that?" Susan asked honestly.

"They're scared of getting pecked," Sarah Jane answered as a matter-of-fact.

Voices heard from the open porch were those of the little fellows who were being previously discussed. With a joyful demeanor, the pair wrestled open the kitchen door and placed the egg basket on top the counter. "We gathered the eggs," Jack Junior announced with an overflow of self-satisfaction. His sister whispered a silent snicker.

"We all are proud of you boys," Abigail stated. "Now, go wash your hands while we set the table and bring in the food. We're having hot biscuits and plenty of strawberry preserves."

CHAPTER TWO

F inal touches were underway as Abel and Amanda made preparations for their trip to Statesville and Jack Leffingwell's farm. Abel always looked forward to visiting his friend and Civil War comrade. The importance of this journey went beyond fellowship. Abel needed his friend's opinion on a decision that would transform not only him but also the rest of his family's lives. Faced with what could be good fortune or catastrophe needed the stalemate broken; and, the mountain man remains the only voice that can move the needle.

Abel hitched the conveyance to the same horse he rode while traveling from Richmond, Virginia to Statesville, Tennessee after the war ended. The animal was more than able to make a trip of twenty miles and seemed anxious to be on his way. It was early enough for the more brilliant stars to still be visible in the first blush of morning. Their two-year-old daughter Abby, wrapped in her warm blanket, was still in the arms of Morpheus.

The way to Statesville was a familiar route having been traveled several times previously. At a leisurely pace the Strawn family expects to arrive at their destination sometime in the early afternoon. Amanda had packed a lunch for the midway rest stop—a shady glade by one of the countryside's quiet murmurs of trickling water. It was a good place to rest the horse and give it a drink for the second half of the jaunt. It also provided another opportunity for Amanda to convince Abel that it was worthwhile having Pearle, her twenty-year-old brother, with them should they decide to make a move. Up 'til now the young man has shown few signs of settling down; a major concern for Abel, should he agree to the worrisome undertaking now tormenting his thoughts.

"You know Pearle thinks the world of you, dear. In fact, he idolizes you," reminded Amanda as she spread out the picnic blanket.

"He's engrossed by the war and associates me with it. Pearle is caught up in the idea of adventure. It's exciting for him, but that's not what war is all about. Because of his youth, he doesn't see the real side of war or the horrible atrocities that make up the truth," Abel replied, while holding Abby, who is now wide-awake and hungry.

"He listens to you and only needs to be around you more," she said tersely.

"I'm not even certain that we're going west. A lot depends on what I learn in Statesville," Abel responded. The subject was put in abeyance while Abby drew their attention. Finally, Abel got to his feet, stretched his tall frame, and inhaled a deep breath while admiring his surroundings. The area, on which he stood, was once used as a hunting ground by Cherokee, Chickasaw, and Shawnee Indians. Itself, a mildly rolling low-lying area, surrounded by the western and eastern Highland Rim. The Cumberland Mountains rise to the east, and the state capitol, Nashville, rested a few miles to the west. Nashville became an important Confederate stronghold at the beginning of the Civil War, only to become the first major Confederate city to fall to Union troops. Under Union occupation, Nashville was used to support the Union Army with supplies, weapons, ammunition, and medical care. The population of the city greatly expanded with soldiers, runaway slaves, and wartime entrepreneurs. The cotton-state faithful unsuccessfully made an attempt to recapture the city from the Union Army in December 1864. It marked the last significant offensive action taken by the South. Abel loved

Tennessee and cherished its lofty mountain heights; another reason for uneasiness over the move to the endless prairie of a new home.

* * *

The entire clan from the two farms met them as their surrey pulled to a stop in front of Jack Leffingwell's open porch. Hope and Abigail ran to help Amanda and little Abby down from the buggy. Jack and Melvin shook hands with their visitor and the three men led Abel's horse to the corral. Jack's maintenance barn will hold the gig for the duration of this year's visit. Travel to and from Statesville will either be in the box wagon, Leffingwell's carriage, or on horseback. Naturally the men preferred the latter, however, when the whole family was involved, the women held sway. As customary, the talk mainly consisted of social amenities, such as, each other's health, fall harvest, and their wives and children. The main topic for Abel must wait for a more suitable time, perhaps at night once the children were in bed.

On the way back to the house, Abel received a heartfelt greeting from Abigail. As long as they both draw breath, Abigail will have no friend more genuine. She will always be indebted to Abel for whom she believes saved her marriage. Their relationship, which began in Richmond, Virginia, at the Robertson Hospital, turned out to be a blessing. Although fate played a more significant role, the mountain man's wife will everlastingly think otherwise.

That afternoon, the families took supper out of doors á la picnic style. Two wooden stands had been constructed for such an occasion. Resting atop the tables was the customary rural fare with fried chicken and an assorted array of fruit jars containing bounty from last year's canning session. On one end stood a vessel holding fresh lemonade made previously and stored overnight in the fruit cellar. Even in the absence of ice, it achieved a soothing coolness.

The children loved eating outside. Mothers tended to be more lenient while dining in the open air. It was like eating in the middle of their play area. They quickly gathered together at the table with the most jars of jam and preserves, planning to concentrate their appetites on fresh baked bread and the sweetened fruit spread.

During that momentary pause before digging in, Abigail requested Abel to give thanks. Rising to his feet, he asked that every eye is closed and all hearts open before saying,

> *"Dear Heavenly Father be present at our table this special day. We come to Thee to give thanks for all our many blessings. We're thankful for our many earthly gifts. We're thankful for Rebecca and Abby. May we be granted the wisdom to raise them according to Your Will. We ask Thy blessing on this food for which we are grateful. Watch over all of us Lord and keep us in Thy loving care. Through Jesus' name we pray, Amen."*

As the October sun moved well past its apogee, sounds of muffled conversation, the tinkle of spoons touching plates and dishes and a mild argument between Sarah Jane and Jack Junior, over a jar of strawberry preserves, was the only audible noise until well into the late afternoon. Determining the main meal over, Abigail lifted the lid from the large pastry plate and announced, "We have chocolate cake for dessert."

Few had left room for the moist and delicious patisserie; however, once coffee cups were refilled with the steaming brew, everyone accepted a small piece.

Approaching the conclusion of a wonderful day, Hope and Abigail got to their feet and began to clear the tables. Amanda and the two pre-teen girls joined them. At this point, Jack turned to Abel and said, "I understand you have something to tell us this afternoon."

"Yes, that's true, but it will take a little time to relate the whole story," Abel replied.

"Then let's walk down by the lake and build a fire. I know a perfect spot to tell long stories," Jack stated while smiling reassured.

On the way to the lake Abel was reminded of the black bear and asked, "Do you still have the big bear?"

"We sure do. In fact, it was a female and now we have two cubs," Melvin interjected.

The animal in question is an American black bear first noticed when Jack bought the property three years ago. At that time, there was little concern for the safety of the cattle. The bison, cougars, and elk that once roamed Middle Tennessee have now disappeared, and the only large mammals remaining are the black bear and white-tailed deer. Timber wolves can still be found in the mountains, but they, too, are reduced due to lack of large prey and being hunted for bounty.

The American Black Bear is a medium-sized ursine found throughout North America. They are not always black, although, generally believed to be raven-colored with a white, star-shaped mark on the chest. Actually, its color ranges from black to brown, cinnamon, beige, and even pure white.

Smaller that Northern Brown Bears and Grizzlies, female black bears can still weigh up to 300 pounds. Males have been known to tip the scales at 600 pounds. Ironically, cubs enter the world weighing less than one pound.

Jack Leffingwell identified the black bear before actually seeing it. Such animals have plantigrade feet (both heel and toe touch the ground) making their tracks easily identifiable. Five short, curved, sharp claws on each foot allow for effortless tree climbing. The forested portion of the mountain man's farm is an excellent habitat for the omnivorous beast feeding on berries, acorns, herbs, carrion and insects. Since one end of the lake is open, and faces the woods, it's possible the black bear occasionally dines on small fish.

Horace Waterman, at Jack's request, had joined the other men visiting the lake. Having a wild bear living on your property has piqued his imagination and curiosity.

"Aren't you fearful for the cattle with a black bear nearby?" he inquired.

"Sort of," Jack replied. "It has lived here for three years, that I'm aware of, and hasn't bothered them. As long as there's plenty of food I believe the cattle will be all right. I guess it's the mountain man in me that wants to keep it here. You may not understand; all the same, it gives me a sense of freedom."

"I understand perfectly. The bear serves to remind you of a way of life that cannot ever be forgotten. A happier time without the pressures of responsibility associated with a wife, children and the farm," stated the elder gentleman.

"I love my wife and children. I wouldn't change it for anything," Jack affirmed.

"Of course you wouldn't. The other is only a reminder of something else you love. It stays buried in the past and the presence of the black bear evokes your memory," Horace explained.

"Now you sound like my Indian friend, Yalata."

"There's a great deal of wisdom passed on within an Indian tribe," the senior guest confirmed.

"Luckily, we only need to worry about the bear half the year. It hibernates for over six months," Jack said, laughing.

"There's two more now," Melvin added.

"True, that lets us know about how old she is," Jack stated. "Females usually don't give birth until they are five or six years old, and they don't conceive again for two or three more years."

"How old will she get?" asked Horace.

"She could produce young until she was about 25 years old; however, most females only live for 10 years or so. Her two cubs tells us there is also a big male roaming around and he concerns me most of all," asserted the mountain man. "They don't usually prey on humans, but they could attack when protecting their space, food, and young."

"We don't let the children fish the lake alone," Melvin announced for the benefit of his father-in-law. With that, the men set about gathering dry branches to make a cheerful fire. A clump of hardwood trees near the main timberland provided an abundance of fallen branches and enough brushwood was about to help kindle a warm and friendly blaze.

Soon, the group sat around a crackling campfire illuminating their images, while the shortened autumn daylight began to disappear. They reposed in silence for a short time, listening to the sound of fish breaking the surface of the lake's placid water, and feasting on insects floating above. At first, the expression on their faces was strained from the initial heated glow. Once accustomed to its fume and radiance, they began to relax.

Jack Leffingwell was the first to speak, "Abel, we've been anxious all day to hear your story. Men who share the Lord's love for you encircle this fire. They are willing to risk their lives, if need be. In the comfort of that knowledge, please feel free to share with us the matter disturbing your peace."

Abel cleared his throat and began, "It started several days ago when I met a man after Sunday services. My father holds a welcome reception and invites those in the congregation to stay for refreshments. It gives them a chance to meet new members. Well, I met a fellow named Jubal Myers. He told me he recently homesteaded a farm in western Kansas, taking advantage of Abraham Lincoln's Homestead Act. He now holds title to it, free and clear; all the same, determined to give it up."

"Things went fairly well the first year. He and his wife built a cabin, using trees on his property. The second year, crops suffered from drought; nevertheless, he managed to reap enough to get through the winter. He told me you can depend on a good harvest at least one out of three years; and, the third year's crop was the best thus far. The year the Civil War ended, the land was attacked by flying grasshoppers. His neighbors called them locusts. The swarm was so thick it blackened the sky and his wife and children battled just to keep them out of the house. Once it was safe to go outside, they found the crops devastated. Locusts had eaten everything for miles around. That winter, his wife and children came down with a fever—a condition not uncommon among the pioneering settlers. Unfortunately, they didn't recover. Now, with his family gone, he has come back. He talked of returning to Ohio and restarting a life. Maybe, after being with folks he previously knew, he might find the right woman and get married again. One thing is certain, he will not return to the farm."

"He asked me if I possessed a pioneering spirit, and I told him that I thought I had. He then offered to sell me the farm for $150 dollars in gold," Abel stated, formally.

"Do you have that kind of money?" Melvin asked.

"Not really. Amanda and I have been living with my mother and father. Being assistant minister doesn't pay well; however, I still have most of the money Lomas Chandler gave me."

"Lomas seems to be doing pretty well back in Richmond. We got a letter from him last month and he said he was the city councilman for his district. I think he'll be mayor one of these days," Jack volunteered.

"I wrote him and came right out asking for a loan," Abel confessed.

"What did he ask for collateral, your daughter Abby?" Melvin questioned, bluntly.

"None of that. He wrote me back and the envelope contained $300 dollars in Yankee greenbacks, plus a note saying—*spend some of it on women and whiskey*," Abel replied, restraining a smile. "On the surface it looks like a good opportunity. On the other hand, Amanda and Abby fill up my fences and I wouldn't want to do anything that might bring harm. If I stay where I am, the best I can hope for is to just wait for my father to retire and take over the ministry. Should I let that happen, I would have forfeited the chance to construct something of my own."

Opinions varied in the minds of the campfire listeners. Finally, Jack Leffingwell broke the silence by saying, "Farming on the Plains is a lot different than plowing soil here in Tennessee. From what I've been told, you always have the weather against you. It seems like Mr. Myers found that out the hard way. For years the general thought was that civilization ended at the tree line. Even so, thanks to Lincoln's Homestead Act, people ignored the absence of timber and pioneered into the flat open spaces. Those homesteading near water proved more successful than others who didn't."

"Who told you these things?" interrupted Melvin.

"Two men I hold in the highest regard. One is Yalata, my Choctaw Indian friend and the other, Tobias Taylor, who taught me about the mountain life. Today Tobias is a wagon master taking people west to the land of which we speak," Jack answered and continued, "Ever since gold was discovered, there is a steady stream of wagons heading west. Not only settlers are included amongst them. All sorts of mankind want to get rich quick and think little of human life in order to achieve it. Farther west, the towns are made up of this pedigree, adding another kind of danger to the homesteaders. At last, there are the Indians who resent all trespassers on their land and stand as a constant threat to attack."

"Myers said there was a tribe close by that makes camp along the Arkansas River. He told me they were friendly," Abel acknowledged.

"They might be peaceful, but you're close to the Indian Territory and bands of unfriendly warriors might take a notion to pass by some day," Jack warned. "The only reason I'm telling these things is to make sure you are aware of all the negatives."

"I appreciate what you say, Jack. For all that, there are a lot of positives if I make a go of it. I can have my own land, build a better future, and maybe raise a few cattle, along with planting crops."

"Abel, I hesitate in giving you a yes or no answer. The only suggestion I will give is, if it were me in your place, I would take the chance," the mountain man honestly stated. "I'm concerned as to what caused the Myers family's demise. It sounds like cholera. The first thing you need to do is dig a well and boil the water until it gets dug. I'll be visiting Yalata soon and will run everything by him. He usually has something to add. When would you leave if you accept Myers offer?"

"Not for a couple months or so. There's a lot of gear I'll need to purchase first."

"Melvin and I will furnish a couple mules to pull the wagon and help with the plowing," Jack pledged. "I also think you need a plan B in case things don't work out. I'd give it three years, and, if you haven't made progress, come home."

The fire had burned down to the point of a few ashes and smoke. The foursome made their way back to where the rest of the family was waiting. Tramping toward illuminated windows, Jack declared, "We have got an extra box wagon in Melvin's barn. It won't take much to make a prairie schooner out of it. We'll bring it over when it's finished."

Rural friendship and generosity brought Abel to the point of tears. He managed to choke back, swallow audibly, and sincerely thank Jack for the offer.

Even though oil lamps were lit, the women remained outside enjoying the fresh air of evening. As the men approached, Melvin asked, "Amanda, did you bring your guitar this trip?"

"Sure did. I played cradle songs for Abby on the way down," she replied.

"How about playing a song for us grownups?" Melvin returned.

Amanda Sparks was taught to play the guitar when she was six years old. Her father, Wesley was accomplished with not only the guitar but fiddle and banjo as well. Wherever group music was heard around Lebanon, Tennessee, you're sure to find Wesley Sparks. In fact, it would be lacking without the sound of the instruments he selected to play. Amanda used her talent at church and in the Methodist choir. Her nimble fingers were light as a feather; yet, each note gave a firm crisp sound. The congregation sat spellbound enjoying a lifetime experience. It was as though the angels of heaven had landed in their midst and the assemblage held their breath so as not to miss a single note. They received a second blessing whenever Amanda sang. In perfect accompaniment with the guitar, her soft, dulcet intonation made gospels come alive. Many of the churchgoers felt as though the service was lacking without her musical performance and judged the sermon accordingly.

Every living thing suddenly became hushed. Crickets stopped calling their mates and the nightbirds made no sound, as if in anticipation of a magical moment. Amanda's voice was both sharp and sweet as it broke the inaudible calm.

> *"Oh take me back to Tennessee,*
> *To my dear home once more;*
> *Where the river runs so merrily,*
> *Down by the cabin door.*
> *And when I see those fields again,*
> *How happy I shall be,*
> *To hear the darkies welcome song,*
> *Dear land of Tennessee!*
> *Oh! I can never here remain,*
> *There is no joy for me.*
> *This land I'll leave, and back again,*
> *I'll go to Tennessee.*
> *There is no joyful music now,*
> *To glad my list'ning ear;*
> *The banjo's happy tone is mute,*
> *No dear old songs I hear.*
> *Oh! I will never here remain,*
> *No pleasure now I see,*
> *Farewell! I must go back again,*
> *To dear old Tennessee.*
> *Oh! I can never here remain,*
> *There is no joy for me;*
> *This land I'll leave, and back again,*
> *I'll go to Tennessee."*

Grace Waterman reflected on bygone days on her father's plantation and the rich tones coming from the slave quarters at night. Voices were much deeper than those with a high nasal pitch she now hears in church back in Richmond. Tonight, in this balmy October darkness, Grace is convinced the sound, caressing her ears, is the most beautiful of all. She turned and looked directly at her daughter Hope, who held her sleeping granddaughter, Rebecca. While still in her meditative state, Grace wondered, *"Where did the years go since you were born? Where was I when it all happened? It seems like only yesterday when I was holding you wrapped in a warm blanket."*

She was quickly awakened from her melancholy trance by cheers of approval when Amanda began to play Dixie.

Jack leaned his shoulder against Abel and said, "Take a gander down at the corral. It looks like your wife has a couple four-legged fans." Two horses, with their ears pricked straight up, stood motionless listening to the music wafting in their direction.

"Amanda is a natural. They're going to miss her the most, once we're gone," Abel replied.

"Then you've made up your mind?" the mountain man asked.

"Jack, you're the one who told me to sleep on the more important decisions. I'll know for sure in the morning," Abel said, emphatically.

By the time the children were put to bed, the bewitching hour had passed. A grand evening had come to an end. Though the guests were weak from fatigue, their mental disposition made sleep hard to come by. Inmost thoughts kept mulling over the previous activities and conversations. Subjective angst varied within each bedroom. Jack Leffingwell was first to pull the covers, while Abigail twisted the oil lamp wick to its lowest point and gently blew out the flame.

Lying in the absence of light, Abigail was updated on the lakeside meeting and made aware of Jack's concerns. He had confidence in his friend's ability and physical prowess but wondered about his mental strength in the face of adversity. Amanda, with all her talent and charm, seemed distant when it came to her husband. That recognizable gaze Abigail had for him wasn't visible when Amanda observed Abel. Then again, it could be only his imagination. Abigail also noticed a similar hint in her facial cast but remained silent. A prayer was given for Abel and his family before the Leffingwells drifted off to sleep.

Grace Waterman, still maudlin over years gone by, had donned her nightgown and crawled into bed. Horace raised the window slightly allowing cool evening air into the room. Sitting on the bed, he removed his shoes and socks; stood again and hung his shirt and trousers on the curved metal hook behind their door; extinguished the lamp resting on a chest of drawers; and joined his wife.

"It seems as though the Strawn family is moving to Kansas. Abel hasn't made the decision definite, but, from all indications, I believe they're going," Horace stated, while plumping the pillow.

"Is he going to continue in the ministry?" asked Grace.

"He's buying a farm and plans to till the soil. He talked about raising cattle," Horace replied.

"Abel doesn't seem like a farmer and his wife certainly appears better suited to city life," Grace replied.

"I know. It will give Abel an opportunity to possess a house and land all his own. The previous owner had built a cabin and, from what he told Abel, it will suit a young family quite well."

Autumn moonlight found its way through the bedroom window, making objects therein more visible. Horace leaned forward to give a goodnight kiss and asked, "Darling, have you been crying?"

"I'm a little sad tonight, that's all. Time seems to have passed me by. When I look at Hope and see how grownup she's become, I don't remember when it happened. It's like I wasn't even around during those years and it breaks my heart."

"At times it's that way for me, too. All the same, look at what we have now. Susan will become a teenager soon. Hope has given us Rebecca and I'm sure she and Melvin will have more children. The good times of our golden years are just beginning. Remember that there's still 24 hours in a day, even though the clock tends to move quicker the older we get. Best of all, I love you more today than ever before," Horace confided, while putting an arm around his wife and gently kissing her wet cheek.

"Have you been told lately what a wonderful man you are," whispered Grace.

That night, the visitors from Richmond slept in each other's close embrace.

CHAPTER THREE

The following morning Abel announced his decision. He will accept Jubal Myers' offer and move his family west after the first of the year. Jack Leffingwell and Melvin Kaufman reminded their friend that they also still retained some of Lomas Chandler's gift. Abel thanked them for their generosity but refused the offer. With Lomas' loan he had more than enough money to buy the necessities and make the trip.

Traveling back to Lebanon lacked the jubilation felt during the initial trip to the Leffingwell farm. Abel, deep in thought, was silently creating a list of things to do and mentally establishing when to do them. Amanda, pondering the future, also found herself subdued in thought. She had never been as enthusiastic as Abel when it came to Jubal Myers' offer. Somehow, she never believed it would be accepted. Her ploy in having her brother Pearle join them would guarantee Abel's refusal and instigate an argument to thwart the whole idea. John Steinbeck, adapting from a line by Robert Burns, may have said it appropriately, "The best-laid plans of mice and men often go awry." Much to her chagrin, Abel accepted her younger brother; after all, another pair of hands is always needed on a farm.

Unconsciously thankful little Abby was sleeping, having been sedated by the steady sway of the carriage, Amanda reflected on her current existence. As each quiet mile rolled by, she was positive about one thing—she wasn't happy with her prosaic life. From the first day she sought asylum with Abel's parents, Amanda has lived in a bubble. There was no other choice. Her lover at the time had departed, leaving her desperate and in dire straits. Finding refuge with the Strawns made sense. After all, she was still married to their son and he was away fighting in the war. Smothered in Christian kindness, the next four years allowed her to maintain respectability while supposedly awaiting the return of her husband Abel. Talented with the guitar, she was able to fine-tune her skills by playing in the Methodist Church choir. Doing so gave a modicum of satisfaction; however, never enough to last the week—a week of constant battle with the natural female desires of a woman her age. She looked forward to the evenings the minister and his wife were at the church. Only then could she completely relax and relieve herself of physical need by sensual stimulation. After her peak of pleasure, Amanda usually felt nausea, most likely from guilt; however, it didn't last long due to the mental relaxation, followed by induced slumber. By the time the Strawns returned, she had awakened with her physical desires in balance.

Once Abel returned from the war, she became pregnant. The myth that children will bring two people closer together has been annihilated. A child only serves as another lock and chain to keep Amanda imprisoned in the life from which she desperately wants to free herself. Abel seems anchored no matter what the storm. Always at home, wherever he is. Each morning continuing where he left off the night before. Resumption after resumption into the lackluster of another dull and mediocre day. Wanting a rich and varied life away from all this, she subconsciously screams, "Help me. Anybody, help me before I die."

The last time she reached the heights of sexual fulfillment was over six years ago; nevertheless, if Amanda had to make a choice between Abel and any other man, she would choose her husband. No single other has treated her with so much love and immeasurable kindness. In fact, the men she had taken to her bed treated her badly with embarrassing sexual demands and sometimes administering physical cruelty. All the same, deep within her psyche lurks the brash desire for forbidden pleasure, which she willfully nurtures in hopes of one day surrendering to it.

A short distance ahead, the roadstead oasis came into view, marking the half-way point of their trip home. Recognizing the familiar sward, Abel guided the horse and carriage off the road and to the pleasant site.

"Whoa," he softly whispered as the rig rolled to a silent stop. Turning to Amanda, he calmly said, "Wait a minute so I can help you down."

She seemed light as a feather as Abel hoisted her up and out of the surrey. While still holding the bundle containing their sleeping daughter, Amanda was gently placed vertically to the ground. "You're awfully quiet this morning," Abel stated, more like a question.

"Me, you haven't said two words since we left the Leffingwell farm," she retorted.

"I'm sorry sweetheart, I must have been engrossed thinking about our move to Kansas and what an opportunity it will be for us," he replied, offering an apology.

"I was doing a little of that myself. You know how I have to be around people. Being stranded out in the middle of nowhere alone isn't my cup of tea. Worrying about being scalped by Indians doesn't help matters either. The only good thing about it is we will finally be away from your parents and that damn Methodist Church."

Her words made Abel wince and cause his left eyelid to twitch. He frequently said that words are very heavy; if birds could talk, they wouldn't be able to fly. Amanda's words can hurt to the very quick, but he never would return in kind.

"Darling, we won't exactly be stranded. There will be plenty neighbors and our farm is near Fort Dodge making it safe from Indian attack. The whole area is building up with towns a lot bigger than Lebanon," he said reassuredly. "We won't start out for a few months and, by then, I think you will look forward to having a place of our own."

Amanda walked to the nearest hardwood tree and sat with her back against it, a subconscious symbol of defiance. Her position was given, and with the buttress of an arboreal foundation, securely moored.

"Let's see what Abigail has in the picnic basket," Abel said, ignoring her petulance and reaching for its wicker handle. "This is heavy," he called out, walking over to Amanda and sitting beside her.

Covering the contents was a checkered picnic ground cloth. Inside was a virtual cornucopia of rural harvest—fresh baked bread, fried chicken, potato salad, pickles, deviled eggs, boiled beans and pork, apple pie, and three jars of various fruit jam. In addition was a personal note from Abigail telling them how much their company was enjoyed and appreciated. With the ground cloth removed, the aroma of such a picnic feast was too much for Amanda to resist. Placing a temporary halt to her intransigence, and, while occupying her daughter, she sat down beside Abel and the mid-day feast.

By the time the ant colonies got wind of the abundant banquet, Abel was repacking the osier basket and the travelers were soon back on the road.

CHAPTER FOUR

November is a gray month. Autumn leaves have fallen and tree branches appear as skeletons against the backdrop of a cheerless sky. It's a time of hard morning frosts and biting winds. The senior Waterman family has concluded their visit and are now back in Richmond, Virginia. Hope still feels the pang of absent parents. Having a two-year-old daughter to tend and duties on the farm soon demand her attention. This morning, her husband Melvin is currently standing next to Jack Leffingwell and assessing the wagon they plan to convert into a covered land schooner.

"Do you think it can travel a thousand miles?" Melvin asked.

"It will once we get done with it," Jack answered, confidently.

The large barn, on Jack's farm, is ideal for performing maintenance on machinery. That was the thought when he first built the oversized outbuilding and, now, it will serve exactly as previously planned. The two men took hold of the wagon tongue and rolled the four-wheel conveyance to an unencumbered place.

"What will we do first?" Melvin was eager.

"First, we need to remove the wooden wheel shafts and have them enlarged. Most likely, we can still use the old spindle skeins, but we'll need the blacksmith to put them back on and make sure they're secure," Jack replied. With that they rolled the wagon on its side and began unbolting the axle hardware.

Curiosity may have killed the cat, but it didn't take long before Jack's two sons appeared on the scene healthy and ready for action.

"Can we help?" asked Jack Junior.

"Sure can. You and Jozef start picking up the bolts and nuts and put them in that bucket over yonder," their father replied. With that, the two youngsters started rooting round the wagon like nursing piglets and soon the area was void of all metal items. The bucket now contained not only the axle nuts and bolts, but also a sundry of wire and rusty nails plus, two corncobs, thanks to little Jozef. The boys now gave irrefutable evidence of work. Both were soiled from head to foot.

"I think it's best they don't let their mother see them for a while," Melvin said dryly.

"You're probably right. Let's put the axles in the active wagon and head into town." Jack averred. "Best we bring all four wheels for the blacksmith to inspect. They look good to me, but he's better trained on these things and it's a far piece between Tennessee and Kansas."

"How come the front wheels are smaller than the back," asked Melvin, honestly.

"Well, we know that larger diameter wheels make it easier for the animal to pull. So a wagon with 48-inch wheels pulls easier than one with 24-inch wheels. In many cases, the wheel size determines what animal is selected for the job—oxen, mules, or horses. Now if all wagons had 48-inch wheels, front and rear, we would have a mechanical conflict. When we try to steer the wagon, the front wheels would stride the wagon body and reduce the turning radius. To overcome this hindrance, we lower the height of the front wheels just enough to level the wagon and increase the turning radius," Jack explained.

"The way you tell it, it makes good sense," Melvin acknowledged.

"Remember, I had to learn it from somebody myself," reassured the mountain man. Don't forget to bring the wheel hubs and hub-wrench. Go tell Abigail that we're going to town for a while."

Melvin slowly sauntered up the steps to Abigail's kitchen and shouted, "Jack and I are taking some stuff into town. The boys are coming with us."

By the time he finished his oral message, Abigail was at the doorway.

"How long are you going to be?" she asked. "I just gave the little ones a bath so they'll look good in town."

"Jack says it will just be a couple hours and the boys look fine," Melvin answered and turned away to stride down her steps, cross the yard, and climb in the waiting wagon.

* * *

Statesville was all abuzz with the presidential election. Andrew Johnson, their favorite native son, carried too much baggage to win the nomination. By 1868, he had alienated many of his constituents and been impeached by Congress. The nomination went for Horatio Seymour, former governor of New York. Ironically, Seymour didn't want the nomination and refused it several times. After his last refusal he rose from his seat, walked out, and waited in the vestibule. While waiting in the anteroom, the convention nominated him unanimously. Francis Preston Blair, Union Army General and Senator from Missouri, won the vice-president slot. Seymour lost the election by a narrow margin to Ulysses S. Grant and Schuyler Colfax, Speaker of the House of Representatives. With many southern white men unable to vote, the election would have been much closer.

Jack Leffingwell was unsure if he would be allowed to vote and sat this one out. He would have voted for the Democrat constituent. Nevertheless, Tennessee, surrounded by states voting for the republican nominee, voted for Seymour/Blair, the eventual losers.

Jack pulled the wagon to a stop at the blacksmith forge. When we think of a blacksmith, our mental image is one of

Henry Wadsworth Longfellow's, *The Village Blacksmith*. Ryan Gosling is the antithesis to the mighty man with large and sinewy hands and brawny arm muscles as strong as iron bands. Ryan is small of build and stands about five-foot-seven. All the same, he equals any smith in ability and better than most. Ryan and Melvin became friends the first time they met, tossing a few beers ever since. Today will be no exception.

Jack explained that he was repairing his old wagon and wanted the axle wood made stronger and maybe new spindle skeins cast. Further, he brought in the wheels and hub nuts for Ryan to inspect and repair, if necessary.

Ryan, nodding at each suggested repair, finally asked, "What are you fixing the wagon for? If you're just planning to use it around the farm, you might get by with these hub nuts," the blacksmith said, while holding one in his hand.

"It's for a soldier buddy of ours. He bought himself a farm and Melvin and I plan to make a prairie schooner for him and his family to travel in," Jack replied.

"How far away is his farm?" the smithy inquired.

"It's over in Kansas," Melvin replied, with a wince.

"Hell, that's over a thousand miles from here," Ryan emphasized. "Now it all begins to make sense, your hub nuts look a little beat up for such a long trip. I recommend that you get new ones. They don't cost that much. You probably can still use the old hub wrench."

I better not chance it. Make me a new one and I'll give him both," Jack replied.

"No problem there. I got the best axle grease you can find anywhere and I'll give you plenty. When do you want this to be ready?"

"We don't plan to take the wagon over to Lebanon until after the New Year," Jack answered.

"That's good for me. I think I should have all the parts ready for you in a couple weeks," Ryan stated.

Now that the blacksmith has agreed to the needed repairs Melvin inquired, "Hey Ryan, can you take a break for a couple beers. It's my turn to buy?"

"I can always make time for an oat soda," was Ryan's grinning reply.

"You two go on over to the tavern, I need to go to Riberty's Hardware and buy some planks for the wagon bed. Abigail also wanted me to pick up a package for her next time I was in town and, more importantly, the boys were promised hard candy for the work performed in the barn. After I run them errands, I'll be over rightly," Jack said.

"Okay by me and Ryan. You'll be behind at least three beers by the time you get all that done," Melvin affirmed.

"One thing is certain, I don't plan to try to catch up with you two," Jack said jokingly.

Since the war, Statesville has grown. The occupation by the U.S. Army and, now, reconstruction increased the population; albeit, mainly with Union soldiers. Nevertheless, the Statesville taverns increased by one. It turned out to be the favorite of the locals, and was the shortest distance from the blacksmith's forge, a fact most pleasing to Ryan Gosling.

When Melvin and Ryan opened the door, a transformation took place. Today, having a rare bright sun outside made it difficult to see well, after stepping into the subdued darkness of the tavern. Roosting at the bar, made it easier to navigate, while looking for a place to sit down.

"Knocking off kind of early today, Ryan," the bartender quipped.

"Nope, just taking a break with my friend," he replied.

"What can I give you boys?" the tapster asked.

"I'll have a tall glass of beer," Melvin requested.

"I know what you want, Ryan," the bartender stated.

"No you don't. I'll have what the fellow on the floor is having," Ryan said with a snicker.

"Don't make me come around this counter."

"Just remember, I've been drinking the shit you serve here ever since you opened. You come around this counter and I'll let a fart that will kill you," the bantam smithy replied. That rejoinder brought a laugh from everyone in the saloon. Even the barkeep couldn't help liberating a grin.

"Just give me a 'skirt raiser' and pour another right away. All this foolish talk is putting me behind schedule," Ryan stated.

* * *

The ambience in Riberty's Hardware is more radiant. Brought about by the large front windows, washed daily. Even so, lights were on inside to better exhibit merchandise, displayed in a fashion to attract prospective buyers. Maryellen Riberty-McKnight still works part-time for her father, on duty today as Jack and his young sons entered the store.

"Hello, Jack, is Abigail with you?" she asked.

"Not this time, Maryellen. I brought the boys with me to give her a break," Jack replied.

"I can see that. How did they get so dirty?" she inquired with a smile, and gave Jozef a hug.

"They helped me work in the barn before we came into town. Is your father here, I need to buy some board for a wagon bed," Jack stated.

"They would be in the lumber shed. Just go pick out what you want and I'll get my little buddies some hard candy." Maryellen suggested. "My dad's out making deliveries."

Jack picked out some of the best pieces and loaded them in the wagon, now parked in front. "I got five eight-foot pieces of lumber and don't forget to ring up the candy," informed Jack. "Does Abigail have a package for me to pick up?"

"Yes, and it's already paid for," she relayed and found it behind the cash register.

"How much do I owe you?" Jack inquired, while reaching for his wallet.

"The lumber comes to $1.68 and the candy is on the house," she said.

"Is the lumber from around here?"

"I don't think so. Dad found good prices from somewhere up north."

Actually, during the spring of 1868, lumber prices fell like a brick. With lumbermen receiving a dollar a day for their labor, and the cost of shipping to a sawmill added in, it didn't pay to cut and deliver the timber.

"Maryellen, would you be kind enough to watch my boys while I meet Melvin and your blacksmith for a beer? I promise they'll be good and I'll pick them up in a half-hour," vowed Jack.

"I'd love to keep them. Take a little longer if you wish."

Before Jack reached for the tavern twist grip, it seemed like a party was going on inside. Sounds of robust laughter preceded his opening the door. Once he turned the knob, any questions were immediately answered. Most of the patrons were standing in a half-circle and gathered around two men, sitting on stools. His vision, blocked by the roisterous group, hardly impaired the identification of the source of merriment. It's human nature for people to turn their heads when a front door opens. Recognizing the Tennessee mountain man, the revelers shouted in unison, "Come on over Jack and we'll buy you a beer."

The partiers were in full accord with that statement, especially Ryan Gosling, the fiery blacksmith, who uttered, "We need you to settle this argument for us. Ole Fritz Adler here, the bartender, says President Grant was a better general than Robert E. Lee. I told this sorry excuse for a southerner, that he's been eating too much Wiener schnitzel."

The din increased in volume as Jack was nudged closer to the stool, made available for a desired affirmation.

"Now Fritz, you're gonna find out who the best general really was. Draw our friend a beer, and you might as well bring me another 'butt slapper' while you're at it," Ryan ordered.

After taking a long swig, Jack slowly wiped his mouth with the back of his hand and calmly said, "The history books will tell the factual story after more time passes. Right now, there are more opinions than ticks on a wild hog."

"We don't give a damn about history books. I doubt if Fritz can read. What we care about now is your opinion. Who do you think is the best general?" Ryan questioned.

The mountain man paused for a second, momentarily hesitant, as if searching for the right way to disclose his innermost thoughts regarding this senseless debate. Although, he must confess, it is one in which has caused him many a sleepless night. He knew no matter what he said there would be rambling divagations that most likely would go on for hours.

"Many people, here in Tennessee, believe Robert E. Lee was the best general and Ulysses S. Grant was a drunken butcher with four times as many soldiers. As you know, Melvin and I fought this awful war with General Lee in Virginia. The boys from Wilson County made up the 7th Tennessee Regiment. You couldn't find a more honest, noble, and gentlemanly man to serve under. We would walk through the gates of hell for him and a lot of us did. Nevertheless, before you can properly evaluate people you need to take a look at their basic character and the causes that make them the way they are.

Robert E. Lee's old man wasn't exactly a pillar of mannerly society. Yet, Lee was able to overcome his father's abandonment and misspent life of financial failure, to learn about the consequences of a lack of self-control. After his father's disappearance, the plantation was lost due to his debts and young Robert's family was forced to survive on the good will of relatives. Spending late adolescence in genteel poverty, young Robert was the only child left at home to take care of his ailing mother. It's been said that if the stick doesn't break your back it will make you strong. That old saw was proven in Bobby Lee's case. It stiffened his backbone."

Jack's soliloquy was interrupted long enough to wet his whistle. The party crowd remained frozen in time and absorbed in interest. Melvin found Jack's story reminiscent of those former days in which the mountain man recounted the news from Virginia newspapers.

"How'd you ever come up with so much information about Robert E. Lee?" Ryan asked, while making a circular motioning with his forefinger to the barkeep.

"I've always been an avid reader. Never missed an opportunity to pick up a newspaper. The rest was learned by talking with two men. One of them is Melvin's father-in-law, Horace Waterman. Horace is a retired college professor and worked as an editor for the Richmond Dispatch during the Civil War. His credentials, in academia, stand-alone. The other man is my own father-in-law, Hyrum Adams," Jack replied, as empty glasses were replaced by others having white frothy foam running down their sides. Fritz was quick to follow the orders of a twirling forefinger.

"Ain't he the Methodist Minister?" questioned one of the revelers.

"Yes, and the wisest man I've ever had the privilege to know," Jack affirmed. "We all can use more of the Good Word laid on us."

Those sitting at the bar began to lean their heads toward the speaker as Jack continued, "Robert E. Lee's first love was a planter's life, working the soil; but, his father's dishonest actions took care of that. He had an interest in the field of medicine; once again, no money to attend medical school. Finally he earned an appointment to West Point military college and, from that foundation, his life changed for the better.

Lee married into the wealthy Washington/Custis family. His wife, Mary Anna Randolph Custis, was the great-granddaughter of Martha Washington, by her first husband, Daniel Parke Custis. After a successful 32-year antebellum military career, Lee was recognized as one of the nation's leading military officers. When the Civil War erupted, Lee was the best officer available to head the Union Army. The commanding Union general, Winfield Scott, told President Abraham Lincoln that he wanted Robert E. Lee for a top command. After Lincoln's call for troops to put down the rebellion, Virginia quickly seceded. Lee turned down an offer as a major general, resigned from the Army, and took command of Virginia's state forces."

"You said it right there. Robert E. Lee was the best officer available in the North. That makes him better than all the rest," said Ryan, believing the debate over.

"Not so fast, Ryan. We've just been talking about Lee's character. It's impossible to make an intelligent determination without first evaluating Ulysses S. Grant, using similar logic," Jack confirmed.

Outside the toasty confines of the Statesville favorite alehouse, November weather has slowly taken a turn for the worse. Early bright sunshine had changed into the more normal dark and gloomy climes of the gray month. The grizzled sky prohibited sunlight from any chance of display, and, coupled with fast moving fall days, indicated the rapid approach of evening. In such an atmosphere, Anodos would certainly lose his multifaceted shadow.

Inside the public house, any sense of time-lapse was obscured by interest in what the mountain man was saying. Thus far, his description of General Lee's character meets approval to a man. Now, anxiety builds as they wait the distinguishing between he and General Ulysses S. Grant. Jack knows the time has grown late, but there's no way he will be allowed to go without settling the primary argument.

Leaving his young sons in the care of Maryellen any longer is an act of tactlessness. He debated over excusing himself and retrieving his boys, then finishing his story. Perhaps they could sit at a vacant table until time to return home. That thought faded in a puff of smoke when his shoulder angel struck a stern discord on its harp, clearly an indictment that would result in another negative entry in his life-ledger. Nonetheless, Abigail would never approve of her sons frequenting a tavern at such an early age. Jack's dilemma was interrupted when the entry door pulled open and Frank Riberty walked in.

Because of his generosity during the war and present largesse in reconstruction, Frank Riberty became one of the leading citizens in Statesville. As owner of the general store, he extended credit to those in need to the point of personal deprivation. In fact, many now sitting with a beer in their hand find their name in his journal. Today, reflecting the status of their gradual reduction of indebtedness.

Amid well-wishers, offering to buy him a beer, Frank angled toward Jack Leffingwell and said, "My daughter asked me to give you a message. She wants to keep your boys tonight and bring them out to the farm in the morning."

"Maryellen is an answer to my prayers," Jack replied. "I'm in the middle of a debate as to who the greatest general is between Lee and Grant and time has gotten away from me."

Frank Riberty nodded, in a sign of understanding, and declared, "I'm sorry I missed the first part but I definitely want to hear the second."

Apparently, Fritz Adler was still under the whammy of that twirling finger as he quickly plunked down refills and the opener for Frank Riberty. Men sporting a mustache temporarily exhibited a frothy appearance under their noses. By now, few took the pains to wipe it away, knowing it will soon dissipate on its own. Jack Leffingwell took a deep breath and began the second half of his narrative.

"Grant, like the rest of us, is from more common stock—no plantation life for him. He was born in Point Pleasant, Ohio in 1822, and the oldest of two brothers and three sisters. Ulysses was raised in a devout Methodist family holding to traditional beliefs. Hyrum Adams explains that its emphasis on helping the poor and the average person, characterize Methodism. Building loving relationships with others through social service is a means of working towards the inclusiveness of God's love. Because of people, deep rooted with such beliefs, my son Jozef is accepted and loved unconditionally even though not one drop of Abigail's blood flows through his little body."

Ryan was beginning to slur his words. Even though he sat only inches away, he drew his face closer to Melvin and asked, "Now, what the hell does he mean by that?"

"I'll tell you later," Melvin replied. There never was cause, in their friendship, to relate all of Jack's experiences with amnesia.

Owing to the amber brew and zealous distribution, Jack found himself beginning to ramble. Prudence being the better part of valor, he slid the full ones down the bar and continued, "General Grant's mother, Hannah Simpson Grant, was a strong, reserved, religious woman, and held to these principles. Some observers believed that her son's strength of character and reserve were traits inherited from her.

His father was a tanner by trade and we all know what that entails. It's a business located in the poorest section of town and away from people. Working with animal skins reeks from the foul smell of rotting meat. It's a noxious and odoriferous trade of which young Ulysses wanted no part. Everybody is aware of Henry Lottinville's hog farm; especially, when the wind is in the right direction."

"I know exactly what you mean," Fritz Adler chimed, while rearranging full beer glasses in order to determine who gets the next one. "Whenever he comes in here, he stinks the place up."

"I think pig farmers get it in their skin and it never leaves them," said a man at the end of the mahogany counter. "Don't they go to your church? How does Ole Hyrum handle that?"

"Actually, the church ladies came up with the answer. They commiserated with Livy Lottinville and gave her some of their homemade soap. On Saturday nights the whole family gets a good scrubbing. When they attend church the next day the sanctuary smells like roses. Sometimes little Henry Junior manages to hide from his bath and his folks can't find him. Once they come to church we all know where he is." Jack said, jokingly.

The hour has reached a critical point. For those in attendance supper is resting on the table and the one who prepared it now looks across the steaming fare to a vacant chair. Her emotions run the gamut. At first she is wrapped in anger, soon to be replaced by fear, the sensation that makes her realize that even though she rules the home and everything in it, her kingdom may only be temporary in her not always happy life. Women with children force a smile and say, "Looks like daddy is going to be late. Let's eat while the food is still hot."

Men in the alehouse reached the conclusion that supper is forsaken. They now form a queue that begins at the latrine and extends into the barroom. Jack has been commanded not to utter a word until they return. A public house toilet has magical powers. It can alleviate human distress, transforming it into renewed vigor, comfort, and comprehension. The frowns of concern have been buffed to a happier glow.

Released from his directive, Jack continued, "As a young boy, Grant was small for his age. And, typical in such cases, other children made fun of him. They mistook his quietness for stupidity, nicknaming him *Useless*. Bullied by classmates, Ulysses took little interest in local schools. He would rather be on his father's farm taking care of the animals. In so doing, he developed skills in managing horses. In fact, he soon gained a reputation in the area for taming the most unruly broncos. Around here he would have been called a horse whisperer.

Well, his father knew Ulysses would not follow him in the tanning business and the family didn't have money for college. He also knew his son could get a good education at the United States Military Academy, in return for army service after graduation. So, without Ulysses' knowledge, Jesse Grant applied for an appointment to the Academy on his son's behalf. He was accepted. When Jesse told his son about it, Ulysses refused to go—not totally unexpected from someone as self-effacing and shy. Eventually, young Grant recognized the favorable aspects of West Point and agreed to attend.

The unassuming youth from Ohio found the Academy difficult. He did well with math and drawing; however, the remainder of his studies branded him a mediocre student. He did stand out when it came to horses. His skills were unrivaled and he astonished everyone with his riding abilities. Talent in this area seemed sure to win a coveted spot in the Army's cavalry, its horse-soldier elite. Since assignments were determined by class rank instead of aptitude, it didn't happen. Instead, after graduation Grant was assigned to the infantry."

"Ain't that the way it always goes," said a listener. "The army brass seems to always make the wrong assignments. They put people in positions they weren't trained for. In our division we had one of the best engineers around and they put him peeling potatoes. I think he was still peeling spuds when the war ended."

"I think many times the army just assigns people because of an emergency. They don't care who it is as long as the vacancy gets filled. Officers don't take the time to consider the talent a soldier has, so, lots of times we end up with a square peg in a round hole," expressed another.

The mountain man appreciated an occasional interruption and this time excused himself for a needed trip to the 'magical' chamber. Patrons, who had been sitting down, took the opportunity to stand and stretch their aching legs. While on their feet, the grandfather clock behind the bar struck seven times. Upon his return, the standing crowd divided itself, making a path for Jack Leffingwell to reach his seat.

After things settled down, he resumed, "Now let's see what we have. Both men attended West Point. Robert E. Lee graduated second in his class, without one demerit in four years. He was assigned to the Army Corps of Engineers. Ulysses S. Grant, because of his grades, was placed in the infantry. His first assignment was Jefferson Barracks, near St. Louis, Missouri. While in Missouri, he spent time visiting the family of his West Point classmate, Frederick Dent, and getting to know Dent's sister, Julia. Before long, the two became secretly engaged. Then, when Texas was annexed into the Union, and tensions rose with Mexico, Grant was shifted to Louisiana as part of the Army of Observation.

The Mexican-American War broke out in 1846 and the U.S. Army entered Mexico. Never content with his quartermaster duties, Grant made his way to the front lines to engage in the battle. He participated as though he was in the cavalry and took advantage of his excellent riding ability. On occasion, he carried dispatches through sniper-lined streets, Indian style, with only one foot mounted in the stirrup. Grant drew praise from his superiors and was transferred to Winfield Scott's army, the main command of the offensive. Shortly thereafter, Mexico agreed to peace before Grant had a chance to demonstrate his ability any further.

Around the end of 1848, Grant and Julia were married. Over the next few years, he was assigned to several different posts. The first, after the Mexican War took him and Julia to Detroit and Sackets Harbor, New York. He and Julia claimed to enjoy that assignment the most. In 1852, Grant traveled to Washington D.C., to prevail upon Congress to rescind an order that he, in his capacity as quartermaster, reimburse the military $1,000 in losses incurred on his watch, for which he bore no personal guilt. The same year Grant was sent to Fort Vancouver in the Oregon Territory."

The blossoming question in the minds of most listeners was how Jack became so knowledgeable about Ulysses S. Grant. Finally, a voice asked, "How come you know so much about the Yankee General? You call out dates and things only a schoolteacher would understand."

"I'm no schoolteacher but, as I said earlier, I read a lot. Most of what I'm recalling today was found in last week's *Lebanon Herald*. If any of you read it, you would remember that it gave a full background of Grant when he was elected president," Jack admitted.

"I remember seeing it, though, I was too disappointed to read the whole thing," confessed a man standing. "Who did they want to win the election?"

"They endorsed Horatio Seymour. All the same, after the election, the editor called for calm, unity, and peace," Jack assured. "There's a little more to tell about Grant before we compare them as generals. Do you all want me to continue?" asked the mountain man.

Collectively, the listeners wanted Jack to finish, although, some in the crowd began to think they may disagree with the ultimate selection. Others remained confident that, since Jack and Melvin fought with Robert E. Lee, there could be no other choice. While the murmuring din was going on among those sober enough to make sense, Melvin turned to Jack and expressed, "You're not making many friends here tonight. Let's make a run for it before it gets nasty."

"Don't worry, I know what I'm doing," Jack replied, as he turned his stool to face his audience and raised his hand to continue. "Now, I believe I left Ulysses at Fort Vancouver when we stopped. While at the fort, he resumed duties as the quartermaster. His wife Julia was eight months pregnant and could not accompany him. Being absent at such an important time in their lives was stressful enough; coupled with the fact Grant's military salary was inadequate to support his family, resulted in a quite unhappy soldier. He attempted several business ventures to supplement their meager income, only to have every one of them fail. Rumors circulated that the tanner's son was drinking in excess. Shortly after being promoted to Captain and assigned to Fort Humboldt, Grant was accused of being intoxicated while off-duty and sitting at the paymasters table. The fort commander had warned Grant several times to stop his drinking. In lieu of a court-martial, the fort commander, Lieutenant Colonel Robert C. Buchanan, gave Grant an ultimatum to sign a drafted letter of resignation. Ulysses never gloried in the ideals of war and mourned his lost comrades and the waste war caused. Being transferred often to distant locations in which he couldn't bring his family only increased his grief. Even though he strongly rejected the accusations of intemperance, on July 31, 1854, Grant resigned from the army."

"The guy was a drunk," slurred Ryan Gosling, as he accidentally tipped over the full-glass resting to his left. The cleanup job gave Jack Leffingwell time to consider the best way to finalize Ulysses S. Grant's character. After Fritz Adler cleaned up the mess and replaced the tipped glass, he admonished Ryan with his final warning. A futile effort since, to a man, the crowd preferred Ryan.

Silence is holy and leads us to wisdom. Just as the stars, moon, and sun move without sound, true understanding cannot be found in noise and restlessness. Therefore, Jack waited for the next moment of hush, which gave its consent for him to proceed, "After leaving the army, Grant returned to his wife and children in Missouri. He was 32 years old with no civilian vocation. Ulysses' father, Jesse, offered him a position in their Galena, Illinois branch of the tannery business on condition, by which, Julia and the children live with either her parents in Missouri or the Grants in Kentucky. The senior Grant knew, in the beginning, purchasing or renting a family home would be too costly. Both Ulysses and Julia were adamantly opposed to another separation, and declined the offer. Instead, Grant took a crack at farming. First, on his brother-in-law's property near St. Louis, using slaves owned by Julia's father. Even though Grant worked hard at it, the endeavor failed. Grant may have failed his initial effort but his enthusiasm remained undaunted. Two years later, Grant moved his family to a section of his father-in-law's farm and built a log house for his family. It turned out to be a rather crude structure Ulysses called 'Hardscrabble' and Julia secretly hated.

Convincing his wife the dwelling was only temporary, Ulysses took another stab at agriculture. Prospects brightened since the land was given to them, along with a 35-year-old knowledgeable slave named William Jones. Nevertheless, planting and harvest required extra labor and Ulysses would only hire free blacks— perhaps, an early window, looking into his deeper feelings regarding the southern institution of slavery. Once again, Grant found no gold at the end of his farming rainbow and was forced to give up the ghost. Now, badly in need of money, it was suggested he sell his newly acquired slave—since an intelligent, 35-year old man, would command a high price. Instead, Grant set him free.

When their fourth child was born, the Grants left the farm and moved into a small house in St. Louis. He worked at several jobs without success. Then, after pawning his watch to buy Christmas gifts, Grant was faced with the painful reality. He could not support his family.

By 1860, the time had come to "eat crow" and appeal to his father for help. He went to work for his younger brother in the Galena, Illinois leather shop."

Melvin Kaufman knows firsthand about giving up the ghost. After losing his arm at the battle of The Wilderness of Spotsylvania, he was transferred to Chimborazo Hospital in Richmond, Virginia. An empty sleeve for a left arm, the young soldier had hit rock bottom. Life was the pits. He only envisioned a future sweeping out taverns and being called Gimpy or the Gimp. All that ended when Hope Waterman arrived on the scene, and the rest is history.

Melvin pivoted his stool and stated, "I know all about giving up the ghost. Been there myself. Like him or not, that had to be very humiliating for Grant to eat crow in front of his old man and ask for help." Turning to Jack Leffingwell he continued, "If it wasn't for this man, and of course, my wife Hope, I'd probably be sweeping up this place or one like it, at quitting time. Jack taught me that all honest ventures are honorable. You just have to know when to quit."

"Well, it seems like Ulysses S. Grant was short on common sense," came a voice from the crowd.

"On the contrary," said another. "He tried lots of ventures and, when one failed, he tried another."

"Yeah, that only makes him normal but unlucky," answered the first.

"He was a loser then and is going to be a loser when he's president," came a third voice. "What do you think, Jack? Is Grant a loser?"

"He certainly had a long string of bad luck in civilian life. Yet, he married a good woman and raised four children. And, don't forget, he became president of these United States. I remember an old saying that *things do not change; we change.* Apparently, it took him seven years to figure that out. Perhaps the most important part of Grant's life lies ahead of him. His only fault, which I feel strongly about, is he doesn't recognize a man's character soon enough," Jack answered.

"What do you mean by that?" several asked in unison.

"Well, Grant had seven years in civilian life and appears to have failed in whatever attempts he made. Many times we humans let our egos take over. As soon as things start to go wrong, a defense mechanism prevents us from removing the word quit from our vocabularies. A friend of ours, by the name of Lomas Chandler, explained it in terms of playing poker. He called it chasing your losses. When a poker player loses, he's more prone to attempt winning it back by making more risky bets than he normally would. Good poker players sense this right away and take advantage of it. Grant failed at farming so he tried farming again. If the repeat was the result of his ego, not wanting to appear as a loser, then he has a character flaw. I might add this kind of character flaw we all possess. Most times it's best to take your lumps and try something else, or take a different approach."

The revelers seemed to accept Jack's explanation, especially those having the second best hand at poker all night.

The original idea just to have a couple beers had turned into a much larger group intent to hear the mountain man's opinion as to who was the greatest general in the war. Jack Leffingwell had only planned to stay less than an hour. However, his narration started first with a description of each man's characters—a time consuming soliloquy that has finally come to the point of comparing the performance of the two generals.

Before speaking, Jack took a quick glimpse at the bar room clock. It now read half-past eight and both he and Melvin shared the same concern—their unsuspecting and anxious wives wondering about the cause of their tardiness. It's going to take at least another hour to finish; therefore, might as well be hanged for a sheep as for a lamb, and Jack continued.

"The South seceded from the Union and formed the Confederate States of America. After the surrender of Fort Sumter in Charleston, South Carolina, Lincoln put out a call for 75,000 volunteers. The Civil War had begun and, suddenly, the North needed experienced Army officers. Recognizing this, Ulysses Grant contacted those in authority to see if he would be offered a commission. Included were George B. McClellan and John C. Freemont. There was no interest, ostensibly due to his alcohol-related exodus from the army in 1854. A meeting was called in Galena to encourage recruitment and the Illinois governor appointed Grant to lead a volunteer regiment which no one else had been able to train. Grant established badly needed discipline, focusing on the regiment main goals and overlooking minor details—a style readily accepted by the rank and file. Winning the men's respect and allegiance, Ulysses was subsequently appointed to brigadier general of volunteers.

Robert E. Lee, on the other hand, was in demand and had his choice of the prized assignments of either side in the war. His mentor, Union general-in-chief Winfield Scott, offered him command of all Union armies. Lee declined the offer, resigned his United States commission, and immediately took command of Virginia's military forces. He soon was appointed the second-highest-ranking operational full general in the Confederate army. So when comparing the two men, one might say, in the opening months of the Civil war, Grant started at the bottom, while Lee started at the top."

"That's an odd way of putting it," Frank Riberty said. "From what I've heard so far, Grant shouldn't have been in the army. Period."

"We'd have been a hell of a lot better off if he wasn't," interjected Melvin.

"I'm beginning to see where you two are heading. Tell us right out, who do you think was the best general?" demanded the merchant, with a slight tone of anger in his voice. Frank Riberty rarely drank. When he did, the alcohol tended to alter his personality. He has never been called a happy drunk. Fortunately,

Frank is fully aware of this fact and limits liquor libation during the holidays and, even then, only one or two drinks. That's not to say he avoids the Statesville tavern. He sometimes pops in to be neighborly, especially if a meeting of sorts was taking place. It's always important to know what's going on around town. During those occasions, Frank usually sips a sarsaparilla. His presence this afternoon was basically just to deliver his daughter's message. Once he learned the subject under discussion, he decided to stay and listen to the conclusion of the mountain man's rendition, being constantly aware of balancing his challenge with the skills of Fritz Adler.

"General Lee found himself behind a desk in Richmond. While effectively supervising the Virginia operations of other Confederate generals, he became frustrated for personally missing field action. It all came to a head after our victory at First Manassas (Yankees called it Bull Run). Jefferson Davis, for all his faults, recognized this and gave Lee command of a mission in northwestern Virginia. The Union Army had built a citadel atop Cheat Summit, named Fort Milroy. Its location offered an excellent view of the surrounding area and the main turnpike crossing about one hundred feet below. At the time, the 7th Tennessee Regiment had spent several weeks camped at Big Springs, Virginia, and was ordered to participate in the Cheat Mountain campaign."

"Did you see Robert E. Lee?" someone asked.

"No, but we knew he was there," Jack replied, flatly, and continued. "At times the weather in northern Virginia can be annoyingly changeful. Union forces began construction on the fort in July; however, due to its high elevation, they faced a number of winter-related miseries. Snow began to fall in August, and even horses froze to death by mid-September. The Yankees kept at it because, due to the precipitous descent and dense laurel growth, it was believed to be impregnable.

Marse Robert was determined to prove them wrong and devised a complicated plan to attack in a five-column assault. It required complete cooperation from those officers serving under him. Conditions couldn't have been worse. The summer had been wetter than usual, in a normally wet region. Mountain roads were muddy and unserviceable. The streams were overflowing and cold enough for ice to form. Attempts to avoid the soggy mountain roads, by traveling through the wilderness, promised to offer severe punishment for those who tried.

Supply wagons sunk to their hubs in mud. Such conditions made it almost impossible to supply the columns or ever feed the Southern soldiers. Many of Lee's commanders wished to abandon their entrenchments and move to a more accommodating location. The inclement weather contributed to heavy outbreaks of measles and fever, depriving units of needed manpower. Without food and medical supplies, it was almost impossible to prevent the spread of disease or control such illnesses. It appeared as though more soldiers were coming back than going forward. In fact, over one-half of Lee's army was too sick to fight. In spite of the present situation, General Lee held firm to his battle plan.

Under the command of Colonel Samuel R. Anderson, from Davidson County, the Tennessee Brigade moved along the elevation's west side and succeeded in securing the turnpike as it crossed the last ridge of Cheat Mountain. We had moved so noiselessly that we surprised unsuspecting Union soldiers and captured them with an enclosing maneuver. After which, our marksmen struck Yankee artillery crews from a long distance. I favored the Whitworth rifle and its elongated bullet that made a ghostly whistle finding its mark. That eerie screech must have scared the hell out of them knowing someone might kill them from over a mile away.

At last, the other columns had achieved their positions and all that remained was for Colonel Albert Rust to attack the fort. The first step was to reconnoiter the area, a simple task that became onerous. Lee couldn't get General Loring to do so. That in itself was foreboding enough to have warned the Old Man of impending disaster. With Loring's insubordination, Lee was forced to personally search out the routes through the mountains that could flank the fortified Union positions. Once the cold weather broke enough to allow suitable reconnaissance, Lee discovered that he couldn't unite his forces. The columns were located on both sides of the mountain with no readily connecting paths.

Rust's assault was doomed from the beginning. He had previously told Lee of finding a pathway up the mountain from his own personal reconnaissance of Cheat Summit. It was that information which made Lee decide to attack the fort in the first place. Rust had lied. For thirty miles, the soldiers under Rust were forced to march single file through the wilderness. By climbing, hacking, and wading, as icy rain continued to pelt them, they slowly drew near their goal. By the time they reached Cheat Summit, the southern boys were hungry, tired, and in miserable condition.

Instead of attacking immediately, Rust encountered Federal supply wagons, less than a half-mile away. They were coming with three hundred men to supply and support the fort. Rust engaged them in the dense woods, lost his nerve, and ordered a retreat. His men willingly retreated, throwing away their rifles and abandoning equipment. All Rust would say later was that he had become convinced he was facing an overwhelming force. At that point, there was nothing left for Lee to do but pull back to winter quarters.

For his failure at Cheat Mountain and loss of control in the mountains which would become the new state of West Virginia, Lee was returned to an advisory position by Jefferson Davis.

All his life, Robert E. Lee had lived with gentlepeople, where kindly sentiments and consideration for the feelings of others were part of the noblesse oblige. One trait that became clear in his West Virginia operations, and one which would follow him throughout the war, was his inability to discipline rebellious, subordinate officers."

You could hear a pin drop. Revelers were in a state of shock, and their silence spoke volumes. The tavern's muteness also gave additional credence to Jack Leffingwell's authority and judgment. None of these things escaped the ken of the Tennessee mountain man, who took a tiny sip of beer, then tried to make eye contact with his listeners. For the moment, they would have none of it.

The Polish poet, Czeslaw Milosz got it right when he wrote, *"In a room where people unanimously maintain a conspiracy of silence, one word of truth sounds like a pistol shot."* Jack's listeners had never heard a recount of Robert E. Lee's first field command and subsequent failure. Pained expressions were borne throughout as they wrestled with assimilating this unwelcome revelation.

The sequence of silence ended when Jack Leffingwell began, "The 7th Tennessee Regiment returned to Big Springs and awaited our next orders. We spent some time at Raleigh Courthouse before being ordered to join Major General Thomas J. "Stonewall" Jackson's brigade at Winchester. With Jackson, on January 4, the 7th participated in the expedition to Bath, Virginia, for the purpose of destroying the railroad bridge near the point. Controlling the Shenandoah Valley was of prime importance to General Jackson. He drove the Union forces out of Bath and into Hancock, Maryland. Not wanting to leave Virginia, "Stonewall" chose not to pursue them. On February 24, we were ordered to Manassas, to join General Joseph E. Johnston's Army. At the Manassas winter quarters the regiment spent the rest of the bleak weather training and preparing for future battle.

Meanwhile, Ulysses S. Grant was making hay. Not the kind he failed at for the past seven years, but the kind more suitable to his best abilities—soldiering. I need to back up a little bit in order to set the table for what comes next.

You'll remember that Kentucky stayed neutral during the Civil War. All the same, it was a key border state and birthplace of Lincoln, his wife Mary Todd, and President Jefferson Davis. Kentucky governor, Beriah Magoffin, was loyal to the southern cause, but the state legislature favored the Union. Both Abe Lincoln and Jeff Davis recognized the strategic importance of Columbus, Kentucky, since it was the terminus of the Mobile and Ohio railroad and its vital position along the Mississippi River. Our boys were miffed over Kentucky's decision to stay neutral and decided that Columbus was too important militarily to be ignored. Those controlling it would possess a strategic advantage.

On September 4, 1861, Major General Leonidas Polk violated their neutrality by ordering Brigadier General Gideon Johnson Pillow to occupy the city. His action prompted the Kentucky legislature to petition the Union for assistance, placing the state solidly under Federal control.

Polk constructed Fort DuRussey in the high bluffs of Columbus, and equipped it with 143 cannons. Always one to dramatize, he called the fort 'The Gibraltar of the West'. The Fighting Bishop also stretched an anchor chain across the river from the bank in Columbus to the opposite bank in Belmont, Missouri. Each link of chain measured eleven inches long by eight inches wide and weighed twenty pounds. The mammoth metal links never got a chance to prove their worth since the chain soon broke under its own weight."

"How the hell did we get a chain that big across the river in the first place?" interrupted Ryan Gosling.

"Probably using barges," Jack returned. "One thing's for certain. He didn't walk it across."

"Was General Polk really a preacher?"

"Yes and a whole lot more. When the war broke out he was serving as the bishop of the Episcopal Diocese of Louisiana. He and Jefferson Davis were good friends and even though Polk had no military experience, Old Jeff made him a General. With his lack of experience and ample ineptness, Polk managed to infuriate much of the brass. In spite of it, Confederate soldiers loved him, probably because he wouldn't take orders from anyone.

Kentucky governor Beriah Magoffin accused each coalition of violating the state's neutrality and called for their immediate withdrawal. However, the General Assembly passed a resolution ordering the withdrawal of only Confederate forces. Magoffin vetoed the resolution, but both houses overrode the veto. The

United States flag was raised over the state capitol, declaring its allegiance with the Union.

In response to the Confederate invasion, Ulysses S. Grant moved by riverboat from Cairo, Illinois, to attack the Confederate fortress at Columbus, Kentucky. The following morning he learned that southern troops had crossed the Mississippi River to Belmont, Missouri. Grant landed his men on the Missouri side, tromped to Belmont, and crushed the surprised Rebel camp. Though badly shaken, our scattered boys in butternut managed to reorganize, and, supported by heavy artillery fire from across the river, counterattacked. Amid cannon shells whistling overhead, Grant determined the enemy would eventually find the proper range and retreated back to his riverboats. He took his troops to Paducah, Kentucky, and seized the city. Full of fight, Grant requested permission from Theater Commander Maj. Gen. John C. Fremont to attack Columbus, but no answer came.

Polk was unable to be present at the skirmish yet suffered a serious wound. While watching a showing of the largest cannon in his army, it exploded during the demonstration. The explosion stunned Polk and blew his clothes off, requiring a convalescence of several weeks. The next two months saw a lull in the action, outside of minor feints and skirmishes.

Grant visualized the merit of controlling the Tennessee and Cumberland rivers and suggested to Major General Henry Halleck that a joint navy/army force capture Confederate forts Henry and Donelson. Halleck told him such a campaign was none of his business and dismissed Grant's suggestion out of hand. However, after Lincoln got fed up with General George B. McClellan's procrastinations, commanding all Union forces forward, Halleck authorized the attack on Fort Henry.

No grass grew under Grant's feet. Within days, the expressionless general and Navy Flag Officer Andrew Foote launched an upriver strike and quickly took possession of the fort. On his own initiative, Grant then moved on to Fort Donelson. Even though it was a much better defended fortress, within two weeks and a hundred cigars, Grant captured it along with a 14,000-man Confederate army. The occupation of these forts was a major blow to the left flank of the Confederacy and marked the first significant Union victory in the war."

"How could anybody make that claim so soon? The two armies haven't even faced each other yet." Ryan Gosling asked. Amazingly, he appeared to be sobering up, a definite denial of sound scientific protocol and logical reasoning.

"Consequential because it opened two great rivers, as avenues of invasion, to the heartland of the South. It also earned Grant a promotion to Major General of Volunteers," Jack replied.

The crafty bartender was fully aware these men had foregone supper to hear the mountain man's recollection of the Civil War. For them, the war was over once the Union occupied western Tennessee. Interest, however, was never dampened and any lengthy conversation eventually returned to the War, no matter the initial subject. Fritz Adler could see the lighted windows of the café across the street and took notice of some tables still occupied with guests. If his patrons decided to call a recess and hot foot it over for a late bite to eat, chances are they wouldn't return—a big loss in revenue.

Er ist kein holzkopf. He's no dummy and, during the last bathroom break, sent a reliable errand runner over with a written food order. Everything came to a sudden stop when the tavern door swung open and a man, struggling with an overladen tray, entered sideways through the portal. A rich, full aroma emanated from beneath the checkered cloth covering the contents, still warm from a previous kitchen.

"Just put it on the table over there," Fritz directed, while motioning to the desired destination. "I suspect you all are starved by now, so help yourself to some roast beef sandwiches. On the house."

If there is one-thing tavern partygoers love to hear, it's free food. Immediately, the room was filled with the jumbled sounds of scooting chairs and discordant praise for their Teutonic tap puller. The congregation didn't stand around the food table after spotting freshly poured glasses of foaming lager resting atop the newly wiped bar.

The impromptu history lesson has reached mid-1862 and Jack Leffingwell took a timeout for tavern occupants to consider what they have heard thus far. Even the most partial southern patriot has to agree, the bearded man in blue has outperformed the cotton state's hero. Most likely, that will change once the revered Confederate general returns to the battlefield. That day came on May 31, 1862, when General Joseph Johnston was wounded at the Battle of Seven Pines—called Fair Oaks by the Union. Jack and the 7th Regiment sharpshooters took part in the battle. Having actually participated lends a great deal more credence to the mountain man's version of events. Another moment of stillness gave the signal for him to steal their ears and continue his disclosure.

"With the rail splitter on his ass morning, noon, and night, George McClellan reluctantly began the first large-scale offensive in the Eastern Theater. He cooked up a plan to quickly move up the peninsula, and by circumventing the Confederate army, capture Richmond. Easier said than done, considering we had established good defensive positions and held him off for a month. So much for his quick advance. Restrained, Little Mac called for a siege. The Confederates were now under the command of General Joseph E. Johnston, who began a steady withdrawal toward the capitol. Each time McClellan moved, he found southern defenses and plenty of resistance. So much so that his losses began to add up.

Nevertheless, he reported each engagement as a victory in spite of suffering the most casualties. We, here in the South, celebrated the standoff.

General Johnston learned that McClellan's reinforcements were diverted to the Shenandoah Valley, leaving us with the biggest army—about 50,000 soldiers to 30,000 for the enemy. At that point, Old Joe decided to do some attacking himself.

Unfortunately, the plan was mismanaged from the start. Johnston issued some of their orders orally while other generals received theirs in writing. General Longstreet, as was his habit, chose to modify his orders without informing Johnston. Making matters worse for both sides, was a severe thunderstorm the night of May 30, which flooded the river, destroyed most of the Union bridges, and turned the roads into a morass of mud. Written orders didn't specify the time of attack, resulting in less than desired forces operating in unison.

The 7th Regiment sharpshooters took part in the surprise attack. We were positioned behind the Confederate artillery. It wasn't as wide a front as General Johnston originally detailed, but the other troops were yet to arrive. Once the firing of artillery and musket opened up, the hostilities became fierce. I now employed the telescope General Jackson had given me and I put it to good use, primarily hitting targets on horseback. As a result, the horses in my field of vision were soon riderless as several officers took a dirt nap.

Because of the conditions, fragmented columns, and McClellan's reinforcements, the battle stood as a stalemate and the Confederates finally withdrew.

During the battle, General Johnston was struck in the right shoulder by a bullet, immediately followed by a shell fragment hitting him in the chest. He fell from his horse and was evacuated to Richmond. Shortly thereafter, General Robert E. Lee was named commander of the Army of Northern Virginia. Marse Robert hit the ground running.

General McClellan had lost his pluck when he could no longer advance and started to move his troops back down the Virginia peninsula. With the bulk of McClellan's army arrayed in a line south of the Chickahominy River, Lee now was on the offensive. Again, he devised a complicated plan requiring exact coordination between our

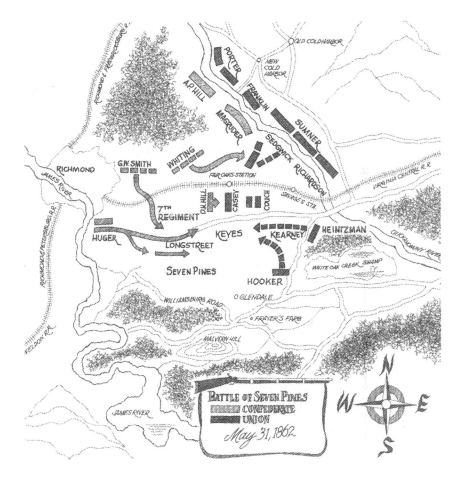

BATTLE OF SEVEN PINES
CONFEDERATE
UNION
May 31, 1862

forces. Since the Union's northern flank was most vulnerable to a well-planned foray, Lee made it the focus of his battle tactics. It would concentrate about 65,000 southern troops against 30,000 Federals.

Stonewall was to begin the strike early on June 26. At the same time, A.P. Hill would advance, and clear the Union Pickets from Mechanicsville, then move to Beaver Dam Creek. General's Longstreet and D. H. (Daniel Harvey) Hill were to pass through Mechanicsville and support Jackson and A. P. (Ambrose Powell) Hill.

Lee's complex plan fell through immediately. Stonewall Jackson's men ran over four hours behind schedule. By early afternoon, Ambrose Hill grew impatient and began his attack without specific guidelines—a frontal assault with 11,000 men. Unbeknownst to us, the federal forces had strengthened their right flank. The 7th Tennessee was held in reserves. A. P. Hill faced 14,000 well-entrenched Yanks. Union troops repulsed his repeated attacks and delivered substantial casualties. Thrust and parry continued for most of the afternoon, and as the sun began to set, we in the 7th infantry were called to make a final assault. A whole lot of southern boys met their maker that day. In 30 minutes, most of the company commanders, and half of the regulars were either killed or wounded.

When Stonewall Jackson finally arrived, late in the afternoon, he ordered his troops to bivouac for the evening, ignoring the major battle raging within earshot. The proximity of his men to the Federal right flank caused McClellan to withdraw to a point five-miles away. Little Mac feared his supply lines were threatened and shifted the base of supply to the James River. General Lee's diversionary tactic of feigning attack south of the river worked like a charm. McClellan imagined he was facing 200,000 rebel troops and abandoned Richmond, but not before burning up the telegraph wires and reporting the same to Washington.

Overall, the battle was a Union tactical victory. Confederates suffered heavy casualties, due to the seriously flawed execution of Lee's plan. Instead of over 60,000 men crushing the enemy's flank, only about 15,000 men saw action. Our losses were four times that of the Union.

From June 25 to July 1, 1862 Lee launched a series of attacks against McClellan's retreating forces. His incursions, marred by clumsy tactical performances from divisional commanders, resulted in heavy Confederate casualties. Nevertheless, Marse Robert's aggressive behavior so unnerved McClellan that he retreated to the James River and abandoned his Peninsula Campaign.

General Lee now turned his attention to McClellan's second army lumbering across central Virginia. It was under the command of a Kentuckian named Maj. Gen. John Pope who had success in taking our New Madrid, Missouri, position of the upper Mississippi. For that, the Yankee's made him a major general."

Pope was his own worst enemy. An unlikable sort, abrasive, conceited, and loud mouthed; constantly rubbing people the wrong way. To his credit, he had a zeal for fighting—the type most favored by Lincoln. When Pope took over the Union Army of Virginia, it was divided into three corps and scattered across northern Virginia. His first move was to concentrate his troops, giving him 40,000 men in one group.

Pope believed the Southern people should pay a price for the transgression of secession and civil war. When his army advanced, he issued orders instructing officers to live off the fertile land, taking foodstuffs and supplies from the civilians. He also implemented stern punishments for guerrillas, and directed that all male noncombatants encountered along the route of his march, be required to swear an oath of allegiance or be arrested and expelled from the region. If they returned, they would be prosecuted as spies. Finally, Pope announced that any man or woman who corresponded with anyone in the Confederate Army, even a parent writing to a son, would be subject to execution.

When Lee got the news of this, he labeled the Union general a "miscreant" and entrained two divisions under Old Blue Light

(Stonewall Jackson) and later, Maj. Gen. Ambrose Hill's division, telling Stonewall, "I want Pope to be suppressed."

* * *

"Following a wide-ranging flanking excursion and with his "longer" arm[6] held up to "equalize" circulation, Stonewall Jackson captured the Union's supply depot at Manassas Junction. Withdrawing a few miles to the northwest found Jackson, sucking on a lemon, and taking up defensive positions on Stony Ridge. On August 28, he attacked a Union column just east of Gainesville, at Brawner's Farm, resulting in a stalemate. On the same day, the wing of Lee's army, commanded by The 'Old War-Horse', General James Longstreet, broke through light Union resistance in the Thoroughfare Gap—a water gap in the Bull Run Mountains—and approached the battlefield.

Pope was strongly convinced he had trapped Jackson and concentrated the bulk of his army against him. On August 29, Pope launched a series of assaults against Jackson's position along an unfinished railroad grade. The attacks were repulsed with heavy casualties on both sides. At noon, Longstreet arrived on the field from Thoroughfare Gap and took position on Jackson's right flank. On August 30, Pope renewed his attacks, unaware that Longstreet was on the field. While Confederate artillery devastated a Union assault by Maj. Gen. Fitz John Porter's V Corps, Longstreet's wing of 25,000 men counterattacked in the largest, simultaneous mass assault of the war. The Union left

---

[6]   Thomas Jonathan "Stonewall" Jackson was one of the most successful southern generals. That said, he also had his idiosyncrasies and ailments. Believing one of his arms longer that the other, he often raised it above his head to equalize circulation. Occasionally falling asleep while eating, and with food in his mouth, indicates Jackson may have suffered from narcolepsy. His serious hearing loss was contributed to previous service with the artillery; however, Asperger syndrome may explain his difficulty communicating during social interaction. Jackson loved fruit and was frequently seen gnawing on a lemon, his favorite.

flank was crushed and the army was driven back to Manassas. At that point, Pope quickly retreated to Centerville.

He was removed from command within a week and what was left of his army, absorbed into McClellan's Army of the Potomac.

Blame for the disaster fell squarely on Pope. He had promised much and delivered little. He, in turn, attributed the defeat to a conspiracy among the officers of the Army of the Potomac, particularly, Fitz John Porter. The military court found Porter guilty as charged, and he was cashiered from the army."

* * *

No longer had Granny Lee, the Confederate general, returned to the field as a firebrand and, after McClellan's retreat, defeated Union General John Pope at Second Manassas, he moved the battle lines from six miles outside of Richmond to 20 miles outside Washington.

At this point, intoxicated with complacency, Lee overextended his army by invading Maryland. Just as a victorious Muhammad Ali shouted, "I'm the greatest" Lee believed, even though his army was half-sick, half-clad, half-starved, and half-shoeless, they were the greatest soldiers and could defeat any foe against them. That being said, no doubt the rank and file would have preferred moving back to Richmond or out to the lush Shenandoah Valley to rest and provision the army. To do so, however, would lose the recent military gains and return the initiative to the Federals. The King of Spades would have no part in that. Discounting the risk, Lee only thought of the possibilities and led his troops across the Potomac; set up camp near Fredrick, Maryland; and, to maintain inertia, sent Stonewall Jackson to capture an isolated Union garrison at Harper's Ferry. Lee had learned that the Federal garrison had not retreated after his incursion into Maryland, and, since he had the inordinate advantage of troop numbers, he decided to surround the force and capture it. After Confederate artillery was placed on the heights overlooking the town, the Union commander surrendered the garrison of more than twelve thousand soldiers. Harper's Ferry provided the southern coalition with a large amount of supplies, including clothing, shoes, thousands of small arms and ammunition, and over seventy pieces of artillery. The remainder of Lee's army then crossed South Mountain and headed for Hagerstown, about twenty-five miles to the northwest.

After entering the Old Line State, the Confederates received little support; rather, they were met with reactions that ranged from cool lack of enthusiasm, to, in most cases, open hostility. Robert E. Lee was disappointed at the state's resistance, a condition that he had not anticipated. Although Maryland was a slave-holding state, Confederate sympathies were considerably less pronounced among the civilian population, which generally supported the Union cause, than among the pro-secession Maryland legislature. Furthermore, many of the fiercely pro-Southern Marylanders had already traveled south at the beginning of the war to join the Confederate Army in Virginia. Only a "few score" of men joined Lee's columns in Maryland.

Maryland and Pennsylvania, alarmed and outraged by the invasion, rose at once to arms. Pennsylvania governor Andrew Curtin called for 50,000 militia men to turn out, and directed General John F. Reynolds to command them. This caused considerable frustration to McClellan and Reynolds's corps commander, Joseph Hooker; but, newly appointed general-in-chief Henry Halleck ordered Reynolds to serve under Curtin and told Hooker to find a new division commander. In Maryland, panic was much more widespread than in Pennsylvania, which was not immediately threatened. Baltimore, which Lee incorrectly regarded as a hot bed of secession, merely waiting for the appearance of Confederate armies to revolt, took up the war call against him immediately.

In a lethargic pursuit, McClellan moved out of Washington on September 7, with nearly a 90,000-man army. Naturally cautious, he assumed he would be facing over 120,000 Confederates. Starting out with relatively low morale, their spirits were boosted by the friendly, almost tumultuous welcome by the citizens of Maryland.

* * *

"How did the rejection of the confederate soldiers in Maryland make you guys feel?" asked Frank Riberty.

"The whole thing was bizarre. We all were told there would be a joyful welcome with a huzzah and flowers. So we marched in singing *Maryland My Maryland* and, without our knowledge, by late 1862, pro-Union sentiment was winning out. Citizens generally hid inside their homes, as we passed through their towns, or watched in silence. Those who were outside had a fixed expression of hatred on their faces. Aesop, the ancient Greek storyteller, had a saying, *'A doubtful friend is worse than a certain enemy. Let a man be one thing or the other, and we know how to meet him.'* Speaking for the 7th regiment, looking into those deadpan kissers gave us a weird feeling. I knew, then and there, the northern excursion was the wrong decision and the cold reception was a portend of worse things to come," Jack replied.

"General Lee had to see the same things you did, why did he continue?" echoed some in the gathering.

"Obviously, after such an exhilarating triumph, he felt it would demoralize his army to withdraw; and, remember, he was hopeful of catalyzing the enlistment of droves of Marylanders into our ranks. Besides, we all knew General Lee was itching for a fight. Picturing in his own mind, 'those people' had been dealt a powerful punch to the solar plexus, and still can't straighten up. He was determined to finish them off, on their own soil. Lee knew McClellan's army was much larger than ours; all the same, he was relying on the fainthearted Little Mac to continue overestimating our numbers. As long as McClellan believed that, he wouldn't achieve force concentration.

Luck deserted us when a couple of Union soldiers found a mislaid copy of Lee's battle plans. I've often wondered who could have been so careless as to have wrapped it around three cigars and lost something so important. The order indicated that Lee had divided the army and dispersed portions to Harpers Ferry, West Virginia, and Hagerstown, Maryland. With our forces isolated, McClellan could defeat them if he moved quickly enough. We were saved by the fact McClellan was in charge. He waited a day before deciding to take advantage of this intelligence. That gave time for Lee to deploy his available forces near the town of Sharpsburg behind Antietam Creek. The terrain provided good cover for infantrymen with outcroppings of limestone fences and swales. On September 15, about 18,000 troops were under Lee's immediate command—a third of the size of the Federal army.

Two Union divisions began to arrive in the afternoon of September 15 and the majority later that evening. An immediate attack would have been overwhelming because of McClellan's advantage in numbers. Believing Lee to have as many as 100,000 men at Sharpsburg caused Little Mac to delay his attack for another day. This gave the Confederates time to prepare defensive positions and, more importantly, allow Longstreet's corps to arrive from Hagerstown and Stonewall Jackson from Harpers Ferry. They immediately took up positions covering Lee's flanks, both north and south.

On the evening of September 16, McClellan ordered Union general Hooker to cross Antietam and probe the Confederate positions. After several probing actions, enough information was gathered for the cautious Union general to devise a plan of action. McClellan planned to overwhelm Lee's left flank. He reached his decision because of the configuration of bridges over the Antietam. The lower bridge was dominated by Confederate positions on the bluffs overlooking it. The middle bridge was subjected to artillery fire from the heights near Sharpsburg. The upper bridge was located two miles east of the Confederate guns and could be crossed with the least amount of danger to his soldiers. With that knowledge, McClellan proposed to commit more than half his army to the assault. Once Union troops skirmished in the East Woods, Lee became aware of McClellan's intentions and prepared his defenses accordingly. Union commanders were given orders for their own corps, but not general orders describing the entire battle plan. Therefore, the assault essentially was three separate, uncoordinated battles. This lack of concentration almost completely nullified the two-to-one Union advantage.

Yankee general Joseph Hooker opened the battle at dawn on September 17, with an attack down the Hagerstown turnpike. Abner Doubleday's division moved on Hooker's right, James Rickett's on his left, and General George Meade's men at the center and slightly to the rear. When the first Union men emerged from the North Woods and into the Miller Cornfield, an artillery duel erupted. A fierce battle raged back and forth. At first, our artillery stunned the Union forces; however, only after they brought up their own guns. We also took a beating. At times the fighting was at very close quarters. Every time one side gained an advantage, reinforcements arrived to alleviate it. After the first two hours, Hooker suffered 2,500 casualties and ended up back where he started. The Cornfield had changed hands 15 times and was now a scene of total devastation. Hooker attempted to gather the scattered remnants of his corps to continue the assault, but a Confederate sharpshooter spotted the general's conspicuous white horse and shot the bluecoat commander through the foot. With him removed from the field, the morning phase ended. Casualties on both sides were about 13,000, including two Union commanders.

By midday, the action shifted to the center of the Confederate line. This sector of Longstreet's line was considered the weakest, but General D. H. Hill's division was in a strong defensive position on elevated ground. The first three Union attacks were driven back with only rifle fire. All the while, reinforcements were arriving on both sides. Finally, the Union managed to penetrate our line of defenses allowing them to establish enfilade on the Confederate line. Many southern soldiers thought the line was lost and fled toward Sharpsburg. Longstreet hastily arranged artillery that stopped the Federal advantage, and, with Hill's counterattack, stemmed the collapse of the center.

Failing to take advantage of the breakthrough in the Allies line, McClellan missed a great opportunity. If the broken sector was exploited, Marse Robert's army would have been divided in half and defeated.

Action now moved to the southern end of the battlefield. Hoping to draw Lee's attention away from the main Union attack in the north, General Ambrose Burnside was to conduct a diversionary attack. He also was to wait for explicit orders before launching. The orders arrived at 10 a.m. Previous movement of units to bolster Lee's left flank weakened the southern state's line. Only four southern brigades guarded the ridges near Sharpsburg and 400 men remained to defend Rohrbach's Bridge (later called Burnside's Bridge), a three spans, 12-foot wide, 125-foot-long, stone structure being the southernmost crossing of the Antietam.

Burnside found crossing the bridge a difficult problem. The road leading to it ran parallel to the creek and was exposed to enemy fire. On the west bank, a high bluff and stone from an old quarry gave enemy infantry and sharpshooters good cover. Burnside seemingly ignored the fact that this sector of the Antietam was seldom over 50 feet wide, with several stretches only waist deep, and out of rifle range.

The Yankee, Ohio brigade made the first attempt to clear the bridge in order for another brigade to cross and assault the South's defenses on the bluff. The effort lasted about 15 minutes before the Union withdrew, losing 139 casualties—about one-third of their strength. A second assault also fell prey to rebel sharpshooters and artillery, ending with the same result.

McClellan was losing patience and sent several couriers to motivate Burnside forward.

A third attempt was by the New York and Pennsylvania corps, who managed to set up artillery support and charged downhill, taking up positions on the east bank. Maneuvering a captured light howitzer into position, they fired double canisters down the bridge until they got within 25 yards of the southern allies. By 1 p.m., our ammunition was running low and word reached command, the Yankee soldiers were crossing the creek on the Confederate flank. After holding their position for over three hours, and costing the Federals more than 500 casualties, the rebels were ordered to withdraw.

The Union assault stalled again. Burnside's officers neglected to transport ammunition across the bridge. Now a bottleneck with soldiers, artillery, and wagons was causing another two-hour delay.

Burnside's plan was to move around the weakened Confederate right flank, converge on Sharpsburg, and cut Lee's army off at Boteler's Ford—their only escape route across the Potomac.

General Lee used this time to bolster his right flank and ordered up every available artillery unit.

The Federals were completely unaware that 3,000 new men would be facing them. Their initial assault pushed the Rebels back past Cemetery Hill and to within 200 yards of Sharpsburg. Farther to the left, another Union brigade came under heavy shellfire from a dozen rebel guns mounted on a ridge to their front. In spite of being confronted with hail-like fire, they kept pushing forward.

Confederate reinforcements commanded by A.P. Hill arrived at 3:30 p.m. and prepared for a counterattack. Ten minutes later they met the Federals in a farmer's cornfield. The Union soldiers were green, having only three weeks training, and their line disintegrated with nearly 200 casualties. A second unit arrived, became confused, and also broke and ran. Burnside ordered his men back to the west bank of the Antietam, where he urgently called for more men and guns. By 5:30 p.m., the battle was over. Both sides had suffered an enormous amount of casualties—a total of 22,719 wounded and 3,653 dead.

On the morning of September 18, Lee's army prepared to defend against another Union assault that never came. Under an improvised truce, for both sides to recover and exchange wounded, Lee's forces began withdrawing across the Potomac to return to Virginia. He left behind a rear guard of two infantry brigades and 44 guns to hold Boteler's Ford.

Shortly before dusk on September 19, the Union sent two regiments across the river at Boteler's Ford and they pitched into the southern rear guard before being recalled. On September 20, two more brigades came across in a well-armed reconnaissance mission and encountered General A. P. Hill's "Light Division" about a mile from the river. We came under a withering hail of artillery fire, which caused a great deal of casualties. After we established our own cannons on the bluffs, the Union brigades crossed the river and met artillery fire. There was a violent clash along the bordering heights and the Federals were forced to retire. For all practical purposes, McClellan believed Lee's Maryland Campaign was over, and determined active pursuit of the enemy was not possible.

President Lincoln was disappointed in McClellan's performance. He believed his general was too cautious and devised poorly coordinated actions in the field, resulting in a draw instead of a crippling Confederate defeat. McClellan was relieved of his command of the Army of the Potomac on November 7. General Ambrose E. Burnside was named his successor. Whether or not a draw or victory, Lincoln claimed victory and took the opportunity to announce his Emancipation Proclamation on September 22, which took effect January 1, 1863.

Burnside had a plan. He would race his army down to Fredericksburg, Virginia, cross the Rappahannock River and get between Lee and the southern capitol, Richmond. Anxious to impress his boss, Burnside beat Lee to Richmond but, in the process, he also outpaced his pontoon bridges and was unable to cross. He had another option. A short distance away, there was a shallow ford up river that cattle used to cross; even so, Burnside ignored it and waited for his engineers to construct pontoons.

During that time, Lee and the Army of Northern Virginia arrived in Fredericksburg and set up on the heights outside of town. When Burnside was finally able to pass over the river, the advantage of surprise was lost. Confederates were now well entrenched on the high ground and sharpshooters stationed in town were able to pick off his engineers laying the floating bridges. The frustrated Union general ordered the shelling of Fredericksburg, an action that infuriated General Lee. Now, across the river, Burnside's plan called for a two pronged offensive. One division would strike the rebel right and the rest of his army would attack the Confederate left, anchored on Mayre's Heights.

The first assault on the right failed. On the Confederate left, Burnside wanted his troops to make their way through the shelled out town, cross an open plain, and move up the long open slopes of the aforementioned Mayre's Heights. He ignored another important fact. His maps disclosed the existence of a canal before troops could reach the heights. Today, it was only partially frozen. Under heavy fire from Confederate artillery, many bluecoats were killed trying to ford the canal and others were ineffective from the ice-cold water.

The Union army charged valiantly up the hill several times; however, not one man reached the stone wall at the top. By day's end, all Burnside could show for his efforts was thousands of dead bodies. Distraught, he decided to lead another foray himself but his officers talked him out of it.

On the right, the Federals found a hole in the rebel defenses and hit Confederate General Archer's line on its flank. Archer's brigade, their line broken, quickly pulled back, suffering heavy losses. The Union needed support to hold their advantage. Due to the dense woods, their troops became disorganized and before they could give assistance, the reinforced Confederates slammed into the Union troops driving them nearly back to the river. The following day neither army moved. Burnside asked for a formal cease-fire to collect the wounded. Many had died from their wounds or exposure to the cold.

The 7ᵗʰ Tennessee Regiment fought in five major battles: Cedar Run, Second Manassas, Harper's Ferry, Sharpsburg and Shepherdstown. In July of 1861, our 7ᵗʰ Regiment left Camp Trousdale with about 1,200 men and, now, we are down to around 250, with a lot of fighting ahead of us."

Jack Leffingwell paused his oration to take an imaginary sip from his empty beer glass, waving Fritz Adler away from rushing to his rescue. Temporarily disappointed, the German tapster immediately recovered and began filling the tumblers of those oblivious to his actions.

The restaurant across the street was now empty and dark. Many of the buildings along the main street were two story structures. Several businesses had living quarters on the second floor. Such was the case with the Main Street Café, whose proprietors resided upstairs. One of their top floor windows, which was illuminated from a unsteady and flickering candle, soon went black. With the exception of the tavern, the Statesville business district had called it a day. Fritz Adler's friendly public-house pub will soon follow suit as a dozen patrons were now stifling yawns. The scene was one of tired Tennesseans stubbornly hanging on until the mountain man said uncle.

"I've come to the end of 1862 after General Lee's Army of Northern Virginia ended with a defensive victory over Burnside at Fredericksburg," Jack said flatly.

"Ulysses Grant also ended the year with significant victories at Belmont, Fort Henry, Fort Donelson, Shiloh, Iuka, and Corinth, Mississippi, setting the stage for the eventual capture of Vicksburg, Mississippi and the last Confederate bastion on the Big Muddy. In accomplishing these victories, Grant kept his casualties at around 20,000 while effecting 35,000 on the southern volunteers.

I, personally, feel General Lee's Maryland Campaign was ill advised. While casualties were about even, they placed a greater drain on our limited manpower. Their replacements took men away from the Western Theater, making it easier for Grant and the other Union generals out west."

"Gentlemen, at this point we need to postpone the remainder of our comparison until another time. It's been a rather long day and Melvin and I still have a ride back to the farms ahead of us."

"How soon will you be able to come back?" asked Frank Riberty.

"That's up to Ryan Gosling. He's doing some work for one of our wagons and we'll be back once he finishes," Jack replied.

The feisty blacksmith became the center of attention and quickly responded, "I have to get parts out of Nashville. I ought to be finished in a couple weeks."

"Okay, let's plan on meeting here in two weeks. Ryan, when they pick up the parts let me know and I'll get the word out. How will you let Jack know when you're ready?" Frank questioned.

"I usually tell Reverend Adams. He's out to their farm at least twice a week to see his grandchildren," said Ryan.

"We're all set then. Let's settle up with Fritz so he can get a little sleep tonight," Frank continued.

"I'm paying for Melvin and Jack," stated the scrappy blacksmith.

Frank nodded in agreement and turned to Fritz, "Total it up and tell me what the damage is."

If there's one thing a bartender always remembers it's a person's bar tab. Fritz kept a running total all evening and quickly said, "After Ryan's tab, it comes to nine dollars and I'm not charging for the sandwiches."

Frank opened his purse and removed a folded ten-dollar greenback, straightened it out on the flat mahogany surface, and said, "Keep the change."

* * *

The night was crispy clear as the two sharpshooters slowly walked to the stable barn to fetch their wagon. Without the bright winter moon, a November night is the blackest. Fortunately, this evening was not the case; however, the air was biting cold, demanding coat collars be turned up to protect their faces. Above, the moon had evolved into an expressive sphere of light, making it easier to find the way home.

"Yalata called the November moon the Beaver moon because it was the last time to set the traps before the swamps froze over.

It assured there would be warm fur during the winter," Jack interjected.

Four wagon wheels creaked softly as the jolt-wagon turned onto the main dirt road. Coming from the warm stable, the horse emitted white vapor into the air by virtue of the colder temperature. Once the equine established a pattern of movement, Melvin said, "Hope is really going to be pissed off when I get home."

"We need to explain ourselves right away," Jack expressed.

"I'm more frightened of Hope than I was at Fredericksburg," confessed Melvin. "You don't know what she's like once she gets mad."

That brought a smile to the face of the mountain man. He, too, was concerned about the pending reception and how Abigail would react. Resolved to the fact she will never accept any excuses, after being in the Statesville tavern all day, explained his frown.

* * *

Back at the farm, Hope distressed to the point she walked across the field to commiserate with Abigail. Melvin had never done anything like this before and she worried he might have been hurt, or even worse.

"How can you be so calm?" she asked.

"It's only on the outside, Hope. Inside I'm mad as hell, but I don't believe anything bad happened to them, otherwise we would have been told a long time ago," responded Abigail.

"Are you going to raise Cain?"

"That would let him off too easy. I learned a long time ago that the best way to get even with a man is to ignore his attempt to explain and go on about your business as if nothing happened. Men must have the last word and that will drive him crazy."

"Then, I'll do the same thing," Hope affirmed, icily.

The two women sat silently at the dining room table. Light from an oil lamp illuminated their faces in a Rubenesque fashion.

Hardly plump and voluptuous, nonetheless, they were as attractive as depicted by the Flemish painter, Peter Paul Rubens. Behind them, the glow created mysterious shadows that took elongated shapes with the slightest movement.

"That commotion we hear outside is them. They'll fiddle round in the barn until they get their stories straight. Now remember, don't let them tell us," Abigail instructed.

Jack was the first to scale the porch steps and slowly opened the door, kicking himself for not greasing the hinges when he had the chance. Melvin fell in line directly behind and spotted his wife sitting at the polished dining table.

"Where are the boys?" asked Abigail.

Jack's throat suddenly went dry. He forced a swallow and replied, "They're spending the night with Maryellen. It was her idea. She'll be bringing them home in the morning. Don't you want to know what happened?"

"Not really. We best let the Kaufman's get home. The night's going to be short as it is. Hope, take one of the lanterns off the porch. I'll see you in the morning. We'll have breakfast when Maryellen arrives."

On their way home Melvin said, "This is the reason we're so late —"

Hope interrupted, "Never mind, enough has been said for one night."

"But, I need to tell you why we're late."

"Melvin, I said I don't want to hear about it," Hope stated with conviction.

CHAPTER FIVE

A manda Strawn's brother Pearle is the happiest young man in Lebanon, Tennessee. Under a few stipulations, put forth by his brother-in-law, Abel has given permission for him to accompany them on next year's trek to Kansas. Now, treated as an adult, Pearle can take part in the planning stage. Unquestionably, another pair of hands, on an endeavor such as this, is worth its weight in gold. Even with a cabin already standing, there will be much more required just to make it through the pending winter, let alone planting and harvest before the snow flies.

An assortment of useful items began to collect in the storage shed behind the parsonage. Outside of wooden barrels, destined to hold water, Abel's most prized item is a brand new John Deere cast iron plow. John Deere, an Illinois blacksmith, had just incorporated his business, and is the favorite manufacturer of pioneer farmers for the vital implement designed to cut through the tough prairie ground. The style chosen by Abel is called *The Grasshopper*. Whenever beyond the vision of curious eyes, he would stand behind it and practice. It was at such a time when the shed doors creaked open and a familiar image stood in the intrusive sunlight.

"Mister Strawn, my name is Zachary Wheat."

"Yes, I recognize you. Don't you help my father around the church?" asked Abel.

"I help him out occasionally. You might say I'm a jack of all trades and do a little bit of everything, working odd jobs for those needing a little help," Wheat replied.

"Well, what can I do for you Mister Wheat?"

"Word has it that you plan to take a journey to western Kansas next spring. Some say you bought a farm there. I was wondering if you had all the help you're going to need. If not, I'd like to offer my services and go along."

Abel smiled at the thought of Wheat's services and questioned, "I'm not sure we can entertain another man. We're bringing my wife's brother, Pearle Sparks, to help me farm and I won't have money to pay for another."

"Oh, you don't have to worry about money. I don't need to be paid. I've saved up enough to get me through the winter. All I'll be needing is a bed out of the cold," answered the bewhiskered visitor.

"What exactly can you do Mister Wheat?" Abel had grown more inquisitive as he remembered what Jack Leffingwell had told him—to not judge a book by its cover.

"Like I said, a little bit of everything. I can plow and plant. I've been called a water witch because I can find water where they ain't supposed to be any. Naturally, I can help dig a well when I find it. I've driven cattle, broken broncos, and am crack shot with both rifle and six guns."

"I do pretty well in that area myself," Abel interjected.

"I know about the 7th Regiment, but you, of all people, understand the importance of another gun if Indians attack."

"Mister Wheat, where are you from originally? You don't talk like someone from around here," Abel asked.

"I was born in New York and joined the militia when the war broke out. I got captured twice and exchanged both times. Finally, after Antietam, I got sent to Belle Isle, in Richmond, Virginia and released in 1864. Ever since, I've been working my way west. I hope to eventually take advantage of the free land offered by the government."

"You look to be ten years older than me. How old were you when you signed up?"

"I owned a cabinet making business before the war. Just when it started to make real money, the war broke out. Today, my brother runs it and banks my share of the profits for me. I almost forgot. You plan to travel with a prairie schooner, most likely drawn by two teams of oxen. I don't know if you've ever driven oxen before, but they can be ornery at times. It takes a skilled hand to control them and I can do that," Wheat said, confidently.

"Mister Wheat, I'm not going to say no out of hand. Give me a couple days to think it over. I'll know by the end of the month. I must talk to a good friend of mine before a decision is made," Abel asserted.

That evening, at the dinner table, Abel asked his father about Zachary Wheat. About all Joseph Strawn could tell him was Wheat was a good worker and knew the verses. He appeared to be a decent sort. However, the minister had a feeling that Wheat was hiding something. He didn't care to talk about himself and became distant when the subject came up. It was obvious his father didn't know any more than he did and that was when the idea dawned on him. Wheat had said he was a prisoner-of-war, and interred in the Confederate prison at Belle Isle, in Richmond, Virginia. During the war, Hope Kaufman volunteered at the area hospitals and may know a little about Mister Wheat or could find out from her father, Horace. Before the household was deep in sleep, Abel had dashed a letter to the Kaufmans and would mail it first thing in the morning.

November 21, 1868

Dear Friends,

Just a note to let you know we arrived home safe and sound. Sorry for not writing sooner but time got away from me. Our visit was the most enjoyable happening of the year. It's wonderful to be able to have everyone together at one time. Amanda and I couldn't wish for greater hosts than you and the Leffingwells. Amanda's brother Pearle will be joining us on our trip west. He'll be 19 by the time we leave and seems more excited than we are. Each day appears to fly bye faster than the one before and keeps us busy from morning 'til night. I keep going over the list Jack gave me and think I've completed it all.

I have another favor to ask. The other day a fellow approached me and asked to accompany us on the trip. His only demand was a warm bed during the winter. Nobody knows much about him but he claims to be experienced and could be very helpful in getting us started. The man is a Yankee and spent time at Belle Isle. He was released after General Lee surrendered. His name is Zachary Wheat. I'd appreciate anything you might be able to learn about him.

Thanks for everything. I'll be writing to Jack and Abigail so as to mail both letters together.

Your friend in Christ,
Abel Strawn

* * *

Like most boys his age Pearle had an interest in guns. He had never owned one. In fact, he had never even touched one, notwithstanding the weapon carved from a tree branch. Pearle owned a pocketknife. Several times during the week he could be found loitering in front of the gunsmith's display window. Today, the most beautiful revolver he had ever seen, mesmerized the curious youngster. Cupping his hands around his eyes to obstruct the sun's glare, Pearle was preoccupied and failed to immediately notice the reflected image of a man standing beside him. The minute he became aware of another window shopper, Pearle moved to his left, making room, so another could stand closer to the transparent glass. The object of their attention was a new Remington, model 1858, .44 caliber, army revolver.

"That's one damn nice gun," the man said aloud. "I may be needing a good pistol in a few weeks." Turning to Pearle, he asked, "Would you like to go inside and hold the merchandise?"

"I'd love to but Mister Durban would never let me hold it."

"I take it Mister Durban is the gunsmith. Well, if I decide to purchase that gun, he ain't got the say so."

"Are you really going to buy it?" Pearle asked, excitedly.

"I think I will. First, let me introduce myself. My name is Zachary Wheat and I'm on my way west to claim homestead land."

Momentarily stunned by Wheat's piercing blue eyes, Pearle hesitated; and then shook hands declaring, "Happy to make your acquaintance. My name is Pearle Sparks."

Smiling at the awkwardness of a 19-year-old, Wheat continued, "You say you're planning to go west. How does that happen?"

"I'm going with my sister and brother-in-law to western Kansas. They bought a farm there and I'm living with them."

Zachary Wheat nodded and asked, "Would his name happen to be Abel Strawn?"

"Why, yes it is. Do you know Abel?"

"I met him the other day and asked to travel with you guys. All kidding aside, I'm a pretty handy fellow; and, without experience, he'll need all the help he can get."

"What did he say?"

"He didn't say no right off. He said he would let me know in a couple weeks." Wheat replied.

"Mister Wheat, I sure hope you can come along," Pearle stated.

"Now that we're properly introduced just call me Zack." With that, Wheat put his arm around Pearle's shoulder and led him inside the gunsmith's shop.

"Gentlemen, how may I help you?" asked the proprietor. Richard Durban loved guns. They were like puppies to a pet store owner. It broke his heart with each sale. Nevertheless, the transaction had to be made for his business to survive. To him, the Second Amendment to the U.S. Constitution was just as holy as biblical scripture. And Durban loved his Bible.

"We're interested in that Remington you have in the window," Wheat declared.

After Durban ordered a dozen Remington Model 1858s he began to worry. The revolver was new and up 'til now, folks were more than satisfied with Colt's Army Model 1860. Colt Manufacturing suffered a disastrous fire in 1864. The majority of their Hartford, Connecticut, Armory manufacturing facility was lost. During their reconstruction, they were unable to supply product and lost competitive edge to the Remington Arms Company.

"The Remington 1858 has some features over the Colt Model 1860," the gunsmith said, as he pulled out the drawer behind the counter and extracted the hand gun. "It's modified to incorporate metallic cartridges."

"Do you have a place for me to try it out for accuracy?" Wheat asked, as he removed the cylinder and held the pistol to the light so he could view the eight-inch barrel's rifling.

"Unfortunately, I don't. I'm sure you'll find it very accurate; but, in case you're not satisfied, you can bring it back for a full refund."

"That's fair enough. How much will it cost for the gun and 20 boxes of metallic cartridges?"

Durban removed a pencil from behind his ear and began writing numerical figures on the pad provide for that purpose. Finally, he looked up and said, "The total comes to $60 dollars. Twenty boxes is a lot of cartridges."

"I plan to do a lot of practicing," Wheat stated, snidely. "I'll tell you what, you make it $55 dollars and you got a deal."

Durban shook his head complaining about the offer, all the while stacking cartridges boxes on the counter.

"I make that offer assuming there is a second cylinder for the gun," Wheat added, while removing his wallet and counting out greenbacks until $60 dollars lay on the countertop. "Do you have cartridges for a Henry repeating rifle?"

"Yes, I do," answered the gunsmith.

"You throw in five boxes of Henry rifle cartridges and I'll pay the full $60 dollars."

At that moment the bell above the entrance door jingled, as two more customers entered the shop. Durban swiped the greenbacks off his counter and packaged the ammunition in two bags making it lighter to carry. Glancing up he stated, "Thanks for the business and don't forget, Durban offers a money back guarantee on that Remington 1858 for any reason, if you are dissatisfied." He emphasized the money back guarantee part to impress the new arrivals.

* * *

Standing outside the gun shop Zack squinted his eyes looking upward and said, "Not much wind and plenty bright. If you want, we can go and try out this Remington revolver."

"Can I shoot it?"

"Yes, only I need to try it out first. Son, don't get presumptuous. You got a lot of learning before this weapon gets your hand on it," Wheat declared.

"I mean when I learn more about guns," Pearle replied. He knew he just received a scolding. Somehow, it was okay coming from his newfound friend.

"Let's head over to the stable. There's an open pasture directly behind it and a wooded area beyond that. A good place to put this iron to the test," connoted Wheat.

Pearle carried both bags of ammunition. Their weight was beginning to strain the youngster's muscles. Were he by himself, the burden would have been put down a long time ago, to rest his aching arms. Lest his new friend think him weak, Pearle endured the pain. The stable was now a short distance away. Thank heavens Zack quickened his step because they arrived just in time. Once inside, the heavy sacks hit the ground.

"Bring them over to the tack room. I've fixed it up to serve as a bedroom," Wheat said.

"Do you live here?" asked Pearle.

"Yep, its rent free as long as I muck out the stalls and keep the place tidy. I don't mind that at all since I love horses. Do you own a horse, Pearle?"

"No, but I've ridden one before," responded the teenager.

Zack continued, "I think I love all animals including that old goat we keep tied up outside. I got to keep him tethered. If not, he'll eat everything in sight. What was I saying? Oh yeah, occasionally I pick up a little extra when a horse needs to be re-shod. The blacksmith shop is nearby and he lets me use his forge if I have to reshape a shoe. I don't get rich. With all the odd jobs, I do manage to save a little. That's how I was able to purchase this revolver," Zack said, as he lifted the Remington.

Pearle knew firsthand how much money a person makes doing odd jobs. Not nearly enough to spend $60 dollars at one time. His new friend must be a bank robber or something worse. Apparently, nobody knows about it, because they all greet him cheerfully, even Reverend Strawn. He decided to wait awhile and learn more about him before turning him in. Acting nonchalant, he observed the room. It was much larger than the bedroom he has with the Strawns. Everything was spick and span from the floor to the ceiling. A cot, stiffly made, resided on one side and a table stood by the sink. It had three chairs for company and an oil lamp resting on top. There was a chest of drawers against the other wall and two large footlockers beside it.

"Bring the ammo bags over and place them on the table. I'm going to teach you how to load this revolver," said Wheat, interrupting Pearle's contemplation.

Pearle quickly lifted both sacks to the table and Zack motioned for him to draw up a chair and sit down. Holding the revolver in his left hand, Zack moved the hammer to a half-cocked position, unlatched the loading lever, and pulled it down halfway. Using his right hand, he slid the cylinder pin forward until it stopped, then removed the cylinder from the revolver.

"I hoped you paid attention how I removed the cylinder. I'll have you try it before we quit for the day. Now hand me one of those cartridge boxes," Wheat directed.

The youngster quickly removed a box of metallic cartridges, opened it, and slid it to Zack. Ever grateful he will get another chance to learn how to remove the cylinder, since the excitement of learning about the Remington revolver obscured his ability of retention.

"Cartridges have improved considerably. During the Civil War we had to employ percussion caps. The cartridges were made of a powder envelope with the bullet glued on the end. To load it, you dropped the cartridge, envelope first, into each chamber and seated them with the loading lever. After all six chambers were filled you needed to place percussion caps on the nipples at the rear of the cylinder. Now, you were ready to shoot."

"These metallic cartridges have it all in one piece," Zack attested. Turning the cylinder on end he pointed out the milled slots between the chambers saying, "See these slots. They're here for safety purposes. It allows you to lower the hammer between the chambers and prevents accidental discharges when you carry the gun." With that Wheat loaded the cylinder and returned it to its proper place, slid his chair back, and headed outside with Pearle at his heels. They walked across the pasture until coming upon the trees. Along the way, Zack had retrieved an empty tin can and short length of string. He tied the string to the can and suspended it from a low hanging branch. Reversing their steps, Wheat counted 50 paces then turned.

"This is far enough to test its accuracy," he confirmed, as he drew the pistol from his belt. Lifting the revolver Zack commented, "This weapon is a bit heavier than my other guns."

Standing for a moment with his arm extended, he slowly squeezed the trigger. The loud retort was a resounding bang, echoing a temporary shock to Pearle's unsuspecting ears, and leaving a ringing noise that lasted for a few seconds. The tin can moved slightly as the bullet nicked its edge.

"You hit it, Zack," Pearle shouted, excitedly.

"I was a little off, probably due to the weight." Zack said, and raised his arm again. This time Pearle was prepared for the blasting sound. Somehow, it didn't seem quite as resonant, and the tin can flew into the air as the bullet hit dead center. Handing the revolver to Pearle, Zack searched for a target a little closer.

"See that big rock? Aim slow and see if you can hit it."

"That's not very far away," Pearle stated.

"You never mind, just try to hit it."

Emulating his instructor, the teenager raised the weapon and extended a wavering arm claiming, "This gun sure is heavy." Pearle was prepared for the loud retort but not for the pistol's recoil. After which, the barrel flew upward and the novice gunman replied, "I missed the rock."

"Keep trying. This time hold your arm steadier."

Pearle repeated the process until the cylinder was empty of live cartridges. The large rock was never struck. Wheat consoled the youngster and the pair strode back to the stable. Once inside Zack opened one of the footlockers and removed a spanking new Henry repeating rifle.

"I bought three of these when the war ended. Rifle is more suited to you right now. I'll sell you this one and some ammunition for $5 dollars. You can pay me later or work it off, helping me here in the stable."

Pearle was dumbfounded. Holding a brand new Henry of his very own, he didn't care if Zack was a bank robber. In fact, he might even decide to join up with his gang.

"I don't know what to say. What if Abel doesn't want me to have it?"

"Well, until he gets used to the idea, you can keep it here with me and practice on the days you muck out the stalls," Zack suggested, with a smile. Pearle walked on air all the way home.

CHAPTER SIX

A bout the same time Amanda and Abel visited the Leffingwell farm, several small bands of Cheyenne Indians began their annual trek, along the Arkansas River, to find suitable land to spend the winter. Winters on the prairie are harsh and the local food and fuel supply can easily fall short of the needs of the larger summer tribe—a bitter lesson once learned years ago.

Falling Water, the son of a tribal chief, and his friend *Two Trees* lead a band of thirty people. They will travel the farthest, as other bands break off along the way, when a shelter of trees and moving water appear. The winter sojourn will take them approximately 100 miles to a heavily wooded area near Spring Creek, the former location of Fort Aubrey, where a stagecoach station now stands. *Falling Water's* chosen site rests five miles to the north. It not only provides protection from winter weather vagaries, it also affords pasture for the 75 horses he brings with him.

Holding his hand to his brow, in order to shield the sun's glare, *Falling Water* stated, "I see the white man's buildings still stand."

"Yes, but he no longer lives there," *Two Trees* replied. *Two Trees* is not the original name given him at birth. He was once called *Little Fox*; however, after growing a head taller than his playmates, his sobriquet became *Two Trees*.

"After the death of his family, he went east to join others of his kind," added *Falling Water*. "I found him to be a human being."

"Maybe so, yet he still believed he could own the land. It is a strange notion for someone who is supposed to be knowledgeable, since we know that man cannot own Mother Earth," responded the lofty associate.

"In many ways he was strange, all the same, my father said if more were like him, there would be fewer wars."

Riding behind *Falling Water*, on a reddish-brown and white pinto, was his half-sister *White Dove Woman*. She was born the daughter of a captured European female and the chief, *Red Eagle,* and so named for her pearlescent skin color. She favored her mother in features and, at an early age, became the ward of her half-brother, *Falling Water*. *White Dove* has lived sixteen summers and has become an accomplished horsewoman after five. She also is skilled in the crafts. Initially taught by her grandmother, *Valley of Flowers Woman*, she has mastered the traditional women's crafts of beadwork, painting on rawhide, and porcupine-quill embroidery. Her talents did not escape the special craft worker's guild for women, an elite group, within the tribe, of female artisans. Membership affords high status in the tribe and the right to make certain religious items. Her guardian brother felt as though *White Dove Woman* was too young for such an august group and declined their membership invitation. Another year or two, under the tutelage of her grandmother, would serve her best.

The winter pilgrimage travels at a slow pace, covering only eight to ten miles a day. Several of their horses tow a travois loaded down with parfleches containing dried meat and pemmican. Others dragged the two-pole frame with cross bars and a platform near the splayed ends. These carried the poles which, along with the tightly wrapped deer and bison skins, which serve as the framework and cover for their tepees.

Some of the women ride horses dragging travois, laden with tepee components. They also own the tepee and most everything in it. Traditionally, it is their responsibility to take down and erect the tepees each time the band moves. All said, Cheyenne women perform most of the work in any given tribe. Before the Spanish mustang and a nomadic lifestyle, Cheyenne women maintained a prominent role in a horticultural society, cultivating gardens near creeks and riverbeds. In the rich, black soil they grew beans, squash, and most importantly, corn or maize. Like the tepees, the gardens also belonged to the women. As one would imagine, the responsibility of feeding the tribe elevated the female status. Now, frequently on the move, the digging, planting, and harvesting of vegetable patches, belong to a past life. Today, the Cheyenne supplement their meat diets through searching and gathering useful plant life. Once again, an activity primarily conducted by women. Not all their vegetal needs grow wild on the prairie. Corn or maize, perhaps the most prominent, is grown in the eastern portion of the plains by horticultural tribes. Nomads must barter and trade for such items. Fortunately, the Cheyenne possess what the farming tribes want most— buffalo, and all their byproducts. The largest exchange among the Plains Indians occurs during the summer when tribes travel to an annual location and set up tepees for a week or two. These trade fairs bring together both warring and peaceful bands, which, for the duration of the exposition, exhibit a friendly manner. Articles from the four corners of the Americas find their way to the summer spectacle. It is here that *Valley of Flowers Woman* collects enough maize to feed her band for the coming winter. Other plant life is gathered on her way to winter quarters and the remainders during the return trip, since many become more recognizable in the spring. This is especially true for the prairie turnip whose plant produces abundant blue and purple flowers in early summer. The purple flower makes it easily visible among the dense prairie grasses. *Valley of Flowers Woman* uses a sharp digging stick to uproot the edible radix. Although the tubers could be peeled and eaten raw, they are usually dried for further use. After being hung to dry, the roots are pounded into flour and stored for the winter months. Soup is made from the flour and when mixed with certain berries, a very tasty and popular dish results.

Cheyenne women also seek certain medicinal plants found growing on the western Kansas plains. Medicinal herbs, with antibiotic properties, are sought out by those with a trained eye. Among the most popular are: yarrow, snakeroot, and purple coneflower, which are used to treat sores, wounds, bites and stings, and allergies. Some plants are chewed to relieve toothaches, while others are dried, added to water making a form of tea which treat multiple internal maladies as well.

* * *

In line, behind *Falling Water* and his family, two significant warriors rode side by side. Their position in the winter caravan depicts their status. Cheyenne warriors ride their own horses and maintain others among the accompanying herd. *Snake Hunter* and *He Lives Alone* are Dog Soldiers and represent a band within a band of the main tribe. While the main tribe is governed by *Chief Red Eagle*, *Falling Water's* father, the society of Dog Soldiers maintains discipline within the tribe and oversees tribal hunts. Naturally, they are prominent in decisions concerning war. There was a time the Dog Soldiers were outlawed from the camp. Roughly 35 years ago, a party of Cheyenne was attempting to raid Kiowa horse herds and, once discovered, killed by Kiowa and Comanche warriors. *Porcupine Bear*, chief of the Dog Soldiers, took up the war pipe and visited various Cheyenne and Arapaho camps trying to drum up support for revenge against the Kiowa. Shortly after reaching a northern camp, which had recently traded buffalo hides for liquor, he joined them in drinking and singing war songs. Soon, two of his cousins, *Little Creek* and *Around*, were caught up in a drunken fight. *Little Creek* had bested *Around* and straddled him while holding up his knife ready to stab his cousin. Inflamed by *Around's* calls for help, *Porcupine Bear* tore the knife away from *Little Creek* and stabbed him with it several times, then forced *Around* to finish him off.

Military societies have strict rules when it comes to murder and accidental homicide. A society member who committed such a crime was expelled and outlawed. Accordingly, *Porcupine Bear* was dishonorably discharged from the Dog Soldiers and he and his relatives had to camp apart from the rest of the Cheyenne tribe. Since the Dog Soldiers were disgraced by *Porcupine Bear's* act, the other chiefs forbade them from leading war against the Kiowa.

The Masikota, one of the original ten tribes, were nearly annihilated by a cholera epidemic in 1849. Many of the surviving Masikota tribe members joined the Dog Soldiers, effectively making it a recognized faction. When the Cheyenne affiliates camped together, the Dog Soldier band took the Masikota position in the camp circle. Over time, the rest of the tribe began to regard them with respect and no longer as outlaws. For the most part, they stood in opposition to the more peaceful chiefs. Though acquiescent to the chief, they were like a time bomb ready for war and quick to respond to any offense against the Cheyenne.

With gold discovered in Colorado, the white man didn't let them down. During spring and summer countless streams of covered wagons cut deep ruts into the Cheyenne hunting grounds. A myriad of humankind trespassed across the land. Some were trappers, miners, together with men and women of ill repute. Others sought a different life, an opportunity to begin anew on land granted by the government. After losing two thirds of their tribe to cholera, the cause being the intrusion of the white man, just the very sight of the endless caravans made the Dog Soldiers furious. Their theme in the council circle was to take up the war pipe.

* * *

It is well past mid-day and a white winter haze blocks out the sun. Tiny spates of snow flurries materialize as the wind begins to sting any open faces. *Snake Hunter* pulls his fur coat up to cover his head and says. "We need to make camp soon. If the snow starts to stick, the women will find it more difficult to locate buffalo chips. I want a good fire in the tepee tonight."

He Lives Alone, also hunched under the hood of his coat, turned to look for the horse herd and the young braves driving them. It will be his call to assign the night watchmen once the band stops for the evening. Winter is not the most dangerous time for enemy raids; however, the loathsome Pawnee were known to defy tradition and take advantage of inclement weather, especially a snowstorm.

"I recognize this part of the river. *Falling Water* will stop soon because it has several good places to make camp. As I recall, just ahead are groves of cottonwood and willow trees. The women can gather enough branches to make a fire and we can tie the dogs to the willows to help watch over the herd. They will bark if strangers come near and the willows make good cover against the snow," said *He Lives Alone*.

As if on cue, *Falling Water* signaled for the caravan to halt and set up camp for the night. The idiom 'practice makes perfect' is never better demonstrated than when the women of nomadic people set up their tepees. In less than an hour the conical homes snaked along the Arkansas River giving the appearance of being there for weeks. Long before the men set up a corral for the horses and secured dogs to the surrounding trees, smoke began to appear above each tepee signifying a meal being prepared and comfortable warmth within the hide-covered framework.

When a Cheyenne man married, it was customary for him to move into the camp of his wife's band. The Dog Soldiers added to their unique separation within the community by bringing their brides to their own camp. *He Lives Alone* married *Anna Wingbird*, an Arapaho, who now resides with the Cheyenne band of *Falling Water*. In addition to *Anna Wingbird*, the mother, grandmother, and nine-year- old brother, share the tepee. Cold winter nights make *He Lives Alone's* appellation the antithesis of reality. He secretly plans to change his name to something more suitable to his achievements and awaits the proper battle in order to do so.

CHAPTER SEVEN

When Abel retrieved mail from the Lebanon post office he quickly noticed the Statesville, Tennessee, postal mark. His anxiety disallowed his returning home before reading the missive, resulting in the envelope being torn open while standing at the postal counter. As expected, it was from Hope Kaufman. Stuffing the envelope into his coat pocket, Abel began to read.

December 12, 1868

Dear Abel and Amanda,

It's always good to hear from you both. You must be excited planning for the move to Kansas. Melvin tells me the railroad will soon be heading across Kansas and we will be able to visit each other. I've begun saving part of my egg money to buy the tickets.

Around here everybody is getting eager for Christmas. Abigail and I have been making tree ornaments and drinking spiced tea. Naturally, the men folks aren't interested in spiced tea, so we make them eggnog. They don't care for that very much either. The Leffingwells received a gift from their friends in Richmond. It came in a special box labeled, <u>handle with care</u>. You'll never guess what Lomas Chandler sent. It came in a gallon jug and tasted like fire (Melvin let me take a sip). Jack told us it was just apple juice but I've tasted apple juice and that wasn't it! Nevertheless, now the menfolk have their own Christmas cheer.

Abel, I wrote my father about the gentleman you were interested in. I personally don't recall him. Father said he did spend time at Belle Isle and a great deal of which was in solitary confinement. Apparently, he got in a fight with two prison guards and put them both in the hospital. Nobody can remember the cause of the fracas.

Melvin and Jack will be bringing the wagon over in a few weeks. They are waiting on some parts so, most likely, it will be after the first of the year. Abigail and I want to ride over when they do so we can get an idea what a prairie schooner feels like. Someone will have to watch the farm. Jack told us not to fret, because, he will figure something out.

Closing for now,
Your friends,
Hope, Melvin, and Rebecca

Abel read the letter a second time before replacing it in the envelope. The fact Zachary Wheat spent time in solitary confinement concerned him. He doesn't appear to be a violent sort but, like they say, still water runs deep. Pearle thinks the world of the man; be that as it may, you can't risk carrying more trouble than which is already expected. He will need to learn more about Mister Zachary Wheat.

Anticipating a visit by his Statesville friends removed a concerned facial expression and makes him smile. Finding room for everybody wouldn't be a problem. The church's fellowship hall has everything they would need—a kitchen, bathrooms, and plenty of space for the children. Best of all, it's connected to the minister's manse.

* * *

Since the end of the Civil War and Jack's return to Statesville, all holiday festivities, dinners, and family gatherings were held at the Leffingwell farm and supervised by Abigail. Hope Kaufman, less experienced with such things, was grateful to be able to assist the mountain man's wife and make it a learning experience. She was reminded of the seasonal celebrations back in Richmond, Virginia, when her mother arranged such events. Of course, Grace Waterman did not prepare the dishes with her own hands.

Abigail's aplomb came about through a trial by fire. The ordeal of war and being without her husband severely tested her resiliency. The pressure of Jack's amnesia and her determination to regain his love strengthened her character. With the help of her father, Abigail's faith persevered. When it comes to culinary excellence, Minnie Rosenthal must share a great deal of credit. The wisdom of the octogenarian taught Abigail more than recipes. The essentials of being a great cook also included having the right attitude.

"I'm always amazed at how cool you seem when preparing large meals. I still get nervous if Melvin and I expect guests. Even when my folks come to visit I get completely stressed out," Hope confessed, as she peeled potatoes in preparation for the Christmas dinner. "All the things I know how to cook I've learned from you."

"Well, I learned to cook at an early age. My mother died when I was just a child and my father raised me. Accordingly, my knowledge of recipes was limited. The ladies from the church kept us going with a steady flow of covered dishes and invitations to supper. They took us under their wing until I got big enough to make meals myself. Then, the widow ladies volunteered to teach me. Looking back on it now, they were only trying to impress my father," Abigail stated with a smile. "Nevertheless, they taught me how to cook."

"I'll never be able to do the things you do," Hope said with a sigh.

"That all depends. I knew the recipes but it takes more than that to really be a good cook. That part I learned from Minnie Rosenthal. She taught me the emotional aspect of proficient cuisine."

"I don't understand," Hope said honestly.

"Well, first of all, you must make a true commitment to cooking. You've got to love your kitchen. Clear the clutter and let in plenty of outside light. A little lemon or orange oil eliminates offensive odors and gives the kitchen a sweet smell. It tends to improve your mood and makes it an enjoyable place to be in. Then, allow plenty of time for cooking," Abigail explained.

The subject of clutter struck a nerve, revealing its impact by the expression on the young girls face. At the moment her kitchen table was supporting unwashed breakfast dishes and a basket of Rebecca's dirty clothes. It's so easy to utilize the kitchen as a catchall in order to assist daily living. Also, a condition to be resolved the moment she returned home.

Abigail continued, "Minnie taught me that, for those with a modest skill set, it's best to begin with a familiar dish you're comfortable making."

"Is that why I'm peeling potatoes?" Hope questioned.

"You might say that. It's not as easy as you may think. There's skill required in making the final dish. Proper mashing and seasoning ultimately tells the story."

"What is the menu for this holiday's dinner?" asked Hope.

Abigail had previously written down the bill of fare and handed the paper to her young friend. She had listed roast turkey and dressing as the main course, along with mashed potatoes and giblet gravy. In addition, several root vegetables including squash, sweet potatoes, and brussels sprout. For dessert she noted pumpkin, apple, and gooseberry pies, plum pudding and sugar cookies. At the bottom of the page she had underlined spiced round.

"I've never heard of spiced round. What is it?" Hope inquired.

"It's a special beef. I've never served it before, however, Maryellen tells me it has become quite popular since the war ended. It's kind of a holiday dish. I'm not certain if everybody will care for it. Maryellen tells me that men like it most."

The meat dish in question is called *Rinderbraten*. Once the Civil War ended, Nashville became a hub of the meatpacking industry in the South. Many of the post war meatpackers were immigrants and brought old country concepts to America. One of which was spiced round beef that became a holiday staple after being featured at the famous Maxwell House Hotel.[7]

Preparation took a great deal of time. Meatpackers usually cut the beef into five-pound roasts. Then, threaded it with long strips of pork fat, which had been blended with a spice mixture containing cinnamon, allspice, red pepper, brown sugar, and ground cloves. The threading or larding process was performed

---

[7] Once a major hotel in downtown Nashville, Tennessee, it had five stories and 240 rooms. Constructed by slaves in 1859, the hotel featured steam heat, gas lighting, and a bath on every floor. At $4 a day, including meals, the guests enjoyed both ladies' and men's parlors, billiards rooms, bar rooms, shaving saloons, and a grand staircase to the large dining and ballroom. Christmas dinner featured calf's head, black bear, opossum, and other unusual delicacies, including spice round.

using a very large needle. Once completed, the meat was placed in brine (containing the spices) and soaked for several weeks.

Abigail had the local butcher order hers from his abattoir supplier. She planned on baking it in a cast iron Dutch oven and serve it along with the rest of her holiday fare. In the event not everyone in the family is fond of spiced round there will be plenty of turkey. If only the men preferred it, the children will be allowed to skip the meat and replace it with a second helping of bread pudding.

"I don't know how we can do everything on this list. It makes me tired just to read it."

"Well, it comes down to mind over matter. When we get tired we'll go outside for a short walk in the fresh air. That will relax us and reinvigorate," Abigail replied. "And, if we get stressed out, just squeeze the place between the index finger and thumb for 30 seconds. That's an old Chinese method to reduce tension."

With that, the two women went about their Christmas chore made easier with the help of Sarah Jane who also wanted to learn more about cookery.

* * *

On Christmas Eve, a blizzard moved across the Nashville Basin covering the surrounding hills with a five-inch blanket of glistening snow. Fortunately, the families had retrieved their trees earlier in the week. Jack was able to locate a perfectly shaped fir about seven-feet-tall and another five-feet-tall for the Kaufmans. Both trees were conical shaped with dense foliage and filled their living rooms with that familiar piney turpentine-like aroma—a scent most agreeable this time of year.

Abigail's father arrived on Thursday afternoon with plans to spend the night, so as to see the children's expression Christmas morning. After Thanksgiving, it had become a tradition for him to read chapters from Charles Dickens' *A Christmas Carol* during his visits. It always held the children captivated. He also found it extraordinary that the youngsters remembered where he had left off at the time of the last reading. Hyrum conceded that, perhaps it was not so unusual, since the children had his genes and would naturally be bright. That, however, didn't explain Jozef, who seemed the brightest of all.

This year Charles Dickens' description of a cold, bleak, and biting Christmas Eve makes the story come alive. With a mounting blizzard taking place outside, Little Jack and Jozef keep running to the window confirming actual conditions with that in the popular Dickens tale. Although, the ghosts of Christmas past, present, and yet to come, frightened the small boys, the whole family roundly celebrated the conclusion with cheers and happy tears. The entire clan joined in repeating Tiny Tim's benison, "God bless us, everyone!"

The snowstorm made the attendance of Abigail's other guests uncertain. A lot depended on whether or not the road was passable. Although five-inches of snow shouldn't impede horse and wagon, wind-blown drifts are another matter. Yet to arrive were: Maryellen and her husband August; Frank and Rosemary Riberty; and Ryan Gosling. Albert Einstein said, "Time is an illusion" — not so, for Abigail. Time is very real and the hour grows late. The silence in the kitchen became intense. Hope's searching eyes fixated on her friend in anticipation for direction. There was tension building up in the room. So much so that Hope began to sense a ringing in her ears. Finally, Abigail broke the trance-like stillness declaring, "It's time to take a walk."

Bundled in their warmest coat, hat, and galoshes, the pair kicked across the farmyard to the snow-covered main road. Fog-like white mist emerges with each exhale as the duo peers into the distance. At last a tiny dark image is seen through the surrounding whiteness. "It's them," they acclaimed in unison and quickly retraced their steps. Upon re-entering the house, Abigail shouted to Sarah Jane, "Finish setting the table, dear, our company is on their way."

For those inside the house, the noise of elevated conversation and stomping boots proved most agreeable and cheery. Maryellen was the first through the front door and gave Abigail an affectionate embrace. The children's attention was immediately drawn to August, her husband, who was burdened with delightfully wrapped gift boxes. Hope and Sarah Jane helped by taking their coats to Sarah Jane's room and laying them neatly on the bed. The men guided Ryan Gosling's wagon to the barn and unloaded the items he had recently constructed—reinforced axle wood with new spindle skeins, wheel hub nuts, wrench, and large tub of grease.

"How much are you charging me for all this?" Jack asked.

"I think ten dollars covers everything," Ryan replied.

"Sure you're not short changing yourself?"

"No, there wasn't much labor involved," responded Ryan.

The mountain man pulled his wallet from his back pocket and removed a ten and five-dollar greenback. He then handed both bills to Ryan Gosling.

"This is too much, Jack," defied the blacksmith.

"Consider it a Christmas gift," Jack said with a wink.

"I expect this means we'll have to wait awhile before you finish the comparison of generals," Frank Riberty stated.

"I'll make sure to finish the evaluation once we return from delivering the prairie schooner to our friend in Lebanon," assured Jack.

"You might find that interesting, August. Jack's comparing Robert E. Lee and Ulysses S. Grant, as to who was the best general," Frank said to his son-in-law.

"I presume General Lee has won the discussion before it even started," August replied.

"You can't suppose anything whenever Jack Leffingwell is involved. He's about half through and nobody's taking bets," Frank replied, as the group slowly walked back to the house.

Upon their return, Abigail announced, "Take a seat in the living room. Dinner will be in one hour. We'll bring everybody some hot coffee and eggnog while you're waiting."

Jack's fireplace flames twisted in brilliant colors of orange and yellow as they licked around the recently laid logs. The ambient crackle and snap was spellbinding and demanded their undivided interest until Hope arrived with a tray of refreshments.

From an aerial view the Leffingwell farmhouse was like a painted lithograph by Currier and Ives. Wispy white smoke curled out of the chimney only to disappear once it reached its apex. Daylight during December begins to wane early in the evening. By 6:00 p.m. darkness has taken hold of the rest of the day, yet, with the blanket of snow under a transparent sky, there is enough radiant energy to maintain visibility. From the gaiety displayed beyond the illuminated windows, it's clear that nobody is planning an early departure. The sound of singing emanated from the residence, as it carried across the farmyard amidst the crispy winter air.

On this cloudless night, thousands of glittering stars beamed from above awakening memories of an earlier time when three noble pilgrims followed a guiding star to Israel and paid homage to the Christ Child for whom this day is celebrated.

Abigail's holiday dinner was a success. Surprisingly, spice round was enjoyed by nearly everybody, including the children. Traditionally, it was mutually agreed this was the best Christmas ever and as guests made preparations to return home, Hyrum gave a benediction that lifted merry hearts further. The congenial gathering and poignant blessing deeply affected Ryan Gosling who willingly shook hands, while shinny tears streaked his cheeks.

CHAPTER EIGHT

Thus far, *Falling Water's* band was faring well and surviving the winter comfortably. Women found ample buffalo chips to keep the tepees warm during the most frigid days. Copious chips signified the size of bison herds and gave encouragement for their return in the spring. In addition to the dried dung, *Valley of Flowers* and *White Dove* were able to gather cottonwood branches along the creek bank.

While hunting has been better than last year, a recent snowstorm vastly improved prospects. Tracking game is easier after a fresh snowfall since animal footprints become more obvious. So far this winter the band has killed two deer. That, coupled with plentiful jackrabbits, has kept sufficient meat in every lodge. Although, snow cover makes it difficult for horses to graze, the band's herd appears healthy, albeit somewhat thinner.

During the past few weeks, the lodge has seen continuous visitors. Most were traveling north to join Northern Cheyenne and Lakota Sioux. Their constant message contained a dogged resolution for war. Ever since the Medicine Lodge Treaty was enacted, contention existed between Plains Indians and the U.S. Government. First of all, the tribes were assigned much smaller territories than previously agreed by the Little Arkansas Treaty in 1865. While reduced to land south of the Kansas state line, the tribes were permitted to continue to hunt north of the Arkansas

River for as long as the buffalo remained, provided they stay away from white settlements and roads. Nevertheless, tribal acceptance of the treaty was contingent upon ratification by three-fourths of the adult males. Sufficient votes were never obtained. *Chief Red Eagle*, though sad to see white interlopers violating the land of his ancestors, was an advocate for peace. The wise leader intuitively discerned this steady stream of humanity would not be stopped by force. The wisdom of his tenet was passed on to his son, *Falling Water.*

Jumping Fox led a small band of warriors traveling north to join other like-minded people. They had previously visited *Chief Red Eagle* and convinced several Dog Soldiers to join their cause. *Red Eagle* wanted no part in war. Troubled by the news they brought, he still had to consider what was best for all his people. More and more the chief knew a great decision must be made, considering the future of the tribe. In the spring, when all the bands return, he will hold a council with the other principals. If they agree, a runner will be sent to Fort Dodge to ask for help in moving south.

Falling Water offered *Jumping Fox* and his warriors the hospitality of the village. They planned to only stay a short while, and then continue north. That evening, a council was held in *Falling Water's* lodge. The women will spend their nights in neighboring tepees until the council ends.

Falling Water's tepee was the largest in the winter camp. Animal skins formed a skirt, covering six feet of the inside circumference, which gave additional protection against winter winds. It also served as insulation to retain the warmth of cooking fires. Furniture consisted mainly of backrests made from peeled willow twigs and supported by wooden tripods. Several stuffed pillows lay about to be used as seats or headrests. At the rear of the dwelling was *Falling Water's* bed. Saddles, bridles, plus weapons are stored nearby so they can be grabbed quickly in case the village is attacked at night. Holy items adorn the back walls of the tepee. Their beautiful design is a tribute to his sister's artistic skill. *White Dove* slept against an adjacent wall, while the grandmother bed down near the door, where food and firewood are kept and cooking is done. Since the lodge was large, an additional three beds can be made accessible in the event of prestigious guests.

After an official welcome in friendship, *Falling Water* turned the council over to his guest.

"I come here with a sad heart. *Black Kettle* and *Medicine Woman* are dead. The soldiers of "Yellow Hair" Custer murdered them. Our brothers were on the reservation agreed in the Medicine Lodge Treaty and camped along the Washita River. *Black Kettle* had returned from Fort Cobb after informing the father (army agent), Colonel William Hazen, that he wanted peace. He was told he had to talk peace with the Great War Chief, General Sherman and he couldn't stay at Fort Cobb. He was told to return to the Washita River village. *Black Kettle* flew the American flag beside his lodge to signify peace. Before the sun rose the next morning, "Yellow Hair" Custer attacked, killing men, women, and children. Those trying to escape were hunted down and slain. Even the wounded were later shot. He took many women and children with him when he returned to his supply base. This proves the white eyes are liars and their treaty means nothing," *Jumping Fox* stated, as rays of hatred emitted from his black eyes.

Next to speak was *He Lives Alone*. The custom during *Falling Water's* councils was to have a moment of silence between speakers. He believed it allowed time to keep things mannerly, especial when highly emotional subjects were being discussed.

"I'm confused. We have over 6,000 people camped along the Washita. Why did we not come together and rout the "Squaw Killer" Custer?" asked the infuriated warrior.

"'Yellow Hair' used our women and children as shields. Our braves followed him until he reached his supply station and reinforcements, then decided to return to the village for council," replied *Jumping Fox*. By the expression on his face, *He Lives Alone* was not happy with the answer.

"Yes, we have thousands of people at the Washita Camp, but most are not true fighting braves. Most are the aged, women, and children. That is why I am visiting our various winter camps in order to assemble true fearless warriors and join our brothers in the north," *Jumping Fox* continued. "Our northern brothers fight alongside of the Lakota Sioux in war against the white eyes. Great war chiefs like *Crazy Horse, Chief Gall, Two Moons, Big Nose,* and the holy man *Sitting Bull* are united in our cause."

"Both me and *Snake Hunter* are Dog Soldiers. We pledge to join you in your quest, however, first we must return to *Chief Red Eagle's* village and make certain our families will be safe," *He Lives Alone* asserted.

"When will that be? We cannot tarry since the white war chief Sheridan has declared war on the innocent," asked *Jumping Fox.*

Falling Water spoke, "We will not return until the snow melts in the spring, a time when the buffalo herds return. My father, *Chief Red Eagle,* is very wise and by then our tribe will know his wishes."

When *Snake Hunter* time to speak came, he inquired, "It has been said that medicine men can cast a spell on the 'Hairy Mouth's' bullets so they can't harm us. Is that true?"

"So I've heard also," replied *Jumping Fox.* "Nevertheless, we must continue our travels to the other camps and solicit more soldiers."

The guests at *Falling Water's* camp stayed for two more days and enjoyed friendly hospitality before setting out in the early morning. Their visit left a great deal for *Falling Water* to ponder. So much so, that he sent a runner back to the main village to find out what the chief had decided. It would be at least a week before the runner returned. In the meantime, usual activity transpired in the camp; and, although *Falling Water* acted nonchalant, *White Dove* easily read beneath the surface.

"Ever since *Jumping Fox* visited, you have been troubled," *White Dove* said. "What is it that torments your thoughts?"

"It's nothing for you to be concerned about. It has to do with a possible move farther south in the spring," her brother replied.

Time usually flies like a bird. Now that *Falling Water* anxiously waits for spring, time seems almost at a standstill. Days creep past at a snail's pace. His heart aches when he contemplates the future. Each morning, as he welcomes the sunrise, *Falling Water* remembers his people's history and the story of their origin. As retold from generation to generation, the land on which the Cheyenne reside was theirs through religious and spiritual ordination. They and they alone have a divine right given by Maheo, the All Being. An affirmation confirmed by the account of *Sweet Medicine*, the prophet, who lived four years within the sacred mountain Noaha-vose. While inside its rocky core, *Sweet Medicine* was instructed in a system of law and behavior. He returned with the most revered possession of the Cheyenne people—the four Sacred Arrows. They are considered the living manifestation of spiritual power. Besides blessing the people and uniting them as Cheyenne, two of the arrows represent male power and establish proper conduct in daily life as well as war. In the spring, the priests will perform the ritual celebrating the Sacred Arrows prior to any other ceremonies before the season's first buffalo hunt.

CHAPTER NINE

The weather in western Tennessee exhibited what is known as the January Thaw. While during the first month, a normal nighttime temperature is below freezing, but the bite of winter is much greater farther north. Nevertheless, as the coldest month draws to a close, the conditions are ten degrees above normal. Since mid-month, any remnants of snow have become ancient history and today the sun's warmth is enjoyed by both man and beast.

Inside the barn, Jack Leffingwell and Melvin Kaufman proudly stand before their recent accomplishment, a covered prairie schooner. Outside, sitting on the top rail of a makeshift fence, the children were dangling their feet and intently observing the four oxen recently purchased by their father. Ignoring the youngsters, the hefty bovines only concerned themselves with the fragrant hay lain before them.

"They sure have long horns," Jack Junior said hushfully. "I bet they could kill a bear if they wanted to."

Jozef, more cautious than his brother, sat close to Sarah Jane for the added assurance of safety. Equally entranced but considerably more fearful, he held tightly to his sister and pointed to the oxen saying, "Big cows."

"They're not cows, fraidy-cat, and if they ever got loose, they would eat you for breakfast."

"Don't be so mean to your little brother," scolded Sarah Jane. Looking Jozef in the eyes, she softly assured him, "Oxen don't eat people, they only eat grass and hay."

The beasts in question were magnificent animals. Each was at least ten feet long and stood nearly four feet at the shoulder. They weighed slightly under a ton and displayed a set of smooth, two-foot horns, curving up at the end. Altered males, they now were docile and much easier to handle. Pleasing brown, red, and white markings served to enhance their stunning appearance.

The choice to integrate oxen over horses or mules was a wise one. Stronger than a horse, they are also less expensive to maintain since they can live on grass and sage, of which there will be plenty traveling across the plains. Because of their superior strength, oxen can pull a wagon a greater distance in any given workday. In addition, they can pull through mud and are able to swim across streams.

The bell on Abigail's front porch commenced to announce lunch time. Out of habit, Jack pulled his pocketwatch, popped open the spring-hinged metal cover, and checked the time.

"Looks like soups on back at the house. We best be heading back and wash up," Jack suggested.

"I'll give a shout-out to the youngsters," Melvin offered.

"No need. Their ears are better than ours," Jack affirmed.

Soon, both families were gathered around the dinner table with little Rebecca in Sarah Jane's former highchair. Due to the unusually warm day, the women had to open kitchen windows to dissipate heat from the oven. Even so, tiny beads of perspiration could be seen just below their hairline.

"I can't remember a day this warm in January," Hope lamented.

"It happens once in a while, but there are plenty winter days ahead. I hope the weather holds up next week. We're going to take the covered wagon to Lebanon," Jack announced. The children were smiling from ear to ear.

"Are we just going to surprise them?" asked Hope.

"Not really, I wrote Abel last week telling him to expect us the first week of February," Jack confessed. "I've also arranged for Maryellen and her husband to stay here, while we're gone. She and 'Shorty' will get an idea of what farm life is all about."

"They're going to love it. August is saving his money to buy that little farm just outside of town. Maryellen tells me they've already paid a deposit and now waiting for the bank to approve the loan," Abigail added.

"Tell them the rest," Hope said.

After a short pause, Abigail continued, "I told her that Jack and Melvin will help him if he runs into any trouble tending the farm."

"I don't see where we will have any time to help the Yankee city boy tend his farm," Melvin stated.

"Maybe you could help him instead of spending all night at the town tavern," Hope said firmly.

"I've tried to tell you about that night," Melvin said blandly.

"Let's not worry about it now. I'm sure August will be able to handle the farm work," Abigail stated, as she passed a hot bread loaf to Jack and followed it with the serrated knife.

* * *

After receiving Jack's letter, Zachary Wheat once again occupied Abel's thoughts. The mountain man not only gave the time of arrival, but also the need to purchase a box farm-wagon and mules for the family's return to Statesville. Abel offered to ride down and drive the prairie schooner back, but the girls were looking forward to the Lebanon visit, plus, riding in the covered wagon.

Once Pearle got wind of Jack's request, he suggested Zach Wheat and the local stables. Not wanting to be beholden to someone he knew so little about, Abel initially looked elsewhere. He learned that every farm had a box wagon, but none were for sale. Whenever the farmers did sell one, it was taken to the stable to be displayed. Perhaps Pearle's suggestion had more merit than

Abel previously thought, and with visitors expected soon, a trip to the stables was now in order.

After the obligatory welcoming handshake, Abel explained his need for the wagon and mules. He also couldn't help noticing the covered wagon parked against the barn wall. It gave strong evidence of recent repair.

"A good box wagon doesn't last long once it's up for sale. The one you're looking at I bought myself for the journey west. You see, I'm also planning to stake a claim on government land in Kansas. However, my offer to you still stands," Wheat stated.

"I'll know for sure after I talk to my friend. He's the one needing the wagon for his family's return trip."

Zachary Wheat scratched his beard as he thought for a second and said, "I know where there's a wagon that's been in a barn for about four years. I help a widow lady out now and then and she doesn't have much need for it now. Her husband and son got killed in the war. I'll offer her $50 dollars, she could use the money," Wheat explained.

"Isn't that a little steep for a wagon that's been sitting so long? You don't even know what shape it's in," Abel stated.

"That doesn't matter, I can fix it and have it ready by the time your friend needs it. You being a preacher and all, I'm surprised that the price concerns you that much. Didn't you hear me say she could use the money?"

Chagrined, Abel asked, "What will you charge me if it required additional work?"

"Your price will be $50 dollars no matter what," Wheat replied. "Getting mules is another story and might give me a problem. I plan to pull my wagon with mules, since I won't be carrying that much weight; however, the three I have will go to Kansas."

"I'd like you to keep an eye out for them, anyway," said Abel.

"I'm sure your friend will bring a couple horses. Push come to shove, he could hitch them to the wagon. His family couldn't weigh too much, so long as he took care traveling. Just in case I find them, a mule team costs about $75 dollars," Zack Wheat stated, while suppressing a smile.

Abel and Pearle walked slowly back to the church. Each to his own thoughts until Pearle remarked, "I bet that widow lady would give him the wagon for nothing, since he probably don't charge her for the work he does."

"I believe you're right."

They walked in stillness until reaching the parsonage. Pearle's thoughts were occupied by the most exciting adventure of his young life, while Abel was engrossed with concern over his wife. Even though she finally accepted the fact they were moving, her current lassitude was equally troublesome. Before entering, Abel turned to his young brother-in-law and asked, "Has Amanda said anything to you about Kansas?"

"Not really. You would think she'd be happy, considering how much she dislikes living in the parsonage," Pearle said frankly.

"That's one of the reasons I thought she'd be happier about a different life."

"My sister has always been unhappy living a routine. As I remember, she was unhappy at home, then, after she moved out, she remained unhappy. It was as though she searched for some vague contentment. When you returned from the war, I thought she might have found it. Abel, I probably shouldn't say this, but we're talking about two persons. The person you see and the person you don't see," Pearle said fervidly.

Such insightfulness, coming from someone so young, worked to reshape Abel's opinion of Pearle. The lad revealed a bit of wisdom beyond his years. Maybe having him along will be a greater benefit than he previously considered. Abel placed his hand on Pearle's shoulder as they entered the house.

* * *

At the Leffingwell farm, Jack and Melvin were maneuvering the bullocks into yoke and harness. The obliging bovines willingly took their positions along the extended wagon tongue.

"Climb up there and make um go. We need to see how they pull together," Jack said.

"What do I shout?"

"Just yell 'Giddy up' and snap the reins. If they don't move, crack the whip over one of the lead oxen," Jack counseled.

Melvin followed Jack's instructions and the wagon groaned and propelled forward. Satisfied with the distribution of weight, the mountain man climbed aboard and drove the wagon onto the neighboring pasture, shouting, "Gee" and "Haw", as the team turned right and left.

Melvin, riding next to Jack observed, "They sure don't go very fast."

"That's not a bad thing. Can you imagine trying to control these boys if they moved quicker?"

Once they returned to the barn, the team was disassembled and led back to the temporary-retaining corral. Satisfied with their performance, Jack felt safe to say, "We can leave for Lebanon in the morning."

The ride to Lebanon took two days. Even with an early start and mild dry weather the prairie schooner covered only eighteen miles. There were, however, frequent stops to check the wagon and rest the animals. Perhaps a bit overdone, but important to Jack, since he didn't want a major breakdown halfway to Kansas. In addition, there was a rather long stay for a family picnic. All the same, their arrival in Lebanon, on the second day, can be easily done.

Melvin handled the reins most of the trip, yet, everybody got a chance to spend time driving the bullocks. The initial excitement for the children had run its course by the end of the first day. Thereafter, their main concern was, "How long will it be before we get there?"

By traveling on the chosen route, Jack was unable to determine how well the reinforced springs performed. The road was frequently used and rather smooth. All the same, the springs seemed to cushion any bumps they encountered, but definitely not the same as when traveling over a grassland prairie.

When the covered wagon entered Lebanon it created a modest spectacle as a cavalcade of children followed all the way to the town's stables. It marked the first time many had seen two pairs of oxen up close. The bravest of the procession demonstrated their valor by dashing up and touching the massive beasts. Needless to say, they were quick to retreat to a safer distance once demonstrating their act of courage.

Outside bustle alerted the Strawn family to Jack's arrival and Abel promptly met his friend in front of the main paddock barn.

"I've arranged for a holding pen to keep the oxen and the wagon can be parked behind the church," Abel announced.

Sarah Jane and her brothers jumped from the covered wagon and soon became lost in the juvenile gathering. Small town children usually make friends quickly. Such is the case with the Leffingwell youngsters. From a hospitable family they tend to be open, kind, and free with the compliments. Of course, coming into town on a covered wagon, led by four gigantic beasts, helped the sociable introduction.

After Jack learned where Abel wanted the wagon, he turned the bullocks around and proceeded to the church. With Abel directing, he maneuvered the schooner near the adjoining outbuilding, making it more accessible for loading. Contented with the location, they unhooked the oxen and led them back to the awaiting pen.

"They seem rather docile. Were they easy to handle?" Abel inquired.

"Yes, they were on their best behavior, but I made certain they didn't get over tired. You'll need to keep an eye out once the wagon is fully loaded. They may get stubborn if overworked."

When the gate was shut and secured, Abel said, "Come inside. I want you to meet Zachary Wheat."

Inside, under the stable roof, the former rebel sharpshooters were met with the familiar smell of hay and horses. At the far end of the barn, occupying a pitchfork, Zach Wheat was mucking one of the stalls. Absorbed in his work, he failed to notice the two visitors approaching. Startled when Abel called out his name, Wheat gave the guests the once-over and quickly recognized Pearle's brother-in-law. "The tall fellow standing beside him must be Jack Leffingwell," he thought to himself. With all three men harboring personal suppositions, the introductions came off rather awkward. Nevertheless, it broke the ice and paved the way for Jack to say, "My family and I plan to stay in Lebanon for a few days and, if possible, I'd like to talk to you about the Kansas trip."

"I'm at your service," Wheat replied.

"Thank you. Look for me tomorrow after lunch. Say about half past one," Jack confirmed.

Before returning to the Methodist Church, Jack surveyed the condition inside the horse-barn. Impressed by the obvious maintenance he asked, "Does Wheat tend the stables by himself?"

"As far as I know. Pearle sneaks over here once in a while to target practice. He's Wheat's number one fan. The lad thinks I don't know what he's up to. So far, I've thought it best not to call him on it. I'm waiting until you have a talk with Wheat," Abel answered.

"I've never seen a barn this size maintained any better," Jack stated flatly.

That evening supper was served in the fellowship hall. Abel's parents, Joseph and Isela, had never met the Tennessee mountain man. However, they felt as though they knew him based on their son's admiration. Accordingly, the only surprise was how tall he was. Hope and Abigail won them over in short order. They insisted on helping prepare the meal. And, as the men convened around the wood-burning Franklin stove, the pleasant sound of female laughter intermingled with the news of the day.

Amanda's disposition brightened the moment Hope and Abigail got there. She viewed Abigail as a kindred spirit, considering the adversities she encountered and apparently overcame. She, alone, could understand the overwhelming apprehension now controlling her mind. Problems of this nature are best solved by female process and the healing can commence once they can be alone.

Abigail was alerted when the women laid out the dinnerware and Amanda whispered, "I need to talk to you alone. After lunch tomorrow maybe we can take tea in the parsonage."

Unseasonable weather continued the next day as both Abigail and Jack found themselves with independent tasks after lunch. Abigail explained her undertaking to Hope the night before. Though Melvin's young wife had her own assessment regarding Amanda, she willingly agreed to be compliant with Abigail's wishes and took ownership of the after-lunch kitchen chores. Amanda hadn't joined her visitors for the noontime meal, using the pretext of an upset stomach. When Abigail found her, sitting behind an elaborate silver tea set, she was the picture of health.

"I'm so glad you came," Amanda said, while pouring two delicate cups with the steaming brew.

"It's always nice to be together with loved ones," Abigail answered.

"You're too kind," Amanda replied, as she considered the appropriate explanation for the face-to-face chat. Unable to find a graceful approach, Amanda blurted out, "I don't want to go to Kansas."

Now Abigail was the one searching for a proper response. Silence sometimes is the best reply since Amanda continued, "I need to be around people. I need excitement in my life. Living out in the middle of nowhere will drive me insane."

"Have you discussed this with Abel?" Abigail asked.

"I did at first, but he was so excited about a place of his own, I just prayed for the sale to fall through. Then, when Pearle was allowed to go along, there are two against one."

"I'm going to ask you something and I'll swear the answer to confidence. Do you love your husband?" Abigail queried.

Debating her reply for a moment, Amanda finally answered, "Not the way you love yours."

Taken aback, Abigail probed, "Why did you marry him, if you felt that way?"

"I thought I was pregnant with another man's child. Abel was such a nice guy and had a crush on me since high school. I knew if I asked him, he would do the noble thing and marry me so I could avoid shame."

"Love has many ways of expressing itself. We tend to limit it with a singular meaning, yet there are many kinds of love. You can love your children, love your parents, and yes, love your husband with different emotions. When it comes to the man you marry, I believe acts of kindness and concern for feelings tend to make love grow. Before long and without realizing it a brotherly affection can turn into a deep abiding love. These things I know firsthand. My husband returned to me in love with another woman. And, to top it off, he brought a child made from their union. Only with supreme sacrifice could I abide that situation. Nevertheless, I chose to accept them both and, out of kindness and faith, prayed for a miracle. Even though the woman had died, Jack remained tied to her memory. As time passed, his love for me gradually returned. Today, I love little Jozef as I love Sarah Jane and Jack Junior. I'm also certain of Jack's love for me. There's no reason the same can't come true for you and Abel. You must work for it, and pray for the miracle," Abigail stated.

"You're right with what you say, but I've tried. Oh how I've tried, and nothing ever changes," Amanda bemoaned.

"Then you need to try harder. This venture in Kansas might be just what the doctor ordered. You won't be alone. You will meet plenty of other people and make many new friends. From what Jack tells me, the area is growing by leaps and bounds. Just remember, the harder you try, the happier you'll become."

"Abigail, there's one major difference between you and me. I don't want the miracle," Amanda said emphatically.

* * *

Jack found Zachary Wheat leaning against the outside door smoking a cigarette. Apparently he doesn't light up inside the barn. Another point on the good side. After an impersonal greeting, Wheat extinguished the cigarette butt by grinding it against the palm of his left hand and said, "Let's go inside, it will be more comfortable there." Opening the tack room door revealed well-kept living quarters.

"My landlord owns the stables. I get free rent for taking care of the place," Wheat explained.

"From all appearances, you're doing a very good job. I couldn't help from noticing the covered wagon. Were you planning to take it to Kansas?"

"As a matter of fact, I do," was Zack's reply.

"Would you mind if I took a look at it. I've just finished refurbishing a box-wagon for Abel, and it took a lot of reconstruction to make it roadworthy."

The two men walked out into the barn area and Jack scrutinized Wheat's handiwork. Similar to Abel's prairie schooner, the axle and wheel mounts were reinforced. He noticed the driver's seat had a new flatspring, however, the wagon shock absorbers were new, but not reinforced.

"When I revamped Abel's wagon, I reinforced the mainsprings. I noticed you didn't do that," Abel stated.

"With a large family traveling, what you did makes sense. It's going to be an arduous journey. I thought about doing that, but since it's only me, I just reinforced under the seat. My load won't be near as heavy," Wheat replied.

"I see you have another wagon in the barn," said Jack.

"I've had it for a couple days now. Been working on it. It turned out to be in better shape than I originally figured. As far as I know, you folks will be riding back to Statesville in it," explained the former bluecoat. "Let's go back to the tack room. I got some hot coffee waiting."

Next to deep breathing, a cup of hot coffee is a natural tension breaker. Perhaps it's due to having something inanimate occupying your hand. Any object draws attention away from immediate concern and allows the natural flow of life to stabilize. In any case, it seems to be working for the mountain man and Zack Wheat.

With long legs stretched under the table, Jack took a sip and said, "I understand you've offered to join the Strawn family and help Abel for a period of time. From what I've observed around here, you have talents essential for such an endeavor. Many of which my friend lacks hands on experience. He has asked me for my opinion, and, from what I can tell, there's only one fly in the ointment. You have admitted being on the other side during the war. That, in and of itself, doesn't give me any problem. After all, the war has been over for four years. During the combat, you spent a great deal of time as a prisoner at Belle Isle. I can hardly fault you for that. What sticks in my craw is the extraordinary amount of time spent in solitary confinement. There's the rub."

"Our views of the war naturally differ, but that, in itself, doesn't make me a bad man. I've kept the reason for solitary confinement personal. Every day spent in darkness, with four walls my only companion, consecrated my silence on the matter. All I will tell you is, no man would tolerate the situation without reacting as I did." Wheat insisted.

"Tell me about the fight."

"There were two guards at the prison that had a reputation of ….how can I say this…..deflowering the manhood of certain prisoners. When they came upon me, I warned them not to touch me. When one reached for my arm, to twist it behind my back, I spun round and kicked him in the chest. While he knelt, coughing, I grabbed his revolver and struck the other before he had time to react. At that point, with both of them down, I shouted for help. I had presence of mind to toss the revolver before other guards arrived. In fact, I was sitting with my back against the wall when they showed up. They asked what happened, but with one guard still coughing and the other out cold, I was the only one who could answer. They didn't want to hear from me."

The mountain man understood and accepted Zachary Wheat's reason for solitary confinement. While his coffee cup was being refilled, he said, "My main concern is whether your presence will help my friends or harm them in any way."

"Oh, I've got my sins and vices. I fear if I eliminate all my vices, I run the risk of my attributes dying with them. We all are two persons, nobody is all bad or all good, but, by nature, somewhere in between," Zack declared.

"It's hard for me to say this, but I understand you. There are some things I choose to push back of my consciousness. No matter what I do, they're always there. If truth be told, I don't want to eliminate them either."

"That doesn't make you a bad person," Zack replied.

* * *

Later that evening, Jack told Abel he could find no reason to discourage Wheat's offer. Mistakenly, Abel felt as though the biggest stumbling block to a successful pioneering journey had now been removed. He will inform Zachary Wheat immediately, and ask him to join in the final stages of planning. Now, feeling as though a great burden has been lifted from his shoulders, Abel's high spirits resulted in inattention to Amanda's veiled reluctance. Fortunately, for the minister's son, the heart-to-heart she had with Abigail, compelled her to at least make the trip.

Jack sat in on the strategy sessions until the time of his return to Statesville. At that point, the Leffingwell party bid fond farewell to a best friend and wished them all, God's blessing. Abigail hugged Amanda with a stronger embrace. Tears glistened on her cheeks from knowing the inner conflict, waging war behind her pleasant outer mien.

Winter had returned to western Tennessee. In spite of falling temperatures, the sky remained blue and cloudless. By the time the Leffingwell's were back on their farm, settled around the fireplace, Abel and Zack Wheat were slowly driving covered wagons to Saint Louis, Missouri. With each mile they cover, the metal rimed wagon wheels leave deep grooves.

Like a signature of whence they once have been, wagon tracks give evidence and testimony for those seeking a better life.

CHAPTER TEN

Using maps acquired by Zachary Wheat, it was determined that Saint Louis, Missouri, was 337 miles away. Without mishap, a distance easily covered in just over two weeks. The men took turns driving the oxen wagon, switching positions after each stop to rest the laboring beasts. And, thanks to an early start, the travelers reached the Cumberland River by the end of the first day.

Not wanting to venture a late day crossing, Zack Wheat suggested they camp for the night. At first light, he would scout ahead and look for a shallow stretch to ford the watercourse.

The cold and crispy night air surrendered to the flames from the cooking fire, and those encircling the dancing blaze were reminiscent of a family picnic outing. The watchful outsider, Zachary Wheat, made a final check on the grazing animals before adding a few timber logs to insure live embers in the morning. Sitting by the rejuvenated warmth, he examined his rifle and verified the loaded revolver. Others will be in the arms of Morpheus before he catches forty winks.

During breakfast the following morning, Zack said to Abel, "I've found a shallow stretch about a quarter mile to the east. There are plenty of wagon tracks leading to it. I fathom others have crossed at that point, so I'm recommending we ford there as well."

Wheat's supposition proved accurate and the water was only knee deep. Avoiding sandbars, Abel guided the covered wagon across without a hitch. Open land lay ahead; however, the pace was slowed somewhat due to the terrain. Though less severe, as the eastern part of Tennessee, the landscape still consisted of rolling hills, which occasionally tested the oxen. Fortunately, fertile valleys and freshwater streams more than compensated for the undulating trail.

The third day on the road, progress came to a forced stop. Around noon, the skies ahead began to blacken at the horizon. Once it was determined that the dark clouds were rolling toward them, it was agreed to leave the trail and find shelter. Safety was located amidst a stand of hardwood trees, ideal place for hobbling the animals and battening down the schooners. Zack Wheat scoured the area and collected several fallen boughs, tossing them inside the back end of his wagon.

It began with a few scattered raindrops loudly spattering across the landscape. And then, after a vibrating thunderclap and strong wind gusts, it became a lashing rain—the kind that stings uncovered skin for those unlucky enough to be caught out in it. Luckily, the pilgrims were under the protection of oil-treated canvas, and remained dry. The cloudburst only lasted for a few minutes, thereupon slackened to a steady drizzle. Contented his freight remained dry, Wheat climbed down and dashed to Abel's Wagon.

"Did you guys get wet?" he asked.

"Whatever Jack used to seal the canvas worked like a charm. We're dry as a bone in here," Abel replied.

"We won't be able to travel for a while so we might as well cook supper and spend the night. If things dry out a little, we can get on the road tomorrow."

"Probably can't start a fire with things as wet as they are," Abel posited.

His fellow companion knew better. In the rear of his covered wagon there was enough dry wood to start a proverbial bonfire.

Wheat squinted briefly at the sky then hurried back to shelter. Once aboard, he lit an oil lamp and unfolded the travel charts.

"Are you sure you were only a private during the war. The way you keep studying those maps I'm beginning to think you were a general," Pearle joked. Abel's young brother-in-law had weathered the storm in Zack Wheat's prairie Schooner.

"Son, I study these maps for two reasons. First, they're hard to understand. And, secondly, I don't want us to make the same mistakes of those who traveled before us," Zack answered without looking up.

"I've got a compass. Wouldn't that be all anyone needed?"

"It might come in handy once we reach the Great Plains. Now, a good map is more important. Some of these trails are five miles wide," Wheat emphasized. "If you take the wrong route, you could get lost and lose a week. At the end of each day I mark down where I think we are and look ahead for any hindrances."

"Do you see any so far?"

"Only a couple of big rivers, depending on the way we go."

Later, the clouds broke apart exposing the remnants of daylight. As promised, a roaring fire brightened the advance of darkness and provided warmth against the pending chill of night. Two iron skillets, resting on rigid tripods, sizzled and snapped as though arguing with each other. One of them retained bacon, while the other held potatoes, and resting near the fire sat a glass jar of green beans. Abigail and Hope spent the day before returning to Statesville helping Amanda and Isela Strawn canning viands for the trip.

Abel, holding little Abby, asked, "Where did you find the dry wood?"

"I picked it up before the storm hit," conveyed Zack, grinningly.

In the morning, conditions were such that the wagons rolled again. And, by the end of day, the pioneers had stopped in a forested area east of Clarksville, Tennessee. They also arrived at a point requiring a critical decision. An oil lamp burned well past bedtime while Abel and Zachary Wheat studied the maps.

Tracing the direction with his finger, Zack said, "We could continue going west and loop around what the chart calls, 'Large Water Basin' and head for Paducah, Kentucky. They have a well-established ferry port to cross the Ohio River. The only drawback is, it requires crossing the Tennessee River in order to get there.

The other route goes north to Hopkinsville, Kentucky. We might have to pass over the Red River twice, but probably ford with the oxen. The chart indicates the rivers are shallow. Even though the trail points up to the Ohio, we may not find ferry transport. In that case, we would need to build a raft."

"Wouldn't the safest way be to Paducah?"

"You might say so. There's added danger building a raft and guiding it over deep, fast moving water."

"I'm for going to Paducah," Abel stated.

"So be it," Wheat confirmed.

Thus far, the maps Zachary Wheat obtained have proven accurate, no unforeseen aggravations other than small creeks and fallen timber. Navigation over the Tennessee River was conducted by flatboat, at a modest fee. Eight days from point of departure, the journeyers find themselves waiting their turn to be loaded on a ferryboat, large enough to transport cattle.

Although Kentucky remained neutral during the Civil War, Union General Ulysses S. Grant captured Paducah in order to take control of the Tennessee River. The port became a depot for massive Union supplies, as well as dock facilities for Federal gunboats. By 1869, nearly 7,000 inhabitants resided in the city. Its economy was thriving.

* * *

After traversing the Ohio River, Abel took the reins of his covered wagon, Pearle guided Wheat's conveyance, and Zack walked alongside the bullocks into Illinois. Their next destination is Marion, Illinois.

On many levels, Illinois represents the positive features of the whole country. The state rests entirely within the Interior Plains and its central portion consists mostly of prairie—meadows of long grasses. Beneath these fertile fields lies the Illinois Basin, a sedimentation deposit formed three hundred million years ago. At a time when an inland sea covered the area, sediments were compressed by weight of the layers above, forming sedimentary rock, rich in minerals. Residing in the basin rocks is coal. Evidence of which surrounds the town of our wayfarer's next destination.

When mining the vicinity around Marion, Illinois, hand shovels were put to use until coal descended too far into the ground. At that point, horses, mules, and wheeled scrapers would strip the earth deeper. Due largely to coal mining, the population had grown to one thousand inhabitants, at which time the Kansas—bound wagons pulled into the community.

Recognizing the feed and grain barn, Abel directed the oxen toward its location. Drawing closer, he was happy to see the blacksmith shop and livery stable.

"Can I help you folks?" asked the farrier.

"Yes, one of our horses needs a shoe and I'd appreciate it if you'd check the mules," Abel replied. "My name is Strawn, Abel Strawn, and the fellow with a beard, sitting in the wagon behind me is Wheat, Zachary Wheat. We're on our way to Saint Louis, then Kansas. I bought a farm there."

"You've got a long trip ahead. I'll give the wagons the once over while you're here," the brawny blacksmith stated.

"Much obliged," Abel expressed. "Where do I fine the post office?"

"It's further down the main street on the right-hand side. In case you're interested, we got two general stores in town. The mining company owns one, and people named Swanell own the other. I recommend that one."

"How long will you be?" asked Abel.

"Y'all come back in one hour. I should be done by then."

The travelers stood briefly outside the smithy's shop then began strolling up the street, heading for the post office. With his daughter in his arms, Abel slowed as they passed Swanell's hardware.

"If you want, we can stop here after the letters are posted," he told his wife.

"Give me Abby and you go on. The letters are yours anyway. We'll go inside and have a look around," Amanda replied, while Abby was being exchanged.

The tavern across the street caught Zack Wheat's eye. Since Abel agreed to post his letter, and the general store posed no attraction, save buying some licorice, Zack decided that a libation was in his best interest.

"I've always found that a tavern can be better than a newspaper when you want to learn what's going on," Zack stated. "Besides, I think I feel a cold coming on and a sip of the spirits always prevents it from taking hold." With that, Zack stepped off the wooden sidewalk and traipsed toward the friendly door. To nobody's surprise, Pearle followed like a hound dog tracking quarry.

"What will you have, gents?" the bartender inquired.

"Shot and a beer," Wheat answered.

"I'll just have a beer," Pearle chimed.

"You boys here to work the mines?" the barman queried further, while pouring Wheat's shot glass.

"No sir, just passing through. We're on our way to Kansas to take up farming. The mining business must be pretty good."

"Good for the mining companies. Not so much for the miners."

"How's that?" Wheat's curiosity was piqued.

"The miners are paid once a month based on the tonnage they dig. The company holds back two weeks, but gives them credit at their store. They pay them about 85¢ a day and work them 10 hours. The coal is dumped over a screen, separating larger pieces from the small ones; miners only get paid for the larger pieces. Besides that, they deduct a percentage for dirt and such. No matter how clean the coal is, they still subtract a set amount. The company sells the small pieces to the local community. If miners complain or don't shop at the company store, they get fired. Plenty newcomers are trucked in every day. As far as the town's businesses are concerned, it would be better if they weren't here."

"We have coal mines where I originally come from. Working in a mine didn't appeal to me then, and definitely doesn't now," Zack confirmed, as he emptied his beer glass. "Pearle, let's go find your brother-in-law."

* * *

The Marion blacksmith found both wagons in good order, and after settling up, the pioneers were on their way, reaching Pinckneyville as the calendar turned to the month of March. In order to accomplish that feat, two rivers had to be crossed. Ironically, both were the Little Muddy. Forming an oxbow traversing their route, it required fording twice. And, after a brief layover to feed the animals and spend the night, the journey to St. Louis continued.

Zachary Wheat's charts showed fifty miles of prairie grassland lay ahead, with the only obstacle being the Kaskaskia River. When the Tennessee homesteaders reached this tributary to the Mississippi, they found a few other pilgrims waiting their turn to cross. A sturdy rope was attached to each side of the waterway by which the flat bottom scow was towed back and forth.

"Just pull in line behind those other wagons. We can only carry one at a time, so it's going to be a spell. Y'all heading for the Oregon Trail?" asked the barge operator.

"No sir, we're traveling to Kansas," replied Abel.

"No matter, it'll cost you two dollars to cross the Kaskaskia," said the ferryman, while holding out his open palm.

Propelling the ferryboat was a slow process. Depth of the muddy water couldn't be readily determined; all the same, the operators used oars most of the way. Were the river shallower, spiked poles would have been utilized.

It took the better part of two hours before both wagons reached the other side. Now, the biggest challenge of all lies ahead—navigating the mighty Mississippi River. A distance of about 25 miles separated the travelers from the East Saint Louis ferry depot. The major portion of which was covered before nightfall.

Considerably more traffic employed the road, making the next morning's early departure essential. In so doing, would reduce the amount of wagons in front, when reaching the depot.

East Saint Louis, Illinois is situated directly across the Mississippi River from Saint Louis, Missouri. While its Missouri sister boasts 300,000 population, East Saint Louis has 5,000 inhabitants; however, many sectors of commerce are blossoming on the Illinois side. Stockyards and meatpacking, considered nuisance industries, are concentrated there, with the blessing of their Missouri neighbors. Many factory stacks emit a somewhat darker smoke plume—the result of using local Illinois coal as fuel.

Settlers, passing through the area, also have the opportunity to see numerous ancient earthwork mounds, constructed by Native Americans, who long inhabited the area, thousands of years before.

Even with an early start, several wagons lined up ahead of the Tennessee pioneers. The ones in front appeared to be on similar missions. All were covered with weatherproof canvas and gave the appearance of being primed for a long journey. In addition, several impatient women and children were milling about, anxious for their pending boat ride. Abel and Zack walked to the ferry depot and asked the attendant, "How do we find a wagon train going to Kansas?"

"First, you got to get across this river," he answered. "Once on the other side, you can't miss it. There will be wagons lined up for a mile."

"Yes, but how do we find out where they're going and join the one bound for Kansas?" Zack inquired.

"They all will be going to Independence, Missouri. That's where you connect to the Oregon Trail. At that point, some will continue on into Kansas. When you fellows are on the other side, ask for a man named Tobias Taylor. He'll either be a scout or wagon master. You can't miss him since he sports a full beard and stands six and a half feet tall. Most likely he'll be wearing a bear skin coat."

"Sounds like a mountain man," Abel stated. "What side did he fight on during the war?"

"Don't know, and I'm afraid to ask him," added the depot operator. "That'll be $5 each for the ferry. The boat's pretty big, but a wagon with four oxen adds too much weight to carry both of you."

CHAPTER ELEVEN

A s March winds ripple against the conical lodge, *Falling Water* and several Cheyenne braves hold council. The mood is solemn and with each gust, the expression on their tawny faces becomes grimmer. The wind poses little danger since the lodge design prepares for it. On the windward side, lodge poles are placed a little closer to the center, creating a steeper surface, while the opposite side has slightly more slope. This, along with the tepee's weight, improves stability against the wind. Regarding weight, the poles alone total over 400 pounds and the buffalo hide cover adds another 150. That and a surface display of painted geometric shapes, sacred animals, and battle scenes, exhibits the status of the resident. *Falling Water* is addressing the council.

"Soon, a new season will arrive. The buffalo shall return from the mountain valleys and we will celebrate another hunt. For reasons beyond my wisdom, white men have insulted the Great Spirit and occupy the land of our ancestors. Land that *Maheo* has entrusted to us. Each day they multiply and grow stronger. At first, the settlers came and plowed up the land killing food for the buffalo. Now the bluecoat soldiers come riding the iron horse. Our chiefs made war to stop their progress, but their numbers are too great. They have war medicine our shields cannot defend against. As leader of our band, I must decide what is best for all the clan and children. *Buffalo Horn*, the medicine man, must sing a song for safety and wisdom. Each of us should do the same, since my decision will be painted on the skins of permanent record."

Snake Hunter, an aggressive warrior, was next to speak, "What my brother says is true. His words come from the heart and I honor them, but they sound like someone who has lost faith. Are we not a free people? Are we not fierce in battle? Hairy mouths tremble with fear when we paint our faces. The buffalo are part of our existence, given to us by the Great Spirit long before the memory of our grandfathers. Are we to deny a gift from *Maheo* and cower like frightened children?"

"When the white eyes made war on each other, many of our braves joined their armies and fought alongside of them. Mostly with those who wore gray coats because they promised us our traditional lands. Now, the people called 'Confederates' are prisoners in their own villages and guarded by bluecoat soldiers. White men desire the same fate for the Cheyenne and our Arapaho brothers. Long knives force us to give up the life we have and live as the settlers do. To plant crops and raise pigs. I, *Snake Hunter*, will not willingly submit."

Black Wolf, *Snake Hunter's* closest friend, agreed with what he said and passed the smoke-pipe to the brave sitting at his side. Thus, it continued, with most of the warriors agreeing with *Snake Hunter*. Any remaining items requiring council approval were reviewed and ruled on without lengthy deliberation. For the most part, *Falling Water's* remedy was accepted without debate. Each member took a puff from the calumet (peace pipe) signifying accord with decisions, and prepared to adjourn.

Falling Water took solace in the fact his decision can be postponed for a while. His friend, *Two Trees*, remained seated after all had filed out. Conditions outside had dramatically turned for the worse. Blowing winds were mixed with heavy snow. Flakes were large and adhering rapidly to trees and earth. Running to his lodge, *Snake Hunter* scooped up a handful and packed it into a snowball. He intended to playfully toss it at *Black*

Wolf, but changed his mind, since he could barely see the tepees through the blizzard.

When *White Dove* and her grandmother pulled open the doorway flap, *Falling Water* was adding more wood to the central fire. The women also carried an armful of dry branches. In spite of the winter storm, the tenants will be warm tonight. Shaking the snow from their coats, they politely acknowledged *Two Trees,* and then took residence away from the men. *Two Trees* was always welcome in the lodge. His honest loyalty and courteousness made him a favorite.

The men spoke in subdued tones even though *White Dove* and her grandmother were occupied with their beadwork. During the council meeting, *Two Trees* was reserved. Whenever he is the center of attention, his voice freezes; an embarrassing problem since early childhood.

"Well old friend, it looks as though we must soon give up our hunting grounds and conduct our lives in what the yellow eyes call, Indian Territory," *Falling Water* said frankly.

"You do not plan to join the Dog Soldiers and go north to fight?" questioned *Two Trees.*

"Thus far, *Maheo* has given me no sign to favor this. I must consider all our people. Fighting the bluecoats has only resulted in our women lamenting the loss of husbands and sons. Our numbers have shrunk while the enemy continuously grows. A new life may be the only way to save the Cheyenne from total extinction."

"Will I be able to catch eagles in this new land?" *Two Trees* seriously asked.

"Yes, if they build nests in the land where we live," *Falling Water* replied compassionately.

With the most bothering question seemingly answered, *Two Trees* was relieved.

The next issue, in which he found troubling, concerned *Snake Hunter.*

"I do not like *Snake Hunter,*" *Two Trees* stated tersely.

"He can be irritable at times," said *Falling Water.*

After a lengthy hesitation, *Two Trees* quietly recounted, "One day I saw him under a blanket with another man."

Falling Water smiled at his friend's disclosure and said, "Perhaps he was hunting a shorter snake."

At first, Two Trees stared blankly, and then began laughing once he understood the joke. "I have only mentioned this to *Buffalo Horn*, the medicine man."

"And, what did he say?"

"He said, *Snake Hunter* was not a two-spirit person. He had once seen him bathing in the river. What I saw had to be just a queer encounter and think no more about it."

"I believe that is good advice, my friend," replied *Falling Water*.

CHAPTER TWELVE

This side of Heaven, the one thing Hyrum Adams looked forward to, was a visit with his grandchildren. Abigail's youngsters matched his enjoyment whenever he stopped by. Little Jozef seemed to also share in their delight. Melvin Kaufman was mystified by it all. The Reverend Adams never brought them candy and the only gifts came once a year at Christmas. He compared the situation with his own as a child. Best he could recollect, a frequent visit by his grandfather didn't cause such a celebration.

He and Jack were in the barn building additional foaling stalls. One of the preferred mares dropped her foal in the field. A circumstance Jack always wants to avoid. By his own design, the month of March is foaling time. The idea came from what he learned about the Kentucky horse breeders. A foal is considered one year old on the day it's born. Therefore, since the gestation period ranges between 320 and 350 days, selective breeding needs to be such so as the foal drops early in the year. Jack deeply regrets missing the birth of this particular foal. There are three other mares, bred by Rambler, his prized stallion, and they will be brought inside for easier observation.

"You ever notice how the young'uns get all thrilled when Hyrum comes around? You'd think it was Christmas," Melvin asked.

"Yeah, I've seen that. It's probably because of the way Abigail feels and the kids sense it from their mother," Jack replied, while tightening a screw on the gate hinge.

"That must be it. Shit, I hated to see my grandfather come around. He gave me more lickens than both mom and dad together."

"Was he an abuser?"

"Nah, I deserved every one," Melvin replied, with a self-satisfying grin.

"Let's saddle up and go wrangle those mares," Jack said, earnestly.

Roping and leading the mares to the barn took longer than either man anticipated. March winds might be great for flying kites; however, frequent surges play hell with throwing a lariat over an unwilling horse. After failing a few times throwing the lasso, ala rodeo style, Jack convinced himself it would be better to ride up to the mares and drop the noose over their head. Still, this method took a considerable amount of time out of a day with shortened hours of light. Once the last pregnant mare was safely in a new stall, it was dark outside. After congratulating each other for a job well done, two tired buckaroos limped slowly toward the lighted windows of the rural abode.

Hyrum was sitting at the kitchen table talking to his daughter when Jack entered the house. Abigail called out, "Is Melvin with you? I've got a pot roast in the oven."

"No, he went on home. It's been a pretty tough day for both of us. I asked him to fetch his family and have supper with us, but I think he was too tired."

"Well, go wash up. Sarah Jane is setting the table and we'll have supper in a half-hour. I'd appreciate it if you'd see what Jack Junior and Jozef are arguing about. They're getting kind of loud."

The noise suddenly ended the minute Jack opened the door. Satisfied with his parenting skills, he entered the wash room and reached for a bar of soap.

Difficulties running a horse farm were explained in detail to this father-in-law. By the look of him, it was obvious Jack was worn out. Horace said grace and asked the blessing on the food and those who prepared it. Abigail's cooking injected energy in the mountain man, and he soon had that familiar sparkle in his eye. A serving of peach cobbler created the finishing touch.

As Abigail and Sarah Jane cleared the table, the boys went back to whatever they were fighting about. Jack and Hyrum removed to the living room, took comfortable chairs, and relaxed with a cup of coffee.

"There's something I've wanted to talk to you about. A couple church members approached me the other day and said some former Confederate soldiers were pressuring them for support. It concerns me a great deal," Hyrum stated. "Have you heard anything about the Ku Klux Klan?"

"Not much. I figured it was mostly just talk." Jack replied.

"Apparently, it's a lot more than the usual complaint. None of us are happy with the way the Reconstruction is being handled. All the same, most people are against violent insurgence. After four years of that, it's time to move on. Not everybody agrees with me. People who call themselves Klan members are trying to form a statewide organization throughout the South. Our own General Nathan Bedford Forrest claims to be the national leader and calls himself, Grand Wizard. Their *modus operandi* is intimidation through threats of violence. In some cases they resort to murder. The government has passed laws to counteract the Klan, but it's not effective. Knowing the average southerner as I do, chances for a national organization are slim to none. Unfortunately, the majority is made up of former Confederate soldiers and they have broken up into local splinter groups. They claim to be dedicated to the removal of scalawags and carpetbaggers, but we know black men have been lynched. Once the vote is returned to us, we can rid ourselves of this vermin using the ballot box. This bunch is bad. I plan to contact Lieutenant McKnight with any information I might pick up and you should do the same," Hyrum expressed.

"Maryellen and little Augie are frequent visitors. I'll make a point to discuss the Klan and offer my help."

"Son, you might forget the adjective 'little' when you refer to a grown man. Since the Lord made all of us, He must have a reason for some to be smaller than others. Lieutenant McKnight probably resents being called 'little,' but holds his tongue to be polite."

Jack's ears began to redden at the top, an outward sign of embarrassment. Understanding his father-in-law was a man of the cloth and wouldn't consciously say anything to hurt someone's feelings, he nodded in the affirmative. At the same time thinking, *"I've got to remember not to say that in front of Hyrum, little Augie will just have to live with it."*

With the kitchen chores finished, Abigail entered the room and took a chair near the fireplace. Sarah Jane gave her grandfather a kiss on the cheek and retired to her bedroom with a book.

"Spend the night with us, Hyrum. You can go back in the morning after breakfast," Jack said.

"I better not this time, my horse and carriage are tied up in front."

"Your horse is in one of my new stalls and the carriage is parked in the barn. I'll hook you back up when the rooster crows," Jack replied, knowing he has pleased both Abigail and her father.

"Have you folks heard anything from your friends traveling to Kansas?" Hyrum asked, as Abigail refreshed his coffee.

"Yes, we received a letter the other day. I guess everything is going okay. It's frustrating for me since I can't answer them back. Jack tells me they won't have an address for three months, so accept things the way they are."

"Your husband is right, dear. Best thing we can do for them is keep them in our prayers."

Chapter Thirteen

Tennessee wagon wheels now rest on Missouri soil. The ferryboat agent was 'on the money' when he predicted there would be plenty schooners lined up. With one behind the other, Abel and Zack positioned their caravan in an established queue, untethered their riding mounts, and set about looking for Tobias Taylor.

People on this side of the river were in much better humor than folks yet to cross. It seemed, with each wagon they pass, people would wave and shout greetings. When they came alongside a schooner filled with rambunctious children, the driver shouted, "If'n you boys are looking for a wagon master, just head for that feller over yonder." He motioned toward someone on horseback that was holding a bunch of colored pennants. As Abel drew near him, he barked, "Who are you looking for?"

"My friend and I seek a Mister Tobias Taylor," Abel replied.

"That'd be a wagon master," he determined, and handed Abel a green pennant. "Just plainly display the green flag, and he'll be along shortly."

Returning to the wagons, Abel thought the idea of colored flags was darn smart. It prevented a passel of people blocking the road while trying to talk to the wagon train leader. Instead, he came to them, one at a time.

Arriving at his wagon, Abel stood in his stirrups to extend his height and fastened the green banner to a conspicuous spot above the front seat. Curious, Amanda questioned, "What's the flag for?"

"It's so the wagon master knows that we want to talk to him," Abel answered.

All of a sudden, the train of wagons moved forward and Abel prompted the oxen to keep pace. From a distance, the cheers coming from those in front began to swell. Even though the immediate destination was unknown, the activity had a thrilling effect.

Traveling for the better part of two hours, the caravan came to a stop on a grassy plain near a shallow branch of the Missouri River. The advantage gave Abel a clearer view of the line of wagons.

"Best I can make of it, there are forty prairie wagons ahead," Abel told Zack.

"And another five behind," Zack replied. "Looks like folks are lighting cooking fires. I guess we spend the night here."

Rules of a covered wagon train are strictly enforced. This also applies to breakfast, lunch, and supper. Apparently, the pioneers were simultaneously making their evening meal. The Tennessee trekkers were no exception. Amanda and Pearle gathered bramble near the riverbed and soon a crackling fire commenced. Abel placed their iron tripod over the flames and his wife hung a pot from the upper hook. It contained ample water along with potatoes, dried beef, a glass jarful of canned tomatoes, and salt. Circled around the fire, the family waited in anticipation. It was then that a rider approached saying, "That sure smells tasty." No mistake about it, based on the extended length of stirrups, he had to be Tobias Taylor.

"I see the green pennant. Do you want a word with me?" said the rider.

"Yes sir, our party is going to western Kansas. We've never made a trip like this before and are ignorant to the correct procedure," answered Abel.

"Every one of your associates is in the same boat. First, you're in the right place; however, all of your neighbors aren't traveling to Kansas. Some desire to go farther west. They'll be taking a different trail once we reach Independence, Missouri. From what I've noticed, at least a dozen of you are heading to Kansas and I'll be your trail boss. I went over the mountains last year." Leaning over, he handed Abel a sheet of paper and said, "This here is a list of the rules. They were written by folks just like you, based on their experience. In a day or two, most of your questions will be answered. If you need me along the way, just fly the green flag," he called out as he rode off.

"We didn't ask him if we had to pay him," Amanda reminded.

"That might be learned tomorrow night, after we form a circle," Abel said.

"With this many wagons, the center diameter is gonna be plenty wide," Zack added. "We might even keep animals in it."

"Time will tell," Abel remarked. "How much longer does the pot need to boil?"

Amanda tested the contents with her two-pronged cooking fork before responding to her husband. Finding the meat tender, she said, "Bring your plates boys, and I'll dish it out."

Once the men were eating, she prepared a plate for Abby, then ladled another for herself.

"There's plenty left, I fixed enough for seconds," Amanda announced. Three Tennesseans rose in tandem and began scooping the hearty stew. They made sure to break off a hefty chunk of bread before returning to their stools.

With the exception of children, most pioneers didn't sleep well that night. Looking forward to the first day of actual train travel created sufficient restiveness to keep them awake until the wee hours of morning. And, just as they began to doze off, it was time for the camp to rise.

The disturbing night resolved itself with the light of dawn, and the camp became a dynamo of energy. After a quick breakfast, men tended to the animals and women replaced their furnishings so as to be ready when the wagon master shouts, "Wagons forward." Even Amanda, whose demeanor is usually blasé, appears to have caught the fever and was bouncing on the seat when Abel cracked the whip.

The state of Missouri can be divided by two extremes. North of the Missouri River are rolling hills and rich fertile soil, formed by pre-Wisconsin glaciations, millions of years prior. South of the twisting watercourse lies a dissected plateau with sharp relief, likely caused by the glacial ice sheet. Subsequent uplifts are similar to mountains. This high and dissected tableland is heavily forested and inaccurately called mountains—the Ozark Mountains.

Tobias Taylor will lead the caravan across the central portion of the state. In so doing, he will avoid the heavily wooded areas, yet keep creeks and streams nearby. The principal encumbrances could have been crossing the Meramec, Gasconade, and Osage Rivers, a task he has successfully completed twice before; however, the chosen route will circumvent them. Nevertheless, he will encounter the Missouri River again, in three or four days, weather permitting.

On the first full day of combined wagon travel, the train rolled over winter grassland and covered 22 miles before calling it a day. There were neither major incidences nor accidents. The novice pioneers handled themselves smartly, much to the satisfaction of those leading the group.

In addition to a wagon master, a caravan this size had eight outriders, who monitored the train's alignment and progress. Also, there were a few teamsters to drive the wagons of inexperienced wagoners, along with a railroad company cartographer and two doctors.

Remuneration for the covered wagon crew usually amounted to $75/month for the captain, $50/month for a scout and $20/month for others. In most cases, a collection was taken for the wagon boss, which boosted his pay a great deal. All in all, not much of a salary when you consider a bounty hunter received

$300 dollars for catching a stage coach robber. Yes, dissimilar occupations, yet, both dangerous professions.

Soon, the space within became active with people tending their cooking fires. Men fed their animals and watered them at a nearby creek. People in neighboring wagons made introductions, but the chilly March winds kept socializing at a minimum, as most sought warmth under the cover of canvas. On warmer nights there will be singing, storytelling, and, once the musicians are located, square dancing.

Problems tend to dissipate after a good meal. And, for those who walked a good portion to the day, avoiding the constant bounce of their wagon, sleep came quickly.

The additional shock absorbers, installed by Jack Leffingwell, made Amanda's ride much smoother; even so, her covered wagon was dark soon after eating. That being said, all dreams came to an abrupt ending at dawn's early light.

The routine continued for the next four days until Mother Nature intervened. After traveling a few miles near Fulton, Missouri, a heavy rain stopped any advancement. The cloudburst came on quickly, then, much to the disappointment of the pilgrim pioneers, slowly turned into a deluge. There was nothing to do but seek shelter and wait it out. Tobias Taylor and his outriders sought safety inside spare wagons, while all the canvas covers were put to the test. Zachary Wheat braved the elements and sat several buckets out to get watered. For some time, Amanda had been curious over what occupied Zack in his wagon. She asked her brother who, in his own mind, found nothing unusual. Zack took care of several chickens, caged on the side of the wagon, and nursed some potted plants inside, under the canvas cover.

The potted plants were actually young saplings growing in buckets. The immature trees were started over a year prior, since Zack knew the first couple of years were critical to a saplings survival. He selected five of the most healthy to make the trip— two each apple and cherry, plus, a black walnut. Even though they appeared in good shape, a little time exposed to a spring rain wouldn't hurt. The chickens, however, required special treatment. Zack had clipped their wings to keep them grounded and brought along a roll of poultry netting (chicken wire) to fashion a small coop whenever the opportunity presented itself. Thus far, they too were doing well. In fact, Zack occasionally gathered a few eggs.

The heavy rainstorm left the trail a sodden and muddy corridor. Once the wagons were able to resume travel, their pace was considerably slower. It took four days to cover the next 50 miles and reach the Missouri River at Boonville, Missouri.

A vote was taken as to what manner they wished to cross. The choice was between flatboat ferry or fording the fast moving water. Using the ferry won out, but only by a narrow margin. Apparently, many were concerned about the expenditure, ignoring the potential damage the river might cause. Charges ranged from $3 for a loaded wagon and team, to 50¢ for a man and horse. Other animals, such as sheep and cattle, cost 5¢ each.

After crossing the river, the pace quickened and Independence, Missouri was reached on March 20, 1869. At this point, Abel and Amanda have traveled nearly 600 miles and the majority of prairie schooners will disport for the Oregon Trail.

Tobias Taylor, and a reduced crew, will lead twelve wagons across the state noted for its sunflowers—Kansas.

Before embarking on the tallgrass plains, the shortened caravan spent a day in Independence, restocking their larder and other essentials. Zack Wheat purchased three bales of hay from a livestock feed store; Amanda picked up a few toiletries; and Pearle bought a western hat, similar to the one Zack wears. Abel stayed behind and looked after his daughter.

Tobias Taylor made a point to ride by each wagon and inform their owners that he planned to follow the Santa Fe Trail through Kansas and leave at daybreak. He also suggested everybody get a good night sleep, knowing full well that wouldn't happen. The next morning, before moving out, he gathered families in the center of the wagon circle and explained some of the discomforts expected along the way.

In his mountain drawl he enumerated, "Kansas ain't as civilized as from where y'all came from. There are still unfriendly Indians about, although I haven't heard of them causing trouble lately. All the same, the outriders with me now are all crack shots and experienced with Indians. Eventually, the government will move them all to the Oklahoma Indian Territory; but, right now, there are still a few die-hard renegades hell bent to raid farms and wagon trains. If we ever encounter these bands y'all just form the circle. My men will do the rest."

"Another nuisance, here in Kansas, is rattlesnakes. Their bite can kill you, so make sure you're wearing high-top leather boots, when on foot. If you see one, just drive the wagon around it. Don't take any unnecessary chances. At the end of the day, when we make camp, patrol the center circle just to be safe. Build a fire in the middle for social gatherings. Are there any questions?" he asked.

"With the possibility of Indian raids, should the menfolk carry weapons?" asked Zack Wheat, mainly for the benefit of others, since he will carry his pistol and keep the Henry loaded in the wagon.

"I don't think y'all need to carry, but I do suggest you keep weapons where they're easily within reach."

The woman in the schooner in front of Abel questioned, "Do the fires drive rattlesnakes away?"

"I wouldn't bank on it. Snakes are cold-blooded creatures. On chilly days the heat might attract them. One thing for sure, human activity tends to drive them away."

"Well, we haven't had a good old fashion hoe-down since we've been on the trail. I've learned we got several fiddle players and I've done a little calling myself. Let's all get together after we camp and had supper," said a man on the other side of the circle.

"That sounds like a darn good idea," Tobias Taylor stated, while mounting up and riding to the front wagon. Turning sideways in the saddle he shouted, "Wagons forward in five minutes."

By the end of the day, the caravan reached the banks of the Kansas River and made camp. The wagon master favored crossing larger waterways in the morning, when dray animals were well rested. Anticipating an evening frolic, wagoners seemed more enthusiastic as they formed the required circle. Once the covered carriers were in place, the diameter between was meticulously tromped to assure no hidden reptiles were about. From the river bank, wood and other tinder was collected and placed in the center for a bonfire, which will give added light, as well as provide a little warmth to the cool night air. The evening meals were eaten in haste and shortly thereafter, the sound of fiddle strings being tightened and the plunk and twang of instrument tuning filled the surroundings.

Abel and Zack were still eating when Amanda insisted, "Watch Abby while I get cleaned up." When the men finally finished, she continued preening. At last, Amanda appeared dressed to the nines.

"Wow, look at you," Pearle embellished.

"I'm gonna have some fun for a change," she said defiantly, and headed toward the jubilant crowd.

Zack Wheat found it difficult to look Abel in the eye. Pearle rescued him by saying, "Come on Zack, let's do a little dancing." Zack turned to Abel, who stated hoarsely, "You guys go on. I'll watch my daughter."

It was obvious this wasn't the first time the musicians played a hoedown. Much to the delight of the dancers, there was something for everyone, whether a square dance, reel, polka, or waltz. The night turned out to be warmer than usual for this time of year. That, coupled with a bonfire and lively dancing, had perspiration on nearly every brow. Women found Zack Wheat a commendable partner and had him skipping and hopping to every set until he nearly collapsed from fatigue. Much to the chagrin of his partners, he cried 'uncle' and sat on the closest barrel to recuperate. Pearle, unfamiliar with most of the styles of music being played, tripped the light with the more youthful girls, whenever a waltz came up.

Amanda was the belle of the ball and drew the attention of all participants, especially mothers and wives. She also was the most beautiful woman on the trampled grass dance floor. Constantly approached by the male shufflers, the most frequent happened to be one of the wagon train's outriders. Tall, dark, and with a gleaming white smile, Amanda enjoyed his company the most. It also became apparent to Pearle that his sister was giving this stranger too much attention. Pearle bristled when the cowboy leaned forward and gave her a lingering kiss. No sooner had that happened, while holding hands, the couple walked slowly to the far side of the bonfire and temporarily vanished from sight. With the bonfire's light inside the circle, the outer edge became dark. And, the outside length of the prairie schooners had very little illumination. Now, devoid of light, Amanda was totally rapt in the moment. With a heartbeat rapid as a wild bird, she willingly returned his kiss. Both were breathing heavily, and as his hands began to find forbidden places, Pearle's voice broke the silence.

"She has a husband and three-year-old daughter back at the wagon."

Stunned and straining to see where the voice came from, the cowboy backed away saying, "I didn't know she was married. She didn't tell me. I'm sorry this happened." He hurriedly made tracks.

Pearle, angry with his sister's exhibition, blurted, "Once a whore, always a whore."

"You didn't have to interrupt, I can take care of myself," Amanda uttered.

"Yeah, if I didn't intervene, he would have had you on your back in the grass," he snapped. "Abel is a good man. My future is tied to his generosity. You danced with that guy too much. Everybody saw you holding hands and walking to where it was dark. You're a married woman and I'm justified."

The indiscretion was another moment of moral weakness. Amanda, filled with the romance of the occasion, had no thought of adverse repercussions. In her own mind, it was the only excitement she'd experienced in months. With no feelings of remorse, she returned to the wagon and went to bed.

* * *

A positive outcome of the previous night's festivities was the pioneers became better acquainted with their neighbors. Abel learned that Elijah Love and his wife, Lisa, occupied the prairie schooner in front and Niels Blankenberg and his wife, Tessa, the one behind. In addition, Theo and Mildred Van Ronkle and Rainbow and Angela Calloway introduced themselves, and in so doing, Abel learned their destination was Fort Dodge. In all likelihood, they will become neighbors. Each had a passel of small children, guaranteeing Abby some future friends.

The following day, the expedition lingered until Tobias Taylor and his scout returned from reconnoitering the riverbank. Faced with two methods by which to cross the moving current, he thought it best to again let the pilgrims make the decision.

"I've had a look see down the river and found a spot where the water is only knee deep. Fortunately, the spring rains haven't happened yet. It's my belief y'all can ford it without a lot of trouble. I also found a ferry barge that can handle your wagons but not with the team tied to it. They would need to be swimmed across. The ferry man said he would charge $2 a wagon."

"Why can't he take the wagon and team?" asked a curious teamster.

"The barge can't handle the weight. It looks as though about three dugouts were covered with logs to make a platform. There's a rope tied on each side of the river and the ferryman uses a pole to propel the contraption," Tobias explained.

At that point, there wasn't any doubt as to the manner of crossing and the wagon master led the caravan to the aforementioned area. Abel insisted that he be the one wading the water to guide the oxen. Reluctantly, Zack climbed back on his wagon and instructed Pearle to help Amanda. The water was deeper than Tobias suggested; nevertheless, all made it to the other side, but not without wet and dripping contents.

The train was led a short distance from the river, then stopped for those with water damage to dry off. In some cases, nearly all the cargo had to be removed. Abel and Zack had no water seepage, thanks to the extra caulking performed when the wagons were retrofitted, back in Tennessee.

Rather than continuing on the journey, it was decided to form the circle and spend the rest of the day with a central bonfire. Saturated belongings were placed at a safe distance from the flames to evaporate the moisture. Fortunately, it was a clear night and the natural desiccant did its job. Dried possessions were repacked and the train was ready to travel when Tobias Taylor called for the vehicles to move forward.

* * *

Abel Strawn had been told that Kansas was flat as a pancake. Now, as the caravan enters the eastern part of the state he sees, with his own eyes, what he was told isn't exactly true. The land gradually rises from just under 700 feet to over 4,000 feet at the Colorado border; while the eastern sub-surface consists of horizontally dipping sedimentary rocks. It has many hills and forests. The Flint Hills, for example, stand well above the lower plains. Its bedrock strata are crossed by deep valleys and streams. True to its name, the land beneath the hills consists of thick flint or chert, which supports the topographic relief. The largest region of prairie tallgrass occurs in this eastern portion. In the summer, tallgrasses extend beyond the height of an average man.

The western two thirds of the state is in the Great Plains of the United States and made up of mid-grass prairie. Its elevation gradually moves westward until reaching the foothills of the Rocky Mountains, a response to tectonic processes millions of years ago. The region east of the Rockies was home to great herds of American Bison, whose existence is being threatened by hunting and the railroad, which is rapidly laying tracks across the state.

* * *

As the caravan moved southwest, Zack Wheat was quick to notice some fallen timber, uprooted or broken at the tree bole or trunk. It was evidence of windthrow and how strong the winds in Kansas can get. A point he will tuck away for the present until the time when he's building a structure on the open plains.

For the following two days, the expedition encountered several streams, but none were a particular problem. The Wakarusa River was a different story. A tributary of the Kansas River with many off-shoots, its main branch lies well below the rolling limestone hills.

These limestone outcroppings presented great challenges to the early emigrants, attempting to ford the stream in their wagons. Often, the wagons were dismantled and lowered down the limestone walls using ropes. Reaching the bottom, they were towed across the gentle current, and then lifted by rope to the opposing bank.

From his previous experience, Tobias Taylor knew Indians routinely made a river crossing. On an earlier excursion, he located their main passageway. The route was precipitous; however, if an Indian pony, dragging its travois, could accomplish it, so could a wagon train.

Pioneers stood atop the ridge looking down at the stream. They were momentarily entranced as the water separated at the larger boulders, sending white spindrift into the air, amid the constant roar. Turning to Abel, Theo Van Ronkle said, "People actually crossed this river from where we stand?"

"According to Tobias Taylor they did. Lucky for us, he knows of another place further north, for us to cross," answered Abel. "The slope is steep, but he's sure we can handle it."

While the pilgrims were talking, Tobias Taylor rode up and barked, "Okay, you folks have seen what you don't have to contend with. Now, let's make a detour and head north. When we come to some wetlands, there's another place to cross."

The wagon train traveled nearly five miles before the ground began to get soggy. Shortly thereafter the Indian passageway was reached. It also had a high limestone embankment, but the trail had a kinder slope. For safety purposes, the wagoners tied a rope to their rear axle and then around a nearby tree, preventing a possible runaway. The idea was the brainchild of Zack Wheat and supported by the tall wagon master. The winding river was shallow at that point, making the ford a smooth operation. Once all vessels were across, daylight began to wane. By the time the five-mile detour was backtracked, it was time to circle the wagons.

On March 28, 1869, the wagon train made camp on the bank of the Neosho River and a community called Council Grove. The area, with its water, forests, and tall grass prairie is beautiful. It is also home of the Kaw Indian tribe, living along the river. A pleasant group that allowed settlers to pass through on their way farther west. Pioneers gathered at a grove of trees waiting for others to arrive and band together for the trip west. In all likelihood, that was the reason for the town's name.

Council Grove became a stopping point for teamsters, traders, and peddlers of every stripe on the Santa Fe Trail. Once wagons were properly arranged, the present travelers mounted their horses and rode down main street investigating the amenities the town had to offer. Abel Strawn was pleased to see a post office. He dismounted and walked inside.

"Good afternoon stranger. How may I help you?"

"I have some letters to post. How long will it take for them to reach Tennessee?" Abel inquired.

"We're pretty fast nowadays. Should get there in less than two weeks," the clerk replied.

Zack had composed another letter to his brother and asked, "How about New York?"

"Less than three weeks."

The postal clerk was handed the letters. He examined each one and hit the upper right corner with the appropriate postal stamp.

"That comes to the total of one dollar, or 25¢ for over 450 miles.

Abel refused the offer of additional stamps, but found the new pictorials interesting, especially the Abraham Lincoln 90¢ issue. With postal chores completed, they rode back to camp and sought the wagon master.

Tobias Taylor was preparing a list of supplies for the camp. After everyone enters their particular needs, he will assign a teamster to take the empty supply wagon to town. Wanting more oats for his mules, Zack offered to assist the driver.

After Zack had left for town, Pearle was beside himself and wished he were allowed to tag along. Since that day in front of the gunsmith's display window, the two have been close friends. It was easier to discuss things with Zack. After all, Abel is a man of the cloth and certain things are too embarrassing to mention in front of him, especially the antics of his sister, Amanda. Pearle believed that certain decorum should be practiced among adults. Zack agreed, but said, "Life doesn't always travel on a straight and proper road. We desire the journey to be stable; however, the path is full of pitfalls. The choices we make dictate the life we lead. Remember that the pull of life is very strong. Give pause before you condemn others."

Abel noticed the forsaken look of his marooned brother-in-law and consoled him by saying, "I understand Zack has a couple fishing poles in his wagon. He wouldn't be upset if we borrowed them. Tobias told me he fished the Neosho and caught good size catfish."

Pearle knew exactly where they were kept and retrieved them in short order.

"We don't have any bait," he stated.

"Tobias said to just turn over rocks. There's plenty bait underneath," Abel replied.

Once they found a suitable shoreline, the wagon master proved accurate. Upstream, the Neosho River coursed through several winding bends slowing the flow passing the two hopeful Tennesseans. So much so that cork bobbers were incorporated closer to the embankment. The cork bobbers waggled against the current for a few minutes then went under at the same time. Unattended at the moment, the poles, supported by a large rock, arched downward. The amateur anglers dashed to their bamboo rods and, much to their surprise, extracted two small catfish.

"Do you think they're keepers?" asked Abel. "Tobias would probably toss them back."

"They're plenty big for me," Pearle answered, while running a new worm through his hook.

The initial catch proved to be the smallest taken that afternoon. They returned to camp with a stringer that made their arms ache. Pearle also thought he heard Abel cuss when he was unable to land a large bass. The youngster smiled to himself. Beneath the façade of pietism, a real man did exist.

When Zack returned with the provisions, the only disappointment expressed was, "I sure wish I was with you guys."

All the pioneers, thanks to the considerate piscators, enjoyed tasty firm catfish. Amanda had learned from Abigail Leffingwell how to improve her cooking with special herbs for seasoning. A little onion, lemon juice, and oregano improved the sweet flavor. Tobias Taylor, making his evening tour of the wagons, was offered a taste at each stop. Without a doubt, the Strawn wagon had the tastiest fish. Of course, it was a fact he kept to himself.

The next morning the journey resumed. Entering the central plains, the pioneers came to the realization that this flat expanse of grassland, extending to the horizon, was a sight they were experiencing for the first time. It was as though they walked on a strange planet in which the familiar sun rose in the distant horizon each morning and, in the evening, set on the skyline's edge.

Traveling at the rate of two miles per hour, the endless monotony had a lethargic effect. His or her torpid state of mind was interrupted once when the lead wagon walker shouted "rattlesnake" but by the time the end prairie schooner passed, no one else had seen it.

The time of year was in their favor. During summer, the landscape of grass would be like a desert. Tobias Taylor made a concerted effort to avoid rivers and seek out fast moving streams in order to water the animals and replenish wagon barrels.

Even with his efforts to minimize undue hardship, the grueling trek, without the slightest deviation, was punishing to the point of monotonous exhaustion. Several of the wagon walkers, as if in a stupor, drifted away from their conveyance. Outriders were forced to herd them back to the side of their own covered wagon. Some held on the sides of the wagon, in order to avoid becoming a stray.

Evening cooking fires grew smaller due to the lack of timber, and socializing more tedious. Some claimed to have seen a herd of buffalo, but Tobias assured them it was only a mirage. He did admit, however, that the area is a favorite territory for grazing.

The ensuing five days, each a duplicate of the other, found the caravan plodding along until it reached the Little Arkansas River near the town of Lyons, Kansas. They made camp in an area said to be where Coronado, in 1541, rested his army of one thousand Spaniards on his quest for *Quivira* and its treasures of gold. Three hundred years later, Abel Strawn and Zachary Wheat were also on a mission, but somewhat less ambitious—they only sought a home of their own.

The sheer fact that civilization was just a few miles away changed the disposition of the pilgrims. They now seemed more animated. Wood along the river made for a central fire to the delight of everyone. Zack Wheat managed to load a few large limbs in his wagon for future use.

Around midnight, a gentle spring rain fell upon the circular camp. The patter of raindrops induced restful slumber and dawn found them still engaged with the sandman. Tobias decided another day of rest was good for the pilgrims and sent a message that no wagons roll until the morrow. The interlude did wonders for their disposition. It also allowed the travelers to take stock of their belongings. Many will need to build a dwelling before winter arrives. Necessary tools omitted at the start must be obtained here at Lyons or Fort Larned, the next destination, 50 miles away.

Abel and Zack sat under a rainproof tarp stretched from the side of Wheat's wagon. Zack put his dry timber to good use and a small fire sputtered in the misty air. Animated by the hissing sound of the coffeepot, Zack rose to pour each of them a cup full of the heady brew.

"Too bad about Bertram and Annaliese Keller," Wheat said flatly.

"Why so?"

"Hear tell of it, their rear axle wood cracked. They won't be going with us in the morning."

"It shouldn't take long to fix it. They can catch up with us afterwards," Abel responded.

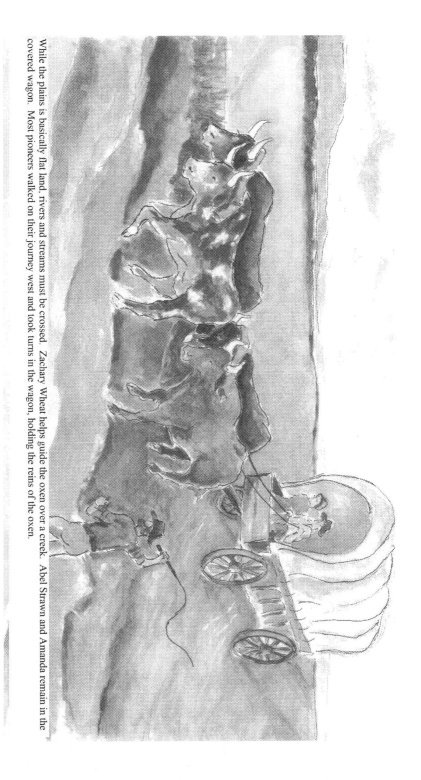

While the plains is basically flat land, rivers and streams must be crossed. Zachary Wheat helps guide the oxen over a creek. Abel Strawn and Amanda remain in the covered wagon. Most pioneers walked on their journey west and took turns in the wagon, holding the reins of the oxen.

"That's only the half of it. These folks are poor as church mice and too proud to let on. I wouldn't be surprised if they sold possessions, repaired the wagon, and returned to wherever they came from."

"Used possessions don't bring much money," Abel stated.

"They do own a cow. A damn good-looking animal. I wonder how much they can sell it for," Wheat pondered.

"Back home, a good dairy cow sells for around fifty dollars."

Both men leaned back and became thoughtful as they sipped the hot coffee. Zack produced a slender cigar, clipped the end off, and took an ember from the fire to light it. Abel withdrew a pipe, a gift from Jack Leffingwell, and packed in a little tobacco saying, "Pass me the ember when you're done with it."

"If my eyes don't deceive me, you're a preacher who smokes."

"Oh, even I have my little sins," Abel confessed.

"Yeah, I heard about one of them from Pearle. Do you kiss your mother with that mouth?" Zack said, while suppressing a grin.

"I better have a long talk with that kid," Abel finally said.

The next morning, the train pulled out minus the Keller wagon. Loosely tethered to Wheat's conveyance was a dairy cow. Before retiring the night before, he visited Bertram and Annaliese Keller and offered them $100 dollars for their female bovine.

On the second day of resuming travel, the immigrants had a shocking experience. Beginning after the usual morning routine and again rolling on the prairie, they were startled by the faint image atop a distant rise. Indian braves, astride their multi-colored ponies, stood like silent sentinels in the smoky haze. The spectacle was enough for the pilgrims to hear their own heartbeat pounding within their chest.

Tobias Taylor called for the wagons to circle and for readiness before he and his scout rode slowly to meet them.

"They seem to be just talking with their hands," Pearle said excitedly.

"Sign language is used when you don't speak the dialect. I know Tobias speaks Choctaw from his Tennessee days. Jack

Leffingwell told me," Abel said, while squinting his eyes to improve the view. Ultimately, the powwow ended and the wagon master and scout returned to the circled wagons.

"I counted twenty braves. They say they are a hunting party looking for buffalo. Nevertheless, they wanted our horses. I managed to convince their leader to accept only five. You must decide which of your horses will be given up. I'll take three from the outriders, and I'm looking for two from you folks. Right now, we're open for volunteers, but, if there isn't any, I'm authorized to select them myself."

Just as Abel was about to offer his, several men stepped forward.

"You can acquire replacements once we reach Fort Larned. I'll see to it that the railroad company pays for them," Tobias promised. With five horses on lead ropes he rode toward the waiting braves. They, in turn, screeched an ear piercing victory shout and galloped away with their loot in tow.

The ensuing days had everyone on high alert. Fortunately, more Indians were not encountered and the party reached Fort Larned on April 5, 1869.

Fort Larned was established to protect both the immigrants traveling the Santa Fe Trail and the budding commerce that followed. It was located in an area where the government held land free from any burden of Indian treaties.

Construction began October 22, 1859, on a site near the Pawnee River fork, and only eight miles from its confluence with the Arkansas River. While the buildings were partially completed, a more suitable location, three miles to the west was agreed upon. The permanent site was completed during midsummer, 1860. Now, the sod buildings and earthworks rested on the south side of the Pawnee, with a big bend of the stream affording a natural barrier. Named for Colonel Benjamin F. Larned, U.S. Army Paymaster, the fort was garrisoned with 160 soldiers.

The Kiowa and Comanches were dissatisfied with their treaty annuities being distributed in Oklahoma and wanted a station on the Arkansas River. As a result, Fort Larned was chosen for this obligation and became a Indian post.

Efforts to relocate Cheyenne and Arapaho tribes farther south were ineffective, especially when a previous treaty granted them land they currently occupy. In an attempt to resolve the situation, Congress authorized a negotiation to be held at Fort Wise—later named Fort Lyon. Chiefs from several tribes attended and came to a controversial agreement calling for annual annuity payments and a new reservation farther south.

Plains Indians do not congregate their villages in any one place. Being nomadic hunters necessitated their dividing into smaller groups for their constant pursuit of sustenance. Accordingly, full representation at any treaty conference was rare. Such was the case at Fort Wise.

From the beginning, many tribes complained that they were misrepresented and refused to honor the treaty. The U.S. government was learning that confining Indians to a permanent location was onerous. Keeping them there proved futile.

At first, the establishment of Fort Larned seemed to have influenced the Indians to show more respect for travelers on the Santa Fe Trail. It was short-lived. As more white people came to the area, the buffalo supply diminished. And, with their principal food chain dramatically reduced, Indians resorted to looting for survival.

The Civil War also had a significant impact on the lives of the Indians. Experienced troops were reassigned and garrisons became undermanned. Soldiers that remained, lacked an understanding of the Indian's predicament, and as a result, the fragile peace began to deteriorate. The Chivington massacre of the Cheyenne at Sand Creek compounded the situation. Strained relations between whites and Indians grew progressively worse until an all-out war started.

With the Civil War over, the U.S. government could give more attention to the warring tribes, and in 1867, called for peace negotiations to settle the matter once and for all. The Kiowa, Apache, Comanche, Arapaho, and Cheyenne came together to attend the conference at Fort Larned; however, the tribal chiefs were uncomfortable at the military post and it was moved near

Medicine Lodge River. The attending tribes were divided into three groups and each group negotiated their own treaty. Basically, the treaties were similar in terms and conditions. Simply stated, the Indians would sacrifice traditional territories for smaller reservations in Oklahoma. Doing so, they would be given allowances of food, clothing, and weapons, plus, ammunition for hunting. Contingent on the ratification of these pacts was the approval of ¾ of the adult males in each tribe. It never happened. Among tribal bands, the emphasis that reservation assignment must be considered temporary, with a permanent reservation made at a later date, was too vague and unacceptable.

Continued depredations by roving bands of Cheyenne prompted the War Department to plan an extensive campaign to chastise the hostiles—called Dog Soldiers. In 1868, the government abandoned the annuity distribution at Fort Larned. Fort Cobb, in the Indian Territory, inherited this function. 1,400 men, including four companies of the 7th cavalry under General George Armstrong Custer, increased the Fort Larned garrison. That however, is another story.

Spring wildflowers began to flaunt their colors of red, yellow, purple, and white. A parade of bluebells, yellow groundsel, wild indigo, plum, and locoweed now dotted the grassy landscape. Pioneers found them beautiful, none the less, Tobias Taylor cautioned them to avoid certain plants especially locoweed. If their future pastures contained these poisonous flowers, they should be removed before cattle and horses are permitted to graze. This was a monitorial some will ignore, and as a result, learn the hard way.

By now, the immigrants had learned that Abel Strawn was a minister of the Methodist Church and beseeched him to lead them, giving thanks for their safety thus far. Gathered within the wagon circle he stood, holding his bible to his chest, and acknowledged gratitude, then asked the Lord's blessing. Now, only a few days away, a new life is imminent, one in which each will be tested. Happiness, hardship, satisfaction, and grief await them all—no one will escape.

CHAPTER FOURTEEN

Jack Leffingwell was readying the wagon for a trip into
town. Melvin Kaufman led the dray horses from the barn.
Asking them to lower their heads, he gently placed the bit in
their mouths and tightened the nosebands. At that point, Jack
positioned the breast collars on the quiet animals. The saddle
was placed on the equine's backs with tails pulled through the
rear loops. Then, the harness breeching was attached to the
apparatus. Melvin moved the wagon behind the cobs and ran the
tongue attachments through the saddle loops. All buckles were
connected and straps tightened.

The operation was a testimony to teamwork. And, of course,
experience, since the procedure was repeated a hundred times.
The women will not accompany the men today, assenting to a
little time on their own. Still, Abigail and Hope had put together
a list of items for them to purchase. With spring planting just
around the corner, Jack intended to buy both seed, and grain for
the animals.

Melvin wouldn't miss a trip to town for the world. It affords
him the opportunity to visit his blacksmith buddy, Ryan Gosling.

Strange how locals seem to mysteriously know when farmers
come to town. Naturally, more rational minds dismiss any claim
to clairvoyance and attribute it to somehow word reaching
them by traditional means. In the case of Jack Leffingwell, his

father-in-law learned of it, during one of his visits, and innocently mentioned it to Frank Riberty. That's all it took for the wheels to start turning. By the time Jack's wagon came into view, the patrons of the Statesville tavern had taken their positions, and, with a foamy glass of beer in their hands, awaited the entrance of the Tennessee mountain man.

"You do realize we won't be able to get out of town until you finish comparing Robert E. Lee and Ulysses Grant. Are you prepared?" asked Melvin.

"All I need is for someone to tell me where I left off," Jack consoled.

Entering town, the wagon was guided to the main street and came to a stop in front of Riberty's general store. Handing the women's list to Melvin, Jack said, "You get the things on the list and I'll go down to the farm and feed barn. When I'm done I'll pick you up."

"You'll find me at the blacksmith's shop. I'll gather what the girls want and leave them by the door so we can load um easier," Melvin stated.

"Sounds like a plan. After everything is loaded, we can park the wagon in Gosling's building."

By happy chance, Maryellen (Riberty) McKnight was helping her parents in the store. In all probability, it would have taken Melvin two hours to find the items on the list. Three yards of chintz, the first item on the list, stopped him in his tracks.

When Maryellen looked up from counting inventory, she observed the plaintive gaze of Hope's husband. Despite the fact several customers were in the store shopping, he looked as though he'd been trapped on the proverbial deserted island. Offering her most reassuring smile, she secretly thought, *'Men, how they make it through life is a miracle. They can build a house, plant a field, provide for their family, and even fight in a war; but, give them a simple chore, along feminine lines, and they're like a deer confronting a mountain lion.'*

"Give me the list, Melvin, I can find things a lot faster," she affirmed.

It was as if the marooned cast-away spotted the sails of his rescue boat. His entire disposition changed to one of relief, as he placed the list in her outreaching hand.

"Could you have someone stack the items by the door? I need to see the blacksmith about something," he requested. "Jack has the wagon and will be back shortly."

"It will all be there when you return, that is, if we're not closed by then," she said knowingly. "I can't wait for you boys today. August is home, so I'll need to make supper."

"Would you kindly mention to him that Jack is in town and we'll be at the Statesville tavern? He wanted to be there when Jack finished his comparison of the generals."

"He'd never forgive me if I didn't," she replied.

* * *

Ryan Gosling was standing in the doorway, donning a dark apron and holding a heavy hammer. The look in his eyes declared the workday has come to an end. The two friends greeted each other with playful jabs to the breadbasket before throwing arms over respective shoulders and marching to the popular alehouse.

Once the door opened, a dramatic change took place. The sober, diligent attitude of the street became a boisterous jangle of shouts and laughter. As Ryan barked his request toward Fritz Adler, the line at the bar separated at the center, making room for the new arrivals. The demeanor in the room was contagious. It was as though the sorcerer's wand had been waved over the entire crew and the slightest animosity disappeared. For those revelers, under the barkeeps roof, it was a special event. Many saw it as the day of Robert E. Lee's vindication, others were not so sure. Nevertheless, the day was significant, and the argument may soon be settled.

Concluding his business at the feed store, Jack stopped by Riberty's before heading to the blacksmith shop. By now, he knew that Melvin was with Ryan Gosling and occupying a stool at the tavern. Frank Riberty, having similar plans, offered help in loading the items Melvin purchased.

"We can drive the wagon to Gosling's barn. He never locks the doors. Your team should be okay for a couple hours," Frank advised.

"I can't stay all night, like last time,"

"Then we better get right at it," Frank declared.

Heads quickly turned to the front door each time the entry knob moved. Apparently, it was an exercise for which none grew tired. Finally, their efforts were rewarded, and a chorus of good-natured cheers welcomed the anticipated visitor.

Shutting the door behind them, Frank Riberty elbowed Jack and nodded toward the table resting near the wall. August McKnight, in civilian clothes, sat with two regular barroom patrons and appeared to have been arguing the debate long before Jack Leffingwell entered the scene. Augie's admiration for Jack was well known by the locals. No one was surprised when Jack joined him and drank the first glass at his table. Aristotle said, "Patience is bitter, but its fruit is sweet." The rowdy crowd, drinking at the bar, soon could care less what some old Greek claimed, even if he did teach Alexander the Great.

The chant for Jack started out softly and then grew like weeds in a flower garden. Revelers chanted Jack, Jack, Jack and kept time with the bottom of their beer mugs. Finally, Frank Riberty uttered, "You better go over there before the windows start cracking. I'll stay here with my son-in-law."

With the sound of Jack's chair scooting on the tavern floor, the incantation dwindled. Melvin, sitting next to Ryan Gosling, was allowed to move over and make room for the mountain man. No sooner had Jack sat down, Fritz Adler placed a fresh draught in front of him.

After a short swig, Jack questioned, "Now, where did we leave off?"

The answers came as a cacophony of mumbles. Coming to the rescue, Jack stated, "I believe it was the end of 1862 and the defensive battle of Fredericksburg. My actual experience is still a little hazy. You might recall that I was wounded, hauled off to Richmond, and suffering from amnesia. Accordingly, my knowledge of what transpired is mostly from conversing with those who were there and reading newspaper accounts.

All the same, it was a major victory for Robert E. Lee and the Army of Northern Virginia. Our newspapers called it, 'A stunning defeat of the invader and a splendid victory to the defender of the sacred soil.' Marse Robert was jubilant, as were the rest of us. On the other hand, Yankee General Burnside was so mad, he could spit fire. He also was desperate to restore his reputation and immediately set about making preparations for a new offensive. Unsurprisingly, it involved feints at Fredericksburg's upstream fords while he took the bulk of his army across the Rappahannock. The plan included a cavalry operation on a grand scale, even though the Confederate mounted force was vastly superior.

Just as his scheme commenced, Burnside received a telegram from President Lincoln stating, 'No major movements are to be made without first informing the White House.'

Old 'Sideburns' smelled a rat and was livid. Only those closest to him knew of his plans, and it seems they were the informants. He quickly headed to Washington to investigate. Burnside later learned his suspicion was valid but President Lincoln refused to disclose the informants. He threatened to resign. Lincoln talked him out of it.

Upon returning to his troops, Burnside revised his previous plan by changing the Rappahannock crossing points. At dawn on January 21, the Union engineers were to push five pontoon bridges across the river, followed by two grand divisions, or about 30,000 soldiers. Meanwhile, another division would distract the Confederates at Fredericksburg.

Burnside must have been born under a bad star. Heavy rains fell the night before and, by morning, the riverbanks became a quagmire. By the 22nd, the artillery, caissons, and wagons were swamped in the mud, bringing the operation to a standstill.

The delay allowed Robert E. Lee to line the opposite shore with troops in gray. Sharpshooters picked off men in blue at will, until Burnside became resigned to his fate. Lincoln replaced him with Maj. Gen. Joseph Hooker on January 26, 1863."

Jack took a moment to gather his thoughts and couldn't help smiling at Augie's emotional roller coaster. He and Melvin made it a point not to discuss the war with him. At times, not doing so, left them with a terrible itch to rain all over the undersized Union officer. Out of respect for Abigail and Maryellen, however, they held their tongues. This evening is a different story. Jack is able to frame the generals in whichever light he has a mind to. There was one indisputable problem, Jack's personal character. No matter what the occasion, the mountain man would always do what's honorable and fair.

"Hey Fritz, you're falling down on the job. Straighten up boy, or I'll call the Kaiser. You got thirsty men here. Set us up with another glass of giggle water," Ryan shouted. The Teutonic tap puller was two steps ahead of him. He had filled a couple pitchers of the golden brew and placed them behind the counter. He grabbed hold of their handles and sat them on top of the mahogany bar.

"The Kaiser speaks German, not hillbilly, you could never get through to him," Fritz answered. The merrymakers responded with cat calls in an attempt to goad the blacksmith, but Ryan was too busy filling empty glasses. Once he finished the job, Ryan turned to the table by the wall and asked, "Hey Augie, where were you hiding when all that was going on?"

Frank Riberty reached across the table and patted his son-in-law's arm saying, "If these guys didn't like you, they wouldn't take the time to bust your balls."

Augie understood and came back with, "You ought to know, Ryan. We both were hiding in the same spot."

When Jack cleared his throat, the banter quickly ended. He raised his beer glass as a silent toast to Augie and began, "After the victory at Fredericksburg, General Lee took a little time to bask in his popularity, and then rested his army. The

Confederate Army of Northern Virginia took up winter quarters near Fredericksburg for a needed period to repose and recuperate from the most vicious battle thus far.

By the end of January, 1863, both Robert E. Lee and Ulysses S. Grant had won significant victories. The outcomes, however, were quite different. Grant's victories at Belmont, Fort Henry, Fort Donelson, Shiloh, Iuka, and Corinth greatly expanded Union control in western Kentucky and Tennessee, as well as, northern Mississippi. He managed to accomplish this while incurring fewer casualties than those imposed on the Confederates. Meanwhile, Lee's victories at the Seven Days', Cedar Mountain, Second Manassas, and Fredericksburg had foiled the Union's strategic offenses. On the downside, there was a negative aspect. The embarrassing Maryland Campaign lost any possibility of European intervention and nearly cost Lee his army to boot. Mounting casualties, and Marse Robert's constant demand for reinforcements, drained other areas of their fighting men. The end result, unfortunately, made Grant's job much easier.

While we were at winter quarters, General Grant stayed right at it, taking steps aimed at capturing Vicksburg, Mississippi, our last significant bastion on the Mississippi River. Stymied at first, he persisted and ultimately carried out one of the greatest military campaigns in history."

"Where do you come off claiming that," yelled someone in the crowd. He was obviously angry.

"It's not me, my friend, that claim is in print all over the Country. I was about to describe it if y'all are interested," Jack replied.

"Wait until I go get my gun," Ryan shouted, and then motioned for Fritz, while the gathering burst into laughter.

Once the frivolity slowed down, Jack raised his hand, signifying he was ready to continue.

"Grant used three major diversionary feints to throw rebel soldiers off balance. Our boys were so bamboozled, we didn't detect when Grant moved the bulk of his army down the west bank of the Mississippi River and conducted an amphibious crossing to the eastern shore. At that time we outnumbered him but couldn't ascertain his movements or locate his whereabouts. Over the three weeks following his troops' landing, Grant outmaneuvered and defeated us in five separate battles. The Confederate Army of Vicksburg was led by Lt. Gen. John C. Pemberton, who, like many others, resigned his commission in the Union and joined the Confederate cause. After losing the previous engagements against Grant, and suffering heavy losses, he led his men back into the defenses of Vicksburg. Grant made two unsuccessful assaults on the city; then, using better judgment, settled into a siege.

On July 3, 1863, General Pemberton sent a note of capitulation to Grant. At first, Grant demanded unconditional surrender, and later, he reconsidered. It would have occupied his army for months to ship that many troops north. And, not wanting to feed 30,000 hungry Confederates in Union prison camps, he offered to parole all prisoners. Considering their destitute state of dejection and hunger, he never expected them to fight again. *Au contraire mon générale,* most of the prisoners, who were paroled, were exchanged and back in the active Confederate Army soon thereafter.

Abraham Lincoln believed that the fastest way to win the war was to defeat Robert E. Lee's Army of Northern Virginia. Capturing territory was less important. To date, the generals assigned the task have failed miserably. His hopes now ride on General Joseph 'Fighting Joe' Hooker.

Toward the end of April, 1863, we were still ensconced in the winter camp at Falmouth, outside of Fredericksburg, Virginia. We figured a battle was coming when the 13th Alabama was added to the brigade. What we didn't know was that Union General Hooker had crossed the Rappahannock River to make another attempt to capture Richmond. He had developed a plan to have his infantry concentrate near Chancellorsville and another force facing Fredericksburg, a double envelopment attacking Lee from both his front and rear.

The Union cavalry had already begun a long-distance raid against Lee's supply lines, but the operation was completely ineffectual. On May 1, Hooker's army advanced from Chancellorsville toward Lee and the abridged Army of Northern Virginia. Lee had made the risky decision to divide the Confederate army, leaving a force at Fredericksburg to confront and deter Union forces posted there.

At the most critical moment, 'Fighting Joe' lost his nerve and, against the advice of his subordinates, moved to a defensive position around Chancellorsville, thus, ceding the initiative to General Lee. 'Marse Robert' pounced on the opportunity and launched multiple attacks against the Union position. Confederate artillery found a favorable location on a rise, a short distance to the southwest, and battered the Union center.

The 7th Tennessee Regiment played a significant role in the assault. Our marksmen kept a constant fusillade of long-distant accuracy with chilling results. To the Yankees, it was like death came out of nowhere followed by the demonic whistle of the Whitworth bullet."

"Weren't you the only marksman with a Whitworth rifle?" Frank Riberty asked from across the room.

"To the best of my knowledge," answered Jack.

"Then, why didn't you say so?"

"I don't like to brag when there's killing involved," was the mountain man's rejoinder.

Leave it up to Ryan Gosling to brighten the situation when he called out for more beer. It also afforded a lull, during which a line hurriedly formed outside the toilet room door. Those with a less genteel mien just paraded outside to the bushes in back of the alehouse.

Natural bodily functions completed, the audience returned to their previous station and immediately began to duplicate the condition that sent them outside in the first place. With Ryan Gosling leading them on, Melvin Kaufman urged Jack to pick up where he left off saying, "It was similar to the shooting gallery, at last year's County fair. Bluecoat soldiers toppled over steadily until Jack's rifle became too hot to hold."

"What did you do about that, Jack?" someone asked. The crowd had refocused on why they were there.

"I had a bucket of water at my side and just dipped the Whitworth in it. I'll never forget the smell of air filled with cordite. It was like a cloudy gray fog. At times, it got so thick that the sharpshooters temporarily lost their target, until a helpful breeze brought it back in sight.

Meanwhile, General Lee determined that the Union army had, as yet, not refortified its right flank. He divided the army a second time and sent General Stonewall Jackson's corps of twenty-eight thousand men, around the Union right flank, to attack. It required a twelve-mile march over roundabout roads, and done without detection. Well, Jackson's march didn't escape detection, but he continued as though it had.

Hooker believed that General Lee was retreating. When he realized that wasn't the case, it was too late to warn Maj. Gen. Oliver O. Howard, his officer responsible for his right flank. Howard's only defense against a side assault was two cannons pointing out into the surrounding fields of brambles, thickets, and vines, known as the Wilderness.

When Jackson's rebels exploded out of the woods, screaming the rebel yell, most of the Federal troops were sitting down to dinner and had their rifles unloaded and stacked. A few bluecoats noticed rabbits and foxes fleeing in their direction, but made nothing of it. The Union general made futile attempts to redeem his inadequate preparations, to no avail. Several thousand of his troops retreated to a clearing across the road from the Chancellor mansion, where Union cannons gave them cover to reorganize for a defensive stand. By then, the momentum of Jackson's attack had passed.

Stonewall wanted to press his advantage before Hooker and his army could regain their bearings and plan a counterattack. He was well aware of the disparity in numbers and how quickly the North was able to add more troops.

It was a clear evening and the moon was full. Jackson led a small reconnaissance party to determine the feasibility of a night attack. Traveling beyond the farthest advance of his men, they were incorrectly identified as Union cavalry on their return. Tragedy occurred when southern guards, thinking them the enemy, opened fire and three bullets struck Jackson. Incoming artillery rounds prevented stretcher-bearers from quickly delivering Jackson for treatment. Once doctors saw him, his left arm had to be amputated before moving him to Fairfield, a plantation near Guinea Station, Virginia, where the beloved southern hero died from complications.

The two halves of Lee's army were still separated. Union General Daniel E. Sickles' third corps was positioned atop high ground at Hazel Grove, blocking Jackson's men. Once that obstruction was removed by a questionable order from Hooker, the frontal attack on Chancellorsville began in full.

Initial waves were beaten back by Union troops stationed behind strong earthworks. However, the men in butternut continued to press forward. It marked the first time, in the war in Virginia, where Confederate cannons held a decided advantage over their Union counterparts. Similar to manpower, the North had a lopsided advantage in cannons. Lee arranged each scrimmage so they never had the opportunity to put them all in use at any given time. In the battle of guns, Lee's cannon on Hazel Grove and the Plank Road dueled Hooker's artillery on neighboring Fairview Hill. The Federals soon ran low on ammunition and, as Confederate sharpshooters picked off the gun crews, the Union was forced to withdraw.

Hooker's so called double development at Fredericksburg, in the end, suffered a similar fate. Yankee forces made two attacks against the infamous stone wall on Marye's Heights, and both times were repulsed with numerous casualties. A party under a flag of truce was allowed to approach to collect their wounded. While close to the stone wall, they were able to observe how meagerly the Confederate line was manned. Upon their return, the Union soldiers shouted, 'They got hardly anybody behind them walls. They are bluffing us.'

A third attack was successful in overrunning the Confederate position. The road to Chancellorsville was now open, but the bluecoats wasted time in forming a marching column. Their dalliance allowed us to set up delaying lines to hold them until reinforcements arrived. The Union army couldn't break our lines of defense and finally were forced to withdraw across the Rappahannock.

General Lee, despite being outnumbered by a ratio of two to one, won arguably his greatest victory of the War. But, he paid a terrible price for it. By losing some 22 percent of his fighting force meant the future army would necessarily be smaller. They could not be replaced, a profound example of the war of attrition.

Nevertheless, his remarkable victories in Virginia demonstrated superior leadership and military skills. Against overwhelming odds, Lee won out facing Hooker at Chancellorsville. Even Union prisoners cheered him as he rode in front of his troops. The modest general was now euphoric and became his own most ardent cheerleader. In his mind, no army could defeat him.

The mood in the south was varied. The celebration of Lee's victory was overshadowed by the loss of their most beloved hero, Stonewall Jackson. In Washington, President Lincoln was shocked and angry. General Hooker was quick to blame his subordinate, General Howard. Others recalled ill-fated decisions made by Hooker. In spite of the turmoil, Lincoln chose to retain Hooker. But, obviously, unsure about his sobriquet, Fighting Joe.

Looking forward, the sheer numbers of active-duty Union troops outweighed southern forces by nearly 300 percent. And now, 150,000 black soldiers had been added to Abraham Lincoln's military.

After the costly battle of Chancellorsville, Lee's forces encamped in order to recuperate from the intensity of combat, take care of the wounded, and reassign troops. General Henry 'Harry' Heth was now corps commander of our regiment. We didn't know much about him at the time, other than General Lee called him by his first name. A sure sign the Gray Fox likes you.

Our spirits were at a low level after hearing that our benefactor, Stonewall Jackson, was killed. We had never met him. I had found favor because of my shooting skills, but hadn't exchanged a single word. Because of his personal largesse, I was treated in Richmond and received the best of care. He was a myth to most of us; and, now, every rebel soldier felt marooned in a gloomy sea of gray uniforms.

The first week in camp went without drills. It gave the men the opportunity to set up personal accommodations, clean and repair their weapons, and write letters to loved ones and friends. It was a wonderful time of idleness; nonetheless, we knew how the army frowns upon it.

After the death of Stonewall Jackson, General Lee reorganized the army from two large corps into three smaller ones. General James Longstreet commanded the first, Gen. James Ewell the second, and A. P. Hill (Ambrose Powell Hill) the third corps. Lee was riding high wearing a smile of confidence. Scuttlebutt had it that he was busy planning his next move.

Our army in the western front was coming apart. We were unable to handle Union general Ulysses S. Grant's campaign against Vicksburg. The top military advisers wanted to save Vicksburg, but Lee persuaded Jefferson Davis to overrule them. They indicated that adding James Longstreet's Corps would save the day; all the same, Lee needed him for what he had planned—another invasion of the North. Putting past failures behind him, Marse Robert was well aware that his army was short on supplies. The rich farming districts of Pennsylvania were bursting with resources, and there for the taking. He convinced Jeff Davis that by demonstrating the ability to invade, it would stimulate peace activity in the North.

On June 3, 1863, without the usual pomp, Lee's army quietly evacuated the Fredericksburg camp and began a move west into the valley of Virginia. At this point, the destination was still remaining a secret—rumors abound."

"You mean to say that the officers just told you to march without telling you where to?" Ryan apparently woke from a temporary stupor.

"That's about the size of it," Melvin added. You needn't be listening closely to detect a slight slur in his speech.

"A military camp grapevine kept us ahead of the officers more often than not," Jack added, and then continued, "Not knowing where we're headed isn't that bad. The worst part of being in the infantry, outside of getting shot, is the long distant marches. Making the trek even more difficult, infantrymen tote nearly fifty pounds of gear counting their rifle, double rounds of ammunition, blankets, clothing, a three-day allotment of food, and personal items. We start out in regular military order four abreast. After a short while, under the hot sun, soldiers begin to break down and disperse all over the road. Troops also quickly get fatigued and need to stop often in order to rest, replenish lost fluids, and wait on stragglers who fell off along the way.

At night we camp out in the open and keep our fingers crossed that it doesn't rain. We all removed our blankets from the rucksacks and spread out around a crackling fire. Firewood was plentiful, and, it didn't take long before we realized that the direction we were going was only a diversionary tactic."

Melvin may have been in his cups, but he listened intently, "Jack, you were the only one who figured out where we were going. The rest of us didn't have a clue."

The mountain man took the interruption as a time to pause for a few minutes. Frank Riberty slowly walked to the window and scanned the main street, more for the need to stretch his aching legs than being inquisitive about the goings on in town. Back at his table he stated, "You're losing a lot of business, Ryan. I saw two customers walk away after finding you gone." He was smiling to himself.

"Frank, I'm the only blacksmith within a twenty mile radius. They'll be back," Ryan said confidently. "I ain't no haberdasher."

"The second day of the journey, the 7th regiment met up with General Ewell's corps at Culpeper Court House. As I recall, it was dusk and we remained for the night," Jack continued. "We remained there for a few days while General Ewell and Hill reviewed maps and reported conditions and progress. Then, the two divisions separated again with Ewell continuing in a southwestern direction and A. P. Hill's corps marching due north, thus answering any questions as to where the final destination lay. Marse Robert was taking us to Pennsylvania.

The journey wasn't easy. It necessitated fording the Rappahannock River, which fortunately was at low level and could be done without pontoon bridges. Always a formidable challenge, the Blue Ridge Mountains needed to be crossed for us to reach the Shenandoah Valley. General Hill rested us east of the Shenandoah River to wait for the arrival of General J. E. B. Stuart's cavalry.

Lee's plan called for Jeb Stuart to secure and hold Ashby's Gap to prevent elements of Hooker's Union army from interfering with our tramp toward Pennsylvania. Stuart was delayed. Unbeknown to the Confederate cavalryman, the Yankee mounted troops had pushed aside pickets at Beverly's Ford and surprised our squadron. Several Union charges were beat back before they ultimately withdrew. When Stuart finally reached Ashby's Gap, the weather had turned for the worse. The wind had picked up and rain came down in sheets. Soldiers scattered in all direction seeking shelter.

By morning, the torrent had subsided, but the division faced the problem of fording the elevated waters of the Shenandoah River. While some attempted to wade across, the majority traveled over pontoon bridges built by division engineers. It took most of the day for men and materiel to reach the other side and continue on the northern junket. Toward the middle of June we were joined by General James Longstreet's First Corps, while Jeb Stuart's cavalry screened the Union from locating the main source of Lee's army.

Continuing north we found farm crops plentiful and foraging unburdensome. Cornfields were in full tassel and fruit trees at early ripening stage. Many of the farms featured barns with colorful geometric decorations, painted in order to bring good luck and protection to its owners. These hex signs did nothing to stop the foraging of nearly thirty thousand rebel troops. Fortunately, for the disgruntled farmers, they were troops on the march and soon to be gone.

At this point, General Lee had managed to perplex Union general Hooker, who knew the Army of Northern Virginia was on the move, but couldn't find them. Lincoln, still skeptical of his general's ability, was now concerned about protecting the capital at Washington. This resulted in two armies parallel to each other and tediously moving northward.

Blind to each other's whereabouts, Lee remained undaunted and continued marching his seventy-thousand-man machine steadily toward Pennsylvania. By late June, all three corps came together outside Hagerstown, Maryland and set up camp. The view from above was like a sprawling city made up with camp fires and pup tents. In addition to soldiers, nearly two thousand wagons, over twenty thousand horses, mules, and livestock, made up the southern aggregate.

Marse Robert's main goal of the campaign was for the Confederate army to accumulate food and supplies outside of Virginia with minimal negative impact on civilians. That proved impossible because an army of this size would consume five hundred tons of food and other supplies daily. Even though we didn't take the food outright, disgruntled farmers and merchants were maddened when we reimbursed with Confederate money. General Lee was disappointed by the attitude of the populace in Maryland. Being a sister slave state, he expected a more generous contribution to the cause. Their attitude was no surprise to the rank and file. Americans, no matter what their bent, resent anyone willfully taking their possessions. Be that as it may, since Maryland voted to not allow Union troops passage through the state, General Lee counted on more from them.

Union general Hooker might not have known exactly what Lee had in mind. He was sure of one thing—with the Confederate army gone, the capital, at Richmond, had to be unprotected. All the same, Lincoln ordered him to concentrate on Lee's army.

General Ewell's Second Corps was first to pull out of camp. Shortly thereafter, he was followed by the other two corps. General Longstreet headed north to Chambersburg, then, turned to the east. Our division, under General Ambrose Hill, marched north, and then turned east toward Gettysburg. The fateful battle lay ahead.

Up till now, Jeb Stuart's cavalry had been circumnavigating the Union army. Lee's instructions were for him to guard the mountain passes with part of his force, while the Army of Northern Virginia was still south of the Potomac. His orders also stipulated that he cross the river with the remainder and screen the right flank of Ewell's Second Corps. Instead of taking a direct route north near the Blue Ridge Mountains, Stuart chose to move his three best brigades between the Union army and Washington.

The decision to disregard Lee's orders proved misfortunate. Although he intended to win favor by capturing large amounts of supplies and cause havoc near the enemy capital, the Union army was on the move and blocked his proposed route. Stuart was forced to veer even farther to the east than he originally planned. His misjudgment not only prevented him from linking up with Ewell as ordered, it deprived General Lee the intelligence wing of the army. After several skirmishes along the way, Stuart finally reached General Lee at Gettysburg on July 2, the day after the battle began.

Prior to the battle at Gettysburg, Union general-in-chief, Maj. Gen. Henry W. Halleck planned a countermove to take advantage of the lightly defended Confederate capital. Two corps, commanded by General John A. Dix, was ordered to move on Richmond. Dix was confused. He wasn't actually ordered to attack the town; therefore, he caused as much damage possible by destroying railroad bridges and other unprotected targets. While Dix was a respected politician, he was not an aggressive general and only employed threatening gestures against the city. The net effect did force Marse Robert to hold back some troops to guard the capital.

Hooker's constant complaint over his officers began to involve Halleck. Now the bickering started between Hooker and Halleck and persisted until the contention about defending the garrison at Harpers Ferry. Hooker requested additional troops from the garrison and was refused by the War Department. In a state of pique, 'Fighting Joe' asked to be relieved of the army command. President Lincoln immediately accepted his request and a surprised Gen. George Meade was ordered to replace him. In all likelihood, it was Lincoln's response to Hooker's embarrassing defeat at Chancellorsville and his weakness in reacting to Lee's second invasion north of the Potomac."

Jack stopped for a break and some water. He had become hoarse due to the extensive oral discourse and motioned for Fritz. Ryan Gosling, always ready to assist the German bar keep, shouted, "Hey Fritz, get off you dead ass and bring the man a glass of water. You can refill our mugs while you're at it. Since you can't taste the difference between the two, what you pass off as beer is the one with foam on top." Fritz just shook his head and handed Jack a tall tumbler of water with a chunk of ice floating on top. The hoarseness disappeared after a couple swallows and the mountain man returned to his account of the battle of Gettysburg.

"Thanks to Stuart's disobedience, Lee was in the dark as to how far the Union army had moved north. That alone was unnerving, however, making matters worse, the Confederate army was strung out and miles away from coming together.

Orders were sent to immediately concentrate the forces around Cashtown, a village located at the base of South Mountain and about eight miles from Gettysburg.

On June 30, a brigade led by Brig. Gen. J. Johnson Pettigrew, ventured toward the city and stumbled upon Union cavalry arriving south of town. Pettigrew hurried back to Cashtown to inform Generals Hill and Heth. Although, Lee gave specific orders to avoid a broad engagement, until the entire army was

George Edward Moon

concentrated, Hill decided to mount what he called a significant reconnaissance in force, to determine the exact size and strength of the enemy legions. The following morning, July 1, two brigades of Heth's division advanced to Gettysburg. One of the brigades, General Archer's, included the Seventh Tennessee Regiment, and shortly, Melvin and I, along with the other sharpshooters, would be engaging in the battle.

Union General John Buford now knew the rebel forces were at the gate and fell back to establish three defensive lines on ridges west of town. Since his cavalry division was small compared to the Confederate infantry forces, his main purpose was to confront them with a delaying action, buying time until Union infantrymen could set up stronger defenses on the hills south of town.

Heth's division moved forward meeting light resistance from Union cavalry outposts. As they progressed, his troops encountered dismounted cavalry units firing from behind fence posts using their breech-loading carbines. Cavalrymen choose such weapons because they are shorter and easier to maneuver. The Yankee delaying tactic proved successful; and, the vanguard of the Unions first corps soon arrived, adding more defensive troops.

South of the pike, General Archer's brigade launched out from McPherson's Woods. Our men in gray were moving in double time and giving the rebel yell at the top of our lungs. It probably was the first time most of the bluecoats heard the head-splitting holler. Yankee prisoners agreed that it was unnerving and scared the piss out of them. The sharpshooters took positions so we could concentrate on Union artillery units. We managed to keep cannon fire at a minimum. Any bluecoat on horseback automatically became a prime target. Union general John Reynolds fit the description, and fell victim while directing his troops and artillery placements east of the woods. Still and all, Archer's charge met stiff resistance from Yankee troops, who held their line.

Bolstered by rapidly arriving Union infantry soldiers, the Federals counterattacked and pushed the Confederates back across Willoughby Run. General Archer, exhausted by it all, took cover in a thicket. His hiding place was discovered by bluecoats, who took him prisoner. Archer became the first General officer taken prisoner while under Lee's command.

Now, Heth's entire division was brought into action along with two divisions of Ewell's Second Corps. The additional manpower turned the tide, forcing the Federal positions to collapse, with their soldiers retreating to the high ground south of town. At days end, Marse Robert deemed it a Southern victory, with the enemy routed and in retreat. The facts tend to speak otherwise. It was true, that once the Confederates had superior numbers, we were able to push the first line of Union defense to higher ground, but not without sustaining heavy losses.

With General Archer captured, the brigade was consolidated under General H. H. Walker's command and held in reserve during the second day. Although, not in the battle, the Seventh Tennessee Regiment had to remain alert and ready to resume at a moment's notice. We cleaned our rifles, refilled ammunition packs, and came to the conclusion that Billy Yank has turned into a much better fighter. We also were convinced that some of them had Henry repeating rifles. It can fire off fifteen rounds without being reloaded, making it perfect for fighting at close range, and a good weapon against an infantry attack.

That night, it seemed as though both sides had taken the evening off. Sounds of human pain and misery came from the hospital tents as more of the wounded were brought in. The dead would not be buried this evening, as neither side could claim victory. That unsavory task must wait at least one more day.

Troops on both sides continued to arrive during the night and took their positions on the field. The Union line ran south of town and extended for nearly two miles. Men in blue jackets were atop elevations with such names as Cemetery Hill, Culp's Hill, and Little Round Top. Lee's Confederate line, nearly five miles long, paralleled the Union delineation and curved around the interior defenders. Lee's plan called for Longstreet to attack the Union left flank and move up the enemy line.

The plan may have been a good one if Marse Robert had recent information. Jeb Stuart was still absent and the available intelligence proved to be faulty. As a result, Longstreet failed to circle beyond the Federal left flank and ended up facing Union General Daniel Sickles' Third Corps directly in his path. Taken by surprise, Longstreet reacted out of conditioned reflex and drove into Sickles with such force that they needed immediate reinforcements. Union General Meade, without hesitation, responded with twenty thousand more troops in blue uniforms. The rebel juggernaut pressed against positions with such names as, The Wheatfield, Sherfy's Peach Orchard, and Plum Valley. They even reached the crest of Cemetery Hill, but could not hold their position in the face of counterattacks.

As darkness drew near, the Lincolnites managed to hold on to the major portion of the vital hills. The Union army's interior lines were laid out so that commanders were able to shift troops quickly to critical areas. Even so, many Union brigades lost half their men in their dogged effort to preserve their real estate. Neither side was enthused about fighting at night; thus, the second day ended with heavy losses and no army claiming victory.

There's something abnormal about the lull when two major armies confront each other. The bizarre scene during the gloaming of that second day is one I'll not soon forget. When nightshades fell, the incongruous reality of bands playing music, echoed across each campsite. The sounds of the banjo, fiddle, guitar, fife, and bugle came together to create an eerie respite from the horrendous event which took place just hours before. The dreamlike expression was accompanied by the voices of a hundred different cities singing ballads accustom to their previous purlieu. Once the marital and patriotic songs ended, a more sentimental attitude prevailed; and, before the music stopped, both sides seemed to join in singing, 'Home Sweet

Home.' Hard fighting men with iron wills had tears shinning in their eyes when the sad sound of silence finally took place."

The tavern gallery extracted a dozen white handkerchiefs once Jack Leffingwell pulled his own to wipe his eyes. Across the room, August McKnight emulated the others and loudly blew his nose. No matter how talented the writer or dramatic the narrator, a true description of war falls short of the actual experience. Like Jack Leffingwell and the sharpshooters, August McKnight knows that experience firsthand. Tears do not embarrass such men, when memories are recounted.

"One of Robert E. Lee's greatest assets was his ability to perceive the proclivities of Lincoln's generals. In most cases, outnumbered by the forces against him, Lee responded with skillful, agile, and competent countermeasures. That is why his orders for the third day of battle fell on the skeptical ears of his wary generals. Previous attacks on the Union's flanks had failed the day before. The results of his approach did not dishearten Lee one iota. It only made him more determined to continue with the present course of action. Perhaps 'Granny Lee' was still riding the euphoric surge from his victory at Chancellorsville. In any case, if Longstreet and Ewell must carry out the commander's orders, they can only pray for better results.

On Friday, July 3, 1863, Confederate prayers went unanswered. With the casualties of the previous day still not completely counted, Lee's faithful sons of Dixie renewed their charge against Union fortifications. From the very beginning, the shoe was on the other foot. A smaller army attacked one larger, and well-defended. In order to be successful, the rebels needed at least a three to one advantage in manpower. Unlike Lincoln's other generals, Meade had better instincts, and didn't fear Lee coming up with an alternate plan of brilliant tactics. Instead, he figured Lee would continue the same as the day before, and prepared for it. National troops were reinforced and began an artillery bombardment driving back multiple Confederate attacks. With no progress made, and heavy casualties realized, the futile assaults were discontinued.

Lee was forced to change his plans. General Longstreet would now command divisions of his own First Corps, plus six brigades of A. P. Hill's Third Corps, and strike at the Union line at Cemetery Ridge. About the same time the rebels gave up the ghost at Culp's Hill, all the artillery the Confederacy could muster was brought to bear on the Federal positions at the well-defended elevation. Over 150 cannons began the largest bombardment in the war. Designed to weaken the enemy, the cannonade failed to materially affect the Union position. It also made our situation worse because the low ammunition supply was diminished even further. The National Army held its fire for a short time, allowing the rebels to initiate the contest, then opened up with about eighty cannons of their own, and braced for the insurgent's infantry attack that was sure to follow.

From the very beginning, Confederate General Longstreet was concerned about the strength of the Union defensive positions and advocated a strategic movement around the left flank of the enemy to secure good ground between him and the capital. Such a move would place the onus on Union General Meade and compel him to attack our defensive stations. In so doing, he would find himself in open territory and subject to our armaments. Lee refused the 'Old War Horse' and stood adamant for his original plan.

Now, on that third and fateful day of combat, Lee called for a full frontal attack even though its futility was predicted by Longstreet. It was reminiscent of lines in Alfred, Lord Tennyson's poem, *Theirs not to make reply, Theirs not to reason why, Theirs but to do and die.*

In the early afternoon, about 12,500 Confederate infantry soldiers moved from the ridgeline and advanced over a battle-strewn field to Cemetery Ridge. These heroic young farm boys charged through the enfilade of musket and rifle fire. All the while, Federal cannon balls were bounding through their lines, killing whomever they met. The rebel yell was overmatched by the screaming shells of canisters and grape that brought down eight to ten men at a time. Facing the torrent of 2,000 musket and rifles, being fired in unison, they still managed to momentarily penetrate the Federal line, but were unable to hold the position. Nearly half the attackers lay on the field either killed or wounded.

Nine brigades took part in the assault, but only three were commanded by General George Pickett. Nevertheless, the desperate drive became known as Pickett's Charge. Six brigades from General A. P. Hill's Third Corps also took part. The 7th Tennessee became a component of Pickett's left flank. Two of the marksmen were wounded. Abel Strawn was struck in the shoulder by a minié ball and Melvin Kaufman took a piece of shrapnel in his leg when a canister exploded nearby. Artillery soldiers helped both to the field hospital.

The massive frontal attack lasted less than one hour. Our soldiers were decimated. While the Union claimed 1,500 casualties, we suffered over 6,000, of which, 1,100 were killed on the open stretch.

The luster is off the shine for General Robert E. Lee. His trusting soldiers would follow him through the gates of hell if need be. Today, they did just that. As the third day of battle came to an end, the clouds turned dark and a steady rain came down. The two armies watched one another while the heavy drencher washed across the bloody battlefield. That night, Lee evacuated the town of Gettysburg and reformed into a defensive position on Seminary Ridge. Union General Meade was cautious against reversing the advantage and did not take the bait.

Both armies began to collect their wounded and bury some of their dead. Over the last three days, nearly eight thousand soldiers had been killed and remained on the battlefield.

General Lee's next strategic move was to organize the mass retreat of his army. The dramatic fallback consisted of a seventeen-mile-long wagon train of supplies and wounded men. General Meade's army followed the retrogression but wasn't enthusiastic about attacking it. By the time he decided to advance, the Gray Fox was long gone. Now, only Meade's cavalry harassed the retreating caravan until the Army of Northern Virginia was beyond pursuit.

During the same period Lee was beaten at Gettysburg, Union General Grant captured Vicksburg, Mississippi, and took control of the river. Governing the Mississippi River, coupled with effective naval blockages of Southern ports, virtually guaranteed the ultimate Federal victory. It was only a matter of time. A similar conclusion could be drawn when considering active troop strength. As it now stood, the Union had 611,250 men available for duty while the Confederacy could only muster 233,586. The disparity grew worse when it was announced that over one hundred thousand former slaves were now wearing Union blue.

Outside of a few minor skirmishes, Lee's army returned to their camp near Fredericksburg to quarter for the winter.

In October, 1863, after Grant's victory at Vicksburg, President Lincoln put him in charge of the entire western theater of war, except Louisiana. A few weeks earlier General William Rosecrans and the Union Army of the Cumberland suffered a defeat at the hands of General Braxton Bragg and the Confederate Army of Tennessee at the battle of Chickamauga. Rosecrans withdrew his army to the city of Chattanooga and took advantage of previous Confederate works to erect strong defensive positions. Unfortunately, the supply lines into Chattanooga were at risk and the Confederates soon occupied the surrounding heights and laid siege upon the Union forces.

Grant's first action was to open up a supply line to the trapped army. At the same time he organized three armies to attack Confederate General Braxton Bragg's troops occupying Missionary Ridge and Lookout Mountain. After an extensive battle, Bragg's forces on Lookout Mountain were defeated and surrendered a thousand prisoners. All the while, the Union Army of the Cumberland continued their assault on Missionary Ridge until they also were forced into a disorganized retreat. Having been routed by the National Army, Bragg retreated to Dalton, Georgia and offered his resignation to Jefferson Davis. The Confederate President accepted it immediately.

Ulysses S. Grant received another promotion and was invited to Washington. In the eyes of President Lincoln, General Ulysses Grant was his favorite commissioned officer. Not so much because of his strategic military skills—although he had ample—but at last, here was a general willing to fight. Lincoln still begrudged General Meade for his failure to pursue Lee after defeating him at Gettysburg. Consequently, in March 1864, Lincoln made Grant commander of all Union Armies."

Jack Leffingwell took a breather for a few minutes when a crowd of listeners formed around Melvin Kaufman, who had dropped his trousers to display the scars left by the metal shrapnel shards. It was a brief scene making Jack's story more personal and valid. It also gave the mountain man the opportunity to suspend recounting the final year of the conflict until a later date. Much to their chagrin, the group acquiesced and reluctantly allowed Jack and Melvin to return to the farm.

Not all of the patrons were disappointed. August McKnight, for one, was happy to go home to Maryellen's supper. Somewhat pleased with Jack's version of the rebellion, he will make certain to be in attendance once the story resumes. Obviously, Melvin and Jack were appreciative for similar reasons. Especially since their last outing resulted in several days of female coolness.

Ryan Gosling and a few of his hard drinking cronies remained. After all, the bar won't close for several hours.

* * *

The ride back to the farm was most agreeable. Enough sunlight remained to finish afternoon chores before dark. Moving at a leisurely pace, the dray horse gave a hitch in her step as a family of foxes dashed across the road in front. Scanning the ditch alongside the wagon's dusty pathway, Melvin said, "She must have a den somewhere along the culvert. The babies sure are cute."

"You ought to be glad her den is there, rather than closer to the farm. They'd be preying on Hope's chickens every night," Jack replied.

"I suppose. Not to change the subject, but did you notice how old Augie reacted to your recount of the war? He seemed happier than a pig in shit. Maybe you're making Grant look too good," Melvin suggested.

"Don't worry my friend, things will work out when I finish the tale," reassured the mountain man.

When the wagon turned down the lane leading to the farm, Jack asked, "You folks eating with us tonight?"

"I don't think so. Hope mentioned she would have a nice supper prepared when we got back."

"Then I'll drop you off at your house. I can unharness the mare by myself. If we have a nice day tomorrow, we can put some of this seed in the ground," Jack said.

After unhooking the horse, Jack led her to the water trough, then to a stall where a bag of oats was waiting. Satisfied with the surroundings, he closed the barn door and headed for the house. About halfway there, Sarah Jane and Jozef came running, worked up over some previous event.

"Daddy, mama made Jack Junior stay in his room and not come out," Sarah Jane quickly confessed.

"Uh huh, and he will never be able to come out to play with me," Jozef was in tears.

"What happened?" Jack tried to look serious.

Sarah Jane put her hand to little Jozef's chest and said, "Let me tell it. Well, Jack Junior and Jozef were walking around the farm, up to no good, when they spied something little down at the lake. They ran down there and found a tiny bear cub. Well, Jack Junior picked it up and brought it up to the house. When mother saw it, she told Jack to take it back because its mama will be very unhappy finding it gone."

"So far, I haven't heard anything that would precipitate being sent to his room," Jack said calmly.

"Well, Jack Junior called mother an old meanie," Sarah stated.

Suppressing a smile, Jack said, "Now, that could result in being punished."

Jozef was still whimpering.

"Stop crying, Jozef. You guys will be back at it tomorrow morning," consoled Jack, as he hefted him up on his shoulders and the trio walked the final distance to the front porch.

Abigail met her husband the moment he stepped inside. Before she had time to speak, he gently embraced her and pressed his lips with hers. Nearly forgetting what she had planned to say, Abigail collected her thoughts and uttered, "I suppose you've already heard that I'm an old meanie."

"Yes, but I've known that for years. In fact, that's the main reason I fell in love with you."

"Be serious," she implored. "Do you think I did the right thing?"

"Yes, dear, for many reasons. First, the boy must learn to respect his mother. We both know that he loves you, but showing respect is just as important. Secondly, the woods near the lake have been home for black bears before we bought the property. So far, they have left us alone. They're very protective of their young and what Jack Junior did endangered both boys. Bear cubs are not pets. We shouldn't do anything to make bears less fearful of humans. Otherwise, we will need to hunt them down and kill them. That's something I don't look forward to."

"Will you explain that to my sons?"

"Yes dear." It always tugged on the mountain man's heartstrings whenever Abigail referred to both boys as her sons.

The following morning, after breakfast, the boys were outside on another adventure, as if the previous day's incident never happened. Jack and Melvin spent the day in the fields and Abigail and Hope cultivated their garden.

The Leffingwells and Kaufmans lead the typical life of those involved in raising their own food, whether it is vegetable or animal. It is a healthy life in which most of the day is spent outdoors. The fresh air, sunshine, and exercise, reward them with immunities those living in towns fail to receive. This is especially true for children. Exposure to dust, pollen, contact with a sundry of animals, and raw milk, helps develop a more robust immune system against asthma and bronchitis. Like everyone else, they are still vulnerable to contagious diseases. A fact that Abigail and Hope are well aware of, making them keep a constant vigil for early signs.

Sunday is the most active day of the week. Besides the daily farm routine, it's the day both families attend the Methodist Church in Statesville. Certain chores are performed before dawn in order for the families to have time to eat breakfast and dress for mid-morning services. Today is Easter, the day to celebrate the resurrection of Jesus Christ and the most Holy day on Abigail's calendar. It is also the second week Hope has taught Sunday school for six and seven year olds. The regular teacher is recuperating from delivering her first baby. Hope volunteered to fill in and took to it like bees to honey. But there is one drawback. She misses the Sunday sermon, a deprivation she won't endure for long.

Services ended at noon, with half the congregation remaining for the social hour which followed. Women swapped recipes and the men talked about current events. Maryellen and her husband made it a point to accompany Abigail and Jack during the communal time. Besides being with her best friend, it discouraged people from complaining to Augie about the Reconstruction. By the time they all were ready to head for home, the boys managed to have shirt tails hanging outside their pants and perspiration on their brows. An Easter egg hunt had been organized by one of the ladies auxiliaries and Jack Junior and Jozef looked as though they only searched where the conditions were muddy.

By the time everyone returned home, Sarah Jane and the boys were ready for a late afternoon nap. Hope and Melvin embraced the same idea, leaving Jack and Abigail to enjoy each other's company without the usual interruptions. It is a quietude that gives solace to the mountain man and his dearest treasure. Abigail removed to the kitchen and lit the flame under her coffeepot.

"It won't be long before we can have a cup," she said, softly.

Once the pot began to gurgle, Abigail poured each a fresh cup and the couple sat in silent contemplation of the remains of the Sabbath.

It was soon approaching dusk. Another beautiful spring day had come to an end. While work on a farm is never done, it now must pause until the rooster crows. The oil lamps are lit in the Leffingwell kitchen, providing a sharpened view for anyone outside. Clearly visible, Abigail and Jack sit at their kitchen table enjoying another gratifying cup of hot coffee. Both are tired, yet, a special look in his wife's eye gave Jack the satisfaction that tonight had a long way to go before they would fall asleep. Acknowledging her eyes, he reached across the table and took hold of her hand. When a marriage is unshakable and based on love, communication often needs no vocal expression.

"The children went to sleep quickly this evening. They must have been as tired as we are," Abigail improvised. Suddenly, their intimate gaze was rudely interrupted by the sound of commotion outside. Peering from a brightened room into the darkness revealed only indistinct images. Jack pushed back from the table and said, "Sit here while I go outside to see what this is all about."

"Jack, please be careful. I think they're wearing some sort of masks," Abigail cautioned, while straining to improve her vision.

Standing on his front porch, Jack could see much better. Several horses pranced nervously as their riders tried to form a more orderly aggregate. Abigail was correct when she said they were masked. They also were clad in white sheets and the aforementioned mask turned out to be white pillowcases with holes cut out for their eyes.

"What's this all about?" Jack questioned the rider who appeared to be the leader.

"This is just a friendly visit. We mean no harm," he answered. "It's common knowledge that you fought for the Confederacy during the war. That makes you a true son of the South. Right now, the Yankee aggressors have the upper hand and loyal southerners are being forced to give up political offices so that carpetbaggers and scalawags can run the country. They're putting uneducated blacks in positions of authority and passing laws aimed at disrespecting our good citizens.

Men you see here are mostly veterans, like yourself. They have come together to form a secret society called the Ku Klux Klan. Confederate General Nathan Bedford Forrest is working at making us a governmental organization of which he will be the first national leader called Grand Wizard.

This so called Reconstruction is being run by the Radical Republicans. There's no spirit of reconciliation, they just want to punish us. Even if they did win the war, we're not going to tolerate this kind of treatment. A lot of your neighbors feel the same way. As a group, we have power to fight back and reverse the changes the Republicans are making with the help of the Union army. We will strike fear in the hearts of these racketeers whether they be white or black. Our goal is to restore the Southern people to all their God given rights. General Forrest has declared the Klan has 550,000 members and growing every day."

"What do you want of me?" Jack questioned, while scanning the horses ridden by those in white costumes.

"We want you to join up with us," the Klansman answered confidently.

"I, too, am not happy the way this Reconstruction is being conducted, especially the occupation by the Federal troops. It took us four years to realize that change through violence isn't permanent. The lesson learned from the Civil War is that permanent change comes through the ballot box. Our former rights as citizens are slowly being returned to us and I'm willing to wait a little longer. I'm sorry friend, but I must refuse your offer."

Up till now, the Klan leader hadn't been refused outright. The spectacle of hooded riders intimidated innocent targets to coalesce on the spot. Tonight was a different story. They encountered the Tennessee mountain man, who, by his very nature, was slow to make snap judgments. Life is a puzzle, never to be completely solved. It can only be lived best, when the underlying issues of any problem are learned, before making a decision.

"You've got a very nice farm with a beautiful wife and children. It would be a shame if the house and barn caught fire some night," the Klan leader stated.

"You don't threaten me, Mason Poor. I recognize your voice and know some of you men by the horse you're riding. I spent four years fighting in a terrible war and killed over fifty men without batting an eye. Most of them were killed with a Whitworth rifle from over a mile away. If anything happens to my family or farm, I'll come after you first. Then I'll get the rest of you. As for you boys, I have a Choctaw friend who can make you identify the rest. Unless you don't mind being roasted alive or having your skin peeled off, I suggest y'all just ride out of here and don't come back," Jack seriously stated.

When Jack was wounded at Fredericksburg, he was left with a lifetime reminder. The white scar extended from the temple to the hairline on his forehead. With his anger, it now was glowing red. He stepped down the porch steps, walked confidently to his adversary and snatched the hood from his head. Some in the group had already turned their mounts and were riding for the road. Mason Poor could not make eye contact; therefore, he spun his horse around and galloped off.

Mentally, Mason Poor had already made a decision. He will resign his leadership post immediately. However, he still faced another problem. His wife, Julia, was a member in good standing at the Methodist Church. It would be impossible to persuade her to give up the women's auxiliary league. He will just have to skip church for a few weeks and try to figure something out.

When Jack walked back in the house, Abigail was standing by the door with his revolver in her hand. The sight of the determined woman made him smile and love her even more.

"You can put the gun away darling, I think they're gone," he said, while reaching around her waist to bring her closer. For Jack Leffingwell, the biggest disappointment of the evening is that special glint in her eyes has disappeared.

CHAPTER FIFTEEN

It was before sunrise at *Falling Water's* camp. Even though the eastern sky has yet to brighten the horizon, the women were already actively performing their chores. Fires were kindled and smoke curled from tops of the tepees. Next, they hurried down to the stream to collect water for their morning use. The Cheyenne did not use water that stood all night. They called it dead, and would only drink living water.

As dawn arrived, the men and boys joined in the activity. Bolstered by the gradual warmth of spring, they, too, hurried to the creek for their morning bath. A few of them had defied the winter, by breaking the ice, to perform their foreday ritual. Today, with ice and snow melted, all could partake in the traditional ceremony, believing it was not only good for health but made them hardy, plus, it washed away all sickness. *White Dove*, and her grandmother, *Valley of Flowers Woman*, would usually wade out to where the creek was waist deep, in order to bathe. However, they hesitated to do so until the water became more temperate.

After the morning bath, the older boys led the horses, which were tethered near the lodges, to where the less valuable ponies grazed. By the time they returned, breakfast was being served.

During the night, *Falling Water* had determined it was time to return to the main village. The next morning, according to custom, a crier rode through the camp announcing his decision. All were to be ready to move the camp at the ensuing dawn. Soldier warriors were sent as scouts to see if the buffalo herds had returned to the spring grazing region. If they had, it will be news for them to carry to his father, *Chief Red Eagle*, before the balance of *Falling Water's* camp arrived.

In spite of concerns over the belligerent attitude of the Dog Soldiers, *Falling Water* spent the winter wrestling with the fact that he soon will be separated from his sister. *White Dove* has passed her puberty and become a woman. Her father, *Chief Red Eagle*, will insist that she move out of her brother's lodge. No matter how hard he tries, *Falling Water* is unable to reach a respectable solution. When she moves out, she must live with an older woman. If that be her grandmother, *Valley of Flowers Woman*, *Falling Water* must sacrifice not only his beloved sister, but his grandmother as well. In order to not live alone, another solution would be for him to marry. Marriage has been the farthest thing on his mind since it requires traveling to the Arapaho village to seek a bride. He was disinclined because the Arapaho women were considered loose by most of the Cheyenne.

Under the direction of the militant warriors, tepees were taken down and readied for travel. With *Falling Water* in the lead, the tribe began the hundred-mile trek back to the great village along the Arkansas River.

After spending the winter away from the main tribe, returning to the great lodges always filled the people with joy. They looked forward to being back with relatives and meeting babies born during their wintertide hibernation.

On the second day of debarkation, *Falling Water's* scouts retuned with displeasing news. As yet, the buffalo haven't reappeared in their customary grazing territory. That was a disturbing fact in itself, but it also deprived *Falling Water* of announcing gratifying information to honor his father upon his arrival. Deference to parents was of the utmost importance among the Cheyenne.

Thus far, the caravan was blessed with partly clouded skies and intermittent sunshine. Along the river the cottonwood trees were prevalent. Their roots loved the water. *Falling Water* made it a point to linger where the trees are most dense. This allowed the Cheyenne women to collect the unopened leaf buds. Such activity can be done in late winter, but the women prefer the spring, the time in which the amount of resin is highest. Just after a high wind or storm makes the task easier, since many small branches and twigs lay on the ground. The buds are removed from their stems and placed in baskets, later to be washed of dirt and dried.

When convenient to the women, the fragrant buds are placed in a cooking pan and covered with oil—squeezed from the seeds of a sunflower plant—and simmered for a few hours. After which the oil is drained off for medicinal use and the bud scales discarded. The oil has a tendency to congeal and is used as a balm for several ailments. It not only smells good, it protects against infection, calms pain, and has incredible healing properties.

* * *

Good weather held up until the Indian trekkers were about thirty-five miles from their destination. At that point, a heavy spring shower pounded the countryside and forced the band to take cover. No one kept time, but in all probability a record was set in putting up the lodges. The floors of the tepees were dry, since the women began their work when the first drops of rain met the earth. Quick action also assured that the lodge fires could be easily ignited. Insomuch as the Cheyenne were taught emotional balance, beginning at childhood, the sudden impact of a spring storm had little effect on their cheerfulness.

Inside *Falling Water's* lodge the cooking fire was serving two purposes. It not only stews the contents in the pot hanging above, but also removes the dampness in the tepee. On the plains, variation between seasons can be erratic. While the gift of April brings warming days and more hours of daylight, it is a period of unstable weather. The Rocky Mountains stand as a barrier restricting the eastward flow of hot and cold air masses. When these extremes come into direct contact, high winds and severe thunderstorms occur.

What began as a temperate day, now, there is a definite raw chill in the air. *White Dove* and her grandmother, sit with a blanket over their shoulders as they divide the contents of the cooking pot. *Falling Water* has discarded his own after moving closer to the flames. They ate in silence, each to their own thoughts, while the rain made a continuous thudding sound as it struck the skins of their lodge.

The somber mood was interrupted by *Valley of Flowers* when she spoke, "I will talk to my son, your father, when we reach the main tribe. His wisdom will direct us to the proper living arrangements."

"I don't understand why we must disrupt our family," said *White Dove*, timidly.

"It is the Cheyenne custom for brother and sister to separate once she becomes of age," the young chief stated. "It prevents them from becoming too familiar."

"If that's all it is, I could wear the rope[8]," *White Dove* innocently asserted.

Both *Falling Water* and *Valley of Flowers* chuckled out loud at her reply. Each wondering how she learned about the rope. It was a subject yet to be taught by her grandmother.

That night the inhabitants slept under blankets, with enough flame in the cooking fire to emit limited heat, and provide embers to restart a healthy blaze in the morning. Their

---

[8] It is the practice of unmarried Cheyenne women and girls, who have reached puberty, to wear the protective rope. It consists of a thin cord, wrapped around the waist, and tied in a knot in front. The ends are passed backward between the legs and wound around each thigh down to the knees. It is very uncomfortable, yet, gives enough freedom for walking. The rope is worn at night or whenever the women are away from the lodge.

conversation gradually dwindled, as the grip of sleep took hold. *White Dove*, hidden beneath a gift from her brother—a comforter made from the skins of 200 rabbits—expressed her love, and then drifted into the land of fantasy.

The next morning *Falling Water* stood in front of the tepee inhaling the fresh after-the-rain smell. It is a familiar scent that fosters images of cleanliness and renewal. While the young chief attributes it to the works of religion, the aroma actually comes from volatile oils released by the plants and trees. These oils collect on the surface of rocks and earth and react when rain falls upon them. The interaction causes the oils to be carried through the air in the form of a gas. At other times, bacteria spores, which grow in dry soil, are forced into the air by a hardy downpour, rendering a similar aroma.

Two Trees was chosen to ride through the camp and announce that they will resume homeward travel shortly after breakfast. In less than an hour the lodges were dismantled and packed on horses. The entire band was poised to travel when *Falling Water* nodded to *Snake Hunter*, who in turn led the tribe back on the trail.

After the thunderstorm, the dark clouds were swept away by a prevailing breeze. Now, along with a bright sun, a rainbow is revealed in the distant horizon. People were in high spirits as each step brought them closer to home. *Falling Water*, and his sister, rode at the front on a well-worn path, beside the Arkansas River. *Two Trees* rode up alongside of them. *White Dove*, recognizing that the two men wanted to talk, dropped farther back.

"I have given much thought to you living alone when your women move out. Perhaps the time has come for you to marry," said the loyal friend.

"Right now, I'm going to rely on my father, *Chief Red Eagle*. He will decide how I will be facilitated," *Falling Water* replied.

"Well, I know several women in the Arapaho village who would make a fine wife," assured *Two Trees*.

"It's not that easy. I must marry a woman of high standing, and most of all, she must be a virgin."

"I know many virgins among the Arapaho," *Two Trees* stated.

Falling Water smiled at his friend and asked, "Do you know what a virgin means? It means a girl who has never had sex with a man."

"Oh, then perhaps I don't know any virgins in the Arapaho camp," *Two Trees* stated seriously.

Among all western tribes, Cheyenne women are distinguished for their chastity. Girls were rarely seduced and, any that yielded, were disgraced for life. Many of the kinsmen in *Chief Red Eagle's* tribe have similar familial bloodlines, thus, reducing the eligible prospective pools. Well-born braves seek a wife from a different village to guarantee diversified genetics.

* * *

As daylight came to an end, the tribe found themselves a half-day from the main village. According to custom, a messenger was sent ahead of the principal body to alert their arrival. This was done so that a proper reception could be arranged. On this occasion, *Falling Water* chose to ride ahead and take the place of the messenger. His friend, *Two Trees* and the Dog Soldier, *Snake Hunter,* joined him. As they drew near the entrance, they were met by a swarm of children and many barking dogs—a typical scene on such an event.

Once inside the village, the trio guided their ponies directly to the lodge of *Falling Water's* father, *Chief Red Eagle.* The access flap of his tepee was open and inside, the winter skirt had been raised to improve ventilation. *Falling Water* stood before the open doorway and waited for his father to receive him.

"Enter, my son. Come and sit beside me," articulated his father, from the far side of the lodge.

Falling Water quickly entered the lodge and moved to his right along the tepee wall until he reached *Red Eagle*, seated on a cushioned backrest.

"My heart is filled with great happiness for your return. Let us smoke the pipe and tell of the past few months," said *Red Eagle*.

Falling Water, now accustomed to the subdued light, appraised the inner walls of his parents' lodge until he caught sight of his mother, *Singing Bird*. She reposed on the left side of the open doorway and unnoticed when he entered. Their eyes said it all. There was no need to speak. Both will embrace after the visit with his father has concluded. Situated next to *Singing Bird* were two young girls, unknown to her son. One in particular was statuesque and fascinating. Realizing that he was staring, *Falling Water* quickly focused on his father preparing the pipe.

Red Eagle had unwrapped the ceremonial pipe and filled its bowl with tobacco. After which, he pointed the pipe stem above his head, then to the ground, followed by aiming it to the four directions. As the chief gave a silent prayer, *Falling Water* was fully aware of the pipe's purpose. By smoking the pipe the Cheyenne are compelled to tell the truth.

Taking the first puff, *Red Eagle* passed the pipe to his son, and asked, "Have the buffalo arrived?"

"Not yet. I sent scouts to look for them before we left the winter camp. They traveled many miles but caught no sight of them. It appears they will be late this season," the young chief replied.

"When I was a child, these roaming giants thundered across the plains in such numbers that their dust blotted out the sky. Each year they become less and less. In the spring, the cows give birth to their calves. Perhaps that is the reason you have not yet seen them. When we hold the summer Medicine Lodge, buffalo will be an important subject. We will also consider the move farther south as specified in the most recent treaty with the whites. Have the Dog Soldiers discussed this with you?" asked *Red Eagle*.

"Yes, *Snake Hunter* and *He Lives Alone* are determined to go north and fight against the bluecoat soldiers."

"As mighty as the Sioux Nation may be, it is a war that we cannot win. Those who are determined to make battle will either be dead or living in Canada. At least moving to Oklahoma will allow us to hunt on the plains," lamented *Red Eagle*.

"I must assume you will be for moving," stated *Falling Water*.

"Yes, my son. I will argue that point at the summer convention."

The pipe, passing back and forth, was handed to *Falling Water* who remarked, "I notice you have two new faces in your lodge."

"Yes, they help your mother."

"Might I ask, in what manner they came by to reside in your lodge?" asked the son.

"They are captives, taken in retaliation for a Pawnee raid on our horse herds. I've been told that one of them is the daughter of a Pawnee chief," returned the father. "I planned to return them as trade whenever a powwow can be arranged. In the meantime, they are a great help for your mother."

"Which one is the daughter of a chief?" *Falling Water* was interested.

"The tall skinny one," he replied. *Red Eagle* smiled widely at his young son's interest.

Embarrassed by his father's intuition, *Falling Water* uttered, "Oh, I guess she is skinny." After a silent interlude he continued, "Where should we pitch our lodges?"

"I have saved the original area for you. You may erect your tepees where they stood before winter."

"Thank you, father. We will arrive tomorrow before the sun is over head."

Falling Water asked permission to leave and went looking for his mother. She soon was found and a proper welcome ensued. *Singing Bird*, standing well below her tall son's shoulder, embraced her only child and cheerfully welcomed him home.

"Your presence lifts a burden from my heart. I spent the winter thinking of you and grew more lonesome each day," she confessed. "Now that you're home, I am once again happy."

"Tell me about your helpers," he asked.

"They are good girls and a great help to me. I am growing older and find my duties more difficult to perform. The girls are captives from the Pawnee, but more than willing to be of help."

"Father says that one of them is a daughter of the Pawnee chief."

"They are sisters. Both are daughters of the Pawnee chief."

"What is the name of the taller one?" he asked.

"She is called *Chumani* which means *Dewdrops*. Her sister is named *Namid* or *Star Dancing*. What is your interest in them?"

"Nothing mother, I'm just curious, that's all," he replied. "I better find *Two Trees* and *Snake Hunter* so we can prepare the rest to come tomorrow."

When *Singing Bird* and her two helpers returned to the lodge, *Red Eagle* called for begging sticks to be sent to the homes of women renowned for their cooking skills. It is incumbent upon those receiving a begging stick to prepare food for the pending feast, which will celebrate the homecoming of *Falling Water* and his tribe.

CHAPTER SIXTEEN

Even though the place for annuities and allowances for food and clothing had been moved elsewhere, many Indians remained around Fort Larned. It was still a trading post for swapping furs in exchange for merchandise at the agency store.

After what had just occurred, the travelers were apprehensive about moving within the ranks of so many tepees. Tobias Taylor assured them that it was perfectly safe. However, the majority were gun shy and decided to wait until Fort Dodge to purchase their current needs.

With personal assurance from Tobias Taylor, Abel Strawn decided to see the government agent. Cautious by nature, the tall minister explained to Amanda that Fort Larned is the first place to register his deed to the property they now own. He admitted to trepidation, but the neighbors don't appear hostile—children were kicking a ball in front of the agency store—and it's time to get used to having Indians about.

Zachary Wheat was the exception. You might question his wisdom, but his daring was unparalleled. With no particular item in mind, he just wanted to see what the agency store had to offer. And, as long as Zack had a pistol strapped to his leg, Pearle resolved to tag along.

When they walked in, the proprietor was standing behind a counter and arguing with an Indian over the value of his skins. The deal was finally settled when the storekeeper offered to throw in a jug of watered down whiskey.

Abel asked if he had a plat map of western Kansas. The proprietor brought out his plat books and said, "These may not be up to date. Fort Dodge has more recent information."

Abel could see the section marked Myers and noted the two parcels immediately to the west were unclaimed.

"Can I file for a parcel under the governments Homestead Act," Zack Wheat questioned.

"Yes, but as I said, the most recent information is found at Fort Dodge."

"Would my claim be registered as of today's date?"

"Yes, but it might be invalid if an earlier claim was made at Fort Dodge," the proprietor repeated.

"I'm willing to take that chance," Zack stated. "I noticed that the next section is unclaimed. My friend, Mr. Sparks, desires to make a claim on it."

"You gentlemen know that you must build a livable residence on the property and maintain it for five years before receiving a legal deed?"

"We're aware of that," Zach asserted.

Once the paperwork was completed, Abel unfolded his document and flattened it out on the counter top. "This is a registered deed and bill of sale for the parcel marked Myers. It was purchased from Mr. Myers and registered at Lebanon, Tennessee. I'm assuming the federal approval stamp allows you to change the ownership to Strawn, Abel Strawn."

"Yes, I believe it does, however, this is the first I've seen of Homestead land being sold. I'll stamp it here, but in order to make certain there's no confusion, I suggest you present your deed to the agent at Fort Dodge" he suggested.

Abel walked outside with a self-satisfied expression and stood overlooking the internal confines of Fort Larned. His attention was drawn to the government corral where Tobias Taylor and one of his outriders were leading a string of horses. Apparently, he had convinced the army major to replace those taken by the

Indians. Zack Wheat and Pearle were each toting a small bag when they joined Abel.

"Looks like Tobias has the replacement horses," Zack stated.

"I thought the Indians only took five horses. They're leading six," Pearle mentioned.

"Tobias must be a good horse trader," Zack confirmed.

When the men returned to the wagon train, it was decided to make use of the remaining daylight hours. Shortly thereafter, the prairie schooners were under way and traveling west. A constant pace gained twelve miles before dusk, and the need to circle the wagons. In this part of the Kansas prairie, trees are only found along the Arkansas River. No central fire burned this night. Only those who saved a bit of wood had the luxury of the cooking flame. Pearle had thought Zack Wheat was a little 'touched' for picking up branches along the way. Tonight, he realized the wisdom of his bearded friend.

"Anybody short of cooking wood just come to my wagon," Zack announced. It wasn't long before three people stood behind his tailgate. Zack meted out the precious sticks and accepted nothing more than a simple thanks.

Forming a circle within a circle the Van Ronkles, Blankenbergs, and Callaways shared Abel's cooking fire. While their repast would never compare with Noma's in Copenhagen, Denmark, on this night on the barren plains of Kansas, it was a feast fit for a king.

For the next two days, the iron rimmed wagon wheels cut deep into the prairie grass, leaving singular tracks among those left on the trail before them. They stand as a testimonial for courage, hope, and the belief in a better life.

Some will soon experience a different kind of tracks— the tracks of sweat and tears—the tracks of heartache and disappointment. Now, on April 8, 1869, jubilance fills the air as eight wagons stall before the earthen walls of Fort Dodge.

A long journey of over 900 miles has finally reached its end. Abel Strawn and the other transmigrates will circle the wagons one last time. In the morning, they will register their claims and receive directions to their new land. The frequency of cavalry troops, coming and going, gave the pioneers a sense of security. Finding several domiciles outside the fort's barricade evidenced a growing community.

Zack Wheat was quick to notice one large framework, which indicated a two-story building. By the amount of activity, it won't be long before its construction is completed. Aware that the railroad will run a line to Fort Dodge, this building can only serve one purpose—a hotel, tavern, and gambling house. In a short while the clickety-clack of the roulette pill will entertain a lively crowd. Grinning at the thought, Zack Wheat knew that where there's drinking and gambling, there are women.

Before the morning fog lifted, cooking fires were at work. The aroma of bacon frying wafted through the camp as the sentries pulled open the fort's main gate. Most of the pioneers spent the night just turning their pillows anticipating the morrow. As a result they woke with a blunted appetite. Abel Strawn represented a perfect example, and stood waiting in front of the agency door as the key was turned from the inside.

The office of the government agent was located next to the sutler's store. Both facilities were much larger than the ones at Fort Larned. The registrations which took place at Fort Larned were repeated here at Fort Dodge. Abel learned that his homestead lay three miles to the west and reachable by following the road in front of the fort. The Van Ronkle, Blankenberg, and Callaway properties were adjacent to Abel's, with Zack and Pearle's linked to the west.

Abel was elected to present Tobias Taylor with the envelope containing their appreciation for a safe arrival. The tall mountain man was found with one foot on the bottom rail of the corral, and talking to a couple of bluecoat bronco breakers.

"Tobias, on behalf of the wagon train we want to present you with a token of our gratitude for the wonderful job you did getting us here at Fort Dodge," Abel expressed.

"I told you folks at the get go you don't need to do this. I'm remunerated by the railroad company," Tobias replied, as he pushed the envelope with the back of his hand.

"We know that, but we still want you to take this anyway," Abel stated.

"I won't do it. Tell everybody I'm donating it toward the material to build your first church. And that's final," Tobias said firmly. "You can do something for me though, tell Jack Leffingwell I said hello the next time y'all see or hear from him."

"I'll make a point of it," Abel replied.

* * *

When Zack and Pearle walked into the sutler's store, they were greeted by the clanking sound of an unwinding chain. They were frozen in place as a large gray animal charged them and roared with a deep loud bark sounding like wah-hu. The length of chain gave out before it could use its large canines and snapped the beast backward. It still was screeching and baring teeth—as large as a lion's—when the proprietor began dragging it toward its cage.

"What the hell is that?" Zack blurted.

"It's an African baboon," the storekeeper stated. "I bought it off a circus, back in Wichita. I use it to keep the Indians in line. They're scared to death of it. I usually keep it penned up when they're not around."

"Has it ever bit anybody?" asked Zack.

"Only Indians," he replied. "How can I help you fellas?"

"We're just looking today. You have a darn good supply of about everything so you'll be seeing us often."

"You boys just move here?"

"Yep, we arrived with the wagon train parked outside the fort. We have a farm a couple miles west of town," Pearle explained.

At that moment, Abel opened the door and walked inside. Zack was a little disappointed the baboon was put in its cage and winked knowingly at Pearle. Abel slowly perused the ample merchandise until the proprietor asked, "Is there something in particular you're looking for? If I don't have it in stock, I can obtain it in less than two weeks. This area is growing so fast that supply wagons arrive every day," he said.

Abel walked over to him and extended his hand saying, "My name is Abel Strawn. I've recently purchased the Myers farm. Do you remember Jubal Myers?"

"Yes, he was a sad case. His whole family died from the fever and he went back east," the merchant replied, as he gripped Abel's hand. "He was a frequent customer."

Many times the male handshake is a test of masculinity. The firmer the grip, the more convincing it becomes. The burly shopkeeper is a past master, but today he met his match. Abel towered several inches above the man, and, with a grip equal to or stronger, settled that part of the introduction.

"My name is Boris Azarov, I'm glad to meet you," he replied.

"Azarov, is that a Russian name?" asked Abel.

"No, I am a Bulgarian," Boris replied, his face still crimson red from the previous effort. My family was woodsmen and lived in the Balkan Mountains. I came to America for a better life."

"Well, there are not many trees around here," Abel said jokingly.

"Ah, if it's lumber you want, I can have it here in less than two weeks."

"That's good to know. We've just arrived, and, as yet, I haven't seen the property. I'll know more about my needs in a few days," "Abel explained.

An hour later, Abel led three other wagons to the area where his farm stood. The countryside had gained importance and its condition was closely observed. The oxen plodded along at their usual gait giving more time to take note of the river and its outgrowth beside the shoreline. Several mature cottonwood trees were unharmed and posed as custodians over the waterway. Surrounded by many saplings, it augured well for the future. Hindered by the snaillike pace, they reached the access road in about two hours. The encouraging sight of the farmhouse and outbuildings made Abel's pulse quicken. He glanced at his wife and pronounced, "We're home sweetheart, our very own home."

"You silly man. You're all fired up and you haven't even looked inside. I'll reserve my opinion until I've actually seen it," Amanda insisted.

By then, the other wagons left the road and moved on open land in search of markers denoting their claims. Abel, with Zack Wheat closely behind, pulled the covered wagon between the house and a partly constructed barn—it had no roof—and jumped to the ground. When he reached up to assist Amanda, she handed him their daughter and climbed down by herself.

Joined by Zack and Pearle, the four Tennessee pioneers stood before the home and admired its construction.

"It's a lot bigger than I expected," said Abel. "Jubal Myers told me that the house was big enough to raise a large family, but I never considered anything like this."

Three steps led to the front porch. Pearle scaled the first and looked down saying, "What are these steps made of?"

Zack ran his hand across the top footfall and said, "Looks to me like Myers must have made them from adobe and sprinkled tiny colored bits of rock on top."

"Why would he do that?"

"I'm not exactly sure; however, it would help keep you from slipping in the winter. I'm more curious about the porch floorboards and railing. Where did he get the lumber for it? The railroad didn't get this far five years ago."

Abel sat his daughter down and fumbled for the key that Jubal gave him. He held it up and declared, "I hope the door isn't frozen shut." Nervousness caused him to miss the keyhole the first couple tries. After finding the opening, Abel gently turned the key to the left and felt resistance.

"Put a little force behind it," Zack called out.

Abel complied and felt the mechanism give way as tumblers changed position. The door protested with a high-pitched complaint, but relented to its new owner and swung open.

From all appearances the cabin weathered the two-year vacancy very well. Once inside, they found it air tight with no leaks. It did have a mild musty odor that Amanda grumbled about. Granting that, Zack promised it was only stale air and will disappear once the windows are opened.

Further inspection disclosed the furnishings. Kitchen cabinets contained cookware and dishes—not fancy, yet more than serviceable. Much to the pleasure of Zachary Wheat, the bedrooms were oversized and there were two of them. Each had full size beds. Likely, the Myers children shared one of them. In the main room a cast iron Franklin stove occupied a corner. The most surprising feature of the home was its puncheon floors— logs split in half with the flat side up, shaved smooth, and oiled to a shine.

The mystery of the cabin's logs would be solved if the new inhabitants had insight into its history. Obviously, there were no trees in the immediate area; however, telegraph lines run about three miles from where the cabin now stands. Five years ago, the U.S. cavalry was rapidly sinking poles until one morning they unexpectedly ran out of material. Soldiers were at a standstill for two weeks waiting for more long wire supports. Had the cavalry happen to ride over to Myers property they would have witnessed a log cabin being constructed. They did not, and the mystery remains perplexing.

"Come with me Pearle. Let's string a line outside and air out the mattresses and bed linen. We got a nice breeze and plenty of sunshine. They'll be fresh as a daisy when we put them back on," Zack pronounced.

Amanda battled with herself not to be delighted with her own home. She tensed when Abel put his arm around her and stated, "All I can say is this is a hell of a lot better than sleeping in the damn wagon."

"When we get done with it sweetheart, you're going to love it," insisted Abel.

Outside, the animals were freed and grazed nearby. Zack had opened his chicken cages within the walls of the roofless barn.

He tossed a couple handfuls of grain assuring the fowl stayed close, while planning to later stretch his tarp over them, in case it rained.

At the moment, he and Pearle watched the bedding swinging to the force of the unimpeded breeze.

"If you bring in the cot from your wagon, I'll sleep in it and you can have the bed," Pearle offered.

"Do you think I'm too old to sleep on a cot?"

"It's not that, but for what you did for all of us. You deserve to sleep on a bed," Pearle confirmed.

"Well, I want to put a roof on Abel's barn. When I do, I'm going to extend the walls and erect a bunkhouse."

"Then I'll stay with you rather than in the house."

"You're thinking like a cowboy. Remember, we're just ordinary farmers," Zack reminded.

"Maybe so, but you tote a gun. And I plan to do the same first chance I get. Abel wouldn't allow me to carry one if I lived in the house," Pearle confirmed.

The rest of the day was spent unloading the wagons and knocking down cobwebs. Zack and Pearle slept like a log the minute their heads hit the pillow. With Pearle on the cot and Zack enmeshed in bed linens, the sounds coming from the interior gave proof.

Little Abby languished in a baby's bed, found earlier along with a highchair. Amanda and Abel still lay awake. Repelling Abel's natural advances, Amanda imagined being elsewhere. Sharing the bed with Abel continued to be uninspiring. Always perfunctory, tonight she refused to go through the motions as a punishment for bringing her to this God forsaken place. Exhaustion won out and Abel finally dropped off.

* * *

Zachary Wheat owns two roosters. Apparently, they have acclimated to their new surroundings, as they began crowing at the crack of dawn. It will become the clarion call, from this day forward, signifying the time to welcome in a new day.

Abel quietly rose from the bed, careful not to waken his sleeping daughter. Amanda has always slept late, with very little disturbing her.

Padding across the main room's floor, Abel exited through the rear door of the kitchen and, after a short walk, became the first family member to use the outhouse. From all indications, the privy hadn't been used often. Probably due to its being moved from another location. The miniature outdoor building had two open holes in the seat, but both are rarely used at the same time. Typical on rural farms, it was constructed from wooden planks, with a roof to protect against rain. Also, it had a swinging door featuring a crescent moon cutout. That feature drew a smile from its new owner.

Even though the bedrooms had chamber pots, Zack and Pearle chose to water behind the barn, out of view from the house.

Still eating from the covered wagon reserves, they sat at the kitchen table holding hot cups of coffee and listened to the bacon frying. Zack had previously whipped up some hotcake batter and presented a trayful.

"I'll set a plate aside for when Amanda gets up," Zack said. "What time does she usually rise?"

"Late," Pearle stated without consideration of Abel. He quickly realized his gaffe and said, "You gotta excuse me, Abel. I am her brother and grew up with her. She always got up late."

"Being a Methodist minister, I used the time alone to gather my thoughts and read the bible," confessed Abel.

"That life is over. Now, we all must work together if we want this farm to succeed," Pearle stated.

"You're right Pearle, and your sister will do her part," assured Abel.

After Zack stacked the dishes he entered the conversation, "What's the first order of the day, captain?"

"Let's saddle up and have a look at the fields," Abel answered.

"If you don't mind, I'll hitch my mules to the wagon and look for buffalo chips while we're at it," Zack said.

Amanda wandered into the kitchen with Abby in her arms about the time the men were well into the fields.

Zack found lots of chips on the edge of Pearle's claim. In fact, with the others help, he filled the wagon up to the sideboards.

"Until we get some coal or more wood this has to keep the fire going."

"I'm surprised it doesn't stink," Pearle commented.

"That's because it's old and dried out. I suspect it was pretty offensive when it was fresh," Zack chuckled, and then led the mules to a field where Abel was standing. The latter had dismounted and was leading his horse by the reins.

"This looks like last year's grain of some sort," said Abel.

"It's wheat. Help me unload the buffalo chips and I'll show y'all how to gather and harvest it."

With that, the trio of aspirant farmers rode back to the barn. Once the wagon was emptied, Zack covered its contents with a piece of canvas and explained how they could save the wheat crop.

"First, it's too early to harvest your winter wheat crop. We've got a couple months before it will be ready. When the heads turn golden and droop down we will know that it's time. Then we need to cut the stalks and tie them into bundles. I noticed a scythe hanging in the barn. Before we use it, the blade should be sharpened. Have you ever used a scythe?" asked Zack.

Abel and Pearle shook their heads.

"Well, it doesn't take much learning after you get comfortable swinging it," Zack stated. "Threshing takes the most time; however, with three of us working, we ought to be able to complete it quickly. What we don't use ourselves can be sold. Next trip to Fort Dodge we can ask about a buyer. Right now, the important action for us is to plow the fields."

"How about the garden?" Pearle added.

"After the fields are plowed," Abel stated. "Also, Jubal Myers left his plow in the barn. With two plows working together, we can finish that much faster."

"When do you want to get started?" asked Zack.

"First thing in the morning," Abel replied.

"Good. This afternoon, I'm going into Fort Dodge and order lumber to build a roof over the barn. Boris Azarov said he could get it in two weeks. I'm gonna put him to the test," said Zack.

"The cost of that is mine," Abel said.

"I'll just keep track of it for now," Wheat replied, and walked back to the house. When he reappeared, he had retrieved some money and wore his pistol. In the meantime, Pearle had saddled two horses, planning to accompany his friend.

Riding at a leisurely pace, the pair arrived at the fort in about twenty minutes. At full gallop, they could reach there in five minutes. On their way, Pearle was troubled by what Zack had said earlier and asked, "When you buy lumber for the barn roof, are you also ordering enough for the bunkhouse?"

"Yes, but you have to help me build it."

"I'll be ready when you are."

As they approached the main gate, the pioneer riders were startled to see a large number of Indians both outside and within the protective walls. Many were concentrated around the government agency office. Federal soldiers were going about their assigned duties and seemingly paid little attention to the increased number of native visitors. Zack and Pearle hitched their horses in front of the sutler's store, dismounted and sauntered inside.

"What's all the fuss outside?" asked Zack.

"Annuities for the Cheyenne arrived last night. They're lining up to collect," answered Boris.

"Do they receive cash money?" Pearle wondered aloud.

"Sometimes, but it's mostly cattle and food stuffs. I suspect they'll be wandering in here before long. Excuse me while I let my animal out of its cage."

"I'd just as soon you wouldn't. That monster scares me as well, and I got a pretty big order to give you," Zack stated. Boris Azarov ignored him.

Pearle could tell his friend was developing a slow burn. Zack's brow had narrowed and he gave out with an audible exhale. The animal from hell tested his chain before baring his teeth and ending its explosive charge. Zack stood erect and drummed his fingers on the top of his leather holster.

When Boris Azarov returned, he said, "You have a large order for me?"

"Didn't you hear me tell you not to release that devil?"

"Yeah, but you don't tell me what to do. I want him loose when the Indians come in," Azarov stated, with authority.

Wheat gathered himself and unfolded his list for the lumber. "How much will this cost me?"

"You can figure about ten cents a foot," Boris stated.

"I'll leave you with seventy five Yankee dollars and collect any change when I pick up the lumber. I got another question. We got a field of winter wheat. Who would I see about selling it?"

"You can haul it a hundred miles east or sell it to me."

"How much do you pay for it?"

Boris scratched his black beard as if figuring a price and said, "Sixty-five cents a bushel, if it's of good quality."

"We'll have some for you in a couple months," Zack stated. At that point, three Indians paused in front of the sutler's window. Azarov uttered, "These are the worst of all. The one with all the feathers is the tribal chief. The other two are his son and daughter. I hear that the son is also a chief."

"What makes them so bad?" asked Pearle.

"They look at me like I'm cheating them."

"Well, you are, aren't you?" Zack stated. He was still mad from the earlier tiff.

"Yeah, sure, but they got no right to question a white man. That pisses me off."

The bell above the door jingled and the three Indians silently entered the shop. *Chief Red Eagle* was expressionless looking straight ahead. *Falling Water*, his son, was more pensive as if anticipating pending adversity. *White Dove*, his sister, was visibly frightened and tightly clutched onto her brother.

No sooner had they shut the door, the African baboon charged at them howling aggressively. The scene startled the men and petrified the trembling girl. Frozen in the moment, the voice of Zachary Wheat broke the spell as he shouted, "If that animal frightens that little girl one second more, you're gonna have a dead monkey on your hands."

Azarov's eyes spewed hatred. Even so, he knew the bearded stranger meant business and returned the baboon to its cage. The eyes of the Indians were trained on Zack Wheat. What kind of man is this who would defend an Indian girl?

Having struggled with the animal, getting it back in its cage, Boris returned asking, "What can I get for you people?"

Zack wasn't even thinking about leaving until the natives had concluded their business. He slowly prowled the aisles examining the merchandise. From what he could hear, *Chief Red Eagle* was buying cooking utensils—metal skillets, pots, and pans—plus, a bag of salt and flour. Apparently, the Cheyenne did receive some cash money. Once their merchandise was paid for, the trio left the shop. After which, Zack called out to Pearle, "Time to go son." Turning to Boris he affirmed, "See you in a couple weeks."

On the ride home Pearle was animated and in a bother over the attractiveness of the Indian girl. He bombarded Zack with endless questions regarding her good looks and allure.

"Did you take a good look at her? She's the most beautiful girl I've ever seen. Her complexion is as white as milk. How did that happen?" he continued.

Boris Azarov's chacma baboon. It is one of the largest of the species, 45 inches long with a 3 foot tail. A chacma can weigh up to 100 pounds. Azarov used it to frighten the Cheyenne Indians.

"Well, her mother most likely was a white woman. She was probably a captive and kept by the chief. Although that little girl has white features, make no mistake about it, she's Cheyenne through and through," Zack warned. "Son, you just got bit in the ass by the love bug. You best forget about her."

Fat chance of that. The delicate maiden haunted Pearle for days. He lost sleep, he lost his appetite, and he lost weight, because her image was always in the forefront of his thoughts. Finally, though he didn't know exactly how, Pearle made up his mind to meet her—come hell or high water. With that determination, the youngster slept for the first time in several days.

Work on the farm continued. With two plows in the field, additional acreage was cultivated. Reluctantly, Amanda joined in. Her proclaimed excuse for the need to watch Abby was not accepted. As a result, the little daughter was tethered to a wagon wheel under the shade of one of Zack's tarps. She sat perfectly happy playing with her toys while her mother, less happy, assisted Pearle planting corn kernels.

A swift moving creek snaked across the northern edge of the property. Tillable land was located on either side. Abel found the area in which Myers had forded; however, it required loading the plows in the wagon and driving the oxen through about three feet of water. Zack envisioned the stream as a source of irrigation for the fields. Pearle, preoccupied with other thoughts, saw it as a place to cool off on a hot summer day. Because of its clear, fast moving, water, Abel and Amanda saw it as a perfect place to take a bath.

By the end of the second week, the major cultivating was finished. Even the large garden plot near the house had been planted.

Giving full credit to the Lord, Abel commended the decision to permit Zachary Wheat and Pearle to accompany him on his journey to Kansas. He knows now that the task was too much for someone as inexperienced as a man of the cloth.

Amanda never got comfortable using buffalo chips for a cooking fire. Accordingly, the men took turns at the kitchen stove. Unfortunately, their repertoire consisted of only campfire cuisine, an unrelieved diet of hotcakes and bacon.

It didn't take long before Zack volunteered to scout along the Arkansas River and collect fallen wood. Pearle helped him hitch the mules to the wagon, and after their bacon breakfast, the pair began following the river shoreline. It was slim pickings for two or three miles; but, thereafter, things picked up. Fallen branches from previous windstorms began to be found. By mid-afternoon the wagon was overflowing with the jagged limbs of cottonwood timber. And, as the mules turned the wagon, a fish burst from the water and returned with a resounding splash.

"Wow, did you see that," exclaimed Pearle. "What kind do you think it was?"

"Hard to tell," Zack replied. "It could have been a bass or even a catfish. Trout favor shallower water, but it might have been a Brown Trout. They sometimes venture in deeper parts."

"I'm going to remember this spot," Pearle stated.

"That fish won't stay here, son. He probably was just passing through."

"Nevertheless, it makes me want to go fishing."

Smiling, Zack said, "The idea of fried fish is appealing to me as well."

"With all the kindling we picked up, Amanda might even bake what we catch," Pearle said, hopefully.

"We won't be fishing for a while. It'll take the rest of the day to cut up the wood in the wagon. The first batch will go directly into the woodbin by the kitchen. No more excuses from your sister. In fact, once the corn crop is harvested, there will be enough cobs to last her forever."

The next morning, Amanda tried the peach cobbler recipe from the book Abigail Leffingwell had given her. She watched tentatively as the men, who endorsed her cooking with flattery and smacking lips, devoured it.

It had been three weeks since Zack ordered the lumber for the barn roof. That should have given Boris Azarov ample time to receive the shipment. Abel decided to join them and help load the wagon. He left his wife with his loaded army revolver. Amanda was an excellent shot from her younger days and had no fear of being alone. While en route, Zack asked, "Is Armanda going to be all right? This is the first time she's been alone since I've known her."

"Haw, I pity the person who gives her any trouble," Pearle snickered.

Fort Dodge seemed more serene since the last time they were here. Nearly a month had elapsed after Zack had threatened to shoot Azarov's baboon and Pearle was smitten with the beautiful Indian girl.

Boris Azarov caught site of Wheat's wagon through his front window and caged his animal, to play it safe. Just as soon as Zack entered, Boris said, "Your lumber is stacked in back of the building. Use the alleyway to get there."

Abel followed his suggestion and parked alongside the wooden planks. Transferring the load to Wheat's wagon, the lumber was evenly distributed in order to balance its weight. After which, Zack used the money over the cost of lumber to buy nails, anchor bolts, and a bag of cement. Pearle wanted to ask Azarov about the pretty Indian girl, but thought better of it and followed Abel and Zack out the door.

Meanwhile, Amanda had placed Abby in her baby bed for her afternoon nap. The house was quiet. Tranquilized by the absence of noise, she poured herself a cup of coffee and stretched out on her living room couch. Nearly dozing off, she was awakened by the sound of horses. It seemed as though it came from the front of the cabin. Placing her empty cup on the dining room table she peered out the window. For a second her heart skipped a beat. Three Indians sat on their ponies as if awaiting the inhabitant of the house. Two of them had eagle feathers attached to their scalp locks. Remembering Abel's revolver, Amanda removed it from its holster and slowly opened the door.

"What do you want?" she asked, while securing her grip on her husband's revolver hidden beneath her apron. Her instincts told her not to act afraid and soon the old Amanda Sparks kicked in.

"I am *White Dove Woman* and here with my brother, *Falling Water*, and our friend *Two Trees*. I speak your language. My brother understands your words but has less practice in expressing them. He will tell you our purpose," the young girl disclosed, and nodded to her brother.

Falling Water urged his pony a few feet ahead of the others and said, "I have a gift for the man with hair on his face. It is a puppy from my father's favorite bitch. A farm needs a good dog to drive away wolves and other varmints."

As if on cue, *Two Trees*, holding the oversized whelp, moved alongside *Falling Water*, leaned down, and released the animal. Thereupon, the trio galloped away without another word being spoken.

Amanda shook her head in disgust, and walked slowly back to the house with the puppy in tow. For a brief moment she thought about using Abel's gun on it. Instead, she laughed aloud, gathered food scraps in a bowl, and placed it outside the kitchen. One thing for sure, Amanda was going to find out what this is all about.

* * *

The over-laden wagon took 45 minutes to reach the farm. Zack drove the mules at a walking gait so as not to exert them too much. He also paused halfway home to give them a short rest. As he pulled into the lane leading to the barn, a wolf-like puppy met the wagon with a shimmy and a wagging tail.

"What the heck is that?" questioned Pearle.

"Looks like a dog," Zack answered.

Abel jumped down and said, "Just pull the wagon alongside the barn. I'll ask Amanda about it. She must know how it got here."

Just as curious, Zack did as Abel directed, then he and Pearle quick-footed to the house. Amanda and Abel were talking when the other two popped in. They missed the first part of Amanda's explanation; but, being part of the story, quickly surmised the principle cause. She went on to explain that three Indians showed up. A girl and two others rode on the property and sat waiting for someone to come outside. One of them, the one holding the dog, was well over six feet tall. They said they had a gift for the man with hair in his face. That must be Zachary Wheat.

Finally, Pearle interrupted, "Let me explain. Boris Azarov had a baboon."

"Who is Boris Azarov?"

"He runs the sutler's store. Well, this baboon is the meanest animal you ever did see, and Azarov threatens the Indians with it. When a girl and her father and brother came in the store, the girl was so scared she trembled. That's when Zack told him to put the baboon away or he would shoot it."

"Did he put it away?"

"It ain't dead yet," answered Pearle. "Not to change the subject, what did the girl look like?" Pearle asked his sister.

"I don't know. She did speak good English. It's probably the same one you saw in the store."

Pearle was devastated. For a month, she was all he could think about, and the first time he was off the farm, she shows up here.

"Before you get all cow-eyed and lovesick, we got a lot of lumber to unload," Zack announced, as he led Pearle to the door.

After they left the house, Abel was puzzled and said, "I never knew Boris Azarov owned an African baboon."

* * *

While Zack and Pearle were unloading the lumber Abel arrived to lend a hand. Now, there was a fourth entity springing about and begging for a playmate. Pearle took the bait and romped a bit with the oversized pup.

"What are you going to call him?" asked Pearle.

"I'll let you name him, son," Zack replied.

"Then I'll need a little time to come up with a name that fits him."

There was still time to start construction before the sun went down. With Abel and his brother-in-law handing up two-by-sixes, Zack laid them on top of the adobe walls. Once they are anchored down, they will become the joists or base plates to secure sturdy horizontal stringers. One-by-ten flat boards will be nailed to the stringers making a floor for the second story hayloft. From that point the vertical framework for roof trusses will be assembled and nailed in place. Zack has chosen an improvised gambrel design in order to create more room for storing hay. The first truss will be used as a template for the remainder. Made of two-by-six-inch material, the support members were toe-nailed and reinforced with gussets at the connecting points.

At first, construction was slow and methodical. Zack preferred it that way, believing fewer mistakes will be made. Once the men gained confidence in their ability, progress quickened and the basic structure was soon completed. They covered the roof temporarily with flat boards and tarred all seams. It will do until the wood shingles arrive.

The three men sat on the grass looking up, admiring the addition to the barn. On the second level there was an opening in front to allow the passage of hay. Extending above the opening was a four-foot cantilever beam with a rope and pulley attached. It was designed to assist loading hay or bales into the loft.

"Did you ever come up with a name for that dog?" Zack asked Pearle.

"I've been calling him Champ and he seems to like it."

"Then Champ it is," Zack proclaimed. "It suits him fine. He's one of the biggest pups I've ever seen."

* * *

Before the advent of the horse, dogs were the only beast of burden utilized by Native Americans. They would carry the family's belongings, as well as pull a travois loaded with the lodge and its support poles. Since a larger dog could carry more weight, Indian dogs underwent selective breeding. What began as a mix between European dogs and coyotes produced a small or mid-size canine. In Canada, the northern tribes crossed their dogs with wolves and had much larger offspring. Trade between the plains tribes and the northern groups often involved dogs. Obviously, the nomads of the plains traded for the larger animals and bred them to maintain a larger breed. *Chief Red Eagle's* female dog resembled a wolf with a patterned hair color of silver and black. Her offspring grew to stand three feet at the shoulder and weigh nearly 120 pounds. There's every indication that *Falling Water's* gift will grow to at least that size.

* * *

After a few moments of silence, Pearle asked, "When are we going to start work on the bunkhouse?"

"Have you noticed the square forms I've been making with leftover lumber?"

"You mean the boxes with short sides?"

"Yep, those boxes will serve as forms for making adobe bricks. At the end of Abel's property line is a stretch of soil loaded with clay. I believe that, mixed with a little sand, straw, and buffalo chips, will harden up and make pretty good adobe," Zack stated.

"Why the buffalo chips?"

"It keeps the bugs away. Do you recall the bag of cement we bought from Azarov?"

"Yes," Pearle responded. "I loaded it onto the wagon myself."

"I think a scoop of cement, added to the adobe mud, will make the bricks a little harder."

"When are we going to start?" Pearle was anxious.

"If it doesn't rain, we can begin tomorrow."

CHAPTER SEVENTEEN

Though several weeks had passed, Jack Leffingwell had not mentioned the visit from his neighbors calling themselves Ku Klux Klan members. Mason Poor no longer attended Sunday services and the congregation began to imagine all sorts of reasons, none of them correct. Church members, in a rural community, seemed to be wrapped up with the business of others. It appears to be part of their internal make up. That's not to say these God fearing folks are bad. They just have an overt curiosity.

Jack Leffingwell knows the reason and began to have compassion for the unaccounted affiliate. After praying for guidance, he decided to come clean and disclose the entire episode beginning with his father-in-law, Hyrum Adams.

The Leffingwell family usually spent time visiting with Abigail's father after services ended. Jack related that he had something serious to talk over. Leaving Abigail and the Kaufmans to chat with those attending the social hour, Jack and Hyrum strolled to the minister's office. The two men took a seat and Jack began, "Do you recall when we last discussed the Ku Klux Klan?"

"I believe so. It was at your farm."

"Well, a few weeks ago a group of hooded members showed up at my door. They wanted me to join up."

"Naturally, you refused," said Hyrum.

"Of course. They went on to make a threat if I wouldn't enroll. That got me mad. Since I recognized most of them by their horses and the spokesman by his voice, I pulled his hood off just to make sure. It was Mason Poor. At that point, I notified all of them, if any harm came to my family or farm, Mason Poor would be the first victim of my revenge, with the rest of them to follow."

"Was that the end of it?"

"Yes, but Mason Poor hasn't attended church since. I don't know what he has told Julia, but people are coming up with all sorts of reasons and I feel sorry for him," the mountain man confessed.

"That's because you're a good man. I think you need to ride over there and have an honest talk with him. Tell him that you harbor no ill will as long as he isn't an active Klan member," recommended Hyrum. "Tell him he is missed at Sunday services."

"Do you think I should tell August McKnight?"

"Only if he doesn't lead a brigade over there to arrest him," Hyrum replied.

"I'll find the right moment. I'm due to finish my comparison of the two generals. That would be a good time to let him in on it."

The next day, bright and early, Jack saddled up Rambler and rode to Mason Poor's farm. The morning mist still hovered over the fields as Rambler romped and snorted his appreciation for exercise at sunrise. Cantering down the lane leading to the small, but well-manicured farm, Jack noticed Julia standing on her porch with a broom in her hand. As the early visitor drew near, she recognized the rider and shouted, "Jack Leffingwell, what are you doing up so early. It's a fine time to be making social calls."

"I figured you folks get up when the rooster crows. At least, that's what Mason always tells me."

"You know the story, get the reputation of being an early riser and you can sleep late the rest of your life," she stated. "Mason hasn't felt well of late, but I think he's up and about. You most likely can find him in the barn milking the cow."

Jack tipped his hat and turned Rambler toward the milking shed. Mason heard Jack's voice as it echoed from the house and stood in the doorway as the mountain man approached.

"Good morning friend," Jack said, as he swung a leg off the horse and dismounted. "It's a fine morning for a ride, so I rode over to see you. Have you been feeling poorly? Haven't seen you in church lately."

"You know why," Mason said, with downcast eyes.

"Look, I don't harbor any ill will as long as you don't participate in the Klan. That group is wrong and a poor excuse for men of the South. What's happening now is also wrong, but it will end someday all by itself. When it does, I want to be standing with the righteous men of faith."

"Hell, I quit that bunch before I got home," Mason confessed.

"Then start coming to church. With you gone I'm the worst singer in the congregation. Besides, you know how folks talk. They got you run off with the widow lady on the other side of the mountain."

"Have you ever seen that lady?" Mason laughed.

"Can't say that I have," Jack replied.

"Her face would stop a clock."

"Then I don't think I want to see her," Jack chuckled.

"Let's head up to the house and have a little breakfast and a hot cup of coffee," Mason invited.

The pair sauntered toward the dwelling. Mason felt better than he had for the past few weeks and his guest quietly shared an equal relief. Julia, in hopes of the visitor staying for breakfast, baked biscuits, and had eggs frying as the men washed their hands in the outside water pan.

When Jack left that morning, she had wrapped a few biscuits in a small bundle, and, handing it up to the rider, spoke in a softened voice, "I don't know what you said to Mason, but he hasn't been this happy in weeks. God bless you, Jack Leffingwell."

Jack's mind was eased after his heart to heart with Mason Poor. On the ride home he began thinking about generals Lee and Grant. By the time Rambler had his saddle removed, the proper manner in which to end that discussion was firmly set in his basis for proof.

Abigail was standing by the door when Jack scaled the porch steps. Although she supported her husband in meeting with Mason Poor, there still was anxiety as to how it would all turn out.

"How did it go?" she quickly asked.

"Better than I ever expected. Mason quit the Klan that same night before he left our property. He still was so embarrassed he couldn't face his neighbors and stayed at home," Jack said.

"You wouldn't tell others what happened that night," Abigail stated.

"I know sweetheart, but Mason didn't know that. Now he does, and I'm sure we'll see more of him from this point forward."

"Are you hungry?"

"Not really," he replied. "Julia made breakfast. In fact, she gave me a few biscuits to take home," as he lifted the bundle.

"Good, then we'll have them for lunch. Hope and Melvin are going into Statesville and asked us to take care of Rebecca while their gone. Do you need anything from town?"

"Yes, I'd like for Melvin to tell his friend, Ryan Gosling, that I plan to finish the comparison of generals this Saturday. That will give Ryan a little time to tell the others."

The Kaufman's buggy pulled up at the same time Jack finished answering his wife. Both he and Abigail walked out to meet them. Hope Kaufman lifted her daughter and placed her into Abigail's outstretched arms. Jack approached from the opposite side and passed along the same information he earlier gave his wife.

"That's going to make a lot of people happy. They've been waiting a long time to find out which one is the best," Melvin said. "I expect half the town will be there."

"If that's the case, the happiest person of all will be Fritz Adler," Jack chuckled.

* * *

On the appointed day, the good citizens of Statesville began filing into the town tavern. Looking forward to a goodly crowd, Fritz opened his doors at nine a.m., Ryan Gosling being his first customer. Within the hour, nearly every chair was occupied. Frank Riberty made use of the proximity of his general store and the alehouse. After unlocking his front door, he walked to the tavern and reserved the same table he and Augie previously utilized.

Jack Leffingwell's wagon came into view at half past ten and was welcomed with a rousing ovation. Fritz was doing a good job. After several back slaps and handshakes, the mountain man and Melvin were led to vacated stools at the bar countertop. Immediately, two foaming beer mugs were placed in front of the Confederate veterans.

All eyes were on Jack as he took his first sip and wiped the foam from his upper lip. It was as though a signal was sent forth calling for silence.

Clearing his throat, Jack began, "At the risk of repeating myself, I'll start my recollection after the battle of Gettysburg and that fateful charge by General Pickett.

Our army began limping back to Virginia. Most of us were in constant fear of Union General Meade attacking us while we were trying to escape. His lack of enthusiasm saved Lee's army. There's no doubt in my mind that half our soldiers would have surrendered if Meade had taken full advantage of the situation. The Union cavalry did harass the rear of our column, capturing wagons and seizing numerous prisoners, many of whom were previously wounded at Gettysburg. By the end of the month, Lee's Army of Northern Virginia was beyond pursuit.

The Gettysburg Campaign cost our army over 23,000 casualties at a time when there were few replacements."

"Didn't you guys give it to the Yanks just as hard?" Ryan questioned.

"Yes, but the North was in a better position to replace their losses," Jack replied. "Offensive battle is much different than fighting on the defensive. You need more troops, a lot more, maybe three to one. The South could no longer pursue any major offensive. From now on, Lee had to concentrate on reacting only to Union initiatives.

Lee's army returned to their camp near Fredericksburg to quarter for the winter. Marse Robert, tormented by the defeat at Gettysburg, sent a letter of resignation to Jefferson Davis, only to be refused.

The coming winter allowed our soldiers to heal from the rigors of war. We also suffered the agony of defeat—a new experience for most of us in Virginia. Abel Strawn and Melvin Kaufman both returned to duty without complications from their trauma in the battlefield."

Resounding huzzahs echoed throughout the alehouse as a tribute to Melvin Kaufman and Abel Strawn's safe return. Such displays are commonplace when it involves the sons of the South. The ovation for Melvin gave Jack an opportunity to finish off his beer; however, before he could wave off another, Fritz had a replacement sitting on the bar.

"Hey Fritz, buy a round for my friend Melvin Kaufman, a real live Confederate hero," Ryan shouted. In as much as the portly tapster continuously filled all empty glasses, whether or not he consented to Ryan's request will never be determined.

Allowing for an adequate intermission, Jack raised his hands and began to speak, "To reiterate, ironically, at the same period Lee was beaten at Gettysburg, Union General Ulysses S. Grant captured Vicksburg and took control of the entire Mississippi River. His victory so impressed President Lincoln that he put Grant in command of the newly formed Division of the Mississippi, giving him the entire western theater, except for Louisiana.

After the battle of Chickamauga, our own General Braxton Bragg forced Union General William Rosecrans' army to retreat into Chattanooga. Bragg then surrounded the city and trapped the Yankee infantry inside. When Grant learned of the perilous situation, he released Rosecrans from duty and replaced him with General George H. Thomas. Then he personally rode out to Chattanooga and took charge of the desperate situation. His first action was to open up a supply line to the entrapped army.

On November 23, 1863, Grant organized three armies and attacked Bragg's soldiers on Missionary Ridge and Lookout Mountain. The determined Yankee forces drove off Bragg's troops and sent them in retreat.

As far as Lincoln was concerned, Grant was now his favorite commissioned officer. On March 9, 1864, Grant was promoted to Winfield Scott's old position and ordered to come to Washington. Lincoln favored the Illinois tanner not so much because of his strategic military skills, although he had ample, but, at last, he was a general willing to fight. The victories at Gettysburg and Vicksburg highlighted the need for an over-all strategic plan and a general who could carry it out. Lincoln went all in and gave that task to Grant.

By mid-April 1864, Grant had finalized his grand strategy and issued specific orders to each commander of four Federal armies. While General Meade's Army of the Potomac and Burnside's independent corps formed the major attack column under Grant's personal dominion, the other armies would operate in a simultaneous and coordinated effort to his overall plan.

First, Gen. Benjamin Butler's 33,000 bluecoats were to skirt the south bank of the James River, menace Richmond, and destroy railroads below Petersburg.

Then, Maj. Gen. Franz Sigel's 23,000-man-army was to act as a rear guard in the Shenandoah Valley and advance on Lee's rail hub at Lynchburg, Virginia.

Gen. William T. Sherman's 100,000 Federal troops were to march on Atlanta, defeat Confederate General Joseph E. Johnson's 65,000 soldiers, and then move to devastate the resources of central Georgia.

Gen. Nathaniel Banks's forces were to disengage along the Red River and, with Rear Admiral David C. Farragut, make a limited amphibian landing against Mobile, Alabama, with the day to advance announced in May.

Whatever some of us think about Ulysses S. Grant, you have to admit that his overall strategy was impressive. If it can be executed, our chances of survival will be precarious.

Another national election was looming. Abraham Lincoln faced a nation tired of fighting and a Congress leaning toward negotiating for peace. The Illinois rail-splitter still believed that the quickest way to end the war was to defeat Robert E. Lee's Army of Northern Virginia. He has entrusted his cigar chewing general to get it done.

General Robert E. Lee was at his best when defending home territory. A Virginian first and Confederate second, he kept a well-trained eye on the movements of General Grant. Yankee generals Sigel and Butler faltered in their assignments and Marse Robert knew that Ulysses S. Grant will now double his efforts. He also knew that the last hope of the Confederacy was to hold out until the national election in which the new Congress would sue for peace. At best, that was over six months away.

On May 4, 1864, in what became known as Grant's Overland Campaign, the Federal forces crossed the Rapidan River, at the edge of the wilderness of Spotsylvania, in central Virginia. It was an attempt to place the Union Army between Lee and Richmond and force Marse Robert into open battle. Lee, always unpredictable, responded by attacking Grant's larger army in what become known as the Battle of the Wilderness.

Because of the unwelcome terrain of bramble, briar, and thicket, Grant was unable to bring his artillery to bear. His superior numbers became an encumbrance due to the narrow pathways and trails.

For two days both sides attacked and counterattacked as they stubbornly refused to give quarter. Visibility was limited to sometimes only a foot ahead. Yankee soldiers were forced to thrash noisily and blindly forward through the underbrush, making them perfect targets for the concealed defenders. Sporadically, the jungle would open up to a small clearing, favoring no one, due to the corresponding confusion. At times, the fighting was hand to hand turning the skirmish into a melee. Soldiers on both sides were firing their weapons a foot apart from each other.

Confederate sharpshooters were retained in the rear of their regiments; however, the terrain of dense stunted trees and twisted prickly bramble worked against us by camouflaging the enemy. The marksmen from the 7th Tennessee Regiment fired blindly in the general direction of the bluecoats. To make matters worse, exploding shells ignited the woods, and both sides witnessed the horror of wounded comrades being burnt to death. Smoke from the fire was so dense visibility became zero. I instructed my sharpshooters to aim a little high so as not to hit the wounded, which were coming back in a steady stream. It was then Melvin was struck in his arm and walked by himself a half mile to the field hospital. As you know, Melvin's arm was amputated and he ended up at Chimborazo Hospital in Richmond."

Jack stopped briefly in order to slake his dry throat. The intermission gave Fritz Adler the opportunity to announce, "On behalf of Melvin Kaufman, I buy the next round."

"It's about time you tight Heinie bastard," shouted Ryan. Ryan was drunk.

"Me thinks you've had enough," stated Fritz, who filled every glass except the one in front of the inebriated blacksmith. Ryan, with his head on the bar counter, appeared to be sleeping. Two of the men, sitting next to him, picked him up and carried the feisty smithy to a table in back of the room. Ryan was now snoring.

When liquor flows freely, men react in different ways. Some become belligerent, causing their better angels to take leave. Others are remorseful and weep over the way the world has mistreated them. Once in a while, alcohol remarkably makes a few extremely creative and energetic. None, save one, collected in the town tavern, fall into any of these categories. Ryan Gosling just got drunk and passed out, an act he has performed before when the drink was free. It has never occurred while the blacksmith was governed by his own available funds.

"Looks like Ryan will miss out when the greatest general is declared," Frank Riberty stated. Frank suffers from one of the ways I've listed. He's smart enough to acknowledge it and conducts himself accordingly. With the commotion settled down, Jack picked up where he left off.

"The battle lasted for two days and ended inconclusive as to which one was the winner. Both sides suffered heavy casualties.

On the morning of May 7, Grant was faced with the prospect of continuing the attacks against strong Confederate earthworks, rifle pits, parapets of abatis, artillery in position, and entrenched infantry. Instead of slugging it out, he chose to keep up his maneuver strategy. That night, the Union army marched ten miles to the southeast and resumed the attempt to interpose between Lee and Richmond.

Marse Robert anticipated Grant's strategy and got to the crossroads ahead of him, establishing formidable earthworks. At the bloody battle of Spotsylvania Court House, the Union repeatedly attacked Lee's defenses, resulting in considerable losses for one and the other. In a foreboding sign, General Grant did not retreat from the battlefield as did his predecessors. The 'Galena Tanner' crossed the Rapidan River with an aggregate of 120,000 troops. Accordingly, attrition favored the men in blue uniforms and their leader was well aware of it.

Undaunted, Grant moved his army to Cold Harbor, a vital railroad hub which led to Richmond. Lee, however, was able to get there first and entrench against the Union's assault. For thirteen days the bluecoats conducted costly frontal attacks on the superior and impregnable Confederate lines. During the third day of battle, Grant led a continuous onslaught, very much like Pickett's charge at Gettysburg, to no avail.

Thirty days had passed since northern soldiers crossed the Rapidan. During which time 52,788 casualties were brought about. News travels fast, bad news even faster. It fueled the fire of northern antiwar sentiment and caused newspapers to criticize Grant, calling him a fumbling butcher.

Rueful of his faulty decision to charge the southern trenches, Grant pulled out of Cold Harbor and headed for Petersburg, a city crucial to the supply of Lee's army and the Confederate capital of Richmond.

Confederate General P.G.T. Beauregard, trained as a civil engineer, was in charge of the defensive machine around Petersburg. He was able to fend off Grant until Lee arrived with reinforcements and additional security. With Confederate troops ensconced behind Petersburg trenches, Grant's war effort was stalled.

After Grant failed to capture Petersburg, he constructed trench lines of his own that extended thirty miles from the eastern and southern outskirts of the city. The Petersburg siege was fought from June 9, 1864 to March 25, 1865. It was not a classic military siege in which a city is surrounded and all supply lines cut off, nor was it limited to action against Petersburg. Numerous raids were conducted and battles fought in an attempt to cut off the railroad supply lines through Petersburg to Richmond. In order to maintain his supply route, Lee was forced to lengthen the trench lines to the point of thinning his already inferior manpower.

Grant's armies continued to be significantly larger than Lee's rebel columns. After Cold Harbor, Marse Robert was outnumbered two to one. He managed to replace his 20,000 casualties with veterans from inactive fronts. Grant, on the other hand, had lost twice the amount and another 20,000 who went home after their enlistment ended. While a temporary setback, the Union had many men available and reinforced with troops pulled out of Washington, D.C. Although some were either raw recruits or artillery crews unfamiliar with infantry tactics, there were now over 100,000 black troops ready for assignment. In a war of attrition, it is numbers that count, and Grant held all the aces.

The siege that wasn't a siege worked to the Union's advantage, since it contained Lee and prohibited him from sending troops to help defend Atlanta. The Democrat Party had nominated George B. McClellan to run against Lincoln, and featured a platform calling for peace negotiations and a truce with the Confederacy. Seemingly, the conflict was at a stalemate and the war-weary populace longed for change. It's fair to believe, without a significant and favorable event, 'Little Mac' would soon take residence in the White House.

On September 2, 1864, General William Tecumseh Sherman captured Atlanta. The fall of Atlanta had important political ramifications and was covered widely by the Northern newspapers. Atlanta's capture improved Northern moral to such an extent Lincoln won reelection by a large margin.

On April 2, Grant's army achieved a breakthrough in the lines at Petersburg. It became obvious Lee no longer had the strength to defend the fortifications. He advised the Confederate government to abandon Richmond. In the evening, General Longstreet's corps crossed the James River to team up with our boys in Petersburg, as the capital city of Richmond was evacuated.

At that point, Lee managed to move his army across the Appomattox River to Amelia Court House where he could be supplied from stocks being held in Richmond. After which, Marse Robert would meet up with the fleeing Confederate government, then head south to join General Joseph E. Johnson. Considering the situation and rapidly changing events, his plan appeared to be plausible.

The 7th Tennessee Regiment, or what was left of it, was held back to defend the Petersburg fortifications. We weren't there very long before a messenger dashed by telling us to prepare to depart the trenches. Still unaware of Bobby Lee's plan, we all celebrated the fact we were leaving the damn ditches. We rejoined the main body under the command of Colonel Samuel G. Shepard.

When General Lee reached Amelia Court House, the expected rations had not arrived. They hadn't even been loaded on the trains escaping Richmond. The pursuing Union cavalry captured any supplies, traveling by wagon. With 30,000 hungry men to feed, Lee lingered an extra day to send out foraging parties. They returned with few provisions. By waiting to hunt for food, Lee lost the advantage of a head start. With Grant's army pursuing relentlessly and promised rations a three-day march, any expectations of joining Joseph E. Johnson in North Carolina faded away.

The avenues of escape were systematically being blocked, and on April 6, Lee's army suffered a significant defeat at a battle along Sailor's Creek. Union cavalry and bluecoats cut off nearly a fourth of the Confederate Army of Northern Virginia. Our soldiers were hammered by artillery and demoralized by Union cavalry cutting through the lines.

Soundly defeated, most of the 7,700 troops in gray surrendered, along with a dozen of Lee's generals. It marked the last battle between the armies of Robert E. Lee and Ulysses S. Grant.

On April 8, Union cavalry captured and burned three supply trains waiting for Lee's army at Appomattox Station. The Army of the Potomac and Army of the James were closing in on the defenders of the Confederacy.

On April 9, General John B. Gordon, still loyal to the gray haired commander, took the offensive in a last ditch effort. Launching an early-morning attack on Union General Sheridan's cavalry, Gordon's forced the first line back; however, the next line held and slowed the Confederate advance. Gordon's troops managed to charge through the line and take the ridge. As they reached the crest, they saw an ocean of blue as far as the eye could see. It was the entire Union Twelfth Corps in a line of battle, with the Fifth Corps to their right. Upon seeing these forces, Lee's cavalry immediately withdrew and rode off toward

Lynchburg. When the Union troops began advancing against Gordon's worn and frazzled corps, Bobby Lee was left with no alternative other than go and see General Grant.

Grant's Appomattox Campaign was an example of masterful, relentless pursuit and maneuver. None of his predecessors had the fortitude to keep pressing, no matter the result. Lee did the best he could under the circumstances. He made a gallant attempt, in spite of no supplies, tired soldiers, and luck finally running out.

The surrender of General Robert E. Lee was a psychological blow to the Confederacy. By June, 1865, all remaining Southern armies capitulated.

Now, when it comes to which general was the greatest, we have two able men with vastly different personalities and leadership ability."

Jack's soliloquy came to a halt when a voice from the darkness of the room shouted, "Damn it Fritz, where the hell is my beer?" It was Ryan Gosling, steady as a rock, and meandering to this favorite bar stool. He stopped short of the bar's mahogany counter top and said, "Hold up Jack, until I take a piss." After which, he made a pirouette and headed for the urinal.

"That guy is a wonder. He has a bladder the size of a beach ball," Frank Riberty stated. Others took Ryan's interruption as the opportunity to line up behind the scrappy blacksmith, waiting their turn at the comfort station. Those who held back finally relented and found their place in the line. Included among the late comers were Melvin Kaufman and the mountain man.

A marked change in the group's disposition took place once they returned to their chairs. Even Jack seemed to have more life in his presentation.

"For the first two years of the Civil War, Lee defeated the Union at every turn. His genteel manner and obvious military competence won favor here in the South, and also with the northern press. His distinguished performance was romanticized in the Union journals to the point of mythology.

It seemed as though Lee could do no wrong, while President Lincoln was berated with criticism for an ineffective war strategy.

Honest Abe became disconcerted over the performance of his generals. So much so, he replaced McDowell, McClellan (twice), Pope, Burnside, Hooker, and Meade before settling on Ulysses S. Grant."

"Wasn't Grant a drunkard?" came a voice at the end of the bar.

"He may have favored a nip of the grape once in a while, but there's no one in this room who can criticize him for it," Jack replied, with a grin. The general laughter confirmed Jack's statement. "Being inebriated was never proven. Rumors to that effect began to circulate in 1853, when Grant was promoted to captain and assigned to Fort Humboldt, on the California coast. As rumor had it, his commanding officer, at the fort, had warned him several times to stop his drinking. When it was reported that Grant was seen sitting at the paymaster's table intoxicated, he was given the ultimatum to resign or face court-martial charges.

He resigned and nothing to his discredit was stated on the War Department's document.

Most rumors about a man's reputation are near impossible to disprove. The whole truth doesn't fit into the equation. Unfortunately, only a bit of truth spices the rumor. Grant's struggle over the next seven years was discussed during our earlier sessions."

Jack hesitated as if he didn't wish to continue, but deeply exhaled and said, "What I'm going to say next comes from the heart of someone who loved Robert E. Lee and would arm himself in a heartbeat if he summoned me back."

Staring into the eager faces Jack continued, "By June 1863, the Federal armies had gone back into the defenses of Washington. Our army couldn't remain long where we were. We needed to be fed and re-supplied. Lee's decision to invade the North was his biggest blunder of the war. He returned in defeat only to wait for the Union offensive.

Grant, though often faced with costly military stalemates, stuck to his plan and kept the heat on the Confederates. After a year of perpetual onslaught, the southern gentleman had no alternative but surrender.

Now, who was the best general? Lee for the most part spent the entire war in Virginia, while Grant was effective in several theaters. Due to Lee's upbringing, he found it difficult to criticize his generals. Grant, a graduate of the school of hard knocks, removed those who were slow to respond. Robert E. Lee was a graceful greyhound. Grant was a fierce pit bull terrier. Lee was off-course after the death of his compatriot Stonewall Jackson. Grant's fellow countryman, General William Tecumseh Sherman, remained to the very end.

In their head-to-head confrontation, Grant achieved complete success in less than a year. We southerners are attached to Robert E. Lee. To us, he represents the best of the southern tradition and cause. It's only natural to resent the one who brought us down.

But, with a clear head and in spite of how much we wished otherwise, Ulysses Grant is the best general."

Outside of Augie McKnight standing, briefly applauding, and quickly retaking his seat, the alehouse was stricken with silence. No one knew what to say. Even Melvin Kaufman was shocked with Jack's opinion. Perhaps it was too soon for rational thought about the war. Nevertheless, Jack's opinion has been given and a sick feeling developed in the bowels of the audience.

Fritz knew he will serve no more beer today as his customers filed out without speaking.

Had the declaration come from anyone else, the crowd would label him a traitor. They knew better with the Tennessee mountain man, who has just damaged the depths of their souls.

On the way back to the farm Melvin asked, "Couldn't you have at least made it a tie?"

"Did the war end in a tie?" Jack replied.

Both Abigail and Hope were delighted at the reappearance of the men, and Jack's arbitration of the generals over. Digging up the bones of the Civil War has a negative affect on many who survived. It nearly cost Abigail her marriage. She, for one, avoids recalling her personal experiences, and was often-heard saying,

"Nothing good ever came of it." Ironically, many times holding little Jozef when she said it.

Jozef is a mama's boy and finds no substitute for being held by his Tennessee mother. His devotion pulls on Abigail's heartstrings only to strengthen her attachment.

CHAPTER EIGHTEEN

A little time was set aside each day for making the adobe bricks. Progress was interrupted when shingles arrived for the barn roof. With three men high above the ground, that job was completed in two days.

By the middle of June, an eight-foot wall ran along the lee side of the barn. Zack chose that location because of the prevailing winds originating from the west. When winter comes, any sparks from Zack's Franklin stove will be blown away from the buildings.

Pearle liked to sit on the wooden plank floor, lean back against the adobe wall, and admire the structure and Zack Wheat's engineering skill. Extending alongside the full length of the barn, it provided for an oversize bunkhouse.

"I can't wait to move in," Pearle said, coming out of his stupor.

"We gotta put a roof on her before we can do that," Zack replied, while lighting his pipe.

"Gosh, it's big enough for lots of people."

"Only if we have to. I'm figuring on dividing it into a kitchen and living room. Do you remember what I did with the barn back in Lebanon?"

"Yes, you had it looking real nice."

"Well, that's what I have in mind for the bunkhouse."

Pearle broke out into a toothy grin, thinking, "This will guarantee a separation from the main house and allow me to wear my revolver and holster." His grin turned into a frown when he realized Zack Wheat only wore his side arm when he went into town. Pearle's reverie ended when he heard a wagon go past the barn and stop at the house. It was Theo Van Ronkle and his wife Mildred.

Abel walked out on the front porch and invited his neighbors inside. Theo removed his hat and the pair was led to the kitchen table where Amanda was musing over a cup of coffee. Without being asked, Abel placed two cups before his guests and poured the steaming brew.

"There's sugar and milk on the table," he indicated, before sitting down. "I hope your visit will mark the first of many yet to come. Amanda and I love company, especially with our neighbors."

"You've always been so hospitable," Mildred stated, as she stirred milk in her coffee. "Since we've left the wagon train, milk is a rarity."

"Our friend, Zachary Wheat, bought the cow when Bertram and Annaliese Keller decided to return home. I believe he did it as a good will gesture because he paid way too much for it." Abel confirmed. "Zack doesn't appear to be a believer, but there's a lot of good running deep within his soul."

"That's one of the reasons we're here this morning," Mildred said. "When we all were traveling with the wagon train, you took the time to minister to us and quote the Bible. Since moving here in Kansas, we're without a collective religious foundation. Theo and I are here today to ask you to continue preaching to us. We can meet out in the open, while the weather holds up, then possibly inside, later. All the families could bring a covered dish and make a picnic of it."

"How many families would attend?" Abel inquired.

"Four families for sure, including me and Theo. People arrive all the time, and before the summer is over, probably two or three more. Counting the young'uns we'd have fifteen or twenty folks here every Sunday."

"I'm willing to give it a try and see how it works out," Abel agreed. "Amanda plays the guitar like a professional and has a beautiful singing voice."

"The Lord smiles on you Abel. I can't wait to tell the others." Mildred was excited.

"I think we have some lumber left over and maybe Zachary Wheat can set up some benches," Abel offered. He was also a little excited. "I'll hold services at eleven o'clock sharp. Folks need to arrive early to get set up."

"Leave it to me to tell the others. They'll be real happy to hear the good news," Mildred stated, as she and Theo boarded their wagon and drove to the road. After turning to the west, the Van Ronkle wagon rolled across grassland until they reached their property. Steel rimmed wagon wheels have cut ruts in the pathway and frequent use indicates the beginning of a road.

"There's something wrong with the preacher's wife," Mildred told Theo. "She was cold as ice."

"Maybe we interrupted a family squabble," Theo replied.

"That's not it. She seemed that way when the wagons were on the trail. Rumor had it she was sneaking off with a cowboy the night of the dance, when her brother caught her and shamed her back to their wagon."

"Well, if the rumor is true, the problem belongs to the preacher."

"I know, but Abel Strawn is such an admirable man. He deserves better," Mildred concluded.

* * *

Abel could not suppress his satisfaction and joined Amanda at the kitchen table.

"I believe this is what's been missing since we arrived. It will be good to get back into the swing of things," he said, confessing to his wife.

"Don't count on me for any of this. The only good thing about living here is not attending that damn Methodist Church. You aren't going to rope me in again. I'll watch Abby while you all do your thing," snapped Amanda.

"But, darling, you add so much to the service. It's only a couple hours on Sunday," he pleaded.

Circumstances around Abel's marriage to Amanda are masked by his love for her. If pressed for the truth, there hasn't been one day in which she showed honest devotion. Amanda married Abel as a convenience when she thought she was pregnant. Her lover bolted when he received the news. The minister's son gladly married her to protect her reputation. He also had loved her since childhood. Later, when Amanda found she wasn't with child, she made Abel's life miserable.

Once the War Between the States began, Abel enlisted in the Confederate Army. Besides helping the South, it gave him time to heal his matrimonial disappointments. Learning she moved in with his parents, relighted a spark of hope. Since the war, Abel, a deeply religious man, has prayed for Divine intervention. Kindness has no effect on the recalcitrant female. Neither has the birth of a beautiful daughter. Abel is situated upon a keg of dynamite and the fuse is burning.

Later that day, down by the barn, Zack was examining the wide boards in search for the longest. He had already set a couple aside when Pearle and Champ appeared.

"What are you up to?" Pearle inquired.

"Looking for some long ones to make benches. Abel's gonna hold church services this Sunday."

"Don't use stuff meant for the bunkhouse," Pearle insisted.

"Not to worry, son. There's a load in Fort Dodge to be picked up. It has everything we need to finish the job."

"When are we going to town?" Pearle asked.

"Is first thing in the morning too soon?" Zack teased. "Grab a pail and help me water my trees."

Zack had planted four saplings by the creek behind the house. Two apples, a cherry, and a walnut survived the trip and stood waist high. The healthy soil and frequent watering have enlivened them to the point of budding out. From all indications, they should make it through the winter—Zack's main concern.

"I brought a burlap bag full of pine cones. They're all big ones so I suspect they contain plenty seeds. If you want, you can help me sort through them and pick out the kernels. I plan to start them in pots until they develop strong roots."

"When will you plant them?"

"That depends upon how well they germinate. More than likely, it will be sometime next year," Zack answered.

Conversation during the evening meal centered on the pending trip to town. The flickering flame of an oil lamp provided illumination, as darkness began to swallow another day on the Kansas farm. From dawn to dusk, the Tennessee pioneers labor to build and maintain their independent future. For the most part, success depends on personal effort and the will of God. Thus far, the ever-changing weather had been on good behavior. Those, wiping their plates clean with remaining bread, understand things can change in a heartbeat. Such knowledge tends to account for a pervading sense of uneasiness. Zachary Wheat, not exactly a churchgoer, strongly agrees with Abel's decision to hold religious services on Sundays. He also senses there is one at the table who shoulders strong disagreement. When Abel and Pearle excused themselves and relocated to the living room, Zack helped Amanda stack the dishes.

"I'm looking forward to hear you sing and play the guitar on Sunday. Pearle tells me you sing like a nightingale," Zack said.

"You're gonna wait a hell of a lot longer, 'cause I don't want any part of it."

"I tell you what. If you play the guitar on Sunday, I'll take you with me when I go to Fort Dodge. It's been a while since you've been there. The gambling house is almost finished. They were painting its sign a week ago and calling it the Lucky Lady. I supposed it will be the unlucky lady for those spending a lot of time there."

Zack struck a chord. Amanda's heartbeat increased at the thought of a combination hotel, restaurant, and gambling hall. There was no telling how much it might change her life. She leaned toward Zack and whispered, "You're on."

The following morning, while the vaporous mist still clung to the fields, Amanda had awakened and dressed. The men, however, began early chores at the cockcrow. When she padded to the kitchen she found the coffeepot beginning to sizzle. Pearle was the first to return to the house. He was carrying a basket of fresh eggs, warm to the touch. Zack's brood of chickens found the Kansas farm much to their liking and now, a chattering of chicks occupied a corner of the barn.

"This has to be a record. You getting up before noon," Pearle said jokingly.

"In case you haven't noticed, I've been getting up a lot earlier than I used to. Besides, I want to be ready when Zack goes into town," Amanda said frankly.

"We're only going in to pick up a load of lumber."

"That doesn't matter. I want to see how much the town has grown."

"You're going to be surprised. It's growing in leaps and bounds and even got the makings of a main street," Pearle said enthusiastically.

"Zack says the railroad is building a depot there. And that's why it's building up so fast," Amanda added.

Footsteps were heard on the front porch as Abel and Zack washed up for breakfast. Their muffled voices served as a cue for Amanda to move the coffeepot aside and place the skillet on the stove. Abel entered the kitchen and inquired about little Abby.

"She was still sleeping when I got up. I didn't want to disturb her," Amanda said, as she laid out strips of bacon and side-meat.

"I'll go fetch her," Abel said, bending down to give his wife a peck on the cheek. It was avoided as Amanda deftly leaned her head away.

Two hours later, the wagon was on the move. Zack and Pearle waved goodbye. Amanda only stared straight ahead, wrapped in her thoughts. If it wasn't for the rattle of Zack's wagon, the trip, thus far, would be noiseless. Amanda was lost in a daydream about reconstructing her life. Her brother and Zack were embarrassed over the way she treats Abel and found it awkward to start the conversation. Finally Pearle broke the ice and asked Zack, "What's that ground cover you got planted behind the barn?"

"You must mean the sweet potato plants. Their vines spread like cucumber or melons and have pretty flowers. Some folks do plant them for ground cover, but, I plan to harvest the tuber roots. Boris Azarov told me they sell for fifteen dollars a bushel."

"Wow, that's a lot of money," Pearle declared.

"At first I didn't believe him. Considering the trouble planting them, he might be telling the truth. In any case, sweet potatoes are good eating."

"How do you harvest them?" asked Pearle.

"You got to dig them up, just like regular potatoes."

Arriving at Fort Dodge, Zack couldn't help but notice an increase in military activity. Unfamiliar with the everyday practice, he made a mental note to ask Azarov about it. Outside the fort, the fledging community continues its rapid growth. The Lucky Lady was open for business and more men were entering than coming out. Amanda insisted on having a look inside. Zack assured her she would, after their business with Boris Azarov is completed.

Recognizing Wheat's wagon from the window, Boris hastened to pull the baboon back to its cage. Leaving Amanda and Pearle in front, Zack remembered where his lumber was stored and drove the mule team to the rear of the building.

Upon entering, Pearle gave a brief salutation and asked the burly Bulgarian, "Has that Indian girl been in lately?"

"No, she don't come in a lot. Her brother and the tall one do most of the trading," replied Boris. "Anyway, the government plans to discontinue distribution of annuities here and move the responsibility to an agency in the Indian Territory. With a railroad depot coming and the way the town is growing, the

Cheyenne will have to move south. At least, that's what the government plans."

"Won't you lose a lot of business with the Indians moving to the Oklahoma Territory?" Pearle asked honestly.

"It stands to reason doesn't it? I bought a piece of land across from the Lucky Lady. The way things look now, it will face the main street. I'm thinking about a general store with a livery barn next to it. If things go like they usually do, the government won't be moving the Indians for a while. I'll gauge my construction with the growth of the town."

"From the look of things, you won't be waiting very long," Pearle stated.

Zack found the side door locked and walked around the building to get in. A twitch in Boris's left eye said more than words. Ever since the incident with the Indian girl, the Balkan storekeeper had a hatred for Zachary Wheat. When it came to Zack's feelings, Azarov was way down the list. At the moment, he wanted to get the wagon loaded and visit the Lucky Lady. Amanda, quiet as angel wings, was more anxious than the bearded partner.

"How much do I owe you?" Zack inquired, even though his vest pocket held the paper with the agreed upon amount.

"I got to look it up," Boris replied. "I thought you wrote it down."

"I did. I'm just checking up on you," Zack asserted.

"You owe whatever you wrote down," Boris answered.

Zack removed the slip from his pocket and spread it out on the counter top. After which, he opened his hip purse and took out the appropriate Yankee greenbacks.

"When you open that general store, you need to do a hell of a lot better job keeping track of the accounts," Zack said, as he counted out the paper money.

"I plan to have a bookkeeper," Boris said, while raking in the folding money.

"Would you mind if I left the wagon behind the building while I visit the Lucky Lady?"

"That's okay, as long as you don't take too long," Boris replied.

Inside the gambling casino was like visiting another world. Brightly painted walls, new tables and chairs, and a long mahogany bar counter added to the festive scene. On the wall across from the bar a staircase led to the second story and hotel guestrooms. A stage, intended for live entertainment, stood at the far end of the spacious betting house. Floodlights circled its periphery and elegant drapery hangs on each side. The kitchen was concealed from view; however, Zack imagined it was behind the doors at the end of the stand-up counter.

The trio led themselves to the bar and ordered three beers. When the glasses arrived, they carried them to a nearby table.

"This is the most elegant gambling den I've seen since the war ended. Once the railroad gets here, it'll be packed every night," Zack stated, as he drained his beer and announced, "One more for the road."

"None for me," Amanda uttered, rising from her chair to take a turn around the room. "I want to get a better look at the stage."

Pearle joined Zack at the bar. The men standing there were affable. One of whom turned to Zack and said, "Looks like the Indians are acting up again."

"I haven't heard a word about it. What's happening?"

"Raiding parties are attacking some of the farms on the outskirts," the man answered.

"How did you find out?"

"Boris Azarov told me. Hell, he's told everybody within five miles of the fort."

Zack smiled to himself, as he thought, "The bastard purposely didn't mention it to us."

With news like that, Pearle finished his second beer ahead of his companion.

Zack motioned to Amanda for her to hurry back. The look on his face made her cut between tables in order to quickly return. Her path led to one in which four men were playing poker. As she approached, the apparent winner raised his empty whiskey glass and said, "Get me another drink, sister."

"Get your own damn drink. I don't work here," Amanda blurted and continued to where her brother and friend were standing.

"I just learned that a band of Indians are raiding the outlying farms. We need to get home and alert the neighbors."

Zack's mules were put to the test and the wagon reached the homestead in record time. Fortunately, there were no sign of any Indians. After passing the information to Abel, Pearle saddled his horse and galloped across the fields to the Van Ronkle farm. Sharing the news, he rode on to warn the others.

Abel removed his sharpshooter's rifle from above the fireplace and checked its condition. It hadn't been fired since the Civil War. He told Amanda, "Get Abby and return to the fort."

"Where are the soldiers?" she questioned.

"Right now, they're probably out looking for the Indians," he answered.

After Amanda was heading for the fort, Zack appeared, armed to the teeth. I'm gonna station myself in the barn. It will put anyone attacking us in crossfire."

"Let's hope they never come," Abel said, as Zack retreated to the barn.

For an hour an eerie silence prevailed. Then, the sound of hoof beats began to be heard. There was no need for communication. Both Abel and Zack knew what it meant. Off in the distance, the image of several ponies took shape. Abel estimated the band consisted of at least twenty riders. They seemed to be hesitant about attacking the log cabin. Plains Indians are a superstitious lot, and often guided by visions and dreams. The homes of those previously raided were made from sod. Here, in the middle of the endless flat prairie, stood a dwelling constructed of wooden logs. Fearful of bad medicine, the painted assailants were waiting for their medicine man to beseech the Great Spirit to protect them. While one tawny brave danced to what appeared to be a pre-battle ceremony, Abel strained his eyes to determine their leader. Satisfied he was the quiet brave, atop a horse at the rear of the group, the former marksman adjusted his sights for a target over a half-mile away.

Suddenly, six warriors broke from the main party and charged toward the homestead. They were yelling and whooping it up as they followed an arc past the barn and in front of the residence. Abel judged it to be a scouting party sent to reconnoiter the property and determine its defenses. Zachary Wheat had climbed to the hayloft and opened fire with his Henry repeating rifle. One thing for certain, the ex-Yankee soldier was a crack shot. Amidst rapid fire, three riders were shot off their mounts and a fourth badly wounded. The other two managed to escape a second volley from the barn, and dashed to safety.

Taking careful aim, Abel gently squeezed the trigger. There was a short time-lapse before their chief flew backwards, dead, when he landed on the ground. Stunned, and without a leader, the raiding party was confused as to what to do next. That is, until the sound of a bugle made everything clear. With a United States Cavalry unit approaching, they made tracks for the Arkansas River. Several bluecoat soldiers rode up to Abel, now standing on his front porch.

"Has anybody been hurt?" the sergeant asked.

"No, we were prepared for them," Abel answered.

"In the future, it's best to go to the fort. We have a Company stationed there."

Zack had left the barn and joined in the conversation. "I thought *Chief Red Eagle* was for peace."

"He is. Those boys are Pawnee. *Red Eagle* has been at war with them since before the white man set foot on this prairie."

Pearle, returning from his mission, dismounted and walked his horse to where the men were standing. "Who shot all the Indians?" he asked.

"That credit goes to these two men. We got here when the Indians were retreating. The thing that puzzles me is, usually the chief doesn't get so close to the action. From the looks of things, he was wounded and rode to the back of his band, then fell off his horse, dead."

Zack pulled his beard and smiling at Abel, said, "Yeah, that sounds about right."

"I'll send a detachment to take these bodies off your property. We'll leave them a mile or so near the river. The Pawnee will be back to bury them."

"Will they bury them where you leave them?" Pearle asked.

"No, they'll just sneak across the river and take the bodies out on the prairie somewhere. Indians don't dig holes like we do." The sergeant saluted, spun his horse around, and dashed toward the main column to assign the removal detail.

Pearle questioned whether he should ride to Fort Dodge or not, to retrieve Amanda and Abby. Abel gave him the go ahead and the youngster remounted his steed and kicked it with both heels.

When the all clear was given at the fort, Amanda walked to the Lucky Lady, with Abby in her arms. She went inside and asked the bartender where the owner was. He pointed to the table with four poker players. Much to her chagrin, he was the man who had previously asked her to get him a drink. Bold as ever, Amanda walked to the table and stated, "I'm looking for work."

"Well, you sure as hell can't wait on tables," he smirked. "What can you do?"

"I can sing and play the guitar. And maybe fetch drinks, if I have to," Amanda replied.

"You do all that with a little girl hanging on your hip?" he questioned.

"I'm in town this way because of the Indian raid."

"Let me think it over. I've got some real women expected next week. Do you know what I mean by real women? I'm open, but not set up properly. Come see me in a couple weeks."

Not finding her at the fort, Pearle knew exactly where to look for his sister. When he opened the door, Amanda shouted, "Buy me a beer."

"Make it on the house," the owner told his bartender.

CHAPTER NINETEEN

On Sunday, a steady string of wagons rolled to the open area next to Abel's barn. By the time neighbors gathered for services, the threatening morning clouds had blown away. Those attending were still talking about the Indian raid. While only the minister's family was actually confronted by the Pawnee, the sheer incidence of a renegade attack made for lively discussion.

Zack had arranged the benches to avoid direct sunlight in the eyes of either Abel or his congregation. Several makeshift picnic tables were distributed on the grassy lawn, on which the parishioners placed their wicker baskets.

At the appointed time, Abel stood before eager faces and said, "I want to welcome you all to the first meeting of our prairie church. When I woke this morning, and set about my early chores, the skies were darkened by storm clouds. It was not at all conducive for outside church services. I began planning to hold them in the barn, but the Lord had other ideas. The wind picked up and soon the dark clouds were gone. It only proves we have no idea what the Lord has planned for us."

Rainbow Calloway shouted, "Amen brother." The rest began to murmur and a female voice said, "That's right," while the others made affirmative nods.

Abel opened his Bible and referenced the book of Matthew, Chapter Thirteen, and verses thirty-one and thirty-two. Nearly every family brought their Bibles, and the sound of turning pages could be heard throughout the group.

Paraphrasing, the tall preacher said, "Jesus tells us that the kingdom of heaven is like a grain of mustard seed, which a man took and sowed in his field.

Now, the mustard seed is very small. Indeed, it is the least of all seeds. But, when it is grown, it is the greatest among herbs, and becomes a tree, so big that the birds of the air come and lodge in the branches.

Our little church is like a mustard seed. And with faith, and the Lord's blessing, we too shall grow."

Amanda was sitting on a chair alongside her husband. She rose and stepped forward to play her guitar and sing. Her selection was the old English hymn, *We Plough the Fields and Scatter*.

> *We plow the fields and scatter*
> *the good seed on the land,*
> *but it is fed and watered*
> *by God's almighty hand;*
> *He sends the snow in winter,*
> *the warmth to swell the grain,*
> *the breezes and the sunshine,*
> *and soft refreshing rain.*
>
> *All good gifts around us*
> *are sent from heaven above,*
> *then thank the Lord, O thank the Lord*
> *for all his love.*

The quality of Amanda's voice had a soothing effect on the congregation. Her tone was soft, yet strong enough to send shivers of amazement. It had been rumored her voice was special. Today it became a fact.

When Abel finished his sermon, he gave his benediction and a line quickly formed to shake the minister's hand. Zack and

Pearle enjoyed the service, especially Amanda's song; but, now, their interest was the tables, top-heavy with home cooking.

With their sod houses partially constructed, many of the pioneers still cooked by campfire. The food was prepared by simple means using Dutch ovens and boiling pots. Nevertheless, an appetizing array of comestibles found their way to the makeshift tables. Zack focused on meat dishes and Pearle was drawn to pies and cake.

"This stew is delicious," he commented aloud. "What's it made of?"

One of the ladies standing nearby turned to Zack and replied, "I believe it is ground squirrel." Unwelcome news to the bearded bluecoat.

Abel escorted a group on a tour of the homestead. The men were very interested in the barn and particularly the new bunkhouse. Conversely, women admired the log cabin and its accouterments. After the tour, each one took time to tell Amanda what a lucky woman she was.

The fellowship lasted until three o'clock in the afternoon. Everyone pitched in to dismantle the benches and tables. At Zack's direction, they stored them safely for the next Sunday meeting. By four o'clock, the area regained its former appearance.

When the last wagon drove away, Abel stood in the middle of the courtyard feeling better than he had for a very long time. Pleased with his sermon, he also believed the church picnic came off without a hitch. Ironically, not everyone was enthused about a church picnic.

Not only Amanda disfavored it. In July, 1869, the Roman Catholic Church has forbidden picnics in this country. The ordinance against them was issued last year, and this was the first season for putting it into practice. The reasoning for the prohibition was the great number of abuses, which were found to prevail at these festive gatherings. The clergy have exerted themselves in enforcement of their Church ordinance. Fairs and picnics have been denounced from the altar and forbidden under special mandate. The clergy have used all their influence for their suppression and the people have yielded to their voices.

There were some who defied the law and continued to enjoy picnics, but, not without chastisement from the priests.

* * *

During the following week, Abel and his partners finished the construction of the bunkhouse. Pearle was ecstatic. Without furniture and a stove, the elongated empty room looks as if it could be divided into two residences. Zack knows that once the space is filled with his Franklin stove, a kitchen area, and beds, it won't seem as large.

"When are we going to move in?" Pearle was chomping at the bit.

"We've got to build a couple frames for the bedrolls, and then we can give it a try," Zack answered. "It won't be long before Abel starts charging us rent."

"I'm thinking along the lines of making you men partners. With two other sections, we would have a substantial piece of property," Abel replied. "We still need to build suitable dwellings to fulfill claim requirements."

The way things look, I think were safe for at least a year," Zack assured.

On Sunday, June 27, the pioneers met for the second church service. Except for the sermon, it was a rubber stamp of the first one. Amanda sang and played her guitar with verve, much to the validation of Abel. She didn't fool Zack for a second. The complete turnaround in attitude was for a selfish reason, and it won't be long before her secret is revealed.

* * *

As a matter of practice, the trio frequently walked the fields to inspect their crops. Corn was growing fast. It won't be knee high by the fourth of July, nonetheless, not far from it. All three carried hoes, and on occasion, put them to good use hacking weeds between the rows. Pearle volunteered to pull weeds in the garden closer to the house. The activity temporarily occupied his thoughts; however, once it became routine, the vision of *White Dove* monopolized his mind.

Abel's twenty acres of wheat was beginning to turn brown. If the weather holds, in a couple more weeks, it will be ready to harvest. Even with Amanda's help, it will require more workers. Abel knew farm labor back in Tennessee earned around $20 dollars a month. He wasn't certain about room and board. All the same, he would make sure they were fed. Zack estimated with three or four extra helpers, the harvest could be accomplished in three days. With the same workforce, threshing would be completed in another three or four days.

"I've got to go into town to talk to my buddy Azarov about a bull to freshen the cow. If you want, I can ask him about some day-labor," Zack suggested.

"Better wait on that. I'm going to check with the neighbors first. I got an idea. Perhaps a little cash money would come in handy for them. Most are experienced farmers and might appreciate the opportunity," Abel said.

"What are you planning to pay?"

"I'm thinking a dollar a day is more than fair."

"Do you want me to ride over and ask them?" Pearle inquired.

"Thanks but no, I'll do it myself."

Of the three closest neighbors, seven agreed to take the job. Considering their eagerness, Abel hired them all even though he only needed four, at most. He compensated by thinking the job will get done faster and is a push to the bottom line. Zack managed to avoid Amanda and rode to the fort alone.

When Boris Azarov saw Zack on horseback, without the wagon, he became very uneasy with guilt. His politeness was over the top and the bearded Balkan suggested a farm nearby, which had cattle from the east. Zack looked around and asked, "Where's the monkey?" Fearing Zack wanted to shoot it, Azarov said, "He's in his cage. I keep him there most of the time now."

At the recommended farm, the owner was a man by the name of 'Shorty' McCorkle, who had several bulls. One in particular was a small animal which caught Zack's eye. McCorkle, a friendly sort, offered to pen the animal in his corral when Zack's heifer arrived. There was no mention of compensation, though Zack was prepared for it.

"What's all this going to cost me?" Zack finally asked.

"Hell, this is the first time anybody ever asked me for stud service. Since you're the first, consider it free," the owner replied.

"I'll at least pay for feed. My cow might be here for a couple weeks," Zack insisted.

* * *

Abel's next church services fell on Independence Day—July 4. Amanda continued to take part and feigned willingness. She concealed her anger with Zack, for going to town without her, but kept silent on the whole affair. Now, she was just biding her time.

After services, Abel, Theo Van Ronkle, and Rainbow Calloway walked the wheat field to evaluate its readiness for harvesting. Rainbow Calloway had raised wheat back in Missouri, and commented, "It looks to me you're still a couple weeks away. We can get a better idea next week."

With a two-week reprieve, Abel and his partners concentrated on other chores readily found on the farm.

* * *

Pearle and Zack now live in the bunkhouse. Zack plans to build bunk beds in order to conserve space; but, at the moment, he sleeps on his cot and Pearle prefers a stack of blankets on the floor, rather than the bed in the house. Bunkhouse windows are covered with wooden shutters and pieces of cloth hang as a deterrent to flying night pests. A roll of screen wire is on order with Boris Azarov. It will replace the cloths currently being used.

Zack plans to retrieve it when he delivers the cow to Shorty McCorkle's ranch.

"Boy, this sure is the life," Pearle remarked, while staring at the ceiling and both hands behind his head.

"It's a little uncomfortable now. Once I build the bunks, it's going to be quite pleasant."

"If I had to, I'd sleep on the floor rather than in the house," Pearle said.

"By the way, are you still hung up on that little Indian girl?" asked Zack.

"I guess I am. Why do you ask?"

"Oh, I was just thinking. Would you like to travel over to her village and take a chance on meeting her?"

"I sure would, but, do you think we could get in?"

"I'll tell you what. Do you remember when we passed through western Kentucky on the way to meet the wagon train?"

"I think so."

"Well, I stopped there to buy some Kentucky black tobacco blend. It's a mixture of Turkish tobacco with what we grow, and the best combination I ever smoked. The way Indians love to smoke their pipe, I bet old *Red Eagle* would be happy to receive say, three pounds of it."

"What makes it black?"

"I believe it's because of the way they cut and fire it. Never mind that, what do you think of riding over there and make him a gift of some?"

"You don't need to ask me twice. When do we leave?"

"How about first thing tomorrow morning?"

"I ain't going to be able to sleep a wink tonight," Pearle answered frankly.

Before sunrise, the itinerant venturers mounted their horses and headed out to follow the Arkansas River. They were traveling east in search of the Cheyenne village, the exact location unknown. After two hours, when the sun's brilliance glared directly against their eyes, the unveiling of many tepees began to occur. Zack judged that the distance of fifteen miles had been covered.

Approaching what appeared to be the main entrance, the riders encountered barking dogs and several children who quickly retreated from the path. More seriously, men with bows partially drawn stood blocking their way and starred menacingly. Zack raised his hand to signify peace and quietly said to Pearle, "Get down from your horse and with your back turned, remove your holster and tie it to the saddle horn." Zack did the same and together the pair slowly walked forward with their hands held high.

"We are friends of *Chief Red Eagle* and have a gift for him."

Apparently, one of the entrance guards understood and sent a runner to inform *Falling Water*. After an uneasy wait he returned, spoke to the others, and led Zack and Pearle inside the village.

Pearle was like a farm boy in New York City, dazzled by the sights. His eyes were drawn to the river where several women and children were splashing and wading. From what he could see, they were all without clothing. Once he recovered from the initial shock, he saw that the women were only naked from the waist up. After tripping on something in his path, he returned to the purpose at hand. They walked past several lodges in which the inhabitants stood outside to witness the presence of alien visitors—two white men. At last they were met by *Falling Water*. Zack explained the reason they were there and *Falling Water* led them to his father's lodge. Motioning for Zack and Pearle to wait outside, he ducked under the doorway and told *Chief Red Eagle* of their visit.

CHAPTER TWENTY

News of the Pawnee raid on Abel's farm had reached *Chief Red Eagle* at the Cheyenne village. Holding to the proverb, *the enemy of my enemy is my friend, Red Eagle* finds another reason to consider, the man with hair on his face, may be a human being. After years of armed resistance the wise chief has taken a more compromising position when it comes to the white man. After all, a great deal is owed to the interlopers. Were it not for the white man, many items would be unknown to the Cheyenne, i.e., metal utensils such as iron pots and skillets and most importantly, the gun and bullets.

Where the whites are concerned, he currently has the will of his people accepting a peaceful stance. Not all, however, will bend to his volition. Dog Soldiers and a few Contraries oppose him. Fortunately, they are in the minority. *Chief Red Eagle* walks the high wire. At the moment he keeps his balance.

Since their introduction to the flat lands, the white man has been a curious oddity for the Cheyenne. *Red Eagle* is convinced that there is much to be learned from the white man—in particular, the one with hair on his face. Before inviting him into his lodge, the chief sent his son to find his sister. She speaks the language of the whites and can translate the words. It will give him a better understanding of what will be said.

Standing patiently outside the lodge, the visitors watched an increase of activity about them. Pearle asked, "What's going on?"

"I believe the chief is asking for others to take part in the visitation."

Promptly, *Falling Water* and a young woman returned. She had her head covered, masking her identity. Seconds later, the younger chief welcomed them inside. *Chief Red Eagle* was sitting at the back of the lodge and resting against a back support. He was flanked by his daughter, *White Dove*. The guests were led along the right side of the tepee until they reached the appropriate seats. Now *Falling Water* sat beside his father and Zack and Pearle in that order.

Chief Red Eagle was the first to speak. He gave a long opening statement of which the guests were unable to comprehend. At its conclusion, *White Dove* said, "My father welcomes you and asks the nature of your visit."

"Tell him he honors us to be allowed in his lodge and we have a gift for him."

Red Eagle smiled. Ever since the visitors entered his lodge, he noticed the package Zack was holding and became interested in its contents. Zack presented it to the son, who, in turn, handed it to *Red Eagle*. The chief cautiously unwrapped the bundle. Recognizing its contents, he sniffed its essence and slowly broke out in a grin of approval.

"My father expresses his thanks and has called for the pipe to be lit," *White Dove* stated.

Zack turned to Pearle and whispered, "That's a good sign. A very good sign."

* * *

For the Cheyenne, smoking the pipe serves two purposes. It is an important ceremony and also an enjoyable activity. After inhaling the Kentucky Black Patch tobacco mixture, *Chief Red Eagle* was compelled to call for the pipe.

The summer heat cures most tobacco, grown by white men. Black Path tobacco farmers cure in closed barns with wood chip fires. The dark-fired blend given to *Red Eagle* has a sweet aroma enhanced with a hint of nougat and nuts.

The Cheyenne also have natural tobacco, sometimes mixed with dry Sumac leaves and the bark of a willow tree. And, on occasion, buffalo grease is added. The revered chief is a discriminating smoker and soon to have a marvelous experience.

Falling Water carefully handed the pipe to his father. *Red Eagle* said a prayer before filling the bowl with his new tobacco. Zack and Pearle watched intently as the chief removed an ember from the cooking fire and lit the material within the bowl. His response after breathing in the initial puff said it all. After all his years, *Chief Red Eagle* never had such a pleasant experience. He sat with his eyes closed savoring the moment before giving the pipe to his son. Pearle was the last to smoke. Careful so as not to cough, he passed the pipe back to Zack. With no one smoking, it was returned to *Red Eagle* who took another puff and repeated the process until the tobacco had burned out.

"Have you observed the return of the buffalo?" he asked.

"Not as yet. It appears as though they will be late this season," Zack replied.

"Each year they come later and later. I believe it is because their numbers grow smaller and smaller. It takes the herd longer to consume the available grass which remains the same every year," *Red Eagle* stated. "Tell me about the Pawnee raid."

"Well, I got news of it while I was in Fort Dodge. I hurried back to the farm and alerted Abel Strawn, the owner of the homestead. He, in turn, warned the neighbors. We prepared ourselves for an attack. When it happened, I counted about twenty or so Pawnee braves," Zack recounted.

"Who killed their chief?"

"That would be Abel. He shot him with the rifle he used during the Civil War between the whites."

Red Eagle tamped another bowl of tobacco, lit it, and repeated the smoking routine.

"I would like to meet this man with such a rifle," the chief suggested. "While I'm pleased to have an enemy killed, your friend may have interrupted my plans to trade two captive girls I hold here in the village."

"We had no knowledge of this," said Zack.

"I realize that, perhaps my son owes him more gratitude than I do. He has his eye on one of the girls," the chief said, while looking at *Falling Water* who reddened at his father's words.

"I would be grateful if you ate supper and spent the night with us. Your horses and firearms will be tended as if our own. You have no worries in that regard."

"I have a question," Pearle blurted. "What must I do to speak to your daughter?"

White Dove hesitated. The two made intense eye contact and held it until the chief asked. "What did he say?"

"He asked what he must do to speak to me," she replied.

Chief Red Eagle looked perplexed. How strange the whites can be at times. Without turning his head he said, "Tell him he must become worthy."

"My father said you must become worthy."

Zack nudged Pearle and told him to end it. He will explain later.

After the meeting with *Chief Red Eagle*, *Falling Water* led Zack and Pearle to his own lodge. Since returning from winter quarters, his sister could no longer live with him. Cheyenne culture forbids it. *White Dove* now resides with her grandmother, *Valley of Flowers*, in a tepee of their own. She also no longer provides her brother with living water each morning. *Chumani* (*Dewdrops*) now performs the task, much to the approval of the young chief.

The three men conversed for a short while, and then *Falling Water* suggested they rest until the women bring food. The young chief excused himself and left the lodge.

"Where do you think he went?' asked Pearle.

"Most likely, he's out hunting *Dewdrops* and will occupy her time until the grandmother calls her inside."

"*White Dove* probably fetches water for her grandmother," Pearle mused.

"I reckon so," Zack said. "Let's try to catch a couple winks this evening, before we eat."

Silent motion stirred the pair from their light sleep. Women were actively bringing bowls of victuals. Zack and Pearle were famished and consumed the fare without questioning its content. *Falling Water* returned in high spirits and finished off the remainder in the bowls.

Zack had explained Pearle's outburst was offensive to the Cheyenne. When a guest is in his lodge, the chief leads the direction of a conversation. Pearle's infraction was overlooked because he is a white man and unfamiliar with custom.

Early the next morning, as the others slept, Pearle determined he might as well be hanged for a sheep as a lamb. He crept outside and walked to the river in search of *White Dove*. Many women were filling their water vessels. Guided by the magnetic pull of love, Pearle identified his affection instantly.

Standing behind an outcrop of gorse, he held his breath and waited for her to pass. As *White Dove* drew near, Pearle moved in front and took hold of her wrist.

"I must ask one question of you," he stated. "Would you want to speak to me should I become worthy?"

There was music in *White Dove's* eyes when she answered in the affirmative.

* * *

On the return to the farm, Pearle considers their visit a success. *White Dove* not only made eye contact, but also agreed to talk to him. That is, after he became worthy. As to how he will accomplish worthiness, is something he plans to explore further.

Zack was thinking about taking his cow to the McCorkle ranch. Once they arrive home, it will be one of the first things he does.

When the travelers failed to return the first night, Abel couldn't help but worry. Zack was more than able to take care of himself; nevertheless, their absence was cause for consternation. Able stood with a pail of cracked corn, broadcasting it near the chicken coop, as two riders appeared in the distance. Expressing a sigh of relief, the tall Tennessean walked to the stable area to await their return.

Zack gave a full accounting of the visit with *Chief Red Eagle*. He commented on the Cheyenne hospitality and the fact *Red Eagle* would like to meet the man with the special rifle. Zack trod lightly on the activities of Abel's brother-in-law, leaving Pearle to disclose whatever he wished. He did, however, mention taking the cow to McCorkle's ranch in the morning.

Later, when the purple nightshade fell, the men sat on Abel's front porch comparing opinions of the present and future. A great deal has been accomplished in a short period of time. Yet, a major task remained.

"I've surveyed the area behind the house and I wouldn't be surprised if an underground spring passed under it," Zack imparted.

"How deep would we need to dig?" Abel asked.

"No more than ten or twelve feet."

"We could start next week. The week after, our neighbors will be here to help harvest the wheat."

"Perhaps one of them might be willing to help with the well," Zack suggested.

"I'll mention it after Sunday's service," Abel stated.

With that, Zack tapped his pipe against the sole of his boot and stood to stretch.

"I'm going to hit the hay early tonight. In the morning I'll milk old Bossy and take her to meet her new boyfriend," Zack chuckled.

The next day, Zack was gone by the time Pearle stirred. More importantly, before Amanda woke to catch him.

* * *

Living a day in the Cheyenne camp aroused the hunter instinct in Pearle. He saddled his horse, placed the Henry rifle in its sling, and rode toward the northwest horizon.

260

As far as the naked eye could see, the land was flat and heavy laden with rich green prairie grass. The only game encountered was of the feathered variety, very difficult to bag with a single barrel rifle.

Pearle idly pressed onward for another hour, listless from the motion of his mount and preoccupied with thoughts of *White Dove*. Suddenly, he was awakened from his fantasy by what looked to be a buffalo and her calf. Kicking his heels, he galloped toward the animals and witnessed several others grazing. Behind them, in the distance, were hundreds more of the shaggy beasts—the herd has finally arrived.

Overcome with nervous tension, Pearle froze on the spot. Surprisingly, the bison ignored his presence. It was as though he could actually walk up and touch one. It took a while before his scrambled thoughts began to unravel. A mental spark brought him back to consciousness and triggered his decision. He will ride to the Cheyenne camp and sound the alert. Who knows, it might be a step toward worthiness. With deliberate haste, Pearle galloped for *Red Eagle's* village.

The Dog Soldiers, guarding the entrance, recognized the excited youth, yet, made him dismount. Again, one of them led Pearle to *Falling Water's* lodge. Engrossed in conversation with *Chumani*, the young chief was perturbed by the intrusion; howbeit, once he heard the message, he dashed to inform his father.

Tidings travel fast in an Indian camp and soon a general hubbub quickly spread.

Tribal laws governed the hunt. Since the Cheyenne tribe depended on the shaggy beast for food, no individual hunting was allowed—all joined in the effort. In as much as large quantities of food will be killed at one time, it was necessary to be organized. The hunt, as well as the enforcement, was in the hands of the soldier band or Dog Soldiers. Those who violated the law were punished severely.

Chief Red Eagle's band had devised a method to their hunt. Braves with faster horses would ride abreast of the bison herd and cut across in order to surround a portion of the larger group. In all likelihood such a tactic will be employed.

It was decided by *Red Eagle* to begin the hunt in the morning. He issued his orders to the Dog Soldiers and, from that point, they had charge of the hunt. For the remainder of the day, it was cried through the village, that on the morrow, all would assist in the pursuit of buffalo.

Pearle found himself amid the fervor and stayed close to *Falling Water's* every move. Exasperated with Pearle, clinging like a burr, *Falling Water* called for someone to fetch the white man's horse. Pearle refused to leave. He was adamant about going along with the hunt. Turning to an alternate plan, *Falling Water* directed his friend, *Two Trees,* to watch over him. They became an unlikely pair. Speaking scant English and towering a foot over Pearle, *Two Trees* communicated by sign language. Following orders, the towering Indian led his charge to his own lodge. That night it was a tossup as to who spent the most restless sleep— Pearle or *Aponi*, *Two Trees'* mother.

Before the glints of daylight, *Two Trees* readied for the chase. Outside the lodge his pony and Pearle's horse were tethered. Many braves were astride their mounts and moving slowly toward the entrance of the village. Others were dragging empty travois. It appeared as though the entire village took part. The brigade of hunters was composed of those carrying the lance, others bow and arrow, with a few featuring a single shot rifle. The Cheyenne were noted for being good bowmen. In fact, *Two Trees* had once killed two buffalo with one arrow. His bow was an excellent weapon up to five hundred yards away and so powerful, no one in the village could bend it.

Pearle was armed with his Henry repeating rifle and fell in line beside his host for the previous evening. He searched the entourage for a glimpse of *White Dove*, to no avail. The hunting expedition continued in a queue formation for the next two hours. When the bison herd came into view, the column only spoke in whispers, for fear they may startle their prey. At the head of the line, Dog Soldiers issued instructions, and then, experienced braves guided their ponies toward the outskirts, in order to encircle the grazing behemoths.

Two Trees motioned to Pearle and spoke in his native tongue. Pearle understood the imposing red man. Because the fiery little white man had never killed buffalo before, he wanted him to hunt and kill a calf. Pearle would have no part of it. Killing a buffalo calf would never make him worthy. As *Two Trees* dashed to join his fellows, Pearle kicked his horse with both heels and directed it at the 'thunder of the plains.'

Inexperienced in hunting bison native style, Pearle soon found himself in the middle of a stampeding herd, instead of along the edge. His horse instinctively ran at the buffalo's pace. To say Pearle was excited isn't a strong enough word, panicking is closer to the fact. Difficult as it was, he managed to gather his wits only to find a large buffalo alongside, running in tandem.

Pearle had pre-set his rifle before the hunt took place. Swinging it over his charger's head, he took aim just below the great bison's undulating hump and fired. There was a loud retort and considerable transitory smoke, yet, the bull didn't lose a step. At such close range he couldn't have missed. Pearle released the reins, and riding with both hands free, squeezed off two more shots just as they came upon a fallen humpback. The big bull veered to the right, dodging the dead animal, and struck the horse. Pearle was tossed into the air, landing atop the angry beast. Finding himself in a riding position, he grabbed the long hair around the hump and hung on for dear life. Close quarters kept the buffalo from bucking and forced it to ignore the alien on its back.

In a timespan that seemed forever, the gunshot wounds began to tell. With Pearle still holding its hump hair in a vice-like grip, the giant beast finally collapsed on the trampled grass. His chest heaving, eyes startled and watery, Pearle stood and blankly watched stragglers running to catch up with the stampeding herd. One thing for certain, Pearle has switched the tassel to the other side of his mortarboard cap.

Pearle Sparks was bumped off his horse and landed on top of the wounded buffalo. He rode it until it finally died and sent him sprawling across the grass. Pearle's friend Two Trees gave him the Cheyenne Indian name: Boy Who Rides Buffalo.

Two Trees was the first on the scene. The tawny Indian was grinning from ear to ear. With both of his muscular arms raised high above his head, he gave out with an ear splitting yell of victory and approval. Pearle, still dazed and unsteady, tried to emulate his tall ally. However, his throat was parched from the terrifying encounter and his shout came out more like a screech.

By then, others rode up to the celebrating pair. It was at that moment, a small group of Cheyenne warriors gave Pearle his Indian name—*Boy Who Rides Buffalo.*

The sound of thundering hooves began to slowly die away, as the hairy legions ran to safety. A landscape dotted with the carcasses of slain bison was left in their wake. Each one attended by small groups of Cheyenne women. *Two Trees* unsheathed his knife and deftly cut open the humpback, removing its liver. Prior to handing it to Pearle, he rubbed blood on the novice's face as initiation into the club.

"You may have a bite, but, your first kill must be presented to *Chief Red Eagle* as a gift," *Two Trees* stated, as he extended the dripping organ.

"No thank you," Pearle said, while turning his head.

"It is tradition," *Two Trees* insisted.

Pearle, squeamish at the thought, acquiesced. He felt like a cannibal.

* * *

Plains Indians utilized virtually every part of the buffalo. Nothing was left behind. Even the entrails and bones were packed on travois and carried back to the village. Almost the entire animal was eaten, in some form or another. The tongue and nose were delicacies. The liver, sprinkled with gall, was also a favorite. Cheyenne filled the small intestine with meat, which was either boiled or roasted—marrowbones were split and the contents consumed. Even the hide of the bull-buffalo was prepared for consumption.

Bison flesh, along with the back fats, was cut in thin strips and dried in the sun. Dried meat was pounded fine with a stone maul, and sometimes, mixed with dried fruit, i.e., cranberries or currants to make pemmican.

* * *

When the hunt was over, and all had returned to the camp, a ceremonial feast was held in honor of the Great Spirit. Names of certain warriors were also acknowledged for special acts of generosity. Among those, cried out in the village, was that of *Boy Who Rides Buffalo.*

That evening, many of the hunters sat around a fire recounting the chase. Pearle sat with *Two Trees* and a few of his comrades. All were in a festive mood. At last Pearle was able to catch sight of his object of infatuation. *White Dove* and her grandmother were sitting next to *Falling Water* and *Chief Red Eagle.* Pearle's stare was intense until their eyes locked. *White Dove's* demeanor visibly brightened and she fashioned a gleaming smile.

"What else do I have to do to become worthy?" he asked *Two Trees.*

"You must make a sacrifice to prove you are earnest. I will discuss this with *Falling Water* after you have returned to the farm. He is the brother and will make the final decision."

"When will I find out what it is?" Pearle asked.

"I will let you know, after I meet with him. Three days from now at the latest," *Two Trees* said confidently.

Two Trees, Pearle's Cheyenne Indian friend. The tall warrior was a great hunter and renowned for his strength. No one in the village could draw his bow or catch eagles by hand.

CHAPTER TWENTY-ONE

‎

The brouhaha over Jack Leffingwell's declaration of Ulysses S. Grant, being the better general, continued long after the mountain man returned home. In Statesville, all hell broke loose as neighbors took sides. Pronouncements from the pulpit were required to quell the pro-southern perturbation. Better judgment obliged Melvin and Jack to only visit town in cases of necessity—a position most disturbing for Abigail and Hope.

Hyrum Adams, along with the other ministers, sermonized about loving thy neighbor and the First Amendment to the United States Constitution—one of ten amendments that constitute the Bill of Rights.

Attending church each Sunday served as the barometer to determine the general attitude. Finally, when more smiles than frowns welcomed the Leffingwell family, Jack felt it safe to resume normal activity. The day Jack was overheard stating, "I respected General Grant and loved Robert E. Lee," the issue was settled.

On the subsequent occasion to be in town, Abigail exited the post office waving an envelope. It was a letter from their friend, Abel Strawn. She decided to wait until they were at her father's house before opening it.

"Who put a burr under your saddle?" Hyrum joked.

"I'm just excited to receive a letter from Abel and Amanda," she replied, after sitting down and tearing open the envelope.

July 6, 1869

Dear Friends,

At last we are living on the farm. The journey was arduous but well worth it. I now have calluses on both hands plus an aching back – ha ha. Seriously, I've never felt better in my life. There was a standing crop of winter wheat when we arrived. It will be harvested in a couple weeks.

Zachary Wheat is a gift sent from heaven. We could not have done this without him. He's helped us plow the fields, plant corn, and start a garden by the house. The Myers barn was without a roof. Thanks to Zack, it now has one. He and Pearle have built a bunkhouse attached to the barn. They have fixed it up real nice. Pearle pushed the issue since I forbid him carrying a gun in the house. Zack sees to it that he only wears it when they go to town.

There are plenty Indians living around here. Mostly Cheyenne, with a peace loving chief. In fact, Pearle is infatuated with the chief's daughter. Only the Lord knows how that will end up. Everyone is in good health and little Abby is growing like a weed.

Trusting you are all well,

Your friend in Christ,
Abel

P.S. I'm holding outdoor church services for the neighbors. Haven't figured out what to do when the snow flies.
My address is – Abel Strawn c/o Fort Dodge, Kansas

Abigail wiped the tears from her eyes, a reflection of past days and another life. As far as she is concerned, the man is a saint. Learning he is happy brings tears of joy.

The visit was interrupted by a knock on the door—a common occurrence at the minister's manse. When Hyrum opened the portal, he found Mason Poor standing on the steps.

"I hate to bother you reverend, but, is Jack Leffingwell here?" Mason asked.

"Yes, he and my daughter are visiting," the minister replied. "Would you like to step inside?"

"No thanks. I just need to talk to Jack, privately," Mason said.

Hyrum returned to his living room and, looking at Jack, said, "Mason Poor is outside and needs to talk to you."

Placing his coffee cup on its saucer and depositing the works on a side table, Jack walked to the entryway.

"I'm glad I caught you in town. It has to do with what happened a few weeks ago. Last night I was called on by one of those people. He was asking about you."

"Was he alone?" Jack questioned.

"No. Jake Butler was with him but Jake didn't say anything. I believe Jake took over after I bailed out."

"Did you catch his name?"

"No. I did learn he was from Davidson County."

"What did he look like?"

"Tall as you, unkempt and mean as an alligator. I had to let you know right away. Lucky I caught you here. I was going to your farm but this draws less attention," Mason answered.

"Thanks Mason. You're a real friend. I'll keep my eyes open," Jack stated, and returned to his coffee. He sat deeply in thought until finally deciding it was time to give August McKnight all the details.

Outside of telling the mountain man he should have come to him sooner, Augie listened to the story from the very beginning. Noting names, some of which were familiar. Augie was surprised that some of the town's most distinguished residents were involved.

* * *

Dewitt Clinton Senter became governor of Tennessee after the resignation of William G. Brownlow. A pro-Unionist during the Civil War, Brownlow's radical policies of disfranchisement had left the state divided and kindled the rise of the Ku Klux Klan.

In his inaugural address, Governor Senter vowed to aggressively pursue the Klan and quell Klan violence. Several counties were still under martial law, subsequently Nathan Bedford Forrest ordered the Klan to destroy its costumes and cease all activities. Not all Klan members paid heed. Accordingly, anti-Klan citizens banded to form opposition. Faced with the state government plus militant citizens against them, only the staunchest members continued to operate—primarily in the dark of night.

* * *

Later in the day, Abigail, and her friend Hope, walked to Riberty's general store. Jack and Melvin stopped by the blacksmith's shop. As usual, Ryan was in a rare mood, complaining about a customer who thought his prices were too high.

"What did you tell him?" Melvin asked, stoking the fire.

"It wasn't a him, it was a her. She had a bad wheel on her buggy. I told her to run it over to Lebanon. I'm sure she could find someone to repair it cheaper." Ryan chuckled.

"That's twenty miles away," Melvin stated.

"Yeah, I know. She had me fix it and I charged her two dollars. If she hadn't raised such a fuss, I'd have only charged her a dollar."

Turning to the mountain man, Ryan said, "Say Jack, I was over at the town tavern last night and a stranger was asking about you. I asked him why he was so interested and he told me it was none of my business. I think he was up to no good. Nobody said much so he stomped out pissed off."

"Was he a tall guy with a beard?"

"That's him," Ryan replied.

* * *

That night, the Leffingwell's had supper at the Kaufman's house. Hope served fried chicken—furnished by her husband since she didn't have to kill one of her brood. Abigail brought an apple pie. They alternated these dinners once a month. After the dishes are washed, dried, and put away, they played Whist, a popular card game at the time. (Eventually Whist was replaced with a similar game called Bridge.)

The rules of Whist are quite simple. The game is usually played with two decks of cards. While one is being dealt out, the other is shuffled in order to speed up the game. Abigail and Hope, and, Jack and Melvin, play as partners. The cards are shuffled by the player to the dealers left and cut by the player to the dealer's right. The dealer hands out all the cards, one at a time, so that each player has 13 cards. The final card, which will belong to the dealer, is turned face up to indicate which suit is trump.

The turned trump remains face up on the table until it is the dealer's turn to play his or her first trick. The player to the dealers left leads to the first trick. Any card may be led. The other players, in clockwise order, play a card to the trick. If they can, players must follow suit by playing a card of the same suit as the card led, A player with no card of the suit led may play any card. The highest trump in it wins the trick. Or, if it contains no trump, the highest card of the suit led.

When all 13 tricks have been played, the side that won more tricks scores 1 point for each trick in excess of 6. The partnership that reaches 5 points wins the game.

The team of Jack and Melvin ask for sympathy points because of Melvin's lost arm. The girls, perpetual winners, are cold hearted and will only shuffle the cards for him.

Once the game is finished, usually around midnight, the women expanded their lead even further—frustrating Jack and Melvin. Hope maintained a running tab on wins and losses. The men can't figure out how the girls continuously win each month. Melvin figures they have a undetected signal code because they can't be smarter than the men. Jack questions that, since each hand has a different trump. In desperation, they considered bribing Sarah Jane to stand behind the girls and signal if they hold any aces. She flatly refused, and they confessed her complicity was a long shot at best.

Hope cleverly hides the list so that Melvin and Jack can't find it and tamper with the numbers. It all becomes a good natured jest enjoyed by both families.

At this time of evening, the temperature outside has dropped to a cooler level, and, with a slight breeze, it made the walk home quite pleasant. The children sleepily managed the short stroll while thinking of their beds. Jozef had a head start for slumber. He was fast asleep in Abigail's arms.

"What were you and Melvin whispering about?" Abigail asked, as she shifted Jozef to a more comfortable position.

"It had to do with the stranger asking about me in town," he answered.

"You talked to August McKnight, didn't you?"

"Yes, he got the while story from start to finish."

"Maybe you should tell Ezell Williams," Abigail suggested.

"Good idea. The town built him a brand new jail. As yet, nobody's been locked up except Ryan Gosling. And he was just drunk and didn't require turning the key."

There is something warm and forgiving about returning home to your own house. Comfortable and friendly surroundings tend to lessen apprehensions and calm ones nerves. After the children were put to bed, Abigail and Jack fell into their overstuffed living room chairs.

* * *

The following morning foretells another hot mid-summer day. The azure sky is cloudless, without much hope of any cooling shower or rain. Animals in the field stay close to the trees for protection from the sun's relentless heat. While Hope replenishes the water in her chicken coop, Melvin tends to his chores and then ambles to the Leffingwell farm. Finding Jack in the barn, pulling hay for the horses, he asks, "We going in town this morning?"

"I was thinking of visiting Ezell Williams and tell him what I know about the stranger and the Klan."

"Would you mind if I go with you? I ain't seen the new jailhouse," Melvin mentioned.

Ezell Williams had been acting sheriff for as long as anyone remembered. No election was ever held. Ezell was sheriff and that was that. Too old to enlist in the war, he did his part by keeping the peace. As far as the townsfolk were concerned, his authority was backed by the community. Ezell owned a pistol but never had the need to use it. It was loaded, and kept in his desk drawer, just in case. It reposed there for the last ten years.

Jack and Melvin found him sitting at his desk and sipping a cup of coffee. The new building still had the familiar smell of fresh pine, and with the exception of a picture of Stonewall Jackson, the walls were bare. A stack of wanted posters covered half the desk. He was reluctant to pin them up for fear of scratching the knotty pine.

"Good morning Jack, Melvin. What brings you in town so early in the morning?" Ezell asked cheerfully.

"I'm here to talk about the Klan in Statesville," Jack replied.

"Lieutenant McKnight told me you'd be popping in. He also gave me a list of folks he thinks are involved. Insurrection against the Constitution is a Federal crime. The law's pretty clear on that. The acts of the Ku Klux Klan break several state and local statutes as well. My office holds for the writ of habeas corpus; however, a lot of these perpetrators aren't aware of it. I can hold them for a time under suspicion of a crime, and, sometimes, that alone, makes them law abiding citizens again."

"From what I hear, the stranger from Davidson County will take more than that to discourage him," Jack expressed.

"The first time he steps out of line, he'll be visiting my brand new jail," declared the sheriff.

"How many cells do you have?" asked Melvin.

"Come on, son, I'll take you on a tour," Ezell replied. He was very proud of his new slammer.

After the cook's tour, Jack and Melvin walked to the post office to mail Abigail's letter to Abel and Amanda Strawn. With that chore completed, the pair walked to the restaurant across the street from the town tavern. Met by the friendly din of diners, they took an empty table. Ma Mambleau was quick as a wink when it came to waiting on customers. No sooner had the pair sat down, she was turning over empty coffee cups and filling them with the aromatic brew.

"What'll you have Melvin?" she inquired. Apparently he was a frequent customer. Most likely accompanied with Ryan Gosling.

"I already ate earlier. Maybe just a piece of gooseberry pie—a large piece."

"How about you, Jack?" After the soliloquy about the generals, Jack was famous.

"I guess I'll have the same. I can always eat fresh gooseberry pie," he conceded.

Picking up crumbs with his fork, Melvin asked, "You ever think about the good old days when the four of us were together?"

"Many times. I wouldn't exactly call the war the good old days, but, there were plenty of occasions when Lomas made us all laugh," Jack recalled. "On the other hand, he also kept us fearful of ending up behind bars. Lomas was either so dense he couldn't see the forest for the trees, or, so clever that nobody could come close to catching him."

"I'd rather think it was the later," Melvin mused. "He seems to be doing okay with marriage and kids."

"The image of Lomas Chandler with three little children crawling all over him is one in which I have trouble fixing in my mind. Nonetheless, I think he is in hog heaven—married to a beautiful woman, whose family owns a hotel, tavern, and a few gambling tables."

Melvin tried to imagine Lomas with children and broke out in a sentimental smile, and said, "He must be doing okay. He sent Abel lots of money so he could make the trip to Kansas."

"Never use money as a measure of wealth. The love of a good woman, healthy children, and faith in a guiding hand, makes any man wealthy—especially those, for one reason or another, who seem to be less fortunate financially," Jack replied, as he finished off the last drop of coffee and pushed back from the table. "Would you like to say hello to your friend Ryan before we head for the farm?"

Melvin answered to the affirmative and caught Ma Mambleau's attention. She returned to their table and asked if they wanted anything else.

"Not this morning. What do we owe you for the pie and coffee?"

"That'll be 40¢ gents," she answered, while extending an open hand. Jack dug into his front pocket and placed a half-dollar coin against her palm, saying, "A little extra for the excellent service."

"Y'all come back real soon, ya hear. And bring the wives next time. I serve roast beef on Saturdays."

For a few moments, the former sharpshooters stood in front of the café, admiring their hometown. Since the war ended, it has grown appreciably. In addition to the jailhouse, a ladies apparel shop and doctor's office extended businesses on the main street. New faces at church services also tend to demonstrate the town's expansion. Melvin lit one of the pre-rolled cigarettes, Hope had made for him, and he and Jack sauntered to the blacksmith's shop.

Ryan was repairing someone's wagon frame when the duo entered his open doors.

"Are you too busy to talk?" Melvin asked, knowing full well the answer beforehand.

"It's been a slow morning. All I got is this wagon and that horse over there." he replied. "She needs a couple new shoes, but, her owner won't be back 'til tomorrow."

The men made themselves comfortable and rehashed community growth, especially the new lockup.

"I understand you've seen it from the inside looking out," Jack joked.

"That damn Fritz. He told Ezell I was inebriated and getting too loud for the customers. They all had been waiting for the first chance to put me in it and laughed like hell when Ezell did. I could have walked out any time I wanted. The door was left wide open, so I took advantage of it and spent the night. Actually the bed was kind of comfortable."

"You got time for a quick one before we leave town?" Melvin asked.

"I just told ya, I'm having a slow day. But, busy or not, makes no nevermind. I always have time for a short beer," Ryan chirped, while wiping the perspiration from his face and arms. Tossing the rag on his workbench, he joined the other two and traipsed across the street.

"Well, well, look who broke out of jail," Fritz goaded. No one in the room laughed. Obviously, the joke had become stale.

"Just give us three beers and go back to your sauerkraut," Ryan snapped.

"I don't like sauerkraut," was Fritz's feeble repartee. "Jake Butler and that stranger were in earlier. They were asking about you, Jack. The big guy is bad news. He also carries a gun strapped to his leg. Ezell Williams told me to run and tell him if he does anything wrong."

"Jake Butler knows where I live. In fact, he and several of his friends stopped by a few weeks ago. He must be shy about visiting me again. That's probably why they want to see me when I'm in town." Jack drained his beer, turned on his stool, and slapped his knees, saying, "Melvin, it's time we were heading home."

"See you boys later, I'll stay awhile and have another cool one," Ryan affirmed.

* * *

The earth has reached its perihelion[9] with the glaring sun and Jack and Melvin were looking forward to soaking in the fast moving water of their creek. As they trooped to the livery stable, the large form of the stranger, blocking their way, suddenly interrupted them. He certainly fit the bill of a Klan enforcer as well as the description given around town.

"Tell the gimp to take a walk. I got a message from the boys in Nashville," he snarled. Jake Butler stood to the side. Obviously, he was nervous and his eyes were darting as he scanned the street.

"You must not have heard me. I said—tell the gimp to take a walk. What I have to say is personal," he repeated, behind clenched teeth.

Demeaning physical or racial epithets have always galled the Tennessee mountain man. His Fredericksburg scar was slowly turning a throbbing red.

---

[9]   The point in the path of a planet that is nearest the sun.

When the brute slapped his hand against his holster, Jack delivered a kick to the solar plexus so hard he flew backward over the hitching rail and landed on the dirt road—softened somewhat from horse's hooves. Paralyzed by the kick, he couldn't rise nor speak.

Motioning to Melvin, Jack said, "Go pick up his gun. He ain't got much need for it." Turning to the enforcer's companion, Jack found Jake Butler with both hands raised in surrender. He whined, "I don't want any part of this."

"Then pick up your buddy and leave town," Jack ordered. "Remember what I told you boys back on the farm. You can expect to see me one of these nights. Better keep your lamp turned low and the curtains drawn."

By this time a small crowd had formed. Two or three men in the town alehouse witnessed the scene. Though the action was over when Ryan came to the window, he claimed to have seen it all.

"That big ape pulled a gun and Jack gave him a mule kick. The oversized gorilla wilted like a dead flower," Ryan shouted.

At that point, Ezell Williams arrived and asked if anyone saw what happened. One or two acknowledged they had and were invited to come to the jailhouse and put it on paper.

"Somebody get a wagon," the sheriff ordered. "We don't want to carry him. He looks like he weighs three hundred pounds."

Now, with two prisoners safely behind bars, Ezell sent for Lieutenant McKnight. Upon entering the calaboose and reviewing the inmates, Augie took one look at the stranger and said, "This man needs a doctor."

Even with a new doctor in town, folks remained more comfortable with old Doctor Hamilton. It will take time for the medical reins to be handed over and Hamilton allowed to retire. After examining the man from Davidson County, Hamilton stated, "This man is seriously hurt. He has broken ribs and possible internal bleeding. He needs to be taken to the hospital in Nashville."

"My men found a Ku Klux Klan costume in his saddlebags. I'm placing him under military arrest and will see that he's taken to the infirmary," replied Augie. "The other fellow is all yours sheriff. Though I suggest you inspect his belongings as well."

Over-confidence can lead to one's undoing. Such was the case of Jake Butler. Inspecting his saddlebags revealed another Klan attire.

"You got yourself in a whole lot of trouble, Jake. This Klan business makes you a federal criminal. The U.S. Army will probably end up hanging your friend from Nashville—if he doesn't die beforehand. As I see it, you only got one chance to escape the gallows. That's to turn states evidence against the other Klan members," Ezell lamented.

"I ain't killed nobody. The worse I ever done was burn a couple barns," Jake pleaded from behind the bars.

"That's the sad part of the whole matter. Have your neck stretched for just burning a barn," said the sheriff, feigning sadness. "It takes a lot of skill to hang a man properly. Unfortunately, it looks like you will be strung up by a bunch of amateurs. I've been told, if the noose isn't set properly, the fall might tear your head plumb off. Do you think you'll kick much?"

That was the last straw. Jake Butler signed a confession and listed every member he was acquainted with. The wily sheriff managed to frighten Butler to the point of spilling the beans.

For the remainder of the summer, Lieutenant McKnight's men investigated every name on the list. Suspects were in such an anxious state, their stomach turned with every knock at the door. The stranger was never heard from again. Jake Butler was eventually released and left town. Some say he went out west.

By the time crops were ready to harvest, the area was back to normal—if that's possible with Ryan Gosling living amongst them.

CHAPTER TWENTY-TWO

T hings have never been the same since *Chumani* was delivered into camp. She has interrupted the harmonious relationship between *Two Trees* and *Falling Water*. Before her arrival, *Two Trees* could meet with his friend whenever he wished. Now, she occupies his good buddy's waking moments. She has bewitched him. It definitely was justification to seek council from *Buffalo Horn*, the medicine man.

"What brings you to my lodge, my hefty son?" asked the aged shaman.

"I believe *Chumani* has cast a spell on *Falling Water*. What can I do to break her magic?"

Buffalo Horn tried to look serious for *Two Trees* benefit. Aware of the tall brave's simple honesty, he invited him to sit and gave forth with an audible prayer, while vigorously shaking a rattle. *Two Trees* was visibly unnerved. Finally *Buffalo Horn* became quiet, yet, kept his eyes closed for a little longer.

"The spell between a man and a woman is frequently cast over our village. Often, the white tailed deer—especially, a fawn—causes it. *Chumani* is not solely to blame. Human weakness, even that of a chief, can be affected by the many moods of mother earth. The full moon, warm evenings, and even rain may weaken the strength to resist. I have sung a prayer to break the spell on *Falling Water*. Only time will dictate its effect," said the wise healer.

Bolstered by the shaman's words, *Two Trees*, once again, sought his friend. Finding *Falling Water* alone in his lodge convinced him that *Buffalo Horn's* magic was working.

"Enter, my friend, let us sit and talk a while," said *Falling Water*.

Two Trees complied. Pleased to see the young chief reach for the pipe, he was equally pleased it would allow them to speak from the heart. Considering their relationship, the pipe ceremony was brief. From the aroma, *Falling Water* was smoking some of the tobacco given to his father. *Two Trees* was anxious to try it. "Where is *Chumani*?"

"She helps my mother, today," replied *Falling Water*. "How did it end with *Boy Who Rides Buffalo*?"

"I'm happy you asked that question. He awaits your decision to name his sacrifice for speaking to *White Dove*. Shall it be three days without food and water or cutting his arm?"

"Neither. If he wishes to speak with my sister, he must swing to the pole," the young chief said with conviction.

Two Trees thought it was a rather strong sacrifice just to speak to *White Dove*. On the other hand, she was *Falling Water's* sister.

The next morning, the towering Cheyenne brave leaped on his painted pony and rode to the old Myers' farm.

* * *

Missing Sunday's service didn't set well with Abel. Refusing to give an explanation vexed him even further. Zack told Abel that Pearle's absence had to be for a justifiable reason and the young man will explain in his own due time. Abel shrugged his shoulders and walked away mumbling to himself.

Pearle was thankful to return to his chores without disclosing his activities with the Cheyenne. Work, previously considered monotonous and tiring, took on new meaning, since it allowed him to evade more questioning and recall the moments with *White Dove*.

Pearle preferred to skip supper that evening, in order to avoid critical eyes. Zack would have no part of it. He quoted Davy Crockett[10] when he said, "Be sure you're right, and then go ahead." Pearle learned of the exploits of Davy Crockett at an early age. The legendary frontiersman became his hero. To the young pioneer, similarities between Crockett and Zack Wheat were evident. And, to top it off, he and Wheat share the same bunkhouse.

Much to Pearle's surprise, nothing was said about his absence on Sunday. Abel was engrossed over the pending wheat harvest and Zack expressed concern over his cow. As always, Amanda's thoughts were in a world all her own.

Later that night, Zack updated Pearle on the events of Sunday past.

"It was agreed, after church on the 18th, we will begin harvesting the wheat crop. Rainbow Calloway is going to teach us about stooking—or at least the way he did it in Missouri. From what I gather, the bundles get tied with their own stalks. Not to change the subject, but, you look like you've been in a fight. Who won?"

Pearle laughed, "I tried to take on a buffalo bare handed."

"If that's Gospel, I already know you lost."

"Truth is, I went on a buffalo hunt with the Cheyenne. The one I shot bumped my horse and I ended up on top of him. I rode it like a broncobuster 'til he fell over dead. Then, I scooted across the prairie face down," Pearle related.

"Lucky you weren't killed," Zack replied calmly. "Did you get to talk to your girlfriend?"

"Not exactly."

---

[10]   Crockett, a Tennessee frontiersman, lacked formal education, yet, served in the state legislature and U.S. Congress. He was also noted for saying, "You can go to hell—I'm going to Texas." And, that he did—losing his life during the battle of the Alamo in 1836.

Zack learned enough about Pearle's escapades and continued his review of the weekend. "We got several strong fellas willing to help dig the well. Some of them found rocks on their property and agreed to bring them over in their wagons. We can line the well with them."

The aroma from Zack's pipe brought *White Dove* to mind—a perfect ending for the day.

The next morning the silhouette of a tall Indian was beheld through the early mist. Recognizing his newfound friend, Pearle raced to the road. Disinclined to come closer, *Two Trees* relayed the words of *Falling Water*.

"I don't understand what swinging to the pole means," Pearle confessed.

"When you come to the camp, my mother has agreed to teach you. It will take three days," *Two Trees* stated, while turning his multicolored mount and galloping away.

Witnessing the meeting down at the road, Zack surmised something nefarious was under foot. Respecting the young man's privacy, he remained silent. Nevertheless, it did beckon the idea of keeping a closer watch over his young associate.

According to plan, wheat harvest began after church services. At first, progress was rather slow, but as the day went on, the fields were occupied by more experienced reapers. In the early evening, supper was served, and by nightfall, a good portion of the acreage contained numerous standing bundles of wheat.

That night, a dozen tired farmers returned home, washed away the dusty remnants, and fell asleep the minute their head hit the pillow. By the end of the following day, nearly all the wheat stalks were cut and tied into bundles or sheaves.

Counting the neighbors' wagons, there were plenty carts available to transport the sheaves to the threshing area. Abel had selected an open tract near the barn for this step in the harvest— separating the wheat from the chaff. A stiff breeze was welcome to aid in the process.

Threshing mainly consisted of banging the seed heads against the side of a bucket. Full buckets of seed were then winnowed, to better remove the chaff. Stalks were tossed aside to be bound and later used for fuel. Other uses included, livestock bedding, plus feed and fodder. Those working the harvest will take some home to make mattresses.

Upon completion of the harvest, the field yielded 20 bushels per acre for a total 400 bushels. Abel retained about 60 bushels for personal use and replanting next year's crop, plus another 20 bushels as a gift for *Chief Red Eagle*—leaving 320 bushels to market. Zack Wheat had presence of mind to purchase an abundant supply of seed sacks and made filling them part of the process.

"The way it looks, we'll have to make several trips to deliver the wheat to town. I figure it'll take all day and that's counting two wagons. I believe we should tell the neighbors we'll pay a dollar a load if they lend a hand," Zack suggested.

Van Ronkle and Calloway jumped at the offer.

"I need to check on my cow. I'll stop by Azarov's store and find out when he wants us to deliver."

Zack's trip into town was the opportunity Amanda had been waiting for. She immediately invited herself along. "I've got a satchel full of old clothes I'll never wear. Maybe I can swap them for material to make new ones."

Once again, Abel proved that love was blind. Zack saw through her ruse right away and held his tongue. There's no way to postpone the trip and confronting Amanda would probably lose Abel's friendship. He stared at the ground and accepted his circumstances.

Amanda insisted they take the wagon so she didn't have to lug her satchel. Abel gave Zack an approving nod. The trip was rigid and constricted by tension. Amanda, aware Zack was on to her scheme, took deviate pleasure making small talk. There was no reply from behind the beard and the short jaunt seemed to take forever. Zack pulled the wagon in front of Azarov's building, making no offer to assist Amanda to the ground. Once inside, he looked for the baboon. It was sleeping in its cage.

"What can I do for you folks today?" Boris asked, in his Baltic English.

"We have the wheat ready to bring in. It's all bagged up in seed sacks. When do you want it?" Wheat inquired.

"Ya, you bring it in this Saturday," Azarov responded. "What did I say I pay you?"

"You said 65 cents a bushel."

"That's too much. Wheat prices have dropped. I pay you 60 cents."

"Not on your life. Wheat prices have risen. Our wheat grain is in seed bags and we have six wagons to haul it. We want 70 cents a bushel or it gets divided with the Indians and we keep the rest," Zack stated with certainty.

Even though disliked, Azarov knew Zack to be truthful. He faked a mental counting and asked, "How much you got?"

Allowing the 60 bushels for personal use and seed for planting, plus 20 bushels for the Indians, Zack said, "We have 320 bushels."

"Ha, you forgot 10% for moisture. That leaves 288 bushels. I pay $200. No more."

"You got yourself a deal," Zack agreed. And turning to Amanda asked, "You want to do your deal now?"

"I need to look around a little more. Go get your cow and I'll be ready when you get back," she directed.

Zack headed to McCorkle's ranch hoping she would still be there when he returned. He found Shorty leaning on the top corral rung and talking to the two bovines.

"I didn't know you spoke their language," Zack quipped.

"Hell yes, I was just breaking the news to the two lovers that you'd be ending their sexual relationship," McCorkle laughed.

"How'd she make out?"

"They're a good match. I think they got the job done," Shorty answered.

It was like pulling teeth to pay McCorkle for the feed and care. Finally, Zack poked two dollar bills in the rancher's shirt pocket, tethered the cow to the rear of the wagon, tipped his hat, and headed back to Azarov's store. He wasn't surprised to learn Amanda left the store right after he departed to retrieve the heifer. And, there wasn't any mystery as to where he expected to find her. With the cow in tow, Zack guided the mules through the fort's main gate and rolled to the Lucky Lady.

Amanda was sitting at a table with two men. One was the owner, Gus Greeley, and the other, Charles Fontaine, also known as 'Champagne Charlie.'

Greeley gives the impression of someone who's never worked at manual labor. He was soft, but only on the outside. Internally, lived a hard customer, feared by those who knew him.

Fontaine, much taller than Greeley, was a gambler and card sharp. Using skill and deception, he sets up shop at the favorite town casino, and plies his trade.

Privately, Fontaine has told Amanda he plans to work his way to California and she is welcome to come along.

Amanda knows there are strings attached, but finds him exciting. At the moment, her valise rests upstairs on the bed in Charlie's room.

Gus has hired Amanda to work the tables downstairs. Her job is to look good and push drinks. The downstairs girls get a modest salary, plus a percentage on liquor consumption. Gus is still undecided whether he wants her to entertain with her guitar. That's fine with Amanda since she doesn't have it with her and no telling when and if she reclaims it.

At last, Amanda can breathe the essence of freedom. She would have taken a job upstairs to get away from Abel.

Zack noticed Amanda the minute he walked in. It was obvious she knew her company better than he anticipated. What puzzled him was, how did she become that acquainted? The trip to get his cow took only an hour—an hour and a half at most. He snaked between tables until reaching the one she occupied.

"Are you ready to go home?" he quavered.

"I'm not going home. I will never go back to that life again."

Zack was lost for words. At the moment, he could only appeal to her better angels.

"But, you have a husband and a little daughter waiting for you," he said.

"Abel can take care of his daughter. He named her after Abigail Leffingwell. Let them look after her," came her bitter response.

Zack's world was spinning so fast he had trouble hanging on. He thought he had seen it all, but this takes the cake. How will he explain this to Abel? Visibly defeated, he said, "I'll wait outside for 20 minutes, in case you change your mind."

"You're wasting your time."

"You're wasting your life," he expressed, and walked to the wagon.

* * *

On his way home, Zack was at low ebb. The task ahead made him sick in the stomach. He rehearsed several scenarios for telling Abel his wife has left him. None were acceptable. He understood the ups and downs in life, still, for some reason, this was beyond the pale. Perhaps, it was because Abel is such a good man and gave his love to his family without requital. Even with no love in return, Abel persisted, in hopes of a miracle. Zack's own relationship with Amanda was, at best, dubious. One thing for certain, he disliked Amanda even more for putting him in this position.

As the wagon turned up the road leading to the house, Abel noticed there was a passenger missing. He quickly descended the front steps and met the wagon.

"Where's Amanda?" he asked.

"The last I saw of her, she was sitting at a table in the Lucky Lady," Zack replied, wishing he had said it differently.

"What happened?"

"When we were in Azarov's store, she told me to go get my cow and she'd be ready once I got back. When I returned, I found her in the sporting house. She told me she wasn't going back. I did my best to change her mind, but she'd have no part of it," Zack explained. "Abel, I did my best."

"I know you did. I've had problems with Amanda all my life. I love her and I'm going to bring her back," Abel said sternly. With that, he walked to the barn to saddle his horse.

When Pearle saw the commotion, he dashed to Zack's side. "What's happened?" he inquired.

"Problems with your sister," was all he said. "Unharness the mules. I'm gonna saddle up and ride back to town with your brother-in-law. Watch over your niece."

The return to Fort Dodge was made at a gallop. Though only a short distance from the farm, the mid-summer heat and physical demand, lathered the horses to the point of foaming at the mouth. Zack had never seen Abel in such a state of determination. They pulled up in front of the gambling house, dismounted, twirled the reins around the hitching rail, and stepped inside. Abel immediately spotted Amanda. She had remained at the table with Greeley and Charlie Fontaine. He walked to her and said, "Have you given any thought to what you are doing? You have a three-year-old daughter calling for you."

"She's more yours than mine. I didn't want her in the first place. You even named her after Abigail Leffingwell," said Amanda bitterly.

"That's only because you wouldn't give her a name."

"You pathetic fool. Have I ever said I loved you? To me, you were only a port in the storm, and once the weather cleared, I'd be long gone. At last I'm finished with you. Go back to your daughter, your farm, and that damn church."

Gus Greeley had hired two ruffians to keep the peace and serve as bouncers. From the looks of them, they were no strangers when it came to a brawl. One of them marched over to the green felt-top table and put his hand on Abel's shoulder saying, "Come on buddy, stop bothering the lady."

Abel was trembling from passionate pain and grief. Once he sensed the intrusion, he reached across his chest, and grasped the stranger's beefy paw. Emotional adrenaline bolstered Abel's strength to the point where his vice-like grip brought the bouncer to his knees. It is said that the human hand has 27 bones. Greeley's expeller has half of them broken. The other tough reached for his gun, but hesitated when he looked into Zack Wheat's frozen stare. Charlie Fontaine pulled a small derringer from beneath his coat. Zack responded with, "Put that pea shooter away or I'll a blow hole in you the size of Texas."

Customers had backed away for fear of gunplay. A few tables from the scene, two bystanders were speaking in low tones.

"Ain't he the prairie preacher?" one asked.

"Yeah, he's also the fella who killed the Pawnee chief," answered the other.

"Now, I've heard it all—a preacher with a gun. What's he doing in here?"

"Do you see that gal at Champagne Charlie's table?" Well, she's the preacher's wife."

"You're pulling my leg."

"It's the gospel truth."

"She's one of the barroom chippies."

"Sort of. I hear she's Charlie's girlfriend."

"Then who is the other fella with the beard and dead man's eyes?"

"His name is Zachary Wheat. Word has it he's got several notches on his gun. And, he's fast as a rattler."

The tension in the room was nearing the point of explosion. Zack tugged Abel's shirt to coax him way from the table. The first bouncer was still on the floor howling in pain.

"There's nothing we can do right now. Let's return to the farm and figure it out," Zack said.

Abel, heartbroken to tears, conceded and the pair backed out of the building. During the speechless ride home, Zack pondered the inextricable differences between him and Abel. Had this happened to him, he would have shot up the place, and then burnt it down.

Abel was considering the reality of being a single parent. Little Abby will be curious over the disappearance of her mother.

He must come up with a plausible reason for her non-present genitor. There was also a church service to be planned. He will be able to think more clearly once that is over.

For the remains of the day, Abel kept his daughter by his side. He explained that her mother had taken a trip to visit friends.

Zack and Pearle stayed with their comrade until nightfall. Not forgetting the responsibility of caring for a three-year-old, Zack prepared supper. Pearle helped with the after dinner cleanup.

"Our lives are going to be a lot different for a while," Zack said, while swirling water to retrieve a dish. "We got people coming to help dig the well. You best stick around until things settle down. The little girlfriend of yours will still be there."

Pearle was displeased, but knew his friend was right. As long as he could remember, Amanda had caused trouble. He possessed a filial love for his sister, though not at this moment.

On Sunday, July 25, neighbors' wagons began lining up in their customary places. They were aware of what transpired at the Lucky Lady. All were supportive of their preacher.

In preparation for his sermon, Abel had been studying the Old Testament Book of Hosea and his wife, Gomer. The prophet's parable, in many respects, corresponds to Abel's relationship with Amanda. While Hosea equates the marriage between him and Gomer as between God and the children of Israel, Abel can't help seeing the more secular interpretation.

As the story goes, the word of the Lord came to Hosea commanding him to take a wife. Not just any wife but one God had selected. Her name was Gomer, the most beautiful girl in Israel, nonetheless, a woman of questionable character. The Lord instructed that Gomer will bear him three children, yet, she will never be faithful to him. After the children were born, Gomer left Hosea and returned to her former life. She passed from lover to lover until she reached the worst of circumstances. Hosea learned of the man with whom she now resides and gave him money to sustain her. Eventually, word came to Hosea that Gomer was to be sold in the slave market. He was brokenhearted and went to the Lord for guidance. God asked him if he still loved this woman after all she had done to him. Hosea replied that he did. The Lord told him to go and buy her back. Hosea went to the marketplace and watched as Gomer was stripped of her clothing and stood naked before the crowd. He increased his bidding until he had his wife back. After which he said, "Thou shalt abide for me many days; thou shalt not play the harlot, and thou shalt not be for another man: so will I also be for thee." Hosea 3:3

We do not hear the end of the story, other than, Hosea was given a new revelation of God. His love for an unfaithful wife is taken as God's love for His idolatrous people.

In his own mind, Abel finds redemption for an unfaithful wife. Though Amanda did little regarding the homestead, the shear fact of her absence made many things unfamiliar. He battled personal demons against depression. At times, not at all certain he would win.

To compensate, Abel threw himself into the activities of his rural church. The neighbors' wives were a lifesaver. They took care of little Abby when farm work necessitated he be in the fields. At least twice a week one of the neighbor ladies brought covered meals for the preacher and his daughter.

Hours ran into days and days turned into weeks. During the timespan, progress in building the homestead continued. Abel now has a well. Just as Zack predicted, a clearwater spring was found less than ten feet below the grassy surface. It appears to be an endless flow originating somewhere high in the Rockies.

The autumnal tilt of the earth is gradually moving away from the sun, bringing cooler days and less sunlight. Winter's chill is holding, but looms on the horizon. Here, on the plains of Kansas, colorful autumn foliage is lacking. However, reflecting the spirit of fall, the young saplings, which Zack had planted, were doing their part. Only time will tell if they make it through winter.

Abel, and his two partners, have plowed the wheat field and replanted by broadcasting new seed as they walked along.

Neighbors have begun picking their corn. Most of this year's harvest will be retained and stored. From all indications, Abel and crew expect to reap over 20 bushels per acre. Similar to the adjoining farms, they will pick by hand. Two wagons, with high bang boards, will be employed. The men pull off the ears and fling them against the boards. After determining the amount needed to replant, feed livestock, and personal use, they plan to market the rest. Zack learned the government was paying $1.29 per bushel. Prices for the general public will be higher.

CHAPTER TWENTY-THREE

*F*alling Water had noticed his sister's melancholia. *White Dove* was no longer her jubilant self. She wore a long face and languished about as if in a trance. There was no complaint of physical pain; nevertheless, *Falling Water* could abide his sister's condition no longer. He met with his birthmother, *Singing Bird*.

"My sister is ill. Have you noticed her manner of late? When I spoke to her and inquired about her health, she only sighed and said there was nothing wrong. I know better. Outside of father, I am her guardian and responsible for her wellbeing. It is imperative for me to learn the cause of her torment and remove it."

Singing Bird offered an endearing smile for her son's sincerity and concern.

"Your sister is not ill. At least, not as you perceive. *White Dove* pines for *Boy Who Rides Buffalo*. She expected him to come and prove himself worthy. He has not visited the camp since the buffalo hunt. *White Dove* is lovesick and yearns for his presence."

"But he is not a warrior. How could a Cheyenne woman brood for someone who is weak?"

"Many times a woman loves a man for no particular reason. Even a Cheyenne woman can be under love's spell. It makes no difference who or what he is. She sees white when her eyes tell her it's black," *Singing Bird* explained.

"*Boy Who Rides Buffalo* was supposed to come to our village and offer a sacrifice. He must be afraid. That makes him a coward and unfit to speak to my sister," declared *Falling Water*.

"You forget one thing my son. There could be a plausible reason he has not returned. He may be the one who is ill. Other circumstances may prohibit him from visiting. You must learn his reason before claiming he is a coward," implored his mother.

"What you say is wise," he replied. "I will send *Two Trees* to learn the true cause."

Zack Wheat noticed him first. He recognized the tall Native American from their visit to his village. Turning to Pearle he said, "Looks like your friend is here again. I wonder what he is up to now."

"I know what he wants," Pearle replied. "He's here to find out why I haven't returned to the camp. Most likely *Falling Water* sent him to prove me unworthy to talk to his sister. Well, I've got a surprise for him."

Pearle marched down the lane to the main road and without *Two Trees* saying a single word, articulated, "I have been committed to remain here because of the actions of my sister. The man who owns the farm is her husband. His grief forced him to neglect the things we all have worked for. Abel has a three-year-old daughter. I have stayed by her side until her father overcame his sorrow. The situation is better now. I will be at the village tomorrow."

Two Trees held his prosaic expression throughout Pearle's explanation. Once Pearle finished, the red man asked, "Is Abel the holy man who killed the Pawnee chief?"

"Yes, he is the minister of our church and has a rifle that can shoot very long distances."

"There is much talk about him in my village. I should like to meet such a man. Now, I must return and alert my mother of your visit in the morning." *Two Trees* spoke no other words. He turned his pony and galloped for the Cheyenne camp.

The next day, *Two Trees* met Pearle at the entrance of his village. He led the horse and rider to his mother's tepee.

"My mother is called *Aponi*. She will prepare you for the test of sacrifice—the one we call, swinging to the pole."

"Will it be harsh?" Pearle quavered.

"You will be joined by a young brave. He is twelve years old," replied *Two Trees*. Remember, *Falling Water* will be interested in how you perform. That alone should strengthen your resolve."

Aponi spoke no English and tried to communicate by sign language. Pearle understood by her motions that she wanted him to remove his shirt. Then, she handed him a few dried peyote cactus buttons and pointed to her mouth. Pearle took that to mean chew them. Once they were swallowed, she handed him a water bowl filled with a liquid concoction and motioned for him to drink. The taste was very unpleasant but Pearle managed to gulp it down. They sat in silence for a few minutes until Pearle began to feel woozy. His nose tickled and vision slightly became blurred. The young suitor of *White Dove* was uncertain if he was even able to stand. At that point, two other women entered *Aponi's* lodge, removed the remainder of Pearle's clothing, and painted his entire body with white clay.

Barefoot and wrapped in a buffalo robe, Pearle was led to a much larger lodge. It is here in which the ceremony will take place. The outer circle was lined with Cheyenne natives, here to witness his sacrifice. Pearle strained to see if *White Dove* was among them. Their shapes were like a gauzy veil, making them unrecognizable. This time it was *Buffalo Horn*, the shaman, who led him near the center pole on which a long braided rawhide rope was attached. It lay coiled at its base like a large snake. He gently guided Pearle down into a sitting position, facing the pole, and stood behind him.

Buffalo Horn spoke to those inside the lodge, "Whoever wished for this man to do this sacrifice let it be known that he complies. May this man have good luck and live a long and fortunate life." The shaman then filled and lit a pipe and held it to Pearle's mouth—making sure he didn't touch it with his hands. The first puff told Pearle it wasn't the tobacco he and Zack brought to chief *Red Eagle*.

With Pearle still in a sitting position, *Buffalo Horn* knelt beside him and, using a piece of charcoal, made two vertical and parallel lines above each breast. These markings serve as to where the knife will enter and come out. *Buffalo Horn* was joined by an assistant. All the while, Pearle remained in a woozy state— somewhat aware of what is transpiring, yet, not very concerned about it. In fact, he was beginning to see double and drifting into a euphoric mindset, when the shaman's assistant pinched the skin and pulled to stretch it while inserting the knife. Once the breast was pierced, a small straight stick was passed through the slit and a string from the rawhide rope tied to it. The pain caused Pearle to partially snap out of his trance. Thanks to *Aponi's* concoction, it was not excruciating, rather a very sharp sting. All the same, he still had the other breast to go. This time Pearle was slightly observant and the pain, considerably more intense.

After the strings had been tied, *Buffalo Horn* and his helper raised Pearle to his feet and supported him closer to the center pole. The assistant pulled on each breast string to test the attachments, then straightened out the rope. It was then that Pearle noticed the twelve-year-old boy undergoing the same sacrifice. He suffered the test just to be a man. Pearle hoped the Indian lad was furnished with some of *Aponi's* elixir.

Buffalo Horn instructed Pearle to continually walk the extended semi-circle of the pole—the other half belonged to the young boy. He was also told to constantly try to break loose. He would be allowed to rest four times—once in the morning, at noon, in the afternoon, and just before sunset. He could not sit down until the shaman returned. Then *Buffalo Horn* and the assistant left the lodge.

Pearle made several attempts to break loose; but, the skewers would not snap nor his skin tear, it only stretched. With each attempt, the bleeding from his wounds grew worse. From the neck down, the white clay paint became heavily covered with crimson streaks, until his feet were leaving bloody footprints on the half circle pathway.

Aware of the onlookers, Pearle skipped the morning rest period and continued walking until noon. *Aponi's* potion was beginning to wear off and the pain intensified. By noon, Pearle noticed the lad across from him taking a rest. He pushed forward. When the afternoon pause approached, he was determined to continue until sunset. As the natural light began to fade he could no longer feel his wounds and his legs were numb, nevertheless, he continued until he felt *Buffalo Horn's* hand on his shoulder.

The shaman and his assistant each took a side and aided him down to a sitting position. They cut through the stretched skin of his breast and released the skewers, then led Pearle into the nearby sweat lodge. His wounds and the blood on his body were wiped off. That night, only the young boy, who experienced the same suffering, was allowed to eat with him. Each of the next three days they took a sweat. During which they were to give their whole body and spirit to the Great Power. Then, when they left the ceremonial sweathouse, their bodies were wiped off with white sagebrush and belonged solely to themselves.

Pearle recuperated a few days in the home of *Aponi* and *Two Trees*. He would not return to the farm in his present condition. He wanted to wait until his wounds were better healed. For the same reason, Pearle did not seek out *White Dove*.

During this time interval, *Two Trees* went to his friend *Falling Water* to tell him that Pearle successfully preformed the requested sacrifice. The young chief wasn't exactly happy about it. *Falling Water* had observed Pearle's conclusive trial and witnessed him refusing to rest. Even he had not been able to skip all the rest periods. *Falling Water* was compelled to accept Pearle's sacrifice. In spite of his reluctance, he informed *Two Trees* that *Boy Who Rides Buffalo* had his permission to court his sister.

Though Pearle left the village and returned to the farm without speaking to *White Dove*, her disposition changed dramatically. No longer moping about, she virtually danced during the performance of her chores. Her swain may return at his choosing and she knew it would be soon.

* * *

Abel was pleased to see his young brother-in-law return to the fold. He restrained from asking Pearle his whereabouts. It was most appreciated since the lad was enduring the throbbing pain of wounds on the mend.

Zack, on the other hand, was Pearle's best friend. He readily recounted his experiences or, at least, what he could remember.

Gone nearly two weeks, nothing of consequence had taken place. Amanda remained adamant about never reconnecting with her husband and seemed to enjoy her new life with Fontaine and the Lucky Lady. Zack makes it a point to stop for a beer each time he visits Azarov's store. They make eye contact but never speak.

Construction is complete on Boris Azarov's new building. He was in the process of moving when Zack was last there. Boris personally transported his baboon. Everyone else was afraid to even touch its cage.

With crops harvested, winter wheat sown, and the hayloft filled with sweet smelling fodder, the manified farmstead prepared for winter. Their garden was completely plucked of its edibles and, with the help of neighbor ladies, canned for storage. Zack spent several days hauling coal from Azarov's new general store. The crafty storekeeper expected many of the town's new constructions would be heated with coal instead of wood. Subsequently, he maintained an ample supply.

At the Cheyenne village, *Falling Water* prepared for his annual sojourn west and protection of the Rocky Mountain foothills.

His sister *White Dove* chose to remain with the principle tribe.

The young chief will not suffer from the frosty air. He has married *Chumani* and will spend plenty time under buffalo blankets in his wigwam.

No longer under the watchful eye of her brother, *White Dove* also has amorous plans. She and Pearle have gone to *Chief Red*

Eagle to profess their desire to be married. He gave his blessing but the ceremony must take place in the spring when *Falling Water* can take part. *Red Eagle* expressed his disappointment in not having a full marriage. One in which both families take equal part in determining gifts given to each side. Since *Boy Who Rides Buffalo* will not be represented by parents, siblings and cousins, it must be a half-marriage. *White Dove* couldn't care less. She had the approval of her father and began counting the days.

CHAPTER TWENTY-FOUR

A bigail and Hope were having their second cup of coffee and making a list of dishes they plan to cook for Thanksgiving dinner. Over the past four years, Hope has come a long way regarding her culinary skills. Thanks to Abigail, she can hold her own with just about anyone in Statesville and its environs.

"How many people do you think we'll be feeding?" asked Hope, even though she already had a general idea. Her parents would not be attending. Grace, her mother, will be entertaining their relatives from Virginia. The Waterman family, including her sister Susan, will visit during the Christmas holidays.

Abigail contorted her features into a counting expression and mentally added the guests.

"Including the children, I come up with around twenty. There could be a couple more, depending on Jack. You know how he is around a holiday dinner. I fully expect to have strangers at the table. One thing for sure, he'll be inviting Yalata and his wife Aiyana."

"My father would thoroughly enjoy visiting again with your Choctaw friends," Hope reflected.

"Actually, Aiyana is a Cherokee princess. Your father could write a book about their courtship and marriage," responded Abigail, standing up to clear the table.

While the pair was rinsing their coffee cups, they began to giggle over something Abigail whispered, out of earshot. They both were startled when the front door slammed and Jack Junior and Jozef came running in shouting, "Where's dad. Something killed one of his cows and eaten half of it."

"Your father and Melvin went into town. They're due back anytime. You boys stay away from it until they get home. Whatever did this may still be close by," Abigail ordered. Her heart rate, as well as Hope's, was still elevated.

"I'm going to get dad's Whitworth rifle," Jozef declared. That brought a smile on the women's faces. "You and your brother just sit in a chair and wait," Abigail insisted, unable to restrain her grin.

"I think it was a tiger," Jozef stated.

"Don't be silly," his older brother scolded. "Tigers live in Africa." Then Jack Junior considered the possibilities. A tiger could have escaped from a circus. "Well, if it is a tiger, dad will use his Whitworth rifle and shoot it."

Where little boys are concerned, waiting for their father can seem like an eternity. Before long, Jack and Jozef were fidgeting so much Abigail released them, but, only to the yard, not to the pasture.

When the wagon was spotted up the road, both boys jumped with excitement and began arguing which was to be first to tell their father. As it turned out, Jack was told in unison. Even though both were pushing and shoving, he gathered that something had killed one of his cattle. To their maximum disappointment, neither was allowed to accompany the men into the field.

Two opossums were dining on the carcass and quickly departed as they approached. Jack walked around the slain animal looking for evidence left by the killer. He was quick to notice the impressions in the grass. Several of which could only be those of a bear. Not just any bear but a very large one.

"I thought bears hibernated this time of year," said Melvin.

"They do. But this guy must be a rogue and not particular if he sleeps through the winter or not. Take a look at this paw print. I've never seen any bigger," Jack replied.

"How big do you think he is?"

"My guess he's over 600 pounds, maybe 700."

"Are we going to hunt him down?" Melvin inquired.

"We have to. First, we'll need to bury the carcass," Jack stated, as they headed back to the barn to fetch shovels.

Abigail and Hope were standing by the barn when the men returned. Each wore a blanket over their shoulder for protection against the November chill.

"Was it a bear?" they questioned. Jack answered in the affirmative.

"Do you think it's the one with two cubs?" Hope inquired.

"No, this one is a heck of a lot bigger," Jack replied. "We're gonna bury the carcass and ride over to the Choctaw village. I promised Yalata he could join the hunt if a culprit ever presented itself."

"Don't forget to remind Aiyana about Thanksgiving dinner," added Abigail.

The Leffingwell children looked envious as their father and Melvin hoisted saddles on their horses. Jack's stallion, Rambler, shivered with excitement when the cinch was tightened. The veteran charger seemed to be aware another journey lay ahead. Melvin's mount was the same animal given at the Appomattox surrender.

Due to the recent fracas over the Klan, both men were armed. Jack carried his Whitworth rifle in a saddle sling, while each holstered a revolver. The trip will take most of the remaining daylight. Push come to shove, they were prepared to sleep outdoors if need be.

Melvin had never seen an Indian village. He imagined Yalata's community consisted of tepees covered with buffalo skins. Nothing was farther from the truth. In 1830, the Choctaws relinquished the last of their ancestral lands. By signing the treaty of Dancing Rabbit Creek, the majority of Choctaws moved to the Indian Territory. A small group remained to become tenant farmers or sharecroppers on local cotton farms. They worked the farms during the growing season and lived off the land in winter. Yalata and others held title to their own land and survived in a changing world similar to their white, English speaking, neighbors.

They retained their heritage through kinship networks, especially the language. The Choctaws believed the loss of language is the loss of identity.

Being on horseback allowed Jack and Melvin to travel trails rather than roads. Even so, the pathway was seldom used and sections were overgrown with brush, making their progress somewhat slower than anticipated. Night lamps were being lit in the village and Jack and Melvin still had a mile or so to navigate. The sky was clear and filled with sparkling stars. Jack was certain there would be no rain this evening and suggested they camp out and visit Yalata in the morning. They found a small open space protected by pine trees and chose it for the evening stay.

Soon, a crackling fire warmed the surrounding area. The horses were tethered and bedrolls lain out.

"All the comforts of home," Jack declared, as he unwrapped the bundle Abigail prepared for a light repast.

"Abigail sure thinks of everything," Melvin stated, while taking a bite out of his sandwich.

"That's for sure," Jack mumbled, with his mouth full. "She's always been my guiding star."

"*Not exactly always,*" thought Melvin. "*But that is long past. Today, everything is fine. A man couldn't ask for a better friend.*"

"Out here, in the wilderness, I'm reminded of camping back when the war was on," Melvin reminisced.

"This is a little different. Ain't nobody shooting at us," Jack quipped.

"Funny how everything is always changing. Who would have guessed I'd be living with one arm, working with you guys, and tending a farm. Hell, I was merely a leaf on the Kaufman's family tree. Unimportant when compared to those linked to the trunk.

My pappy never had anything but a passel of kids. He had some rich relatives but they never knew we were alive. Then the war came along and everything changed," Melvin recalled.

"That war changed a lot of us," Jack answered. "It altered my life more than I want to remember. If it weren't for Abigail, heaven only knows where I'd have ended up."

"She's the kindest woman me and Hope have ever met. In a way, she had a lot to do with me even meeting Hope."

"From what I was told, Lomas Chandler did not attend the dinner in order to visit the Eagle Inn and Tavern," added Jack.

"That's right, had he been there, things may have worked out differently."

They sat in silence recalling the past. Each staring at the flickering flames until Jack rose and tossed another branch on top the embers.

"Good old Lomas. Remember how he tried to convince me fairies were real? You don't believe that, do you Jack?"

"Something tells me we've had this conversation before. All the same, people have claimed to have caught a glimpse of these magical creatures. I believe some of them to be sincere. I'm not sure about Lomas, but I am about his mother. Personally, I have never seen them. That doesn't mean they're not real. I guess you must have the right perspective. It all comes down to faith— seeing fairies when your eyes tell you they're dragonflies. If you believe in them, they are real."

"What do you think they look like?" Melvin queried.

"Once again, I haven't got a clue. However, the consensus of opinion is that they are small, delicate, and very feminine. Like I said, most people can't see them. Lomas told us you have to have a pure heart. That's why all children can witness them. I've read where certain people claimed to have observed actual fairies and others, in the same group, a white misty shape. If I could have a conversation with Lomas' mother, maybe the entire controversy could be straightened out," Jack replied.

Melvin rolled over and pulled his blanket up to his chin, confused as ever. Jack did the same and shortly the soft purr of sleeping men wafted in the crispy air.

The next morning, the pair rode into the Choctaw village. Melvin was surprised to see log cabins, strategically spaced, boasting neatly attended gardens, recently harvested. In addition, there were well-kept corn fields and properly fenced animals.

Yalata and Aiyana cheerfully greeted their early morning visitors and served a hearty breakfast. Jack reminded them of the upcoming holiday dinner and explained the reason they were there.

Only Jack recognized the expression of approval in the stoic features of Yalata. Long ago he learned his friend's emotions by watching his eyes. In the manner of his ancestors, the Choctaw brave will bring only his feathered lance and bow with a quiver of iron-tipped arrows. After bidding a fond farewell, the trio was again on the trail. This time, in pursuit of a very large black bear.

Yalata led the way on a different track from the one previously used. His pinto pony seemingly moved without human control. It became evident to Melvin there will be no speaking until the first time they stopped. No matter, the undulating motion will give tempo in which he could contemplate a little longer on the existence of fairies.

Each time Jack meets with Yalata his mind changes back to earlier days. He feels more alive. His reason becomes sharper, recalling the imagined freedom of a carefree life.

Like all of us, the memory of previous tragedy and pain becomes less vivid with each passing year. The infrequent pleasures tend to consume our recollections and gradually take their place.

After nearly two hours at a constant pace, Yalata signaled toward a brook trickling across their path.

"We can water the horses and give them a rest," he said, as he dismounted and pulled on the reins, leading the painted pony to the creek's edge. Following his lead, Jack and Melvin copied the Choctaw's actions. Being early November, shade trees were void of foliage, making the area rather stark or plain. Were trees bearing leaves, it may have been magical. Water rippling over various rocks still made a musical sound—quite pleasing to the ear. *"Perhaps a place where fairies might dwell,"* thought Melvin.

The short break ended and the travelers continued uninterrupted until the Leffingwell farm came into view. By the time they reached the home and grounds, it was well into the afternoon and darkness was beginning to take hold. Enough daylight remained for the trio to examine the crime scene. A few carrion birds flew high above, likely disappointed that the carcass rested deep below the earth's surface.

It was agreed the hunt would commence tomorrow at the crack of dawn. This evening will be spent telling lies about various hunts in which each had either participated, or, heard about.

When the children were finally in their beds, sound asleep, the storytelling was still gaining speed. Hope and Abigail sat at the kitchen table capitulating to the inevitable. Rebecca lay in her father's arm undisturbed by the rounds of laughter.

"We might as well start packing food for them. No telling how long they'll be gone. When Jack and Yalata go hunting together, they have a one track mind. From the look of things, Melvin has joined the club. Spend the night here with me. We can catch up on our sleep once they're gone," said Abigail. "Rebecca can sleep in Jozef's little bed," she continued. "He now sleeps in the loft with his brother."

Hope broke out with a mischievous grin. "I'll fetch Rebecca and put her to bed. We have ways to make our husbands pay, once they return from their hunt."

The men slept in their story telling chairs. During the night, when one or the other woke up, he began relating another tale. Finding his audience fast asleep, he too resumed his slumber. A restful evening, it wasn't. Nevertheless, when the rooster crowed, three tired fellows filed out the front door loaded for bear—no pun intended.

Yalata had no problem picking the bear's tracks. To him, it was like tracking a box wagon in a cornfield. Once beyond the forest's edge, the perennial timber grew thicker, along with scrub brush and undergrowth. In some respects, it makes the quarry's trail easier to follow. Claw marks on pine trees, broken twigs, and tufts of coarse black hair kept the pursuers locked onto their goal.

"We're close to the end of my property," Jack alerted.

"Maybe so, but the animal's spoor is recent. His excrement is still soft," Yalata replied. "We must decide if we are going to continue the hunt."

"This bear killed my cattle and will never stop. I have no choice. We have to go on," Jack asserted, as he looked to Melvin for a consensus. Melvin, in full agreement, had a bright red welt across his face. "Don't follow so close. A bramble branch must have snapped back," Jack cautioned.

"I don't want to get lost," Melvin replied.

"You couldn't get lost even if you tried. Yalata can always find you."

At that moment the husky roar of an angry black bear shattered their tranquility. They were frozen where they stood. Another huffing growl and the hunt resumed—this time at a faster pace. Yalata was quick to notice a dark object climbing a tall pine about a hundred yards ahead.

"We have him treed," he shouted.

As the hunters moved closer, the massive creature climbed further up the tree.

"What do we do now?" asked Melvin.

"We wait until he decides to come down," replied Yalata.

"Couldn't we just shoot him while he is up in the tree?"

"That would not be sporting."

Jack and Melvin checked their weapons. Yalata squatted in a position allowing him to face the elevated prey. The bear continued to huff and growl, unnerving all three.

"How long is he going to stay up there?" Melvin queried.

"Until he gets mad enough to come down," said Jack.

And so it went for another two hours. The interval allowed for Abigail's bag of vittles to be opened. Before they finished their first sandwich, the bear had enough of their presence and began backing down the tree. The trio stood ready for the animal's attack. Once upon solid ground, the beast whirled and charged—stopping halfway to rise up, on its hind legs, and give a mighty roar. While Jack and Melvin were taking aim, three arrows struck in succession—twang thump, twang thump, and twang thump. The great beast staggered backward and fell lifeless to the earth.

Yalata let loose with an earsplitting yell, scaring the hell out of Melvin. Jack couldn't help laughing at his friend. "He's just celebrating the kill," informed Jack.

"Shit, I thought I was next," Melvin quavered.

Yalata was already busy removing the thick shaggy hide and confessing it to be the biggest bear he had ever seen. Turning to Jack he said, "You make me young again, Jack Leffingwell. It would be an honor to share the meat."

"Only a small roast and steak. The kill is yours," Jack replied. "My boys would appreciate seeing the hide when we return."

"It will be my pleasure," Yalata stated.

* * *

It took two men to hold up the gigantic bearskin. Jack Junior whistled in amazement over the size of the animal while little Jozef was in awe. Perhaps more so with Yalata than the oversized hide.

Anxious to return home with his spoils, Yalata had to reassure Abigail he and Aiyana would attend her holiday dinner, before she let him go. Once she was satisfied with his answer, the heavy-laden pinto pony began its trek back to the Choctaw village.

CHAPTER TWENTY-FIVE

In western Kansas, a light November snow partially covers the fields. The erratic clouds take credit for the sparse, misty blanket, which serves as a harbinger for things to come.

A windblown plume of smoke wafts above Abel's rooftop chimney, and fades into the frigid air. He peers through his kitchen window, now covered with a circular sheen of frost, and sees the illuminated portals of the bunkhouse—an indication that all is well this Sabbath morning.

The young minister has made breakfast for him and little Abby, and, now, finishes dressing for this morning's service.

The rural congregation no longer meets in the open air. Zack and Pearle have rearranged their bunkhouse to accommodate the Sunday worshipers. Although a temporary fix, it looks as though it will continue until spring. Children are the most satisfied with the present adjustment. Invariably, they manage to drift into the barn in order to pet the animals.

Today, after the morning services, a meeting is scheduled to determine the next course of action. It goes without saying, a stand-alone building is the best solution. The manner by which to come by such a structure is the focus of this morning's gathering.

Anticipating the church meeting gave Mildred Van Ronkle extra energy. She sang in high voice and full lungs when leading the hymns. It was a foregone conclusion she will chair the meeting—she and the minister, of course.

Before giving the benediction, Abel reminded everyone of the meeting after services. They all stayed.

The activity was now less formal. With their empty cups in hand, adults formed a line leading to Zack's Franklin stove, on top of which stood a simmering batch of coffee. While their parents were occupied, the older children were inspecting food baskets, looking for cake or other sweet morsels.

For the next half-hour, the noise level was surprisingly low. Most likely due to the book of Matthew 18:20—*For when two or three are gathered together in my name, there I am in the midst of them.* These pioneer Christians hold true to their bible. Even though they gather in Zack's bunkhouse, on this Sunday, it is their church.

Mildred Van Ronkle drew a chair alongside Abel, who called the meeting to order. She interrupted briefly to ask Angela Calloway to keep notes.

"I don't have anything to write with," she reported.

"Not to worry, there's plenty in my food basket. I came prepared," Mildred disclosed, nodding to Abel as if giving him permission to continue.

"Our church membership has reached the point where a stand-alone building has become imperative. We're here to find a way for that to happen. Does anyone have a suggestion?" asked Abel.

"How much will it cost?" Rainbow Calloway questioned.

"Around a thousand dollars including a stove and furnishings," Zack stated.

"We don't have that kind of money," Rainbow disclosed.

"We have to raise it," countered Mildred. "The community around Fort Dodge is growing as we speak. The town folk have seen fit to furnish a building for a schoolhouse. We have to convince them a church is a necessity."

"The person with the most money is Gus Greeley. We don't want money from him because of the way he gets it."

"He's not the only one in town who could contribute," Zack offered. "I'll have a talk with Boris Azarov and Shorty McCorkle. Between the two we could have a lot of it covered."

Writing furiously, Angela asked, "When will you talk to them?"

"Next week."

"How about us. What can we pledge? Put the Van Ronkles down for five dollars," Mildred offered. Her husband was relieved she didn't pledge more. His back was still sore from digging the well.

"You can count on our homestead for a hundred dollars more," said Abel.

Before the meeting ended, Angela logged $117 in pledges. Mildred made assignments for herself, and others, to visit people living in the community. Filled with the promise of expectation, the meeting adjourned.

When on a mission, it seems as though the women of the church are much more aggressive than their male counterparts. The masculine gender often prefers to keep in the background, especially when organizing a drive to raise money.

* * *

As promised, Zack and Pearle, their mufflers covering their faces against the wind, drove the wagon to Fort Dodge to seek contributions. Shorty McCorkle, born and raised a Baptist, was disappointed it was for a Methodist Church. Nevertheless, he pledged $25. Zack's next stop was Azarov's general store.

"I think old Boris will be a tougher sell," Pearle stated.

"I'm not so sure. If I can make him understand it serves his own interest, he might come around," said Zack.

"No matter what he pledges, we're a long way from a thousand dollars."

"Have a little faith, son. I ain't talked to him yet."

As the wagon approached the fort, they observed the long row of tents on either side of the pathway. Signs, hawking the various services and merchandise, were flapping from the pre-winter gusts. Now that the railroad depot is completed, these canvas complexes will give way to more permanent wooden structures. The embryo of a frontier community will soon give birth to a recognized town.

When Zack and Pearle entered Azarov's store, he had several customers buying merchandise. They browsed until all transactions were completed. Finally alone, Zack strolled over to the counter and said, "In two years you're going to be confronted with all kinds of competition."

"That's why I combine general merchandise with feed and livery," he replied.

"It might work now, with the fort and all, but what will you do when the government closes the fort? They're already talking about moving the Indian annuities to Oklahoma. Just remember, you're not going to be the only general store when the town gets bigger. Hell, we're probably going to have two or three more liveries and a blacksmith forge tied next to them."

"Why so many?"

"To handle the cowboys when they bring up longhorn cattle herds from Texas. We'd be their first stop on the way to the railhead at Abilene."

"I'll hire me a blacksmith," Boris countered.

"That'll just increase your overhead. What you need to do is insure your customer base," suggested Zack.

"How do I do that? Most people don't like me," asked the burly Balkan.

"As I see it, that's the only problem. You need to make people like you, and here's how to do it. No doubt you've heard about the rural preacher, Abel Strawn."

"He is your friend," Boris replied, squinting a suspicious eye.

"That's got nothing to do with it. Abel Strawn's congregation has increased in numbers since he resumed preaching. He had his own church back east."

"His wife left him and now works over at the Lucky Lady."

"That's right. It gives him more time to concentrate on the bible. Have you given much thought about the eternal fires of Hell?"

"I don't like to think about that," Boris said honestly.

"I wouldn't either if I were you. Well, the congregation needs to build a church right here by the fort."

"Nobody's stopping them."

"Yes, Boris, you are stopping them. Let's look at it this way. They will buy all the materials and furnishings from you. All you need to do is give them a line of credit. That alone will assure their loyalty when the community gets bigger. Besides, they can influence the newcomers and there's going to be a lot of them. Shorty McCorkle has already pledged a pisspot full of money."

"How much?"

"I'm not at liberty to disclose the amount. All I can tell you is, he is thinking about the future, and wants to be a major part of it," said Zack.

"Why do you do this for me? You were going to shoot my baboon."

"That was before I knew the kind of businessman you are. Your baboon scares me to death. I suggest you keep it penned up when the church ladies are here shopping."

"They don't shop here."

"That's the point. You do something for them and they'll do something for you."

"Do you think I'm a good businessman?"

"I've only seen a couple like you back east. Unfortunately, they didn't secure their customer base."

"What happened to them?"

"They went broke and had to close up. Some of them might even head west and end up being your competitors."

"If the Indians are gone and I have the church ladies as customers, I will sell my baboon."

"Spoken like the businessman I think you are," said Zack, smiling like the fisherman who feels a hard bite on his line.

* * *

Mildred Van Ronkle and crew took a different tactic. Assuming families with children will be more interested in a church, they planned to present themselves at the schoolhouse to learn the names of parents. The young schoolteacher was a girl named Laurel Harper.

Miss Harper is a blossoming woman with flaming red hair. After her mother died, she came west with her father in search of gold. The effort proved futile since the amount of shiny metal wasn't enough to pay for food, let alone anything else. Living in a tent for nine months, Laurel witnessed her father's failing health. Turning to hard liquor hastened his demise until one day he was found, an apparent heart attack victim, with a bottle clenched in his fist.

Laurel sold their claim and equipment to make a return trek back to Illinois, where it all originated. Her money ran out at Fort Dodge. The inhabitants took pity on her and provided room and board, until such a time as she earned enough to continue her journey.

For Laurel, Kansas was just part of a broken promise land— offering heartache beyond belief. In spite of a physical handicap, her determination was unalterable. In her quiet moments, she resolved that her imperfection saved her from working the miners' tents and taverns. Men, looking for sensual satisfaction, would not desire a woman with a withered left hand.

A new town was forming around Fort Dodge. The Atchison Topeka and Santa Fe railroad planned construction of a depot nearby. Therefore, with the community's expected growth, Laurel was offered the position of schoolteacher, grades one through eight. Her remuneration is set at $20 a month, plus the continuation of free room and board. Beneath the clothing in her bottom drawer, a nest egg grows at the rate of $10 each monthly pay period. She plans to leave the west by stagecoach and ride in style.

Mildred was confident the last child had left the school, and, gently rapped on the door. When Laurel opened the entryway, a gust of wind molded her dress against her shapely frame.

"May I help you?" she asked.

"Can we come in? I can explain our mission better inside where it's warmer," Mildred replied.

The meeting lasted for over an hour. No one took notice of Laurel's left hand. They were, however, fascinated by her dark crimson hair.

"You have the most beautiful hair. It fairly glows," Angela commented. "I've never seen any like it. What color do you call it?"

"I've always referred to it as red," Laurel replied.

The women were humming their disagreement when Mildred questioned Angela, "Did you write down the names of the families?"

"Yes. Fifteen children and seven families," she answered. Angela then asked Laurel, "Miss Harper, do you have any church affiliation?"

"None since coming out west but back home my mother and I attended the Methodist Church."

"Please don't consider me bold, all the same, I'm sure you would enjoy meeting with us on Sunday. We hold services at the minister's farm. He's turned the new bunkhouse into a sanctuary for the occasion. Abel is a wonderful person and I'm sure your heart would be lightened by hearing him preach. I know mine is."

"I appreciate the invitation," Laurel replied.

With that, Mildred thanked the teacher and the ladies traipsed to the door. They will call on the seven families another day.

Upon returning home, Zack found Abel in the barn, sitting on the milk stool, and a vacant look in his eyes. It had been several weeks since his last bout with depression. Finding him in this condition struck heavyheartedness in his bearded friend. Looking about, Zack spotted a blanket draped over a stall gate and placed it over Abel's shoulders. There was no telling how long he had been sitting in the darkened corner. The barn was much warmer than the air outside due to bodily heat of the animals and hay and fodder stored overhead in the loft. Even so, the preacher wore no coat and felt cold to the touch.

"Abel, are you all right?" asked Zack. "Is little Abby in the house?"

"She's with the Calloway daughters. They're bringing her back before bedtime," Abel answered in a low voice.

"Then, how are you feeling?"

Tears began to swell in the minister's eyes blurring the image of his concerned friend. Abel could no longer disguise the burden of loneliness. There, in the barn, in the darkness, he began to sob. His breakdown sounded like a wounded animal—a deep hoarse moan that brought tears to the stony face of Zachary Wheat. Abel's doleful lament lasted until he could no longer produce tears.

He appeared somewhat invigorated from the emotional release; and, withdrawing his handkerchief and wiping his face, he said, "Have you ever felt yourself out in the middle of the ocean with no land in sight? Tempted to chuck it all and let yourself drown, knowing full well the Lord wants you to swim. The unanswered question remains, in which direction. For years, I've just been floating and waiting for divine guidance. It never came. Amanda tested my faith. Whatever she has done, I would take her back in a heartbeat."

"I've never loved a woman that much. Maybe someday I will. One thing I can do is feel your pain. You're going to get through this. That's something I would bet my life on," Zack confirmed.

"We're different people Zack. You're a man rushing forward in the pursuit of life. I'm one who is most comfortable tied to a stake. If you were ever tied down, you would probably wither and die like the flowers in winter," said Abel.

"I guess I just haven't found the right woman," returned Zack.

"Apparently, neither have I."

"Hand me that bucket of oats. I'll finish feeding the horses. You'll love to hear about my little talk with Azarov. I'll be up once I've finished."

CHAPTER TWENTY-SIX

<hr/>

Pearle's sacrifice has elevated his status among the Cheyenne. He no longer is stopped at the entrance of the village. He now passes with impunity and greeted by the Dog Soldiers with a friendly but laconic wave.

On his ride to meet the beautiful bride to be, Pearle conjures up an image of the two of them, in bed, and performing erotic acts of lovemaking. By the time he actually reunites with *White Dove*, the libidinous thoughts are forgotten. Having endured the painful sacrifice of swinging to the pole, Pearle steadfastly resists any sexual encounter until after their marriage. In fact, he intends to wait until they are wedded by his brother-in-law in the Methodist bunkhouse sanctuary—a sacrament he has yet to discuss with the Cheyenne maiden. In no way will Pearle risk a violation of the tribes prevailing culture. At times the choice of chastity also becomes another painful experience.

White Dove couldn't care less about the cultural taboo. Her post puberty hormones cloud her rational, making the idea of waiting to consummate their relationship unimportant and foolish. Pearle must be the strong one, when it comes to protecting their reputations.

"If we find abstinence too difficult, I better stay away until our wedding day," he reluctantly stated on their previous meeting.

"Out of the question," was her response.

When apart, *White Dove* spends her idle hours mentally conceiving methods for eluding her grandmother, in order to be alone with her betrothed. Because of her innate wisdom, plus, years of experience, *Valley of Flowers* has witnessed every bit of subterfuge and nips each attempt in the bud. There is one subtlety she seems to have missed. That is, time together with each under a blanket. Similar to the rural custom of bundling, the grandmother allows the couple to touch each other through protection of the multicolored covering.

A practice since Colonial times, certain pioneer societies wrap one person in a blanket while accompanied by another in bed. The aim was to allow intimacy without the full sexual act.

Usually, the participants were adolescents with the boy staying at the girl's residence. They were given separate blankets and expected to talk to one another through the night. The practice was mainly conducted in winter, and, often, a bundling board further separated the pair. They could cuddle but that was as far as they could go.

While the parents were pleased with the custom, it did allow the participants to engage in heavy petting—a form of non-penetrative sex. Under the overlaying spread, a form of frottage frequently took place. The couples would actively rub their bodies against each other to achieve sexual gratification without actual penetrative intercourse. With every scheme blocked by her grandmother, *White Dove* was determined to put the blankets to the test.

Nearing the village, the landscape offered a slight rise giving Pearle a better view of the river and several hundred lodges. Each had a thick haze curling from their conical tips. The granular snow had increased, yet, he could still make out the vacant plot where *Falling Water's* tepee once stood before moving west to spend the frigid season.

While smoke from the lodges hung heavy over the encampment, it will be short lived as the gray month's wind gusts began to grow stronger.

Upon entering *White Dove's* lodge, the young maiden handed Pearle a blanket suggesting he warm himself from the cold journey to the camp. Once he draped it around his shoulders, *White Dove* did the same and dropped down beside him. So close he could feel her warmth through both coverings. Her brazenness forced Pearle to avert his eyes toward *Valley of Flowers*. Fortunately, she had busied herself with sewing blue beads on a parfleche, destined to be a wedding gift. The couple spoke in undertones, barely audible to the elderly grandmother.

"Lay back so that we can converse side by side," she suggested.

Even though he was aware of her intentions, Pearle obeyed. All the same, he was very concerned over their aged and respected chaperone.

"Do you miss me when you're with your people?"

"I miss you every second you're out of my sight," he replied, all the while feeling her inch closer. So close, he began to be aroused.

"When did you fall in love with me?"

"I believe it was the first time I saw you at Fort Dodge in Azarov's general store."

"When did you realize you loved me?"

"At the same time. Your friend made Azarov put his baboon away but you were the only one I saw."

"You would never know it by the way you treated me," Pearle complained. "I had to go through hell to even talk to you. And then, you wouldn't talk to me. You were dissatisfied with my gifts and gave them away. You're not of my race. You bathe in the river totally naked, where all can see you. And, in spite of that, I can't live without you."

"Is that all?"

"No, there is a whole lot more but I can't think of them now."

White Dove had a dancing light of mischief in her eyes as she wriggled closer and reached her hand under Pearle's blanket. Drawing her face to his, she kissed him with open lips. Rapt in the moment, Pearle lost concern for *Valley of Flowers* and returned her kiss with reckless ardor. With her wayward hand she felt his emotional response. Pearle gently clasped her hand and said, "It would be best if that happened after we are married."

White Dove rose to her feet and said, "I'm tired of waiting. I want to rid myself of this rope." She raised her skirt exposing the milky white flesh above her knees, then, turning slowly, the well-formed curves of her shapely bottom. Pearle was stunned. His breathing stopped and his heart pounded so hard he could actually hear it.

"My darling, cover yourself with the blanket. I want you more than you will ever know, but we have come this far without slurring our reputation. I can't do this on my own, I love you too much. You must help me. Look at these scars on my chest. I have them because of my love for you. Help me not to dishonor them," Pearle implored.

Valley of Flowers, whom they thought was sleeping, had only been resting her eyes. After hearing Pearle's loving exhortation, she gave a satisfying smile and continued as though asleep.

* * *

There were a few new faces in the makeshift church two weeks succeeding the fund raising campaign. One in particular drew specific attention. Primarily due to her captivating hair color. At times the minister's sermon was a bit halting when the fetching smile and florid coiffure distracted his attention. Mildred Van Ronkle had reported her visit with the schoolteacher but neglected to mention her outstanding feature.

The Calloway and Van Ronkle boys, those in their advanced teens, were also drawn to the eye-catching young miss. After the solemn formalities, she found herself among the young admirers, who offered every courtesy, kindness, and service of which they could think.

Once Abel introduced himself, her fan club reluctantly dispersed. He arrived holding an extra cup of Tessa Blankenberg's hot tea. Offering it to Laurel, he said, "I wish to tell you how pleased I am to see you here this morning. You seemed to have brightened everyone's day."

"Thank you, Reverend, the young boys are attracted to my hair."

"Now that you mention it, you do have a very unusual color. Did your parents have red hair?"

"No. My mother's hair was light brown and father's was nearly black. There must have been a traveling salesman about," she joked.

Abel cleared his throat and replied, "You speak of them as if they are no longer with us."

"They are both dead. Mother died when I was younger and father two years ago in the Colorado gold fields."

"You must have an interesting story to tell of your past. I would like to hear it someday," affirmed Abel.

"Reverend, I assure you, it's not that interesting," she replied.

"Call me Abel. That's my name when I'm not standing on the pulpit."

When Abel moved on, she was quickly surrounded by the female committee and remained so until the congregation began to depart.

"Do you need a ride back home?" Angela questioned.

"No thanks, I borrowed a neighbor's horse," she responded. Hearing her answer, Pearle was quickly at her side and said, "I'd be happy to pick you up next week. It's not a problem. You're practically on my way."

"It's not on your way. You live here and I live in town. Thanks anyhow. I'll be here next week and find my own way."

"What if it's sleeting or snowing hard?"

"Now that's a different story. Keep a sharp eye on the weather," she voiced, while walking outside and hoisting herself atop her borrowed mount.

Later, when Zack and Pearle were putting the bunkhouse in order, Zack commented, "I noticed you giving that cute little redhead a lot of attention. Aren't you supposed to be getting married?"

"Of course. Did you notice her left hand? She's handicapped. I was just offering to help her come to church," Pearle asserted.

"Looking from the ground up, I never got that far," Zack quipped. "Seriously, I wonder how it got that way."

"If we can keep her coming to church, maybe we can find out. Do you think Abel noticed it?"

"Hell no. It's a wonder he noticed her hair. On Sunday, your brother-in-law has a one track mind."

Inside the farmhouse, Abel sat with his young daughter on his knee. He was having difficulty getting the fetching redhead off his mind. He, too, wondered how her hand was injured. Taking Abby by the hand, they walked into the living room to find a spot for Zack Wheat's Christmas tree, currently lying lengthwise on the front porch. Where and how he got it, no one dare ask. In many ways Zack reminded the minister of Lomas Chandler, his friend and benefactor living in Richmond, Virginia.

CHAPTER TWENTY-SEVEN

H eavy snow came down on *Falling Water's* winter quarters. Over the last twenty-four hours nearly a foot had fallen. The tawny inhabitants huddled inside their lodges in an effort to keep warm. Outside, the clouded air was thick with large white crystals cascading to the earth. The women gathered snow instead of water for drinking and the morning wash-up. And, though the white blanket will afford an easy hunt, they must wait until it stops before venturing out.

Inside *Falling Water's* tepee a crackling fire emitted sufficient heat; nevertheless, he and *Chumani* remain under heavy blankets and furs. Both are naked and confident they will remain uninterrupted until the snow stops descending. With his full attention on his new bride, he rarely thinks of his sister and her suitor. *Chumani*, on the other hand, is curious about *Boy Who Rides Buffalo.*

"You allow a white man to court your sister? That would not happen with the Pawnee."

"There's more to it than you know. Besides, you are a Pawnee and married to a Cheyenne. That, too, would not happen with the Pawnee," *Falling Water* chided. "*Boy Who Rides Buffalo* has won her heart. When that happens, no one can change it."

Chumani pushed her body against *Falling Water* and sensuously replied, "I know what you mean."

* * *

A few small bands of Cheyenne Indians remain in southeastern Colorado at the Rocky Mountain foothills. One of which is led by *Hopping Toad*, a veteran warrior and medicine man. He has resisted any treaty requirements to move to a reservation. During *Falling Water's* winter retreat, *Hopping Toad's* thoughts can be told to the son, and passed on to *Chief Red Eagle*.

A foot of snow was not near enough to forestall the resolute red-man from visiting the young chief, *Falling Water*. He, and two others, arrived once the pale sun, obscured by cloud cover, reached its mid-point. It gave assurance that morning activities were completed and other interruptions lessened until dinner.

Upon entering the lodge, *Hopping Toad* observed unexpected changes. *Valley of Flowers* and her granddaughter, *White Dove*, no longer reside there. In their place stood a strange woman, looking somewhat like a Pawnee.

"You look surprised, my brother. Her name is *Chumani*, and she is my wife," informed *Falling Water*. "My grandmother and sister did not make the winter journey. They chose to stay with the main village."

"And, your father is well?"

"Yes, very much so. My mother, *Singing Bird*, also enjoys good health. I trust you and your family can say the same," replied the young chief.

"Other than suffering another year older, we do not have complaints."

Chumani crouched by the fire and began reheating food, as her husband directed his guests to sit down. They convened in a semi-circle, next to him, with their backs against the tepee's wall. *Falling Water* reached for the pipe and filled it with his father's gift. After the brief ceremony, the pipe was handed to *Hopping Toad*, whose eyes lit up with the first puff. He then passed it to *Cut Nose* and *Poor Wolf*, getting the same reaction.

"I must obtain some of this tobacco. Who made it?" *Hopping Toad* questioned.

"It was a gift for my father. Given by a white man."

"At least the white man is good for something," said *Poor Wolf*. His humor brought chuckles from all three.

"Does *Red Eagle* still oppose fighting the white man?"

"My father is a great warrior, but he is also very wise. Since the whites quit fighting each other, their numbers are greater than ours, and they keep coming. The iron horse carries them by the hundreds. Their covered wagons trains are unending. The bluecoat soldiers have guns that can shoot for miles—they call them cannon. When our braves kill one, ten take their place. *Chief Red Eagle* is resolved to abide by the treaties."

"And you feel the same way?" asked *Hopping Toad*.

"He is my father," *Falling Water* stated.

"Well, he is not my father. Me and my band will travel north and fight with *Chief Red Cloud*," he responded.

"*Chief Red Cloud* no longer fights. He has signed a treaty at Fort Laramie."

The three visitors were stunned by the news. Their plans to travel north are severely affected if it is authentic.

"You are sure of this?" asked *Poor Wolf*.

"It is common news. My entire village is aware of it."

Hopping Toad was crestfallen. The proud warrior was visibly dispirited, and wanted to cut short his visit. His host would hear none of it. *Chumani* brought the vessels containing the warmed-over food and returned to the fire to prepare something more substantial. *Falling Water* handed each of them a cup, made from the horn of a mountain sheep, and poured liquid from a hidden gourd.

Alcohol had for many years been an article of trade. While desiring its effects, most disliked the taste of hard liquor. It wasn't until the fur traders sweetened the fiery beverage that it became so popular—to the point that nearly one half of furs traded were for whiskey.

With the initial swallows the guests began to flush. Beads of perspiration soon formed on their brows, and, to a man, they stood and removed heavier outer garments. In short order, *Poor*

Wolf began to sing. Sounds of merriment and frivolity echoed from *Falling Water's* lodge well into the night. Any thoughts of an earlier departure were long gone. In fact, the visitors spent two nights with the young chief's band and left with a promise to attend next year's gathering of the tribes.

CHAPTER TWENTY-EIGHT

The Christmas holidays have come and gone. The month of January offers hours of time in front of a fire. People get to know each other better when imprisoned by their frozen clime. Nature no longer provides a vestige of fall colors—replaced by the gray loneliness of the iron-cold pastures and fields. It's been said that 'every mile is two in winter' and, for good reason, when traveling on foot.

Fortunately, Laurel Harper can rely on no other than Zachary Wheat to provide transportation to and from Sunday services. The first time inclement weather occurred on Sunday, Zack snatched the opportunity from Pearle, under the guise of seniority, and controlled it ever since.

Having the young teacher as a regular member appears to have elevated the entire congregation. Mildred Van Ronkle has taken her under her wing and given Laurel a role with the women's fund raising committee. While the older boys continue to seek her recognition, a particular child has fallen in love with her radiant tresses. Little Abby insists that she sit beside Laurel and spends most of her time fixated on her scarlet color hair. The affection is mutual, as Laurel thoroughly enjoys the child's company. Sundays have given Laurel some of the happiest moments since she arrived at the fort, nearly two years ago.

Zachary Wheat has also changed. He has become a little more outgoing—a far cry from the former individual who seldom smiled. His change is imperceptible to the congregation; however, Abel noticed it almost immediately. Obviously, it had to do with the young schoolteacher. The attention he and Laurel show each other has brought out another human weakness in the melancholy minister. He envies and resents their open display of fondness. Something he must atone for when on his knees at bedtime.

Laurel also takes part in rearranging the bunkhouse, after the churchgoers returned to their homes. When it once again becomes a dwelling, she, Pearle, and Zack recline around the kitchen table, finishing off leftovers, and sipping the remains in the coffee urn. It's at this juncture the trio ascertains the most knowledge about each other.

"Zack, were you ever married?" Laurel asked. Suddenly the room became so noiseless you could hear each other's breathing. Finally, Zack quit staring into his coffee cup and looked up saying, "Yes, but she died."

"You never mentioned that before," Pearle remarked.

Ignoring Pearle's statement, Zack continued, "She was run down in a carriage accident. Both she and our unborn child were killed."

"How terrible. You had to be devastated," acclaimed Laurel.

"I was. After five years as a carpenter's apprentice, I opened a cabinet making workshop with my younger brother. We were doing quite well until the accident. Without my wife I was lost. I became of little use to the business or myself, so I hired another wood craftsman and turned the business over to my brother. He promised to continue until such a time I was mentally able to return."

"What did you do then?" asked Laurel sincerely.

"I signed on to a merchant ship," Zack stated, with a chuckle to himself. "That seemed to be the biggest distraction I could undertake."

"How long did you spend at sea?" she inquired.

"Three years," he answered tersely.

"Was it difficult?"

"Oh yes. It was difficult," he complaisantly replied. "A sailor's life is much different than being on shore. You live in cramped conditions for months at a time, totally cut off from the outside world. Every day we faced the danger of storms at sea and menace of angry weather."

"Did you ever get used to it? I've heard that a busy ship is a happy ship," asked Laurel.

"The ship I signed up on was called the *Colonial Flyer*. It was referred to as a Down—Easter due to its oversized carrying capacity. She was designed to transport large loads of cargo and required around thirty sailors to man her. Looking back on it, I'll have to say our sailing master or captain did a good job keeping everything together. When your life depends on the performance of the crew, the ship's officers must maintain strict discipline on board. For the most part, the hard conditions created a good sense of comradeship—everybody towed the line. That doesn't mean there weren't any fights, thefts, and insubordination. Punishment was rare but it did happen. Usually the threat of punishment was enough to maintain proper order; however, on occasion, it had to be administered.

Flogging was the most common form. It was conducted with the whole crew made to watch. That way it would serve as a warning to the others."

"That sounds awfully severe," commented the young schoolmarm.

"Not when you compare it with being tarred and feathered or tied to a rope and dragged underneath the ship."

"Were you ever punished?"

"Yes, once," Zack replied. "When I signed on, the first mate asked me if I had a trade and I told him, yes, I was a carpenter. Unbeknownst to me carpenters were considered, by the crew, to be idlers, since they didn't stand regular watch and lived aft with the mates and steward. Well, one of the veteran sailors, from the West Indies, took exception to a novice holding that position.

He was a surly fellow who threw barbs at me every time we met. I ignored it thinking he will soon grow tired and give up. That never happened. One day, the Caribbean native and two of his friends cornered me out of view of either first or second mates. I told him to get over it. I'm a carpenter and we can't do anything about it. Apparently, he thought he could and pushed me so hard I landed on my back and slid across the deck. His eyes were emitting rays of hatred. When he came at me again, I ducked his punch and gave him a hard pop on the jaw. It was his turn to end up on his back and he did, out cold. The second mate asked who started this fracas. I knew the Caribbean native had been punished before and this time it will be really harsh, possibly keelhaul. So I said that I started it. By the time punishment was administered, my adversary had come to and watched me receive ten lashes. From that point forward he became my friend and protector."

"I suppose there were plenty girls in the ports," Laurel asked, in the form of a statement.

"Lots of women and lots of time. We stayed in the ports for over two weeks, unloading and waiting for cargo to bring back. Carpenters, however, used this time to make repairs. Even so, there was time for sightseeing and other inclinations. As for girls, I wasn't much interested that first year."

"Were the girls beautiful? Men believe the foreign women to be the most attractive."

"Where did you ever hear that?" queried Zack. "There are attractive women everywhere; but, to me, at least, those in the ports could hardly be called beautiful. Maybe in France the girls are more romantic and sensual but for true beauty, those women were found on the voyage to China."

Pearle took notice of the expression on Laurel's face and changed the subject, "What was the most difficult part of living on a sailing ship?"

"For me, it was keeping dry. All ships take on water below deck. It had to be pumped every day. Top side we are confronted with the constant spindrift. Only those tending the sails can avoid it and to do that you must not be afraid of heights. Looking skyward and watching them about their tasks made me dizzy and a little sick to my stomach. Thank heavens I never had to do it."

"Did you ever have to swab the deck?" asked Pearle, half-joking.

"Many times. The captain was good at dividing up the work."

"Tell us about your voyage to China," Laurel specified, reverting the subject back to women.

"New York to China is a voyage that takes a year. It's far different from the trips to Europe where in a little over a month you can reach England or France. Going, we took advantage of the prevailing westerly winds and the Gulf Stream current. Returning, however, would take twice as long. We had to detour north and south to find favorable wind and current.

I first learned about the possibility of sailing to China while we were in port at Buenos Aires, Argentina. The rumor caught fire and before long we were all talking about it. Everyone feared us continuing around Cape Horn and on to California. Cape Horn was known for tough seas and fierce storms. Sometimes it takes two months just to navigate the Horn. Winds blow from the west, straight against the direction of the ship. I asked the second mate if the voyage to China was true and he nodded and smiled.

With our hold filled with wool, hides for leather, sandalwood, and ginseng, we set sail for the Cape of Good Hope on the southern tip of Africa. From there, the destination was Java and the Sunda Strait—then, on to the port of Hong Kong.

Three weeks later, with a cargo of furniture, silk, and tea we returned home. The captain chose a route to San Francisco, California. I suspicioned it was because of opium stashed somewhere on board but that was never proven. His route led us into the French Polynesian Islands. The sailors thought they had died and gone to heaven. It was here, they boasted of the most beautiful women in the world. For my part, Tahiti was the Garden of Eden. When we launched the landing boats to replenish water barrels and procure fresh fruit, the young girls swam out to greet us. There was no modesty when it came to nudity. Their culture made them subservient to men and they happily demonstrated it to the foreign sailors. I have to admit these naked girls were quite attractive, especially after weeks aboard ship.

Our stay not only improved morale, but the food had a healing quality for those lacking in fruit and fresh vegetables."

"How many of these naked beauties did you have in your harem?" Laurel snidely inquired.

"Keep in mind that these girls are mainly attractive during their youth. From ages thirteen to about twenty-five. After that, they take on more homely shapes."

"You didn't answer my question," Laurel stated.

"There was one magical beauty that did draw my attention. She and her friends constructed a grass hut for us to spend time alone. It was very difficult for me to leave when the captain decided to make sail. If I remained, it would mean the gallows for desertion. On the morning of the ship's departure, I kissed her while she slept, crept out of our hut, and swam to the ship."

"And you've been running ever since," said Laurel.

"Not exactly. Once we returned to New York, I left the ship and rejoined the cabinet business. My brother had done a fine job while I was on the high seas and, now, I could better focus on making it even more prosperous.

When the Civil War started, I once again turned my business over to the skilled hands of my younger brother. At that time, we had nearly a dozen employees, some of which enlisted in the New York militia. When President Lincoln asked for volunteer troops, I felt it my patriotic duty to sign up. Later, while wearing the Union blue uniform, I was taken prisoner and sent to Richmond, Virginia, where I remained incarcerated until the surrender at Appomattox.

Once again, I found myself footloose and free. I believed the direction America was growing was west. Accordingly, I asked my brother to take over the business while I traveled west to grow with the country. He promised to put my half of the profits in a bank account from which I could draw upon whenever I needed funds.

I stopped for a while in Lebanon, Tennessee to set my sights for moving on. It was there that I met Pearle and Abel and talked my way into joining their move to Kansas."

"So any day now you'll be getting the itch to move again," said Laurel.

"Not so fast, young lady. I've got a claim on 160 acres west of Abel and fully intend to homestead it. I'll be building a cabin next spring and, with the help of my partners, plow the prairie and plant a crop." Zack attested. "You can plan on me to take you to church for a very long time."

Pearle broke the silence with a question. "With your brother banking half the profits, you must have a sizable amount by now. Might I ask how much?"

"Let's just say, it's a sizable sum," he answered.

On the ride back to the fort community Laurel was arguing with herself. She felt jealous over Zack's affair with the islander girl. Even though it occurred years ago, she resented it—telling herself resentment now was being foolish. There was no trust broken. She didn't even know him back then. Besides, he hasn't indicated or even hinted that he cared for her other than a ride to and from church—something he would do for just about anyone. As things stand, she won't see him again until next Sunday.

"Are you warm enough?" he asked.

"I'm okay. It's not a very long ride, and, besides, it's going to be warm in my room. The folks I live with keep a good fire."

"This spring, when I build the cabin, you're welcome to move in. I won't bother you. If the idea makes you uncomfortable, I can still live in the bunkhouse."

"I appreciate the offer. It gives me something to think about," Laurel replied, thinking, "*Just what I need to bait my traps.*"

* * *

The month of February is considered the frozen heart of winter. In western Kansas, it brought a major blizzard lasting several days. The road to Fort Dodge was impassable as snowdrifts reached record proportions. Active life came to a halt. The pioneers were sustained by the knowledge that beneath the chilly white blanket, lies seed waiting to sprout. At Fort Dodge, things were locked down—no coming or going. Community businesses were closed as well as the schoolhouse. Inhabitants were confined to their homes. Most were huddled around their stoves in an attempt to keep warm.

Abel managed to construct a path to the barn in order to feed and water the animals. Pearle and Zack dug a channel from their doorway to the stable with the same idea.

Finding themselves together in the barn struck the trio as humorous and all had a hearty laugh. Impervious to the conditions outside, the animals were surprisingly calm and went about their morning feed undisturbed. Zack's cow is seven months along and due to deliver in early April. Thus far, she seems to be doing just fine, and gave two buckets full of milk, which Abel will take back to the house.

"I wonder how long we're going to be snowed in," Abel said, as he lifted a fork of hay for the horses.

Folks should be traveling in a week or so. The sun gets pretty warm by high noon. It won't take too long before the roads are clear." Zack replied.

Pearle had climbed to the loft and pushed a bale of hay through the opening and down the ladder steps. "Look out below, me maties," he shouted in jest, as though he were a pirate.

"Come down ye landlubber afore we make ye walk the plank," Zack answered.

Abel was bewildered with what was going on. He assumed it was a joke between those two and grasped the bucket handles to return to the house. The remainder of the day was spent near the stove. In weather this cold, both dwellings heated with coal. Thanks to Zack, they had plenty to see them through.

It took until the last Sunday in February before the benches were full at church. Renewed camaraderie made the sunny day brighter. Mildred Van Ronkle was anxious to resume collections for the new church and set the following Monday for canvassing the town's businesses. Once the service was over and during the fellowship luncheon, Abel approached Laurel and asked to meet with her. Immediately, she was torn between embarrassment and fright. Her appetite quickly diminished and the rest of the social hour she spent trying to control her heartbeat. She thought, "*Why in the world would he want to speak to me in private? I don't recall doing anything improper.*" It seemed to take forever for the last churchgoer to leave the bunkhouse. Finally, she turned to Zack and said, "The minister wants to meet with me at the house. Do you know what that's all about?"

"Beats me. It can't be anything too important or he would have told me and Pearle."

With that Laurel put on her coat and scarf and walked to the house. The minute she scaled the front steps, Abel was standing in the doorway with Abby at his side. He took her wraps and hung them on the hall tree and directed her to the living room. Little Abby was still clapping her hands in excitement.

"Can I get you something, a cup of tea perhaps?" he asked. "It won't take a second. There's a kettle of hot water on the stove."

"If it's not too much trouble," she answered, as Abby climbed in her lap and touched Laurel's hair.

When Abel returned with two cups of steaming tea, he told his daughter to get down and go play in her room. The reluctant tyke obeyed her father but not before expressing a grimace.

"My wife always served tea with a wedge of lemon on the side. I don't have any lemons but you'll find two lumps of sugar on the saucer, if you need them," Abel stated.

"This is fine the way it is," she replied.

"I suppose you've heard about my wife," said the minister.

"Yes, from the women in the congregation. They say you're not to blame."

Abel paused for a moment then cleared his throat, "I've been meaning to talk to you about Zachary Wheat. It's obvious you two have formed a strong friendship. Not to say anything against Zack—how can I phrase this—he's not the stay-at-home type. That doesn't mean he's a bad man. I couldn't have made this move to Kansas without him. I owe more to him than I can say, but, I feel I also owe you some of my limited wisdom."

Laurel was aware of what was coming next. Inwardly, she found the stammering preacher a bit pathetic and actually humorous. That said, she was miffed at being treated as though she was gullible to the ways of life.

Abel went on, "Friendship can lead to a more serious relationship and young girls, such as you, are susceptible to making mistakes that can hound them for the rest of their lives. I don't want to see that happen to you."

Laurel hesitated for a moment thinking of the appropriate thing to say. Finally, she looked up and stated, "I've never felt more secure than when I am in his presence. For the first time in years I sleep the entire night uninterrupted by nightmares. Zack has done nothing to indicate he wants more than a platonic exchange."

The more Abel talked, the more Laurel began to sense the heartrending attempt of a man still suffering over his wife. Here was a man acting solely out of her best interest, with kindness, and without ulterior motive. What Abel said next nearly floored her.

"I worry about my little daughter growing up without her mother. I'm not capable of providing the lessons only a woman can teach. It's no secret how much she cares for you. You have indicated that presently you are living in one room. What I would like you to consider is moving here, in this house, and provide the feminine touch. You will have free reign at no charge. In fact, I will pay you for your effort."

"You forget, I teach school. Living where I do allows me to walk to the schoolhouse," said Laurel.

"I have a carriage in the barn. You're welcome to use it for traveling back and forth. In a year or so Abby will be starting school and she could ride with you."

"And, what will happen when your wife decides to come back?" Laurel asked.

"My wife is never coming back," Abel finally accepted. "Don't give me your answer now. Take some time to think it over. All I ask is that you don't disclose our conversation until you reach a decision."

Fortunately for Laurel, little Abby could no longer obey her father and came running out of her room. She insisted on giving Laurel a tour of the house. While on the tour, Laurel took notice of the unoccupied bedroom. It was much larger than the one currently retaining her bed. Thanks to the church ladies, the whole house sparkled, especially the oversized kitchen.

On her way back to the bunkhouse, Laurel found herself in a conundrum. She now has been offered two houses. One of which is yet to be built. Sleeping the entire night without the interruption of dreams, for a while at least, will be a thing of the past.

* * *

The following day, after school let out, Mildred Van Ronkle and Angela Calloway called on the young teacher. They had collected a grand total of five dollars from three of the families with children. Laurel was to join them when they canvas the businesses along the main drag. Zack gave his approval for them to solicit from the tent merchants along the main thoroughfare, however, issued an admonition about Boris Azarov and the Lucky Lady. He would tend to that himself. Mildred didn't mind omitting Azarov's general store and stable—she couldn't stand the man. The Lucky Lady had a certain naughtiness about it, imposing a particular intrigue. Fundraising gave her the only opportunity she will ever have to see inside. The thought of it gave her a rare sense of impishness—just enough for her to suggest they go inside and solicit from the patrons.

The gambling house was well attended after being closed for the winter blizzard. It appeared as though the customers were trying to make up for lost time. The rowdy din came to a complete halt the minute the three entered the room. All eyes were focused on the entrance. Gus Greeley rose from his table and walked over to greet them.

"My name is Gus Greeley, I'm the owner. How may I help you ladies?"

It took a moment before Mildred could utter a word. She was stunned by the opulent surroundings, the lavish draperies, and exciting colors. At last she composed herself and said, "We're part of a fundraising committee to build a new church. We would like to solicit donations from your patrons."

"There's no need for that. I'd be proud to make a donation on behalf of them all," Greeley offered. He also noticed the girl with the fiery red hair.

"We appreciate the offer but I'm not sure our minister would approve," Mildred replied. "Your patrons have no connection to your establishment, other than their amusement and their donations will be accepted."

"I appreciate your frankness, Miss eh…"

"It's Mrs. Mrs. Mildred Van Ronkle and the other ladies are Mrs. Angela Blankenberg and Miss Laurel Harper."

Without taking his eyes off Laurel, Greeley said, "I'm pleased to meet you ladies." He then walked to an opening between tables and lifted his voice, "These ladies are collecting donations to build the first church in the Fort Dodge community. They will be passing by each table. I expect you to dig deep for such a noble cause." With that he gallantly motioned with his left arm to lead their way.

The previous undertone returned along with the jingle of coins striking the outreaching small baskets. Many, at the card tables, dispensed folding money. When Laurel approached the table occupied by Charlie Fontaine and a woman, she knew

340

immediately it had to be Amanda, Abel's wife. As Charlie placed a five-dollar bill in the container, the two women locked eyes. It was as though female percipience had united them. Without ever meeting, somehow each knew they had entered one another's lives.

Mildred was ecstatic. She could hardly wait to drop Laurel off at her residence and return to hers to count the loot. She and Angela will soon learn they had collected over seventy-five dollars.

That night Laurel was in a whirlwind of commingled thoughts. She felt as though she had accepted Abel's offer and suffered the eventual embarrassment of meeting the wife. On the other hand, she was comparing herself with the woman at the table. Was her feeling of guilt due to the fact she had emotionally accepted Abel's offer without giving it proper diligence or consideration. Her pillow will flip many times tonight before the feint streak of light enters her bedroom window.

* * *

The next time Boris Azarov sought amusement at the Lucky Lady, Gus Greeley called him over to his table.

"What do you know about this new church business?" he asked, while lighting a panatela.

"All I know I learned from Zachary Wheat. He told me about the church and asked me to donate a line of credit. He promised me the members will be loyal when more competition comes."

"I suppose you will sell the materials to build it at your usual discount," Greeley said with a twisted smile.

"I won't pad their bill too much because of Wheat. He will demand a good accounting."

"You're afraid of this Wheat, aren't you?" Greeley said, as he exhaled a ring of smoke.

"I believe he is a gunfighter."

"Have you seen the woman with red hair?"

"You mean the one with the withered left hand?"

"I never noticed that. She was wearing gloves at the time," Greeley conjectured. "No matter. You know that I own land at the end of the strip. My deed is open. I want you to offer enough for a church and grounds to Zachary Wheat as part of their line of credit. Sell it for ten dollars."

"It will be worth a lot more than that," Azarov stated.

"I know," Greeley confirmed. With that he slid an envelope across the table and said, "Don't open it here. It contains $250. I want you to add it to their account. If you cheat me, I will feed you to the Chinaman's pigs."

"Why are you doing this?" asked the Balkan.

"I have my reasons," Greeley stated, then signaled their meeting was over.

Boris left the Lucky Lady wishing he had never gone there in the first place. Now, he not only has Zack Wheat to worry about, but, Gus Greeley and the Chinaman's pigs. He has reached the point of almost treating the churchgoers account honestly. The bit about the Chinaman's pigs has been a rumor since the Chinese came to the fort, while building the railroad, and deciding to stay. They mainly remain to themselves and are represented by a spokesman, named *Bao-Zhi*. Rumor or fact, Boris has no intention of proving it either way.

* * *

The month of March brings the stormy beginnings of spring. Prairie grasses start to green, and daffodils commence to bloom. Creeks and streams are moving faster and the sounds of outside activity can be heard around the pioneers' cabins. Still cold and too soon to plant, it's a time for the earth to be reborn.

Looking to the heavens, at the beginning of the month, the constellation of Leo, the lion, commands the skies. Then, at the end of March, it's Aires, the ram or lamb, which presides over calmer winds. In all likelihood, the adage, *in like a lion, out like a lamb*, is akin to these heavenly bodies.

342

It's a time of anticipation. Lumber to build the church will arrive any day now and Zack has recruited enough workers to complete the job with deliberate speed. Though basically a four walled construction, he has added a few amenities for uniqueness—in particular, a steeple to accommodate a church bell.

It would be incorrect to say Zack was pleased by Laurel's decision. His own cabin is still in the planning stage and Abby needs a woman's signature, especially now. Abel made an innocent and logical request. Zack has no fear of Abel as a competitor, yet he couldn't help the nagging tug of the green-eyed monster.

For Laurel's part, her presence in the preacher's house fit like a glove. Before the first week ended, it all seemed like old hat. Her idle time is no longer confined to one small room. Her new bedroom was large enough to accommodate a desk and chair, plus, a rocker. Now, she had to battle the inviting urge to take schoolwork home.

With all the activity outside the homestead, she often feels useless; but compensates the emotion with the knowledge that soon school will be dismissed for the planting season and summer, when she will be able to lend a hand wherever she's needed.

CHAPTER TWENTY-NINE

A bel and Zack returned from the fields. They had been testing the soil to see if planting could begin. Pearle was mucking the stalls when he heard them outside the barn. He leaned the pitchfork against an adjoining wall and walked through the open barn door.

"How was it?" he queried.

"Still too wet," said Abel.

"It will be two weeks before we can put a plow to it," echoed Zack, after which he and Abel went into the barn to work on the carriage. Up 'til now, Zack has transported Laurel to school and home again. Today being Saturday, Abel expects to have the carriage ready for Monday morning. The little mare is perfect. Gentle and smart, a few miles a day will keep her in good fettle.

Having a woman on the farm again has made a visible change in Abel's daughter, Abby. She is happier and now sleeps without the pitiful sobs during the night. If she wakens, she crawls in with Laurel and sleeps until morning. Abby also rises with Laurel and dresses herself to have breakfast with her newfound motherly friend. Unlike Amanda, the nighttime companion does not disturb Laurel. As Abel had previously suggested, love has the ability to arrive from several avenues.

This morning, after breakfast, the inquisitive pair bundled up against the chilly March air and traipsed to the barn to see what the men were doing. The image of them standing at the entrance had an uplifting emotional effect on the man inside.

"Come take a look at your buggy," Abel invited. "It has a cover to protect you from the elements."

When they walked past the third stall, the little mare stretched her neck to see who the visitors were.

"She's excited," Abel explained. "We're going the harness her, so you can take a spin and try it out."

"Where are Pearle and Zack?"

"They were here a minute ago. They must have gone to the bunkhouse," suggested Abel, as he lifted his daughter to pet the inquisitive horse. "I'll hook up the mare and you two can see how you like it."

Laurel was experienced riding and leading a box wagon. The horse and buggy gave her a thrill by the ease in which the little mare could travel. Swiftly, she drove to the end of the lane and onto the main road. Only tugging the reins to slow the mare down, the horse also could feel a lessor burden. Finding a wider stretch, she turned around and headed back. With a firm grip on the reins, Laurel handed the ends to Abby to hold, on the slow return.

"Oh Abel, it's wonderful. I'll never be able to repay you," she stated, before handing the reins to the smiling father of her joyful passenger.

"You just being here is payment enough," he replied.

* * *

Later in the day, Pearle caught a glimpse, of the setting sun reflecting on the image of the tall Cheyenne. It was *Two Trees* astride his pinto pony. When he got within earshot, Pearle said, "Welcome my friend. What brings you out this day?"

"I am hunting eagles. Would you care to join me?"

Pearle was now aware it would be at least two weeks before he will be needed to help plow the fields. "How long will we be gone?"

"I will spend six nights," replied the tall native. "You should plan accordingly."

The Cheyenne, as well as other tribes, place a high value on eagle-feathers, especially those from the gray eagle. They believe such birds possess great power and a war bonnet made of their feathers will protect them against bullets and arrows.

Two Trees will first seek the eagle's nest. And finding one, he will remove the down-covered chicks to take back to his lodge and raise them. At the present time, two full-grown eagles remain tied to a stake outside the lodge of his mother, *Aponi*.

He has learned that pulled tail feathers will grow back, but only two or three times. And, a fully-grown eagle can produce up to thirty feathers.

Others in the tribe also hunt the majestic birds. Even so, *Two Trees* is recognized as the better. Hunting this early in the season minimizes his chances of finding hatchlings in the eagle's nest; nevertheless, the tall Cheyenne is resourceful and will employ his own technique.

* * *

With the imposing red man waiting outside the barn, Pearle saddled his horse. Zack stepped from the bunkhouse and greeted *Two Trees*. The two men held each other in high regard and enjoyed a friendly chat.

"Isn't it a little early to hunt eagles? You may only find eggs in their nests."

Two Trees stoic expression melted into a smile as he answered, "I have other ways to catch an eagle."

The sound of a door opening made him look up at the house. Standing on the porch was the man with a rifle who killed the Pawnee chief over a mile away. *Two Trees* thought, "Someday I must meet this man." Appearing from behind Abel was a woman holding a sack of provisions. As Laurel drew nearer, the Indian became frightened. The woman had hair the color never seen before and her withered left hand settled it—she is a witch.

Buffalo Horn had instructed him how to detect whether or not a person is a witch. In his mind she fits the description.

Pearle was leading his horse from the barn when Laurel said, "Abel asked me to bring you these supplies. How long will you be gone?"

"The better part of a week," he replied, while attaching the bag to his saddle. "Oh, *Two Trees*, this is Laurel Harper, she's a schoolteacher and takes care of Abel's little daughter, Abby."

Laurel gave him a kindly smile and said, "I'm happy to make your acquaintance."

Two Trees nearly had a heart attack. He was torn between riding away as fast as his pony could carry him, or, pulling an arrow from his quiver. Choosing neither, he only nodded.

Shivering from the cold, Laurel said to Pearle, "He seems nice," and, hurried back to the warmth of the house.

The eagle hunters traveled along the Arkansas River until handicapped by darkness. They found a suitable spot, by a lonely cottonwood tree, and set up camp. *Two Trees* managed to find enough twigs and branches to have a small fire and Pearle had presence of mind to bring his waterproof tarpaulin—the yellow one Abel saved from the Civil War. Between the two they shared pemmican, cornbread, and fried chicken. To the hunters, it was a meal fit for a king.

Pearle had gotten used to his taciturn companion and found no problem in laying back in silence. He made good use of these quiet moments, thinking about *White Dove*. Their long awaited wedding is now just weeks away.

On the second day of their journey it began to spit rain. Not the kind of rain to be expected in April, but the best which the fading month of March could bring. Pearle's laconic escort had his head down and gave no indication of seeking a sanctuary. The misty rain continued all day, and so did *Two Trees*. Finally, when the weakened light began to give out, he brought the second day's mission to a close. Pearle quickly unfolded the yellow tarp and constructed a shelter. *Two Trees* gathered soggy branches and laid them out as if a fire could be ignited. Much to Pearle's amazement, he withdrew buffalo chips from his parfleche and soon a smoky fire was sputtering.

The night was pitch-black. The only time you could see in front of you was when a lightning flash illuminated the area for a moment, only to return to total darkness. After a while, *Two Trees*, always frugal with his words, said, "Tell me about your witch."

"You mean Laurel?" Pearle replied. "She's no witch. She's as normal as you and I."

"She may have put you under a spell. Witches can do that."

"I assure you, my friend, you are wrong to think Laurel is a witch," confirmed Pearle.

"Maybe so, but how did she come by her hair and withered hand?"

"The poor girl was born that way," Pearle sighed. "How long before we reach the eagle hunting grounds?"

"We are here. We hunt when the sun comes up."

* * *

On that same night, Laurel and Abel shared a hot cup of tea. Abby had fallen asleep on Laurel's bed. Abel offered to carry her to her own room, but Laurel assured him his daughter is fine just where she is.

With Pearle gone, Zack decided to hit the hay early, leaving the two at the house alone for an infrequent occasion. The nervous situation caused hesitance with both staring into their cups. Laurel broke the ice, "I want to say how happy I am to have taken you up on your offer. I used to wake up during the night in a panic. Sometimes I felt as though I was no longer there. It took a while to realize I wasn't dead. When people told me to wake up and smell the roses, I only awakened to feel the thorns. I still don't have both feet on the ground. For a while I thought Zack could fill the void in my life; but, now, I see that can never be. I even foolishly thought you and I might make a life together, but you are a minister of the church and hurting over the loss of your wife. So I live in my purgatory, bracing for the next shoe to fall."

Abel was emotionally touched by her words. He slowly digested what he had just heard and said, "A lot of my pain is gone, but I'm not yet ready to conform to its absence. I could tell you to pray for divine intervention. That wouldn't be honest. You see, that's what I did for many years. What I can say to you is to take it a day at a time. The world turns around every day. This spinning globe takes us all for a ride. Only God knows what will confront us mortals when the sun rises. Regarding what the future holds for us, I also have envisioned you and me together for the rest of our lives."

Without another word spoken, Abel gathered the cups and walked them to the kitchen sink. Laurel padded to her bedroom. It will be good to have company tonight. She has a great deal to think about—perhaps to dream of a very happy future.

* * *

The eagle hunters were up at the crack of dawn. *Two Trees* had asked Pearle to kill him a rabbit while he sought the material for his trap and constructed a cage. Pearle admired the dangling ear rings and neck chain the tall Indian wore and took this opportunity to ask about it.

"Did you make your adornments?" he asked.

"Some. Others were made by my mother from stones I gave her."

"The yellow stones that shine are particularly beautiful. Where did you find them?"

"In the very stream by which we now stand. I was hunting eagles and walked up the creek looking for bait. They glistened to my eye and I picked them out of the water and carried them home, along with three eaglets. It was a good day," he replied.

Pearle removed his boots and walked the fast moving water upstream. Those glistening stones looked like gold. This time of year, the current ran strong. Yet, it was crystal-clear. You could easily see the multicolored pebbles worn smooth from the constant flow of water. He didn't travel far before coming upon a larger stone with shiny pieces of the yellow gem imbedded. The farther he walked the more he found. Some smaller pieces were lying loose beneath the frigid water. Pearle removed his kerchief from his neck and made a pouch to contain his hopeful bonanza. Then, as fast as he discovered them, there were no more. He trekked nearly a mile against the unyielding flow. But no others could be found.

(Millions of years ago, the Rocky Mountains were formed during a period when a number of tectonic plates began to slide beneath the greater North American Plate. The angle of subduction—where one plate moves under another—was shallow, resulting in a broad belt of mountains running down the western part of North America. Further tectonic activity, plus erosion by glaciers and rainfall, has sculpted the Rockies into their dramatic peaks and valleys.

By virtue of the Continental Divide, these valleys direct melting ice and rainfall down the slopes to either the Pacific or Atlantic oceans. Rocks on these mountains were formed by sedimentary deposits long before being raised by tectonic forces.

Heavy laden with minerals and metals, ductile portions wash away into the flowing streams. In all likelihood, the reason Pearle, and *Two Trees* before him, found the shiny stones imbedded with precious gold.)

Convinced walking further served no purpose, Pearle stepped out of the water, secured the ends of his homemade pouch, and began the trek back. Along the way, there was movement in the brushes by the creek bank. He paused to cock his Henry rifle. A large gray rabbit sprang forward. Only one shot was required to send the cottontail high in the air and dead when it hit the ground.

Even though the boots were cold, it felt good to put them back on. By the time he returned to the horses, he witnessed *Two Trees* digging a hole—a very deep hole. There are times his tawny friend amazes him. This was one of them.

"Why are you digging such a deep hole?" Pearle inquired.

"So I can fit in it. Did you kill a rabbit?"

When the cavity was deep enough for *Two Trees* to lower himself inside, he tied the rabbit to a cover made from branches and brush and pulled it over him.

"You must move away so as not to frighten the eagles," he stated.

Pearle looked overhead to see several birds circling high above. He moved backwards to the small cottonwood to which the horses were tethered and placed the homemade pouch in his saddle bag. Afterward, he sat with his back against the tree.

For the better part of an hour, there was no activity near the rabbit. Then, suddenly a large gray speckled eagle swooped from the sky and landed on the bait. *Two Trees* let out a shriek and bounced the lid in order to frighten the bird away. He only wanted bald eagles.

It didn't take much longer before a white hooded eagle grasped the bait with its sharp talons. At the same time, the big hand of *Two Trees* reached through the cover and clutched the eagle's legs. He deftly projected himself from the pit and tied the eagle's legs together. Then he placed a perforated leather hood over its head and pulled the cinch.

Pearle observed in wonderment. His friend was actually catching eagles barehanded. Walking to get a better look, he exclaimed, "Wow that is a giant."

"Eagles mate for life. The female will be much larger."

An hour later proved his point. He caught the female using the same technique. It was at least thirty percent bigger—larger wings, feet, talons, and beak. After securing it, in a similar manner, he extended the bird of prey to Pearle so that he could feel its weight.

"It must weigh nearly twenty pounds," he asserted.

"I have never caught one larger," replied his tall friend.

On the trip home, *Two Trees* sang victory songs. They were more like chants than tunes. Nevertheless, Pearle found himself singing along. When they reached the farm, the Native American placed his hand against Pearle's chest, as a sign of affection, and rode to his village.

Pearle didn't mention the rocks tied in his kerchief. He will take them personally to Boris Azarov. That would avoid criticism from Zack in case they were worthless. He couldn't care less what Azarov thought.

Early the following day, and under the guise of visiting *White Dove*, Pearle retrieved the heavy kerchief bag and rode to the fort. He found the unlikable merchant scanning the church builder's account, in an attempt to find areas in which he can skin both Gus Greeley and Zack, without being detected—similar to sinners scrutinizing the Bible searching for loopholes. Looking up with eyes reflecting the strain, he greeted Pearle—silently happy Zack Wheat was not with him.

"What can I do for you this morning?" questioned Boris, whose W's always come across as V's.

"I've got some metallic ore I'd like you to assay."

"You're wise to come to me rather than those assayers in the tents. They are all crooks."

Pearle took that with a grain of salt and hoisted the bag atop the counter. Azarov raised a piece to the light, and then reached beneath his counter to remove his bottled chemicals. Breaking off a smaller piece, the storekeeper dribbled a few drops of *aqua fortis* (nitric acid) and watched the surrounding substances dissolve. Humming to himself, he then let a couple drops of *aqua regia* (a mixture of nitric and hydrochloric acid) fall on the remaining metal which dissolved some of its thinner edges.

"Where did you get this ore?" he enthusiastically inquired.

Pearle could tell by Azarov's expression, he had hit the jackpot. Wisely he answered, "I brought it with me from Tennessee. There's a lot of mining taking place in the mountains. I want you to tell me what it's worth."

Disheartened by learning it came from Tennessee, Boris slid his scales to the center of the counter and began weighing the clumps.

"You've got six and a half pounds. I would estimate it contains at least twenty-five percent gold. There could be more if I broke it all down," knowing full well the yield would be higher.

"How much would it be worth if I sold it as is?"

Boris began to scribble on paper. "Let's see, six and a half pounds equals a hundred and four ounces. Twenty-five percent gold yields twenty-six ounces. Twenty-six ounces times twenty-three dollars an ounce comes to five-hundred ninety-eight dollars."

"I'll take it," Pearle stated.

"I haven't figured in my charges for processing and selling. That would come to five percent or thirty dollars, leaving four-hundred sixty eight."

"That's okay. Give me the money," Pearle said.

"I don't carry that much money here in my store. I'll need to get it from my house. You come back tomorrow and I'll have it for you. I can give you a hundred dollars now and a receipt for the remainder if you wish."

"Okay, I'll take the receipt and will return for the balance tomorrow."

Boris counted out the hundred dollars, mad at himself thinking he could have cheated more. Pearle didn't mention the pure pieces of gold he kept in a smaller leather pouch. Based on Boris's price per ounce, it would come to nearly five hundred dollars. He'll keep that for a rainy day.

* * *

It was the second week in April before the fields dried out enough to accommodate the plow. From that point, the men worked from sunup to dusk. It is a time when the hopes of the pioneers shape the future. With the will of the Lord, it can be predictable to the extent of human effort. Last year's crop was good. Anticipation for an even better harvest reaches to the mountaintop. Neighbors help each other. The oldest Calloway daughter watches Abby while Laurel is teaching school. Older students are noted by their absence. They can be found helping their parents during this critical period.

Laurel teaches until noon then dismisses her class. The enchanting redhead returns to the farm to help out as needed. This routine continues for the next two weeks.

Grassy topsoil, for the first time, is turned over on Zachary Wheat's claim. He has made a plat drawing of the property denoting the location for the cabin, barn, garden, well, and fields. From the looks of things, it will be some time before the itinerate partner moves forward in search of life.

At the end of the first week of hard labor, Pearle's aches and pains began to subside. In truth, he had never felt better. Besides unfettering his mind while undertaking the work, he had a sense of achievement—one step closer to a place of his own.

Several windows of the bunkhouse were partially opened to allow for an April breeze. Not only providing cool air, it also rendered the pleasant smell of spring.

Tomorrow is the Lord's Day. Possibly the last service to be held in the bunkhouse. The new church's roof is completed, making the structure watertight. There's no reason Abel can't preach while the inside details are being finished. The move will be met with mixed emotions. The bunkhouse landlords grew to enjoy the weekly preparations. Now, they will be like the rest of the congregation, and travel to church on Sundays.

Tonight, as they lay on their bunks, the pair quietly reflect on the future. Pearle's marriage to *White Dove* is imminent and he has yet to mention it to Abel. Even though he will undergo the Cheyenne ceremony, in his own mind, the union isn't completed until a Christian ritual. What if his brother-in-law refuses to marry them? He could deny it because the bride is a savage and not a Christian. Where will they eventually live? Approaching a headache, Pearle needed a diversion, "What are you thinking about Zack?"

"Not a heck of a lot, how about you?" responded his bearded friend.

"Oh, maybe a little about the upcoming wedding. I still haven't told Abel and I'm concerned if he will agree to marry us."

"You may have a point there. If you have two weddings in mind, better ask him first. However, that's not the only thing you should think about. You've got stardust in your eyes, and not considering what's going to happen even if he agrees to marry you two. Ain't many people going to accept it. To them, *White Dove* is only a Cheyenne Indian and feelings about the Indians are bad right now. That crowd won't ever accept your wife. It's going to be tough on both of you."

"You're right. I haven't given that much thought."

"You can always live with the Cheyenne," Zack suggested duplicitously.

"That might be okay for a while but I wouldn't want it long term. Ultimately, I want to live in my own cabin."

"None of what you want can take place until you have a talk with Abel," said Zack.

"I'm kind of scared of Abel, him being my brother-in-law and all," confessed Pearle.

"Okay, why don't you have Laurel intercede for you or I'll have a talk with him."

"You've done too much for me already. It's about time I stand on my own two feet. Do you think Laurel would do this for me?" asked Pearle.

"I'm sure she would if you explained your situation," Zack replied.

"Whatever happened between you two? I thought you guys were on the way to becoming a couple. You were going to have her live in your cabin, once it got built."

"I thought, because of her imperfection, she might consider me—kind of a last chance sort of a thing. Moving in with Abel changed all that. She's still a wonderful girl but too young for me. Hell, I got a saddle older than her," Zack admitted.

"You'd be a catch for any woman, and I'm not saying that just because you're my best friend."

"Laurel is at a good age for Abel. If he had any brains he'd realize that. She needs a man more permanent and they don't come any more steadfast then your brother-in-law. He plays all the songs of life in the key of C—day in and day out without modulation. And best of all, he wants it that way. I'm cut from a different clothe. To me, the future lies in front, like a carrot dangling before a burro, I must continue forward."

"You still have a great deal to finish here, in the present. You've got a cabin and barn to build and a farm to develop," said Pearle.

"The present. For me there isn't any present. There's either the past or the future. I don't like dwelling on the past, therefore, the future is all I have. Don't kid yourself about the present. It's only a word for an imaginary state of being."

"Zack, I'm beginning to see what you mean. I'm totally at peace talking with you and find a keeper each time we converse," said Pearle, thinking, there is no subject beyond his ken.

"Well, you better get to it. *Falling Water* will be back any day now. And, he will expect the wedding ceremony to take place soon," cautioned Zack.

* * *

After the final bunkhouse services, Pearle made several attempts to talk to Laurel and lost his courage every time. He finally decided to catch her tomorrow around noon when she returns from teaching school. As it so happened, it turned out to be a good idea. The Calloway girl had taken Abby home with her and Laurel was alone. At least until she brought the little girl back. Pearle took the reins from her and said, "I'll put the mare away. There's something I need to say to you."

"Thank you, Pearle. I'll be up at the house."

It seemed eerily quiet with Abby gone as Laurel led him to the kitchen. The whole house reflected the female presence. It even smelled better. Laurel offered him a glass of water and said, "So, you need to talk about something?"

Pearle took a long swallow and replied, "Yes. You know that I'm sort of engaged to a girl in the Cheyenne village."

"I gathered as much, but you never told me."

"Well, I love her with all my heart and we're supposed to be married once her brother returns from his winter camp."

"Sort of engaged huh? Looks to me like you aren't sort of engaged, you are engaged," she taunted.

"That's my problem. I'm going to marry her the Cheyenne way, but I can't be a true husband until there's a Christian ceremony."

"What does she think about that?"

"Ah, I haven't exactly made her aware of that," Pearle confessed.

"Boy, you do have problems. What can I do about it?"

"You can talk to Abel for me. I'm scared of what he's going to say. He might not want to perform the ceremony with her being an Indian and all."

"Does he have any idea of what's going on?" she asked.

"I don't believe so. I only told Zack."

"And what did Zack tell you?"

"He said for me to talk to you," uttered Pearle, with a fading voice.

Laurel puffed her cheeks and exhaled. "Let me figure out some way to do this. You better go back to work," she advised.

It wasn't until the lamps were lit before Laurel had occasion to talk to Abel. After lighting the fancy globular oil burner, with hanging tassels, the pair relaxed for a short time before retiring to their bedrooms. Laurel handed Abel a cup of tea and said, "Pearle asked me to remind you about the wedding ceremony."

"What wedding ceremony?"

"The one when he marries the Indian girl. Don't tell me you forgot about it," she questioned.

"I don't know anything about any wedding," he affirmed.

"Then you did forget about it," she replied. "Do you remember him visiting her nearly every day?"

"I knew he often visited the Cheyenne village, presumably to see a maiden, but, I don't remember anything about a wedding."

"Well, you've made a liar out of me," Laurel lamented, while dabbing her eyes from imaginary tears.

"How's that, dear?" asked Abel sympathetically.

"I told Pearle not to worry. Abel would never forget something that important."

"Please don't cry dear. When is this wedding expected to take place?" Abel asked.

"After her brother returns from his winter quarters. Pearle will submit to the Cheyenne ceremony, but, not consummate until you perform a Christian ceremony. Because you wanted it that way," Laurel sobbed her crocodile tears. She should have become an actress because she has talked herself into a real crying jag.

Abel placed his arm around Laurel and again pleaded for her not to cry. He innocently took in the alluring aroma of her person—a reminder of life's possibilities. "They can be married in the new church. It will be my first wedding performed in Kansas."

During the following week Laurel had difficulty finding Pearle alone. Being the conveyor of good news and unable to report it was beginning to be nerve-wracking. At first she complimented herself for an effective demonstration of the female guile. Then, remembering how easy it was to deceive Abel, she felt ashamed. He was so sweet and tender at the sight of her tears, it pulled on her heartstrings. Now, when he's around, she has shortness of breath and trembles as if caressed by a chilly breeze. It is a sensation she has never felt before. Yes, one of the symptoms of being in love.

Laurel resolved, no matter how long it takes, Abel Strawn will succumb to her wiles and she will be the wife he has always wished for.

On Thursday morning, Pearle harnessed the horse and led her to the house. Laurel met him as he tied the reins to the hitching post.

"Have you talked to Abel?" he hopefully asked.

"Yes, and he will marry you guys in the new church whenever you're ready."

Pearle felt as though a mountain was lifted off his shoulders. He was ecstatic.

"How did you ever get him to agree?"

"Let's just say it was the woman's touch," she replied.

"Abel would never be affected by the so-called woman's touch, no matter who the woman was," Pearle declared.

"Is that a fact," Laurel stated, as she climbed into the buggy and headed to school.

* * *

From the first gleaming light of the sun until the oil lamps radiated through the cabin windows, the pioneers worked the fields. Mother Nature acted as a full partner and withheld her showers until late in the evening. After which, she allowed sufficient time for the fields to be serviceable in the morning.

Zack promised Pearle that he and his new wife could inhabit the dwelling if he helped build it. And then, when it came for Pearle to build his own, Zack will lend a helping hand. The youngster jumped at the offer. And, for several days their box wagon made trips to and from Azarov's feed and stables barn hauling logs.

"These logs had to cost an arm and leg. Did you buy them on credit?"

"I thought about it. Instead, I wrote my brother to make a withdrawal from my account. My balance was the major surprise. It had doubled since receiving the last statement."

"You sure must have a lot of money in the bank," Pearle surmised.

"A sizeable sum. A sizeable sum." Zack repeated.

* * *

Whenever the men weren't in the fields, and daylight permitted, they were building Zack's log cabin. Foundation footings consisted of wooden forms dug well below ground and filled with cement. Each anchoring outer blocks had an iron rod protruding upward, to which holes, drilled in the initial logs were tightly fitted. The same technique was used on the inner blocks to secure the logs that will support the floorboards. From this point, the four walls took shape by notching and interlocking the logs until reaching a foot, or so, above the area designed for the entrance to the cabin. Thus far, the construction took nearly two weeks.

When the purple shades of night had fallen, and with supper digesting, Pearle and Zack lay on their beds and spoke of the future. "How soon do you think the cabin will be completed?" Pearle asked.

"Oh, another two or three weeks. Sooner if we had more help. We still need to cut the portals, put up a roof, and I want to build a fireplace."

"We don't have any stones for a fireplace."

"*Au contraire*, my friend. You forget the stones left over when we dug the well. Besides, there are plenty stones across your claim, likely the remains from a glacier a million years ago. All we have to do is look for them," instructed Zack. "Are you getting a little antsy? By the way, when is your wedding taking place?"

"Next week. And damn right I'm antsy, you would be too if you were getting married," Pearle responded.

"I suppose you're right," laughed Zack. "But the thing is, I ain't the one getting married. Am I supposed to do anything? Kill a goat or bring chicken bones?"

"Very funny," Pearle replied. "Just be there. You are my only moral support."

"Should I come packing heat? If so, I better oil my guns."

"This is serious, I'm scared. I still haven't told *White Dove* where I want us to live," said Pearle.

"Well, the way it looks, you're gonna live with her for at least a month. That gives you plenty time to tell her."

"You don't understand, I ain't even told her about the Christian wedding. I won't have sex until Abel marries us," Pearle confessed.

"You haven't had sex yet? You're a better man than I am. Are you sure you're not a blood relative of Abel?"

"*White Dove* is as anxious as I am. I plan to tell her on our wedding night. You see, Cheyenne women wear a protective rope to prevent them from having sex. It's not unusual for newlyweds to keep it on for a while so they can get to know each other better. I was going to tell her then."

"That might work. You can spend the first night sleeping in the river."

"Stop being a comedian," Pearle said sarcastically.

* * *

On the day of the wedding, the soft beat of the drums echoed through the village. Its rhythmic tempo was soothing to the ears and intended to be an invitation to the Great Spirit—recognized by the Cheyenne as the formless and omnipresent source of all life. The sun is viewed as the manifestation of the power of the Great Spirit. Soon, the nostalgic sound of flutes began to be played in unison, giving a cacophony of discordant intonations. At first, irritating to the unfamiliar listener; but, eventually, that too became pleasant. Because of rank within the tribe, and no family member present for Pearle, *Falling Water* was chosen to guide the young groom during the ceremony.

That morning, *White Dove* washed herself in the river, to be blessed by the spirit of the earth. Later she wore a blue dress with white buckskin leggings and covered in a white wedding robe. The marriage of the daughter of *Chief Red Eagle* was attended by several hundred guests and well-wishers. Only her immediate relatives could be close by to witness the ceremony. Even then, a large crowd circled the pair as *Buffalo Horn*, the shaman, performed the ceremony. Zachary Wheat and *Two Trees* were part of this group, being friends of the bride.

Standing before the shaman, the couple declared that they chose to be known as husband and wife. Tobacco was offered by *Chief Red Eagle* and accepted by the shaman. *Buffalo Horn* then lit the pipe and the couple took a puff.

Afterward the shaman's young assistant held a basin of water before them. Water is used as a symbol of purification and cleansing. *White Dove* and Pearle have a ceremonial washing of hands to wash away past evils and memories of previous love. Then, *Buffalo Horn* reached out, with his arms skyward, and called upon the Great Spirit to bless the newlyweds. Blue blankets were placed over the couple and they were led to the traditional feast where the ceremony is solemnized.

Because of the extraordinary large attendance, the food is placed on blankets and served buffet style. *Buffalo Horn* gave a blessing at each blanket. The pulsating music increased with singing as the dominant expression. Men in falsetto accompanied by drums, flutes, rattles, sticks, and whistles, sang love songs. Food consisted of buffalo flesh, venison, squash, beans, corn, corn soup, potato soup, and many deserts. The elders ate first followed by the bride, groom, and guests. Merrymaking lasted well into the night; however, at the appropriate time, the blue blankets were removed and the newlyweds were covered with a large white blanket indicating a new life together. It also signaled the couple could steal away to their new lodge and begin the life of husband and wife.

The minute they entered *White Dove's* tepee, she dropped the blanket, raised her skirt and began removing the rope. Pearle raised his hand signaling for her to stop, "Darling, I am your husband now, but, I want you to continue to wear the rope for one more day. In the morning we will ride to the new church in the Fort Dodge community. We will be married again in the religion of your mother—the Christian religion. My brother-in-law is an ordained minister—what you call a medicine man—and will perform the ceremony. Tomorrow night we will be free to make love with the blessing of both religions. Let me repeat, you should not fear because it is the religion of your mother."

The maiden was bewildered and perplexed. This night she has dreamed about for months. The setting was perfect, illuminated by moonlight and the gentle fire in the center pit, intoxicating the senses. And now, she must wait another day.

Sleep was nearly impossible. *White Dove* lay awake counting the minutes. Each restless movement kept Pearle from dozing off. At last, the east side of the tepee began to lose the darkness and out of habit, *White Dove* rose, and went to the river to bathe and fetch water. Pearle was sitting up when she returned.

"When do we leave?" she asked, while combing her hair.

"I told Abel to expect us around ten o'clock. That gives us time to dress and eat breakfast."

"There will be no breakfast until tomorrow," she stated with defiance.

"In that case, we can leave now, and wait at the church," he replied.

Pearle felt relieved when he saw Abel's wagon parked in front of the church. The unspoken ride had increased his apprehensive tension. *White Dove* seemed hesitant as Pearle dismounted, but, with his reassuring hand, swung her leg over the pinto and alighted on the ground.

Opening the front door revealed those already inside. Entering from the outside brightness into a darkened sanctuary made it difficult to see those standing in front. Most easily recognized was Abel positioned at the altar. The others had their backs turned and were facing the minister. Laurel's flaming red hair attested to her presence, and little Abby, the child at her side. The other man could only be Zack, but the woman wasn't affirmed until the pair drew closer. It was Mildred Van Ronkle. She was present at the request of Abel, who knew she would feel slighted not to be invited to the first marriage ceremony performed at the church. Besides, the amiable woman considers herself second in command when it comes to church activities. In addition, Abel knew her presence at the wedding of mixed race and culture will help alleviate resentment among some of the parishioners.

Laurel, with a glistening smile and gentle embrace, was first to welcome *White Dove*. Not to be outdone, Mildred Van Ronkle extended a warm reception of her own. By the time Pearle made formal introductions, the poorly lit church evolved into a friendly and much brighter house of worship.

Abel called the couple to stand before the altar. He had his Bible in his hand, but, knew the ceremony by heart, "Dearly Beloved, we are gathered together here in the sight of God—and in the face of this company—to join together this man and this woman in holy matrimony."

As Abel continued, tears of happiness began to swell in Pearle's eyes. The pathway to this occasion in his life had been strewn with so many strenuous obstacles—some of which likened to physical torture. Turning to the innocent face of *White Dove*, he knew it was all worthwhile. Pearle was not the only one who shed tears. Laurel and even Mildred Van Ronkle had trouble with handkerchiefs keeping up with their overflowing eyes.

The ceremony ended with the exchange of rings—purchased by Zack, unbeknown to Pearle. The reception was abbreviated due to the newlyweds' eagerness to return to the Cheyenne village. Abel, and the others, stood outside to bid the couple a fond farewell as they mounted their horses and headed toward the encampment. Once the pair was out of sight, Abel and the rest went back in the church. Abel dated and signed the marriage document, while Mildred, Laurel, and Zack endorsed as witnesses.

"I'd like us to make another copy for church records and will give the original to Pearle the next time I see him" Abel said.

"When do you think that will be?" asked Mildred.

"In about a week," Zack quipped.

Mildred caught on right away and chuckled, "If that soon."

After the newlyweds returned to their lodge, the entrance flap was closed and they were not heard from for two days. The months of waiting were now a vacant memory. On the third day, *White Dove* could be seen bathing in the river and returning with fresh water. She acknowledged the smiles of her friends before entering the tepee and securing the door flap. It was kept closed until the following morning.

* * *

For a week after the wedding, Abel and Zack conducted all of the farm work. It was hardly business as usual since both men missed Pearle. The youngster had won his way into their hearts and his absence left a mark. Especially with Zack who had lost his bunkmate. No more late night conversations, at the time thought to be annoying.

Abel realized Zack would be hit the hardest and made a point of visiting the bunkhouse in the evening. He usually found Zack lying on his back, staring at the ceiling, with a half-empty whisky bottle on the floor.

"Want a drink?" Zack asked mockingly.

"Yeah, I'll have a swig," Abel replied, as he took the bottle and wiped the opening with his palm. After tipping it to his lips, the amber content bubbled while dispensing a good-sized swallow. Abel grimaced while handing the bottle back to Zack, "I never could develop a taste for that stuff."

Zack was momentarily shocked, "That's probably a good thing, you being a minister and all."

"When do you think your cabin will be livable for Pearle and his wife?"

"In about three weeks. I want to dig a well first. Why, are you missing the lad?"

"You darn right I miss him. The place ain't the same without him around," Abel answered. "I'll see if I can get you some help digging the well."

When Abel returned to the house, Laurel had their traditional cup of hot tea waiting. She stiffened once she smelled alcohol on Abel's breath—a hurtful reminder of the last year with her father. Her disapproving attitude was obvious.

"It's not my habit to partake in strong drink. I found Zack in low spirits and took a swallow on his behalf."

"Did it make him feel better?" she asked snidely.

"You don't understand, dear. I guess it's a man thing," Abel said feebly.

"Just don't make a practice of it," she stated. "Drink your tea."

For some unexplained reason, her commandment made Abel's day, perhaps because Laurel only had his interest at heart.

* * *

As the eastern skies brightened at the horizon, Pearle joined *White Dove* for the morning ablution in the Arkansas River. The pair will make their first trip to the farm as man and wife. *White Dove* had been there once before when the oversized whelp was delivered. Not yet fully grown, the dog they call Champ weighs one hundred pounds. And, the impressive canine was the first to greet them when their horses trotted up the lane.

"Don't be afraid of him, darling. He's gentle as a lamb, if he knows you," reassured Pearle, while Champ bounced around like a goat, now realizing Pearle had been gone. The resounding barks alerted Laurel that company had arrived and she stood on the porch with a dishtowel in her hand as they approached.

"They're all in the fields," she declared. "Come in for a spell before you look for them. *White Dove* can stay with me and help make dinner. It'll give me a chance to show her the house."

White Dove shivered with apprehension as she found herself in a strange world controlled by the woman *Two Trees* called a witch. The pumping of her young heart flushed her cheeks. And, like a bird fresh from the egg, her eyes became wide, bright, wet and shiny, with hesitant doubt as Laurel took her hand to lead the tour. The last time they saw each other, *White Dove* was on the edge of childhood; but, after a week of marriage, the dew was definitely off the rose.

Little Abby had the most calming effect. She took it upon herself to point out the items in the house she personally liked the most. Her innocent sincerity easily won *White Dove's* favor.

Pearle was welcomed back to the homestead amid backslaps and handshakes from Abel and Zack. He thanked them for wishing him well; all the same, he was anxious to resume work on Zack's cabin. Walking to the structure he noticed the pit being dug by the oldest Van Ronkle and Calloway boys. "You fellas need any help?"

"Just keep the drinking water coming," they answered in unison.

Looking up, Pearle saw Zack drawing near to check on progress. Satisfied with the effort thus far, he said, "Boys, take a break for a while. Laurel will be right up bringing more cold water." Then, turning to Pearle, asserting, "Let's you and I go help Abel chop weeds in the cornfield."

Returning to the hoe gave Pearle the sense of belonging. With each whack at the unwanted plants he felt more at home. "*If only Amanda could realize how wonderful a life like this could be,*" he thought. It was the only mental blemish on the return of the newlyweds, still, lasting just for a moment.

At the end of the day, both men and boys sat in the creek. Besides being refreshing, its fast moving water washed away all evidence of toil and grime.

Supper was held outside, attended by family and those who occupied the shovel. *White Dove* assisted Laurel in serving the fare, which was previously prepared. It marked the first time the Van Ronkle and Calloway boys had seen Pearle's Cheyenne bride. They couldn't keep their eyes off her. She was too pretty to be an Indian, making them wonder how the preacher managed to have two beautiful women on his farm. They seriously considered joining the ministry.

CHAPTER THIRTY

In Statesville, Tennessee, it was a perfect day in a perfect young summer. Everywhere you looked, buds were bursting. In another couple months perhaps laziness will find respectability, but not today. While Jack, Melvin, and the boys were in the pasture cutting out a yearling colt, Abigail, Hope, and Sarah Jane—with Rebecca sitting on her mother's lap—were driving the wagon to town. It was that kind of day in which rural ladies had a need to shop. Not for anything in particular, just to satisfy the female gender's innermost psychological urge. Contrarily, on a scale of one to ten, when it comes to men, window-shopping falls to the bottom.

"Do you think Riberty's store will have new material?" Sarah Jane has learned to sew and is allowed to make a simple dress or two.

"I wouldn't be surprised. Maryellen said as much last Sunday in church," her mother answered, in a sort of hiccup when the wagon wheels struck a clump of dirt—an event bringing silly laughs to all three. Riding against the breeze occasionally forced their summer frocks to flutter at the edges, but, sunbonnets kept their hair in place.

It was a familiar sight to see the Leffingwell wagon come to town and their entry drew little attention. Abigail guided the horse down the main street and came to a stop in front of

Riberty's general merchandise. A courteous pedestrian took the reins from Abigail and tied the horse to the front hitching rail. They thanked him, climbed down, and straightened their apparel—misshapen from the vibrating ride.

"Well, my day is complete. It's beautiful outside and, now, it's beautiful inside," Frank Riberty called aloud. He must have visited the tavern for lunch.

"We're shopping for new fabric to make dresses," Sarah Jane announced.

"I believe I have just what you want. We got several new bundles last week," Frank proudly declared.

The young Leffingwell daughter was in seventh heaven, finding each bolt prettier than the one before it. After thoroughly inspecting every bundle, she was totally confused as to which material to purchase. It was a moment requiring a mother's assistance. Abigail selected two cloth patterns and Hope, with Rebecca in her arms, leaned over and picked the third. All three met with the joyful approval of Sarah Jane. The girls browsed for a while, purchased some attractive buttons, and then walked to the post office before going across the street for a bite of lunch at the town restaurant. Abigail held a letter from Abel, debating whether she should open it now or wait until she got home. The waitress settled it for her by reciting the luncheon fare. Abigail will wait until she returned to the farm. Hope was anxious to hear the latest, but understood the decision for biding until later.

The girls ordered egg salad sandwiches and iced tea. Sarah Jane, finding it hard to repose, couldn't resist taking another peek at the material just paid for. Hope fed Rebecca a bite at a time, in spite of her outreaching hands and wiggling fingers. Several customers, on their way to the front counter, stopped to compliment Hope, on her well-mannered baby. After ringing up their tickets at the cash register, Ma Mambleau walked to the girls' table and asked if they wanted desert. Declining homemade pie, Abigail directed the waitress to put all three on one tab. The bill came to 90 cents. She handed Ma a greenback dollar and said, "Keep the change Ma, as always, everything was delicious."

"You all come back with your misters. I ain't seen those husbands of yours in a coon's age," she stated, as the trio withdrew.

Sarah Jane, anxious to cut out a pattern, suggested they head for home. Her mother and Hope had no argument against compliance and boarded the wagon for the return trip.

The envelope in Abigail's purse shouted, "Open and read me" all the way back. The news that Amanda left Abel was not totally unexpected; yet, it caused consternation and increased concern over Abel's welfare. The paucity of Abel's correspondence was troubling to Abigail. She could expect a letter every month, giving her an update on the family's progress. Then, when Amanda abandoned Abel and her daughter, only one letter reached the Leffingwell mail box. The epistle in her possession not only brings tidings, but developments over the last few months. Abigail fought against herself not to open it while the wagon was moving. Hope, also curious, offered to hold the reins.

Home, and at the kitchen table, Abigail slit the envelope with her thumbnail and unfolded the contents.

May 15, 1870

Dear Friends,

First, let me apologize for not writing sooner. Physically, we are all in good health. Our second year's crops are planted and thirty additional acres put to use. Zachary Wheat's cow has delivered a heifer increasing the livestock by one. The cabin, on his claim, is nearly finished and will be habitable in a week or two. More about that later.

I've accepted the fact Amanda is never coming back. For the longest time things were as dark as a mother's womb. With the passing of time, I'm beginning to see more clearly. A young schoolteacher, from Fort Dodge, has accepted my invitation to move in and help me take care of little Abby. The goodness in her young heart makes us forget her disability—a deformed left hand from birth. We have come to an arrangement that is acceptable in the eyes of the Lord, or, at least until my marriage with Amanda is legally concluded. Abby adores her, and has overcome the suffering from an absent mother.

Pearle, Amanda's brother, has married a beautiful Cheyenne girl—the daughter of the chief. Zack has graciously offered his cabin to the newlyweds and I expect them to move in soon. That leaves Pearle's claim next to be developed. The good Lord willing, we will break ground this fall. Thus far, Kansas is nothing like my dreams of Tennessee. Hopefully, that will change over time.

The new church is built and I hold Sunday services, in fact, I married Pearle and White Dove there, making their nuptial the first marriage in our church.

Not a day passes without me conjuring thoughts about my Statesville family. Write soon and let me know how that Tennessee mountain man is doing.

Your friend for life,
Abel
Fort Dodge, Kansas

P.S. The community is growing leaps and bounds. It won't be long before the vicinity stands alone.

Abigail wiped the tears from her eyes, folded the letter, and placed it in its envelope. "I'll give it to Jack when he comes in."

"He seems like such a good man," stated Hope.

"Abel is the most virtuous man I've ever met," declared Abigail.

"How about Jack?" Hope questioned.

"Yes, even more so than Jack."

"I suppose the war changed all the men," Hope suggested.

"It didn't change Abel Strawn," Abigail said in confidence.

"Sometimes you act as though you love him," said Hope.

"I love Jack. I always have and I always will. My feelings for Abel reflect a different kind of love. It's like my love for the children and wanting the best this world can provide them. I've never met a man as trustworthy as Abel. He's the only male friend I've ever had."

"Except for Melvin, all the men I ever met had an ulterior motive," Hope sighed.

"That's exactly what I mean," Abigail concluded.

* * *

Jack found Abigail in the kitchen preparing dinner. After nearly fifteen years of marriage, he still couldn't resist his lovely wife occupied with the culinary demands. Walking up behind, he reached his arms around her waist and turned her gently to face him. Her forehead, dotted with tiny pinpoints of perspiration, only served to stimulate his desire. Their lingering kiss was not typical for a couple awaiting the Crystal anniversary. Catching her breath, Abigail resumed stirring one of the pots simmering on the stovetop. "We can finish this tonight after the children are asleep. Right now you need to get cleaned up—father is joining us for dinner."

"Why isn't Sarah Jane helping you cook?"

"She has been helping me between cutting a pattern to make a new dress. We found some pretty material at Riberty's this afternoon. Look on the end table by your chair—we got a letter from Abel. I think he's doing better, but you should read it yourself."

Jack plopped down in his chair and opened the letter. He was curious about the schoolteacher and walked back to the kitchen. "This schoolteacher business looks kind of serious, or am I reading it wrong?"

"I think you are reading it right. My hope is that everything works out and she remains the way he describes her," Abigail insinuated.

The dinner table was being set when the familiar sound of a carriage met their ears. The boys scurried to the door to greet their grandfather. For a short while, the seriousness of life took a back seat. Hyrum cherished his frequent visits which categorized the pressing concern of secular problems—the Lord first, family second, and whatever else coming in a distant third. He did, however, have an issue to discuss with Jack—Tennessee not ratifying the Fifteenth Amendment[11].

Democrats have slowly taken back the State Legislature and the minister feared a drifting away from the gains for blacks. Not necessarily the right to suffrage, since the state had passed a law

---

[11]   The Fifteenth Amendment to the United States Constitution prohibits the federal and state governments from denying a citizen the right to vote based on race, color, or previous condition of servitude. It was ratified on February 3, 1870, as the last of the Reconstruction Amendments. Requiring three-fourths of the states to ratify, it managed to pass without Tennessee's vote—rejected in 1869, it was finally ratified on April 8, 1997.

in 1867 allowing blacks to vote. Hyrum knows there are other ways to restrict voting rights, and, with Southern control of the state, he fears Nashville might administer them.

After the meal was over, Sarah Jane assisted her mother in clearing the table and returned with sugar coated apple strudel, hot from the oven—a perfect ending for a perfect meal.

"If you want, we can bring the dessert to the living room and you can have it with your coffee." Abigail suggested to her father. The boys couldn't wait that long and dug in the minute the dish hit the table.

"We're two lucky men, Jack. Abigail is as good a cook as her mother," Hyrum declared, while shifting a bite a little hotter than he expected.

Learning from his father-in-law's example, Jack blew on his first bite, saying, "She amazes me and, fortunately, Hope and Sarah Jane benefit from her example."

"Have you read much about what's on in Nashville?" asked Hyrum, as he sat his coffee on the end table.

"Do you have something particular in mind?"

"Yes, not ratifying the Fifteenth Amendment."

"Tennessee already passed a law giving blacks the right to vote. Some say that the only reason our southern neighbors signed the Amendment was to lessen the Reconstruction restrictions."

"Maybe so, but that doesn't excuse our refusal to ratify. Since we are beginning to control state government, I think it is an act of pure defiance—opening the door for poll taxes and literacy requirements. And, as you are personally aware, the Klan will take care of the rest," Hyrum foretold.

"Sometimes, men of good will worry too much about things in the distant future and tend to neglect the wrongs near at hand. How many black families do you have in the congregation? We could take care of a poll tax with contributions. As far as a literacy test is concerned, the church ladies guild can educate the voters," Jack reassured Hyrum.

"Most black families have their own churches. Black households only earn $25 a month. A two-dollar poll tax is way beyond their means and they won't be able to vote—that's exactly why it would be levied."

Jack learned years ago arguing with his minister father-in-law was fruitless. After all, Hyrum had the Lord on his side. His silence signaled concession and he asked, "Would you like another piece of Abigail's apple strudel?"

CHAPTER THIRTY-ONE

T he protracted summer witnessed the completion of Zack's cabin and well. Pearle convinced his wife to move in on a limited basis to see if she could adapt to living in a permanent abode. Zack now found himself residing between two dwellings and often returning to the bunkhouse for a little peace and quiet.

It was a time when pioneers went to bed while daylight remained—also, a time when the farm chores were at the pre-harvest lull, giving ample opportunity to appreciate the lethargic meander of sunrise and sunset. The summer's ghost of September seemed far away as the men found periods to lie in the grass by the creek and listen to the murmur of water snaking through their property. As they viewed the clouds float across the sky, the perfume of intermission conjured up boyhood memories.

"Life can't get any better than this," Pearle professed. The unspoken reply indicated agreement.

"You guys enjoy, I need to go back to the house and use the convenience," Abel stated.

"Use the creek," Zack suggested.

"Normally I would, but this time there's more involved," replied Abel, who groaned getting up and quick-stepped toward the outhouse.

"If you can't make it, just dog scoot in the grass," Zack chuckled, while giving Pearle a friendly shove.

Abel entered the door with the half-moon just in time. Before returning to the others, he decided to look in on Laurel and *White Dove*. He found them sitting at the kitchen table discussing the vagaries of married life.

"Are you women doing okay? If you need anything, just holler."

"We're doing just fine. Would you like a glass of sweet tea?"

"I don't mind if I do," said Abel, taking a chair at the table.

Before his glass was empty, he heard Champ barking at a wagon pulling up in front of the cabin. "Just sit here, I'll go see what they want," said Abel, as he rose and walked to the door. Laurel turned little Abby over to *White Dove* and followed closely behind.

Stepping out on the porch, Abel saw Amanda and Charlie Fontaine and asked, "What do you want?"

Amanda stood up in the carriage saying, "I'm here for my half of the farm. As your wife, I'm legally entitled to it."

"Ownership of the farm is divided among Zack and Pearle. You're welcome to half my share."

"Then I'll take $500 instead," she snapped. "Or I'll take my daughter."

"Amanda, you abandoned your daughter and the farm. You haven't seen her in over a year."

"It's my legal right. You get the money or I'm taking her back," she asserted. "Come on Charlie, let's go." The carriage turned around and made its way to the road.

Abel's thoughts were in a whirl. The prospect of losing his daughter had a catastrophic affect. Weakened by just the thought, forced him to require a chair. Laurel put her arms around him and softly said, "We are going to fight this. Losing Abby is out of the question."

Once Zack and Pearle returned, the situation was explained. Zack knew the fort had no civilian lawyers, but it contained the person who could help him find one—Boris Azarov. The brawny Balkan knew the laws, since he had broken nearly every one of them. Most assuredly, he will know of a lawyer. When it came to something important, no grass grew under Zack's feet. He alerted Abel of his mission and rode to the fort at a gallop.

With Laurel's help, and a cold wet washcloth, Abel regained his composure. Embarrassed by his attack of frailty, he apologized to the women and drew little Abby to his knee. Pearle explained to *White Dove* what she had just witnessed and the family tensely waited for Zack's return.

Boris Azarov was working in the stables pitching hay for a couple new tenants. With a constant flow of people moving in the area, his business has increased to the point of adding an employee. By personally tending the stables, the store is neglected. Even though he tries to keep one eye open for customers, he has missed a few sales. Being the only store in town guarantees their return. With competition, they may never come back. The sound of footsteps on the wooden sidewalk indicated the arrival of a customer.

"I'll be right with you," he shouted. After hanging the pitchfork on the wall and patting a horse on its forehead, he hurried to the general store. Boris stopped short as soon as he saw Zachary Wheat standing at the counter. He began to worry once he noticed the revolver strapped to the bearded man's leg.

"What are you so nervous about? Have you been burying a body?" Zack joked.

"I bury no bodies," Boris said, with a quivering voice.

"I need to talk to you about a lawyer. I figure if there's anybody in the community who knows a lawyer it's you." Zack stated.

"What have I done wrong?"

"Not you, you dumb bastard. Abel Strawn needs to talk to a lawyer."

Relieved, Boris began to calm down. "There is a man in Gibson City who practices civil law. I've had need to use him once or twice."

"Is he any good?"

"He has got me off every time," Boris replied.

"That's what I wanted to hear, because, sure as God made little green apples, you were guilty. What's his name?" Boris retrieved a small box from beneath the counter and began thumbing through the papers. "Ah ha, here it is, I have his business card. In fact, I have three of them." He gave it to Zack.

Holding it to the light Zack read aloud, "Mister A. B. Lucas, attorney at law."

"What has happened to the preacher?" Boris questioned.

"All I can tell you is, it's a domestic problem. I'll be back to go over the church goers credit account later," said Zack, as he walked out the door.

"I know it's okay because Gus Greeley looked at it yesterday," the Balkan blurted, then caught himself, wishing he had kept his mouth shut. Now, he hoped Zack was in so much of a hurry, he didn't hear him.

* * *

Gibson City was a two day ride by horseback. Declining Zack's offer to accompany him, Abel prepared for the journey alone. The trail followed the Arkansas River and was traveled enough to display adequate wagon tracks. Laurel prepared food for the trip and Pearle made sure the yellow tarp was rolled tightly and tied to the saddle. Zack insisted he bring his revolver and long distant rifle, in case of renegade Indians or other scoundrels on the road.

Leaving the protection of the homestead to Zack and Pearle, Abel started out while the moon was still shining brightly.

It wasn't until Abel was on the road for an hour did Laurel emotionally break down and require solace from the rest. Even though Zack suppressed his own fears for such a journey, especially traveling alone, he attempted to console and alleviate Laurel's trepidation.

It was when he placed his arm around her shoulders that his cloistered emotions were liberated. Available women he had met, thus far, were female in the words most supercilious sense—haughty and vainglorious. The wounded bird within his grasp was none of these things.

At this moment, Zack realizes how much he hungers after the female now living under Abel's roof. He manages to constrain his covetousness in hopes others fail to recognize his inner feelings. He also knows, if Abel returns home safely, the time is near for him to continue his quest forward.

When the sun was straight overhead, Abel stopped to water his horse and let it graze on the lush grass alongside the river. He placed the edge of his hand against his forehead, in a salute fashion, and made a circular scan of the area. It gave him the impression of being the only inhabitant of a distant planet—one in which no trees grow—a flat terrain of endless sward. For a second he thought he saw something afar, but, without field glasses, it may have been only a mirage. Purpose and future expectation confiscated the urge of hunger; hence, Abel pressed on, saving his provisions until later. The uniformity of the endless plain brought about boredom to the point of catching himself nodding off. To compensate, Abel began reciting Bible verses.

Hopping Toad rarely wandered this far east searching for game. It so happened he and two of his braves had chased a lone buffalo and calf along the Arkansas watercourse. Hidden by a copse of scrub and bend in the river, they were butchering their quarry out of sight of the approaching vocalist. Needless to say, it was a startling encounter when each became aware of the other. The Bible verses abruptly ended, and for the longest time, they stood like statues. Finally, Abel kicked his heels into his mount's girth and made a dash for it—all the while, inserting a cartridge into his Civil War rifle.

Hopping Toad was torn between giving chase and continuing with the task at hand. He settled on sending the two Cheyenne braves after the strange white man while he finished carving the meat.

Abel hadn't galloped far before he became aware the two braves were following him. However, they were far enough away for him to dismount and use the saddle as a rifle rest. He took aim and gently pulled the trigger. There was a loud echoing report and, shortly thereafter, the lead Indian flew from his horse. As Abel was reloading, the other brave, confused by what just took place, pulled his pinto to a hastened stop. Abel remounted his charger and continued his journey, albeit, at a faster clip. At the end of the day, confident he was no longer being followed, Abel sat in the loneliness of a starlit sky, eating some of what Laurel had prepared. He decided not to have a fire, just as a safety precaution. Then, using his saddle as a backrest, he covered with a blanket and catnapped through the evening darkness.

The following day, the event that transpired seemed like a dream. Nevertheless, remorse began to set in. Killing during the war could be justified. In all likelihood, the man shot off his horse was dead. Similar to the Pawnee chief, both will require a personal atonement.

Gibson City was scheduled to become a switching station for the Atchison Topeka and Santa Fe railroad, whose iron rails were being hammered in place fifty miles further east. As with other rail heads, a settlement had formed in anticipation. The town itself consisted of a combined hotel-tavern and skeletons of buildings under construction.

Abel figured the best place to find the whereabouts of A. B. Lucas was the general meeting place—the hotel and tavern. Accordingly, he tied his trusty steed alongside the others at the hitching rail, scaled the steps and pushed open the tavern's swinging doors.

Leaving bright sunshine and entering the tavern made it appear to be exceptionally dark inside. It was only the interlude in which his pupils adjusted. All eyes were on the tall preacher as he negotiated the smoke-filled room and walked to where a few men stood at the bar.

"What'll you have?" came a friendly voice from behind the counter.

"Just draw me a short beer," Abel said. "I'm looking for a lawyer by the name of Lucas."

"If you'd of come in sooner you'd have found him standing where you are now. Otherwise, he's probably in his office," the bartender stated, while using his thumb to indicate overhead. "His workplace is a room in the hotel. You can use the stairs inside or the one outside. The outside steps lead right to his office."

Abel preferred the outside staircase and drained his beer glass, paid the tapster, and walked back into the sunshine. Mounting the steps, he stood under a hanging sign signifying the person being sought and turned the doorknob.

Bright Lucas was short in stature but carried the demeanor of confidence. His dark, short-cropped hair was beginning to reveal a little gray at the temples, bespeaking a man of experience. Greeting Abel, he directed for him to take a seat across from his desk and returned to his own. Reaching for his cigar, deposited in the ashtray when he received Abel, he took a few puffs to determine if it needed to be relighted, and said, "What can I do for you?"

Abel related the history of him and Amanda, beginning when they were in high school. The husky attorney leaned back with his hands behind his head while listening to the account. There was a minute of silence after Abel finished, as the legal wheels in Lucas' mind began to revolve.

"First your wife has abandoned you, the farm, and her child. Laws in the state of Kansas frown on abandonment. Those guilty of it lose many rights formally guaranteed. Based on what you've told me, she could not win a custody battle. Have you considered a divorce?"

"Not aggressively," Abel stammered.

"You could be granted one predicated on abandonment, if she hadn't set foot in the house for two years," Lucas stated. Abel's hesitation indicted the preacher wasn't ready for that. "Here's what I'm doing for you. Today I'll file a restraining order to keep her off the premises. I'll also petition for full custody based on abandonment. You must make certain she doesn't enter your house for two years, in the event you seek a divorce for abdication."

"How do you file these things without local government?" Abel inquired.

"Excellent question. We have a circuit judge who comes through here about twice a month. I'll present the petitions at that time. However, a duplicate copy will be mailed to the capitol in Topeka. We'll have it covered at both ends. Do you have any more questions?"

"None that I can think of right now. I'll probably have a dozen tomorrow."

"That's the way it usually goes," Lucas said, as he stood to shake hands. "I'll mail a copy to the address you've indicated. Has the railroad built a depot at Fort Dodge?"

"We're expecting it any day now."

"That's going to make my job a lot easier—not only traveling, but sending mail. It'll speed things up quite a bit."

"Not to change the subject, but what do I owe you?" Abel asked

"That will be fifteen dollars. You don't need to pay it all at once. However, I charge three percent a month interest."

For some reason, Abel was reminded of Boris Azarov, but didn't mention him. Instead, he counted out fifteen green backs and Bright Lucas wrote a receipt.

Before reaching the stairway, the attorney shouted, "It may take a couple weeks before your wife is served papers."

Abel returned to the farm a great deal more confident than when he left. His efforts were recounted to the family except for the skirmish with the Indians and his ability to get a divorce on the grounds of abandonment. Zack knew there had to be more to Abel's rendition, but didn't press the issue out of deference for his friend.

Laurel wept tears of sorrow when he hastened off and wept tears of joy on his return.

Zack envied Abel for Laurel's love, and couldn't comprehend his aloofness in recognizing what he had. At times Zack felt like dragging his ass behind the barn and horsewhip him. And, just as fast as Abel made him angry, he would do something to earn the former sailor's respect.

Thank God for the coming harvest. Zack won't have time to ponder the platonic relationship.

* * *

Mary Clemmer Ames, American newswoman, poet, and writer called harvest time, "The dead summer's soul."

In western Kansas, the pioneers experienced the blessing for which they had prayed ever since their first shovel probed the earth. The yield of 1870 had earned the appellation—bumper crop. It didn't come easy. Perhaps worry and prayer consumed more energy than labor; nevertheless, proceeds from the yield will replenish empty bank accounts and restore solvency for another year. Among the neighbors, Abel had a leg up. The old Myers farm was established when he took over. With additional cultivation and Zachary Wheat's claim beginning to produce, profits will more than double from the year before.

By the first week in October, the last wagonload of corn headed for storage. The day had been unusually warm and saw Abel's entire ménage work the fields. The queen of heaven had waxed to its fullest, and cast a rare illumination that lit up both farmhouse and grounds—a phenomenon reminiscent of a midnight sun. They were hot, sweaty, and tired. Their dust-covered faces emitted an eerie metallic appearance. After collapsing on blankets, they surveyed a job well done. *White Dove* was the first to speak, "If I have enough strength to get up, I'm going to the creek and take a bath."

Her words seemed to revive the others. "Would you bathe in front of the men?"

"Of course, the Cheyenne are civilized. I've bathed with men ever since I was a child," she explained.

"Civilized or not, I won't bathe in front of men," Laurel retorted.

"You are ashamed of your body?" asked *White Dove*, and rising to her feet.

"It's not that. I was brought up to bathe privately."

"In that case, the men could wash farther downstream," *White Dove* suggested.

Capturing the full attention of the men, Pearle agreed, saying, "Yeah, we could wash downstream and you girls would be out of sight."

Laurel knew, to be completely out of sight was impossible; but, the idea of *White Dove* being thoroughly refreshed, and clean to boot, weakened her resolve. Her cheeks began to flush with an increased heart rate as she surrendered to the idea. On their way to the creek, the men seemed rejuvenated and happily hummed an incoherent tune. Pearle had given his wife a bar of homemade soap, kept in the wagon for just this purpose. The men often bathed in the creek at day's end. Tonight, the women used it to wash each other's hair. The lathering formed spumes of foamy bubbles skimming the surface and glistening as it rushed to where the men were located. The melodic sounds of female laughter and a slather of froth, propelling against their loins, served to increase carnal desires. It forced them to avert their eyes.

The most vivid image Zack could conceive fell far short of Laurel's actual symmetry. Her maturity, highlighted by effulgent moonlight, was a sight to behold. Even the word exquisite failed to bestow proper justice.

After the fast moving water carried away clinging sweat and dust, the group emerged from the creek, and silently walked to their independent quarters. That night Zack wondered if Abel also found it difficult to sleep.

* * *

The next morning, all the children of their neighbors were needed at home. As expected, Laurel remained to tend Abby while the others went to the fields. She was cleaning the breakfast dishes and reflecting on the night before, when two men directed a carriage to the front of the farmhouse. Wiping on a dishtowel, and taking Abby by the hand, she opened the front door and asked, "Can I help you?"

"Yeah, we've come for Amanda's little girl," said the man holding the reins. The other, a swarthy wretch, jumped down from the carriage, swiftly moved to the porch, and punched Laurel with his fist. The impact of the blow sent her to the floor. Although dazed, Laurel held tightly to little Abby's hand. While she kicked and screamed he struck her again and twisted Abby from her grasp. After dragging the child to the wagon, they quickly drove away.

Hearing her screams, the men abruptly ran to the house. By the time they arrived, Laurel's eye had swollen shut and her jaw was turning purple—possibly broken.

"Who did this?" Abel asked.

"It was two men. I never saw them before," she sobbed.

"What did they look like?" questioned Zack.

"The one who hit me was swarthy with a scar on his face. Things happened so fast, I didn't get a good look at the one driving the carriage."

"They had to be working for Amanda. I'm going into town," said Abel.

"No. We don't need diplomacy. You stay here with Laurel. I'll go into town," Zack asserted, with authority.

When Zack reached the Lucky Lady, the name Zachary Wheat was whispered from table to table like a dust-laden simoon circling across the Sahara desert. They had posted a lookout, to alert those inside when the preacher arrived. Abel never showed. It was the other man, called Zack, who pushed open the door. He walked without pause to the table occupied by Charlie Fontaine and two strangers. The large dark man rose from his chair and stood defiantly. Zack continued forward, pulled his revolver, and shot him at close range. The miscreant's eyes opened wide in surprise as he dropped dead on the floor. The other man shouted in protest. Zack leveled his pistol and squeezed the trigger. The force of the impact sent him flying backward and he, too, lay lifeless on the stylish carpet.

Zack, calm as a brain surgeon, asked Charlie, "Where are you keeping the little girl?" The smell of ammonia drifted from beneath the table. Charlie had wet himself.

"I won't ask you again," Zack said.

"She's in a room upstairs."

"Have someone bring her back down. If you have harmed her, I'll kill you and burn this place to the ground."

With that warning, Gus Greeley interceded, saying, "I'll go get her."

Zack's eyes never left Charlie. He repeated, "Have someone bring her back down." The sound of the hammer clicking made Charlie shout, "Bring the girl back down."

The door of one of the rooms opened and Amanda appeared holding her daughter's arm. Charlie pleaded, "For Christ's sake let her go or he's going to kill me."

Zack walked to the landing and little Abby descended the steps one at a time. With Abel's daughter in his arms, Zack slowly scanned the room and backed out the door.

Gus Greeley pointed to the dead bodies and yelled, "Somebody get a hold of *Bao-Zhi.*" Then, turning to Charlie Fontaine, he said, "You've talked about going to California, I want you out of here by noon tomorrow."

"I don't have the money for both me and Amanda," he whined.

Gus laid $500 on the table saying, "It's worth it to me, having you two out of here."

From one of the occupied tables a voice said, "We need law and order in this community." From another, "Gus should hire a sheriff." With that, Gus Greeley turned and said, "The only man I would hire just walked out of here with a little girl in his arms. Right now, I don't think he would take the job."

* * *

It took until the end of the month before things returned to a semblance of routine. Laurel still sported a black eye and bruised cheekbone, and the perpetrators have disappeared, thanks to *Bao-Zhi* and the Chinese pigsty. Abel hesitated in discussing the episode with Zack but knew, sooner or later, the subject must be broached.

One evening, after supper, he finally made the trip to the bunkhouse for a private conversation. After perfunctory small talk, a more serious discussion began.

"You must be aware how grateful I am for your rescuing my daughter. All the same, I can't condone killing those two men," Abel explained, quoting Romans 12:19, *"Dearly beloved, avenge not yourselves, but rather give place unto wrath: for it is written, Vengeance is mine; I will repay, saith the Lord."*

"That's all well and righteous, but have you taken a good look at that wonderful woman's face. She may be scarred for life. Those men were swine and on their way to Hell, they ended up with their likened selves—in the Chinese pigsty. What do you think would have happened to little Abby had I not intervened?"

Abel only could offer a blank stare.

Zack continued, "Ever since my wife died, I've sought my place in the world. When I lived in New York, I used to look out my window and watch the passing parade. There were bankers, builders, beggars, prostitutes, peddlers, panhandlers, pedestrians, pimps, preachers, shylocks, simpletons, shoppers, sailors, touts, crooks, vendors, wagons, carts, horses, and policemen. I could see their lips moving, but I couldn't hear what they were saying. They all moved fast as if a delay would be a tragedy. I wondered, where are they going? What was so important in their lives necessitating a quick double step? Nothing could deter their effort to reach their purpose. These people passed each other without a look of recognition. I began to grow green with envy. I thought my life was slowly turning me into verdigris. Before I became a statue, I asked my brother to once again run my shop, and began a journey to find what was missing in my life. I pledged that before the years of old age sucked the energy out of me, I would press forward in my quest for life. Somewhere out there a woman is waiting to share what years I have left."

"You talk as though you plan on leaving. What about building Pearle's cabin?"

Zack presented a knowing grin and replied, "Nice try Abel. You know, as well as I, you two are capable. What you don't know is, that youngster has enough cash to hire it built."

"How can you say that?"

"I happened to find his stash one day when cleaning up the place," Zack replied.

Abel had a look of disbelief.

"After what happened at the Lucky Lady, the longer I remain in Fort Dodge, the more trouble I'll bring to you and the farm. Live your life. Cherish what you have. Marry that little redhead and raise a passel of children. You might consider naming a boy Zachary, so you never forget me. In any case, when I find my El Dorado, I might pass through here someday. All I'll be needing is a bed out of the cold."

Abel remembered those were the exact words Zack used when he joined the trip to Kansas. At that moment, he realized what was happening before his very eyes. This man, yes, a sinner by all counts, was singularly responsible for everything he considers worthwhile—the farm, the crops, and, to some extent, that little redhead with the bruised face. Life without Zachary Wheat is unfathomable. His existence leaves an imprint on every person and place encountered. Abel finds himself at a fork in the crossroads in life. It is a time in which he should insist his bearded friend remain with the family. But, unlike Zack, who always views events as an opportunity for action, Abel has difficulty making a spot decision. The tumblers in Abel's mental lock move more slowly as they fall into place. Action is never his first response. It might be the last or never take place at all.

While Abel continued his blank stare, Zack continued, "No matter how hard I try, I can't erase my past. It is written on the pages of my life, like a watermark."

Without saying a word, Abel left the bunkhouse and ambled back to the main house. By the expression on his face, Laurel knew something was wrong. He walked into the kitchen and plopped down on a chair.

"What's the matter? Tell me what's wrong," Laurel demanded.

"Zack's leaving the farm. He's moving farther west."

"Did you try to persuade him to stay here?" she asked. "You didn't, did you?"

Abel only shrugged.

"With Zack gone, our lives will change dramatically. Our affair can't just stand still. It must either go on or go back. I've a mind to ask Zack to take me with him," Laurel threatened.

Abel was pressed for another decision. He wanted to take things as they come, but that won't work anymore. At this moment, Laurel has her hand on the lever and the preacher seemed to be anchored in neutral. Tears began to swell in Abel's eyes and he ruefully looked up to Laurel, pleading, "What can I do?"

"For one thing, tonight I sleep in your bed and tomorrow you see about a divorce."

CHAPTER THIRTY-TWO

The Cheyenne village was in turmoil. After a council with all the chiefs, *Red Eagle* had announced his decision to move the tribe to the reservation in Oklahoma. The council consisted of all major chiefs and lasted for two days. The majority of Dog Soldiers and Contraries challenged *Chief Red Eagle's* recommendation and a fiery debate ensued. Each day, when the group convened, the pipe was lit and those who wished to speak had an open forum.

Snake Hunter and *He Lives Alone* called for moving the tribe in a different direction—north instead of south. They argued for joining their northern brothers and align with the fight against the bluecoat soldiers. Hatred spewed from their lips and their sincerity reached the hearts of many.

On the second day, *Chief Red Eagle* represented cooler heads. He began with a recitation of Cheyenne history, "The old chiefs tell of a time when war was unknown to our people. It was a time when strangers were met in friendship and welcomed into our camp. Yes, there was disagreement and arguments—usually over women or other possessions—but they were not bloody. It was a time before the Great Spirit introduced the horse and we experienced the comfort and freedom this animal could give. Because of the horse, men desired more, but there was only two ways to obtain them—by capturing those running wild or taking those in the possession of other tribes. This became the sole purpose for going to war.

It is drawn, on our history blanket, when the Cheyenne and Assiniboine's came upon the same herd of buffalo—each claiming to be the first. A dispute resulted and that night the Assiniboine's attacked our camp. They had guns. We had never seen them before and ran away. For years, we were continually forced to give up our homes and move south.

That all changed when guns came into our possession. We no longer retreated from our enemies. We now defeated them and drove them away. Having guns turned the Cheyenne into warriors. War became a noble pursuit. Young boys were taught to excel in it. They were taught that nothing compared to the joy of battle and death was considered a glorious result. Men began to seek wars.

Having no fear of death, some of which was ill-advised, too many casualties occurred. But, the Cheyenne did strike terror in our enemies. Our bravery was recognized among all the tribes.

Then, the white man came. He brought many gifts for trade including more guns and bullets. In our custom, we welcomed him to share the bounty of the land. Still, he thought he could own it. We knew that no one could own land. The Great Spirit provides it to be used by all.

The white men erected permanent lodges and fenced off parts of the grazing land to plant corn. In the beginning, these white men were a novelty. Then they kept coming. As our numbers declined, theirs increased a hundred fold. Our land was vanishing before our very eyes—along with the buffalo.

The Shaman foretells their numbers will continue to increase until all the land is overtaken and we will have no other choice but to live as the white man.

We witnessed the power of the hairy faces medicine at Sand Creek and Washita River. There are no more chances to show our bravery. Now we must hide to fight them. Even then, the white man's cannon can reach us. We die while out of range of both rifle and bow. I believe the Shaman. Any of us, who has seen the cannon, knows he tells the truth. I will fight them no more."

Snake Hunter rose to his feet and shouted, "We will not go to the reservation. Those who go south are cowards. We will join *Crazy Horse* and *Sitting Bull* to fight for our homeland."

Two Trees stood up, bringing his six foot eight inch height to its fullest, and said, "I respect the words of my chief. Let any man call me a coward to my face."

Snake Hunter quickly sat down. He knew a challenge to the towering brave meant instant death.

Chief Red Eagle extended his arms and waved his hands downward. All understood it was a motion to calm down, as he said, "I must consider the welfare of the entire tribe, of little children, mothers, the weak or sickly, the old, and those who seek peace. Warriors who desire more bloodshed are free to do what their heart compels them."

The moment of truth has arrived. In three moons the arduous journey will begin. *White Dove* and her husband will spend two nights with her grandmother, *Valley of Flowers*—the required time for them to bid proper farewells. It will take longer for *White Dove's* tears to dry, since her family will soon be living nearly two hundred miles away.

On the second day of their stay, *Falling Water*, *White Dove's* brother, his wife *Chumani*, and *Two Trees*, Pearle's friend, visited the newlyweds.

Falling Water could be overheard saying, "Well, little sister, it looks as though we, too, will soon live as the white man. Our father maintains the old days are behind us."

"If the reservation is anything like Pearle and I have, *Chumani* will love it," *White Dove* asserted.

"The Cheyenne have always followed the buffalo herds. Now, we can only hunt when the herds migrate this far south. They rarely do so anymore. It means an unfamiliar way of life. We must plant our food and raise cattle, an unworthy animal that tastes like a coyote."

"That is because you prefer to eat buffalo raw. When you season and cook cattle properly, it has an excellent taste. I will show *Chumani* how it is done."

Two Trees directed his words at Pearle when he stated, "It will require a long journey in order to hunt eagles. When the time comes, I will stop by your lodge to see if you wish to join me. Perhaps you will find more of the yellow stones."

"It would be an honor. Our last hunt is written on my heart for more reasons than you will ever know," Pearle replied.

The rest of the evening they looked back on their memories, reminiscing on fond and humorous recollections: the time when *Boy Who Rides Buffalo* first visited the camp; *Chumani* and *White Dove* bashfully harkened to the removal of the rope; and how delighted they were without it.

Falling Water recalled the time the bearded man of distinguished valor threatened to shoot Azarov's baboon.

"That's one thing I'll truly miss—not putting an arrow in that boisterous animal," he stated, honestly.

"Perhaps the bearded one will do it for you," suggested *Two Trees*.

"I doubt that will happen. Zack Wheat will be leaving us in the spring," said Pearle.

"Where will he go?" asked *Two Trees*.

"You've heard what happened at the Lucky Lady. Well, Zack feels everybody is better off if he moves on."

"How can that be? His shadow improves everything it touches," *Two Trees* remarked.

"His decision isn't unusual, but it is very complicated," Pearle stated.

The expression on the tall Indian's face indicated his lack of understanding. He registered it under things to discuss at a later time.

Valley of Flowers announced food is prepared and handed each a bowl of stew. The women frowned for her serving too much. *Two Trees* grimaced because there wasn't enough. Knowingly, *Valley of Flowers* patted his shoulder saying, "You can have a second helping."

CHAPTER THIRTY-THREE

A cruel February wind cut its way across the landscape in Statesville, Tennessee.

Jack Leffingwell and his family were arranged in front of their fireplace, tranquilly enjoying the sound of crackling logs and radiated heat. A Franklin stove rested in the corner of the room; but, thus far, the fireplace was doing an adequate job. Jack had built the cabin airtight and no drafts were felt, unless a door is opened. On a day such as this, they remained shut tight, save for the first glimpse of daylight, when Jack checked on and fed the animals in the barn.

The boys were engrossed reading Jules Verne's *A Journey to the Center of the Earth*; Sarah Jane was occupied at the treadle sewing machine; Abigail sat at the dining room table reading the latest correspondence from Abel Strawn and his wife Laurel; and Jack had dozed off, due to the hypnotic effects of a log fire.

According to his letter, Abel had petitioned for a divorce under the abandonment laws in Kansas. His attorney, Bright Lucas, came through in spades. It is uncertain whether or not such a document is honored in other states; nevertheless, Abel and Laurel were married by the circuit judge and will worry about that issue, if it happens.

Removing her reading glasses, Abigail surveyed her family. A smile slowly materialized on her face as she drifted in thought, "Life doesn't get any better than this."

Casting her gaze upon the extended legs of her sleeping husband caused the image to slowly blur. Tears of happiness flooded her eyes forcing continuous blinks in order to bring back a clear likeness. Abigail is a special woman with a special family and for a moment, she was young again, driving a wagon to the Cumberland Caverns. *She had her hat brim turned down and coat collar turned up, hiding her face. Jack walked toward the wagon to get a better look, when she asked, "Are you Jack Leffingwell?"*

"I might be. Then again I might not be. Who the hell are you?"

"My name is Abigail Adams. I am Deacon Adams daughter. My father couldn't make the trip. The good Lord took Pastor Simmons day before yesterday, and the council had to meet for succession talk. I volunteered to take my father's place."

Jack tilted his head to see her face better. "You people must be crazy. There are renegade Indians between here and there. Nobody risks a trip like that alone."

"I ain't actually alone," she said, holding up a rifle in one hand and pistol in the other. "And I can use them better than most men."

Jack saw that he had ruffled her feathers and replied, "Let's go meet the folks you'll be taking to Statesville."

Even though she tried to hide her face, Jack saw enough to determine she had handsome looks. In fact, he found her pretty. After she took off her hat to wipe her brow, he saw she was beautiful.

"Your husband couldn't make the trip either?"

"I'm not married, but if I was, he wouldn't need to come along. I can take care of myself."

Like soap bubbles when she shampoos her daughter's hair, the knock on the front door popped her placid state of reverie. It was Hope Kaufman. She was there to help with making supper. Abigail's father would be along later and possibly Ryan Gosling. Ryan wasn't exactly the women's favorite person in Statesville, however, the men seemed to like his company. And, after all, he was alone and a home-cooked meal was far better than spending the day in the town tavern.

"Let me take your coat," Abigail said. "What's Melvin up to?"

"He's sitting by the fire, sound asleep," she replied.

Looking back at Jack, Abigail gave a brief huff, saying, "Guess who else is sound asleep?"

* * *

Any concerns whether or not Ryan Gosling would be in attendance were dashed when Hyrum Adams' horse and carriage came trotting up the lane with him as a passenger. Complaining about him was the fundamental requirement. Now that he was here, all were pleased to have him as their guest.

Even after many years, his intellect was yet to be agreed upon, not so when it came to the desirability of his company. Ryan Gosling was a veritable cornucopia of information—idly gathered from many hours at the mahogany bar of the town tavern.

The fiery blacksmith was the archenemy of pretentiousness and took pleasure in every opportunity to demonstrate it. That trait, most likely, attracted Melvin Kaufman to be his best friend. Whenever they were together it was like two peas in a pod. Naturally, Ryan was the most ostentatious since Melvin by nature was self-conscious and modest. Nevertheless, when together, it was a laugh a minute.

Out of respect, Ryan always was on his best behavior when under the Leffingwell roof. It was out of this respect he could accept Jack's opinion regarding the two generals and reluctantly defend it.

During supper, the conversation centered on mundane topics, allowing all of the diners the opportunity to take part. Interspersed were comments from Ryan Gosling declaring each item as the best he ever tasted.

The custom of the times called for the more serious discussions to be among the men and take place after the meal is concluded. While both Hyrum and Jack respect Abigail's opinions equal or superior to most men, a custom is a custom, is a custom. Because of the sagacity of his daughter, Hyrum has stated that someday women will actually be allowed to vote—a statement of which Ryan Gosling adamantly contradicts, making certain his words are not within earshot of a female. Like he frequently says, "My mama didn't raise no dummies."

On this blustery and freezing afternoon, the posterior supper subject focused on income taxes. Of those reclining near the sputtering flames of a new log, Jack probably is the most concerned.

"There's a lot of talk about Congress repealing the income tax law," Ryan offered.

"When it comes right down to it, they didn't really repeal anything. Congress just let the time limit run out," said Hyrum. "The way the Constitution is written, a national tax must be based on apportionment of the relative population within each state, making it impossible to impose a direct tax on individuals. The national income tax, instituted in 1861, was falsely called a duty by the legislature. According to the national constitution, a duty is recognized as an indirect tax. Most people believed the tax was unconstitutional, but accepted it because of the war. It was never meant to be a permanent revenue device."

"I'm against all taxation," Ryan stated emphatically. "Why? You didn't pay the tax anyway," Melvin chided.

"Plato is quoted as saying, "Where there is an income tax, the just man will pay more and the unjust less on the same amount of income," Jack recited.

"Well, who the hell is Plato?" Ryan asked defiantly.

"He was a philosopher and mathematician in ancient Greece. Plato helped lay the foundations of Western philosophy and science. His dialogues have been used to teach a range of subjects, including philosophy, logic, ethics, rhetoric, religion, and mathematics. At eighteen, Aristotle was educated in Plato's Academy in Athens and remained there until the age of thirty-seven. Aristotle tutored Alexander the Great. You might of heard of him?" Jack suggested.

"How could I possibly have heard of those guys? They lived in Greece," Ryan answered.

"Did any of them ever come into the town tavern?" asked Melvin, with a serious look.

"Not that I know of," Ryan answered honestly.

At that moment, Sarah Jane walked in with the coffeepot in hand, "Would anyone care for a refill?" They all took advantage of the opportunity to replenish with fresh made.

Hyrum continued, "The bulk of national taxes, a duty on incomes excluded, came from tariffs. Now that the Civil War was over, tariffs added considerably to the government's coffers. Some believed a high tariff insured foreign competition did not injure agriculture and industry. The downside, however, was that domestic prices became artificially high—to the benefit of northern industrial states. You might recall these tariffs initiated the arguments between the states.

Agricultural states suffered most from the war. High tariffs made prices for farm implements beyond the reach of many southern growers. Accordingly, support for the income tax was strongest in southern and western states—trusting the tax would lower the cost of products now under high tariffs."

"I still stand by my comment on income taxes," Ryan interjected.

"And so do many others. I foresee that argument for many years to come," consoled Hyrum.

"What might bring the argument to an end?" asked Jack.

"Most likely it will be the world around us. The Civil War has left the United States weaker. Abroad, Europe and Great Britain now have an opportunity to strengthen themselves militarily while we slowly recover. New and improved weapons are being invented every day. Even Japan is increasing their fleet. In a few more years the national government will be forced to do the same, and, it will cost a lot of money. Whether we like it or not, we haven't heard the last of income tax."

Hyrum's sobering message seemed to silence even Ryan Gosling. Jack Leffingwell and Melvin Kaufman were quieted by thoughts of the previous war and the horrors it brought. Another war was unfathomable.

That night, with the guests gone home, the children asleep in their beds, Abigail softly breathing, her body pushed hard against his own, and all artificial lights extinguished, Jack had assumed the attitude of thankful prayer.

CHAPTER THIRTY-FOUR

In western Kansas, the spring planting was conducted in the usual manner. After the splendid harvest the year before, spirits were at the highest level. Zachary Wheat was an admirable contributor, acting as though his pending departure would somehow never come to pass.

What became known as the 'Shootout at the Lucky Lady' was now distorted to the point of heroic self-defense on the part of a local farmer. Even those who were eyewitness have recounted a different story.

That is, all except Gus Greeley. He envisioned a manner in which a man with such fearless dynamism could help him become the town's first mayor. From that point, a state representative, then perhaps, governor. After that, who knows? Rumor has it the bearded bluecoat had plans of leaving the territory—a hearsay dear to the heart of Boris Azarov. Gus Greeley has convinced himself that Zachary Wheat, as sheriff, would tame the town during its growing pains. A circumstance in which Greeley would receive the credit and insure their votes.

Sitting at his favorite table, he removed a panatela from its case, struck a match on the sole of his shoe, and then placed the flame to the cigar's tip. Inhaling the husky flavor, Greeley contemplated a method to best meet with Mister Wheat.

* * *

From afar, the dust cloud gave further evidence the men were plowing the fields. Having tilled the acreage the year before, gave the mules an easier time of it. Rich black waves of soil rolled over with each pass of the plow blade. It will all be level once the harrow rake, designed by Jack Leffingwell, makes it ready to receive seed. The three men took turns behind the plows—also sharing the fine dust-filled air, making their face and clothing resemble West Virginia coal miners.

Laurel and *White Dove* will join them when it's time for planting. There's a much better sentiment pervading their perspective. Most of the credit must be given to Laurel. Her sempiternal love for Abel has brought about a dramatic change in the irresolute preacher. Abel's confidence increases every day. It takes time to undo ten years of marriage, if you could call it that, to Amanda—an emasculating life resulting in the timorous chipping away of a man's soul. During those years he became dependent and lacked masculine initiative. He slid into a life of lethargy, unable to make definite judgments. When he did, it was under panic of some aghast or irreparable awakening. Laurel has ended all that. She is the woman Abel should have had from the beginning. Unlike Amanda, Laurel expresses her love at every opportunity.

It takes time to repair the afflicted relationship instituted by Amanda. Now it's like building a house with a healthier foundation, and in doing so, a better outcome is a certainty.

White Dove's family is now located in Oklahoma at the Cheyenne reservation. Her tears have finally dried. There's little time for sentimental longing while spring planting is being conducted. *White Dove* has fallen into the ways of the pioneers, and from all appearances, thoroughly enjoys it. There are times, when she is alone in the cabin, the Indian princess yearns for the company of her grandmother, *Valley of Flowers*. And occasionally, there is a twinge of homesickness. With the adventure of young love, that too is soon forgotten.

She has formed a female friendship with Laurel and adores little Abby. The child is attracted to the unique affiliation of *White Dove*, especially when she wears native attire. All in all, the arrangement at the homestead lacks any need for improvement.

The lives of our pioneer families are like a slow burning fire only interrupted by external sources—such as a wind which turns smoldering embers into a glowing flame or the imposition of outsiders. That too, must adjust to the absence of Zachary Wheat, who plans to depart once the planting season is over. From all appearances, Abel is up for the task. His physical ability was never questioned. He broke Azarov's hand in a playful demonstration of strength. Now, with a mental adjustment, the tall preacher is a man to regard.

* * *

In the fields the workday was drawing to a close. Abel wanted to continue, taking advantage of the remaining light, but the western sky had a different idea. It reminded him of the war when the sound of cannon is heard off in the distance. There was a significant drop in temperature when the wind began to increase, making the blackened sky more foreboding. This was Kansas, where a shift in weather conditions might occur without much notice.

"We best call it a day. The storm will be upon us before you know it," Abel called out. Unhitching the mules, the men ran them back to the barn. Plows and the wagon were left in the fields. When the rain came, men with dirty faces sat comfortably in the barn.

It came down in buckets and the sound of each thunderbolt made them jerk. No matter how hard they subconsciously tried not to let it affect them, their reflexes failed to cooperate. To compensate for their own fright, Zack and Abel laughingly pointed at Pearle each time he was startled. Abel opened some of the windows to create a cross draft and let the cool air in. Rain parkas were hanging on hooks close by, yet, they chose to wait awhile before making the dash to the main house.

Both Laurel and *White Dove* were safely inside preparing the evening meal. Every time there was a lightening flash, the porch was illuminated like a beacon for those in the barn. Zack was the first to relent, "It doesn't appear this is going to let up for a while. How about it Abel, I'm for putting on the raingear and running for the house."

"Sounds good to me," Abel replied.

The sound of stomping feet drew smiles from the women and *White Dove* suggested they retrieve some towels for when the men came inside.

"We better hand them towels while they are still under the protection of the porch covering. Otherwise, they will mess up the whole house," Laurel stated. They had just finished scrubbing the floors.

The men had presence of mind to utilize a collection of rainwater to wash the field dust, or rather mud now, from their hands and faces. After drying off, they became more presentable to enter the clean house.

White Dove...daughter of *Chief Red Eagle*, sister to *Falling Water*, and Pearle Sparks' wife.

The cheery group was tackling dessert when the rain turned to steady drizzle and Gus Greeley's horse and buggy splashed to a halt in front, with the folding top pulled down. Abel walked to the edge of the porch to receive an envelope addressed to Zack.

"Is there another message?" Abel asked.

"No sir, just the message for Mister Wheat. I was sent to deliver it sooner. But with the rain and all," the emissary explained.

"I'll see that he gets it. Would you like to come in for a spell and have a hot cup of coffee?"

"I surely would, sir, but Mister Greeley would want to know I delivered his letter, so I best head back right away. Thanks anyway," he replied, and turned the carriage back to the road.

"What was that all about?" asked Laurel.

"It's a letter for Zack from Gus Greeley," Abel answered, as he handed the envelope to an equally puzzled partner. With all eyes trained on the envelope, Zack opened it and removed its contents. And then, spread it out on the dining table. It read:

Mister Wheat,

I have a proposal to make. One in which a man of your talents might find acceptable. At your convenience, I would like to discuss it in person. I believe you know where to find me.

Gus Greeley

Zack spun the note around for all to read and said, "I wonder what he's up to?"

Turning to Pearle, he continued, "If it's still raining tomorrow would you like to accompany me to the Lucky Lady?"

Pearle considered a sensual day in the cabin frolicking with his young wife and replied, "I don't believe so. I would hate to leave *White Dove* alone."

* * *

When Zack opened the door to the Lucky Lady, the interior commotion came to an abrupt halt. You could hear the proverbial pin drop. Only when he spotted Gus Greeley, and sat at his table, did the usual din resume. Zack waved away Gus' offer of a cigar and said, "I got your message."

"How would you like to put your talent to good use?"

"I do that already."

"I'm referring to your ability to control a situation," Greeley said.

"Go on."

"As you are probably aware, the railroad is here. Surveying flags are popping up everywhere. Fort Dodge will grow faster than you can imagine. Cowboys, driving cattle from Texas, will start using the rail head to load and ship east. Obviously, my business will grow with the vertical city. We have no law and order. That's where you will fit in. I'd like to hire you as sheriff for the weekends at the Lucky Lady. Don't worry about the rest of the town. Ford County has a marshal, and that's in his jurisdiction. My concern is to make my establishment the safest place in the community. In so doing, I plan to run for mayor."

"What were you thinking of paying?" Zack questioned.

"$100 dollars a week. Now, that's not bad for one night's work."

"Gus, that's the most tempting offer I've ever received. If I weren't leaving the territory, I'd take it in a heartbeat," Zack confessed.

"You don't have to leave over what happened the other day," Gus said.

"I know. I'm leaving for something totally different," Zack explained. "It has nothing to do with you or the community. It's personal between my future and me. Anyway, I never stay in one place too long."

"I'll make it $200 a week," Gus said.

Zack shook his head and said, "Gus, you're breaking my heart. I don't have time to stick around any longer. These worn out bones are a hell of a lot older than you think. Father Time is running out on me." With that, Zack shook hands with Gus Greeley and wished him good luck. He turned his head scanning the boundary within the room and uttered, "This is the best whorehouse I've ever been in."

When Zack departed, Gus sat alone thinking, "What could be his reason for moving on?" Finally, he decided, "He must be in love with the preacher's wife."

* * *

At a time when Sir Henry Morton Stanley became a journalist, and was instructed to find the Scottish medical missionary and explorer, Doctor David Livingstone, Zack Wheat will embark on his own journey forward in his quest of life. While Stanley headed to Zanzibar in east Africa, Zack will travel further west on this way to California.

The Tennessee mountain man's family and friends are cast in interesting roles as the Country continues to mature. Extending from Statesville, Tennessee, to Fort Dodge, Kansas, they have cleared the land, built homes, raised children, cattle, and crops, and added a Cheyenne princess to the clan.

It will take years before the ruts of iron wagon wheels are finally overtaken by prairie grass. Until that time, these tracks serve as a reminder of promise and hardship, hope and despair, happiness and gloom, and dreams and reality.

Perhaps, the most important is dreams or fantasy, because we all live in two worlds. One is fantasy, the other realistic. How horrible life would be if we didn't have both.

Naturally, we value stability, security, and prudence, but our own lives aren't much different from those living years before us.

Life is always a journey and adventure. We all have personal dragons to be slain, ogres to overcome, and barriers to pass. Each and every one of us must live out an inscrutable tale.

The Leffingwell saga is a never-ending story. As is the segment called, Wagon Tracks Across Kansas.

While we may pause at this point, as they say, "Life goes on."

The Deferment